Praise for Lulu Taylor

'Nothing lifts the winter blues quite like a glam bonkbuster, and *Heiresses* is one of the highest pedigree ... Addictive, decadent and sexy, it'll easily see you through the depths of winter's most depressing month' *Heat*

'This is such great escapism it could work as well as any holiday' *Daily Mail*

'Pure indulgence and perfect reading for a dull January evening' *Sun*

'Wonderfully written and bursting with greed, sex and money – this indulgent read is totally irresistible' *Closer*

'If wealth and glamour turn you on, then turning the pages of this epic bonkbuster will brighten the credit crunch chill for you' *Best*

THE WINTER FOLLY

Lulu Taylor

PAN BOOKS

First published in electronic form 2013 by Pan Books

First published in paperback 2014 by Pan Books
an imprint of Pan Macmillan
20 New Wharf Road, London N1 9RR
Associated companies throughout the world
www.panmacmillan.com

ISBN 978-1-4472-3048-9

5 7 9 8 6

A CIP catalogue record for this book is available from the British Library.

Typeset by Ellipsis Digital Ltd, Glasgow
Printed and bound by CPI Group (UK) Ltd, Croydon, CR0 4YY

Visit www.panmacmillan.com to read more about all our books
and to buy them. You will also find features, author interviews and
news of any author events, and you can sign up for e-newsletters
so that you're always first to hear about our new releases.

To Ophelia Field

Prologue

A strange, ghostly figure moved silently through the darkness, its white gown billowing out behind as it trod lightly along the stony path, never looking down but drifting onwards as easily as though it were a sunny afternoon and not the dead of night.

A large cold white moon shone hard above, casting a chill light and making the inky night sky around it glow navy. Stars glittered like scattered ice and beneath them the world had been leached of colour, leaving only gradations of grey and black.

The figure skirted the lawns of the big house where the grass was the colour of granite, and drifted past the walled kitchen garden. It went down the yew walk where the shadows were thick and huge hedges loomed on either side, then passed through the old wrought-iron gates that never closed, the ones flanked by high pillars with stone owls sitting on top. It walked out onto the bridle path and on into the woods. There were hoots and flurries in the high branches of trees, and brushings and shakings in the undergrowth, the snapping of twigs and rustling of dead leaves. A pair of eyes flashed eerie green and yellow, and there was the dark outline of a fox. The woman in white went on, moving without haste but with utter determination.

She turned off the bridle path and into the thicker darkness of the woods where the beams of the moon could not penetrate, then came out again into a clearing where a large dark form stood on the brow of a low hill – the ruins of an old tower that still reached high into the sky. The woman walked towards it, through its empty doorway and into the darkness beyond. She ascended the rickety broken staircase that wound upwards against the ruined walls, going slowly but surely, taking one careful step after another until she reached the highest point of the folly, where a few floorboards remained, blackened, sodden and slippery. The woman paused and then walked slowly over what was left of the floor to where a missing wall had created a gaping hole in the side of the tower. She stood there, luminous in the dark, her white expressionless face turned outwards, gazing over the trees, her hands still clutching the sides of her nightgown, which lifted and billowed gently against the night sky.

She seemed to stand there for an age. Then she turned her face up to the stars, her chin lifted with something that was either defiance or surrender. She looked outwards again, her eyes blank. Slowly, deliberately, she took one step out into the void and then plummeted, her nightgown fluttering like a flag, her hair spreading upwards. Her arms flew out, her fingers splayed, her mouth opened but no sound came out. Then she vanished, swallowed by the shadows at the base of the tower and there was a hard thud and a crack, sharp as a whiplash.

A deep and dreadful silence followed.

PART ONE

PART ONE

Chapter One

1969

Alexandra called out: 'John! John! Come back here!'

John turned to glance at her, his eyes sparkling as he giggled. Then he carried on running, his fair hair bright against the dark foliage. He was fast, considering he was only two years old, and the excitement of the chase only made him dash on more quickly.

She couldn't help smiling at his merry little face; his soft plump cheeks, button nose and round blue eyes that were gradually changing to grey always softened her heart. All she wanted to do was pick him up and smother that sweet peachy skin with kisses. But she ought to be stern with him if he was going to learn to obey her. 'John, do as you're told!' she said firmly. 'Be a good boy for Mummy.' She walked quickly after him, wishing she'd worn something sturdier than her smart square-toed buckle-fronted leather pumps, which were pretty but not at all designed for speed. They'd only come out to wander about the lawn, John on his new plastic tractor, but he'd climbed off and started exploring. After a time, he'd trotted off down the yew walk, stopping to inspect anything that took his interest, while she followed. Whenever she got near, he would straighten up and set off again, his pace surprisingly fast considering his short legs and little feet. At the end of the walk, those blasted gates were open, of course, the old wrought-iron ones flanked by high pillars with stone owls sitting on top. Alexandra had asked for them to be replaced and given orders that until then they were to be kept shut, but the gamekeeper claimed that they had rusted into place and could not be closed.

'Can't you oil them?' she'd demanded, exasperated. 'It's dangerous with a small child running about.'

But the gamekeeper had simply looked at her with an expression that seemed to imply the child would be better off for being able to escape her smothering and run away into the freedom of the woods. Her orders still carried little weight, even now.

'Don't go through the gates, darling!' she called, but he ignored her and wandered out between them, singing to himself. Alexandra upped her pace, picking her way along the muddy walk as quickly as she could. She didn't like him being on the bridle path alone. Once she was through the gates, she could see him further on, quite a way down it already. He was probably remembering the way from walks with his father, perhaps when they'd taken his bucket and spade down to the river to dig up mud and pebbles, which he loved doing. He was far too young to fish yet and Alexandra had forbidden him being taken out on the river in the row boat. She herself hadn't been down to the river for a very long time. Not even the swimming expeditions in the summer, when it was cool and refreshing, could tempt her. She stayed up by the pool near the house instead, perfectly happy to swim in the turquoise chlorinated and overwarm water, and sunbathe on a lounger on the concrete surround, like a tourist at a hotel. The gamekeeper thought she was afraid of the woods, like some of the old men in the village who claimed that ghosts of Roman soldiers were clanking around in there. Somebody's legions had marched through and the Saxons had ambushed them and cut them to ribbons. They were supposed to be on the march still, homesick, bloodied and bent on revenge. But she didn't believe all that, of course. Ghosts were absurd, and the wails and screeches that came from the woods at night were those of unfortunate rabbits, caught by a fox or in the metal teeth of those awful traps the keeper put out. The stories had no doubt been spread to scare away poachers.

There was another reason altogether why she never went there.

'John!' she called. 'Come here, darling! Wait for me!'

He laughed again, his short legs moving even faster. He turned off the bridle path and began to follow a track. His red dungarees and white jumper were vivid among the dull wintery colours of the dead bracken, the black-leafed brambles and bare branches, and she saw his fair hair in bright flashes as he ran. She stepped in a patch of mud and slipped, catching her balance just in time to stop herself falling. Her snakeskin pumps and their gold buckles were spattered with black. She should have slipped on her boots and usually would have but they'd come out of the French windows instead of through the boot room. If they'd done that, they'd be wearing coats as well. She shivered. Her cardigan was too thin against the winter wind, and John didn't have enough on, he ought to be inside. They ought right now to be climbing the stairs to the nursery, where the fire would be burning and Nanny would have set out his tea: boiled eggs probably, and golden-brown toast shiny with melted butter.

'John! Come back!' She began to make larger strides to catch up with him but he sensed her approach and put on another burst of speed. 'Now, don't be naughty, I shall be cross with you!'

But it was a game to him, she could tell. He had an innocent recklessness; he could run and climb easily enough but had no idea of danger or hurting himself. Only the other day, someone had left the picket gate by the pool unlatched and she'd found John about to take a step onto the tarpaulin that covered the swimming pool, unaware that it would give under his weight.

Now here she was in the woods, the place she disliked so much. Her skin prickled and goosebumped. The undergrowth seemed to be crowding in on her, reaching out to grab her with hundreds of long thorny fingers. She shrank away from it as she went down the path that was mushy under her feet from the recent rain, and gasped out loud when she felt something pluck at her. Turning, she saw she'd snagged her cardigan on a spike of a branch and she fumbled with it until she'd freed herself. When she looked back, John had gone.

'John, John!' She began to hurry along the path, fearing that if he turned off it and scrambled away into the undergrowth, he could be lost, disappearing in a moment into the thickets and bracken. She could see him at once, hiding for fun at first, curled up in a little nest beneath a bush like a dormouse, waiting to be found; then, as the cold grew greater and the darkness came down, he would whimper for her, sobbing out that he wanted Mummy as the animals of the night began to sniff around him. 'John! Where are you?' Her voice quavered but she tried to inject into it as much command as she could. 'Come back at once, do you hear?'

She emerged suddenly into a clearing and stopped short, staring wide-eyed at what she saw before her: a folly, half in ruins, but still imposing, reaching into the afternoon sky. It had once been a high, handsome tower with arched windows and battlements, like a place where Rapunzel might have lived, but now it was mouldering and decayed, swathed in ivy, the few remaining battlements like jagged broken teeth. Most of the front of the tower had fallen away, and old masonry lay in heaps and hillocks, overgrown now, about its foot. It was possible to see that there had once been five floors, the bottom two now vanished but remnants of the others remaining, the fifth being mostly intact, though the old boards were no doubt soft and mushy with years of rainfall, frost and mildew. An old staircase twisted up the inside of the tower, treacherous with its broken and missing treads, perilous where the wall had fallen away. It was dark without and within, dank and cold, the breath of decay all around it, its stones thick with moss.

Horrible, rotten old thing! she thought, filled with a fearful revulsion. *I wish they would knock it down!*

The sight of the old ruin repelled her, and she was overcome with a sense of suffocation that made her want to run away. She saw it often in her dreams, a recurring nightmare in which she was forced to climb it in order to stop something dreadful happening, but she was never able to reach the top in time to prevent it. She hated seeing it in her dreams. The festering reality made her shudder.

She saw a flash of red from inside. John was in there.

At once a horror possessed her, the one she knew from her nightmares: choking panic and a desperate urgency to stop something terrible taking place. She began to run towards the tower. She heard his laugh again, and saw through the gap in the wall that he was climbing the staircase. She knew those stairs from childhood games when she'd been made to go inside: in some places they were as brittle and fragile as a thin layer of ice, ready to snap at any moment, and in others damp, turned spongy and yielding in the centre. A foot could sink down as easily as in wet sand, only below it was nothing at all. She wanted to scream and yell but her heart was pounding in her chest as she gained the interior of the tower. She looked up. It was open to the sky, which showed blue through the remains of the upper floors. Ivy swagged and hung from the old boards and joists, and branches crisscrossed where they had penetrated from outside. It smelt of sodden wood, wet stone and the bitterness of mould.

'John!' she called. He was going steadily up the staircase, one small hand pressed against the wall as he went, his tongue out between his lips as he concentrated on each step. He was making fast progress, his path keeping him close to the wall where the treads were strongest, and he instinctively avoided the gaps.

She gasped, her hands prickling with fear. He was surrounded by danger and with every step he took, its consequences grew greater. Below him were heaps of fallen stones, broken beams pointing upwards and worn to spear-like sharpness, rusty nails protruding from them. She imagined him fallen on one, impaled, and a grim nausea swirled in her stomach.

The little boy was higher now; he'd passed the empty first and second floors and was on his way up to the third. She had no choice. She ran to the staircase and began to climb as fast as she could but her progress was hampered by her need to take care. She was heavier than John – what supported him might not support her. Perhaps he was protected by his childlike faith in his own safety, but she was not and her imagination painted quick scenes for her: she lay with a broken leg or smashed ankle, helpless to reach him. No one knew where they were, no one would know where to look. Panic was threatening to choke her and her fingers trembled with adrenaline as she scrabbled for support on the slippery wall. *Damn these shoes!* she thought. Their soles had no grip, no tread, and she hated them with all her heart. If only she'd been wearing her blasted boots.

'Stop, John, stop!' she called.

For a moment he did stop, looking back over his shoulder and smiling at her, his big blue-grey eyes shining with amusement at their funny game. Then he turned back and lifted his little knee with determination to take the next step.

'John! Please!' Her voice broke on the words. She wanted to cry but there was no time for that luxury. She knew she had to stay in control. She went on from step to step, fearing that at any moment one would disappear from under her. Ahead of her John had reached the fourth floor and was still climbing. She was gaining on him, she was sure, but progress was so painful and slow. Now he was at the fifth, the staircase ended. He stopped again and looked down at her. The fact she was still coming seemed to propel him onwards and he trotted out across the floor.

She pulled in a sharp breath of panic; the floor was broken in places, and there was no telling where it had lost all strength. At this height the entire front wall of the tower was gone. John was walking towards the gap, at least thirty-five feet above the ground, where there was nothing to prevent him falling.

She found speed from somewhere, flying up the staircase two treads at a time, making split-second decisions about where to place her weight, hoping that her pace would not give the boards time to break beneath her. She heard ominous creaking and cracking as she went but there was no time for that now. All she knew was that she had to reach John as quickly as possible.

He was standing at the edge, one little fist on an outcrop of broken stone, looking out over the woods, his red and white figure bright against the black masonry and the dark trees beyond. A buzzing sensation filled Alexandra's head and she felt sick and dizzy. The frightfulness of her beloved boy standing on the edge of the tower went beyond the immediate danger and into a more primal place, a pit where something so awful lurked she couldn't bear to look at it. She was there, at the top of the stairs, on the landing, stepping out onto the boards. She advanced slowly, not shouting now but talking sweetly, calmly to the child as she took each shaking step across the black and slippery floor.

'Now, John, what did Mummy say? This is very silly. Come away now, come back to me. Come on, shall we go home and find Nanny? Shall we go to the nursery for eggs and toast? You know how you like to dip the soldiers in and give them yellow helmets, and Nanny will let you have your favourite little spoon, won't she?'

Each step took her closer. In a moment she would be able to reach out and grab him.

He stared up at her, smiling. 'Neggs,' he said contentedly. 'Boil neggs.'

'That's right, darling, boiled eggs. Shall we go home and get warm? That's enough playing for now, isn't it?'

He nodded his fair head and turned towards her. He looked cold. A bitter breeze was invading the tower and bouncing off its broken walls. It ruffled his soft, straight hair and he gave a little shiver. He was ready to come home.

She smiled with relief and held out her arms to him. He let go of the stony outcrop and made to come towards her. His stout little shoe landed on a slippery wet patch and he lost his balance, beginning to topple. He was going to fall backwards on to his bottom, as he usually did when he stumbled, but this time he would not land with a little jolt, none the worse for it, ready to scramble up and totter off.

She saw his outline against the bare emptiness beyond the absent wall. She knew that he would fall out of the tower. The moment stretched and lengthened as he wavered, his arms held out stiffly, and then began to fall backwards. His eyes opened wide with shock and surprise. With the speed of reflex, Alexandra reached out, strong and fast, and seized the shoulder strap of his dungarees. *Hold, hold,* she told the little buckle, as it took John's weight. It was all that was stopping him plummeting to the earth. It held as she yanked him towards her and the next moment he was safe in her arms.

He was quite still, happy at last to surrender to her, comforted by her warm arms wrapped around him. She buried her face in his hair and hugged him tight, not sure whether she was going to cry, laugh or scream.

'Mummy's here,' she murmured instead, her hands shaking. 'You're all right, my darling. Mummy's here.'

Chapter Two

Present day

Delilah sneezed, once, twice, three times in quick succession. The dust up here in the attics had formed layers of grey wool as thick as a carpet, and she had disturbed so much that the air had turned smoky with it. It swirled about, tickling her nostrils and coating her throat. The light from the bare bulb illuminated the clouds of motes, along with all the trunks, boxes, rolled carpets, old pictures, broken furniture and mountains of general bric-a-brac that filled the attics, a series of four on this side of the house, stretching the length of the east wing.

'Go up if you like,' John had said when she'd asked. 'God knows what you'll find. Mess around as much as you want to.'

It was the only place in the house that she was allowed free rein. When she'd come to live at Fort Stirling six months ago, she'd imagined that she would begin to feel that it belonged to her and that she could control and perhaps even reshape it, just as she had other places where she'd lived. She'd had a childlike excitement in exploring the house, and longed to set her imagination loose on the rooms and restore and refresh them. Everything was new and full of charm then, and she had fallen in love with the lichen-speckled stone pineapples on the terrace balustrade as much as the Louis Quinze chairs, gilded and spindly, in the drawing room. Every window, every corridor had enchanted her, and she'd felt that she had found her perfect setting, a magical place where life would be endlessly beautiful and interesting. But gradually, like seeing the set of a play close up, she'd realised that it wasn't quite as magnificent as it seemed. The rickety furniture on gilt legs looked splendid but the springs beneath were dropping, the silk damask covering was stained and frayed, and there was black caked into the golden carving.

Now she was beginning to understand that newcomers were not permitted to change anything in the house. Instead she had the sense that the house would possess her rather than the other way around; it would tame her and turn her into one of its own, another in a long line of inhabitants, the vanished people who'd walked the same corridors, sat on the same chairs and slept in the same beds. The thought gave her an unpleasant chill.

Up here in the attics, though, where others rarely came, she could do what she liked. Perhaps here she might feel more like the house's owner, rather than its inmate.

Delilah began to look through some of the boxes that surrounded her, finding a morass of odds and ends: a collection of broken picture frames, some discarded lamp stands without plugs, bulbs or shades, puzzling little plastic and wire whatnots that must have been part of something once. She stepped over a stack of chairs, lifted a pile of heavy folded velvet curtains and felt a flash of triumph. Now, this was more like it. A large steamer trunk, black and edged in studded leather, with a flat lid that locked with two big brass catches. On the top in scratched gold lettering were the words: *The Viscountess Northmoor, Fort Stirling, Dorset.* Labels, long faded and turned crisp, were stuck on the lid but it was impossible to make them out now. She drew in her breath with pleasurable anticipation. This was the kind of treasure she was looking for. She rubbed away a layer of dust from the top. Her hands, she noticed, were filthy and her nails rimmed with black. Her palms felt caked and dry, and she rubbed them across her jeans to get the worst of the dirt off before she opened the trunk. She snapped the catches down, hoping that the central round lock had not been fastened for there was no sign of a key and she had a feeling she would never find it. But it opened easily enough and she pushed the lid back until it was supported by its leather hinges. Immediately underneath was a layer of shallow drawers, filled with colourful scraps. There were ties, both knitted and silk, bowties, handkerchiefs, a cummerbund, scarves, belts and fans. Pairs of long opera gloves were folded into clear plastic bags and she could see pearl buttons, kid, silk and velvet.

'Bingo,' she whispered. '*Bingo*.'

This was what she had been hoping to discover. Costumes. After all, she had found a setting, a stage furnished with Chippendale and ormolu, Meissen vases and Sèvres china, gilt candelabra and inlaid cabinetry, marble statuary and vast gold-framed oils, black-and-white marble and ancient polished floorboards. She ate dinner in a perfectly round room decorated with wallpaper printed in a factory that had been destroyed during the French Revolution, and after dinner she sat back on a soft sagging sofa before an Adam fireplace, John's spaniel snoozing at her feet, and read books from the library that no one had touched for a century or longer. But occasionally the art director in her felt there was something missing. Where were the clothes? She wondered what had happened to the silk gowns, the lace and velvet worn by the women in the portraits around the house. Passed on until they fell to pieces, she supposed. It was understandable that the Regency muslins and Tudor bodices hadn't survived, but in the photographs from the last century were opulent furs, smart frocks, evening dresses, large-shouldered tweed coats, chunky black heels, snakeskin handbags and hats of all varieties. A snap of John's great-grandmother showed her in a drop-waist dress with a pleated skirt, a long cardigan, a rose corsage pinned to a string of pearls that dangled past her waist, and a tight-fitting cloche hat over her fashionably shingled hair. Vintage twenties clothes.

She felt a hunger for them, her fingertips tingling with a desire to stroke the fabrics and furs she could see everywhere but not touch.

'They're bound to be about. We never throw anything away,' John had told her idly one day, 'and there's been a distinct lack of daughters in my family.'

The comment had taken root in her mind. The clothes must be here somewhere, packed away or left in a forgotten wardrobe to rot gently on their hangers. She longed to find them. She couldn't help imagining how she would style some skinny, high-cheekboned models and where she would place them in the house to the best effect. She wondered if she could stage a play or an opera in the garden, and use the real clothes as her costumes.

Calm down, she told herself firmly. *You're racing ahead of yourself. Besides, John would never allow it.*

Once he'd seemed to like her ideas for enlivening the place, and opening it up. But she was realising now that he'd never taken any of them seriously.

She pulled out the drawers and put them on the floor. Now she could see what lay within: piles of clothes neatly folded. She began to look through them reverently. They'd been put away with care – she didn't want to disturb them unnecessarily. The colours and fabrics were not twenties or thirties, but sixties and seventies: yellows, purples and greens; short-sleeved knits, A-line skirts, paisley and zigzags and bold prints. They must have belonged to John's mother – she was surely the only woman living here then. Delilah's mouth watered. She had hoped for something older, but this was just the start. She would enjoy these too. Perhaps she'd find some treasures, some designer originals. At the bottom she saw some weighty looking dark cloth, folded so that she could not see what it was. She pulled it up and out of the trunk, trying not to disrupt the layers above it, and then she could see it was a coat in heavy black wool, double-breasted with large black buttons and, by the looks of it, short. It would sit just above the knee, she reckoned. The reason it seemed so bulky was that inside was a matching dress, also black but edged with white around the scooped neckline. It was beautifully made, with perfect seams and a silk lining. The label was not one she recognised but the quality was evident.

Gorgeous, thought Delilah. *So elegant*.

She shook the garments out and sniffed. They smelled of time and dust, of wool left to age in the dark. It was one of her favourite scents. As a girl, she'd thrilled to that slightly bitter aroma in the old dress shop where the eccentrically dressed owner, a woman with wild grey hair, sat sewing silently as Delilah burrowed into the heaps of abandoned coats or the racks of evening frocks. She examined the dress and coat, and wondered if they had indeed belonged to John's mother, whose face she only knew from the water-colour portrait in the drawing room and the few photographs scattered about the house in silver frames. The photographs showed a young woman, impossibly slender, in the fashions of the late sixties and early seventies, with backcombed dark hair and large eyes emphasised by a swoop of black eyeliner and false lashes. Delilah smoothed her hand over the fabric, remembering the strikingly pretty face, its pale skin and elfin features dominated by those huge eyes. She'd been struck by the look of vulnerability in them, and the slight awkwardness in the way the woman faced the camera. How strange to be touching something that John's mother wore all those years ago. How could she have known that one day her son's wife would stroke this dress and think about her?

I wonder what happened to her, Delilah thought. She knew that John's mother had died when he was a boy, but he'd never told her more than that. Sometimes, when she looked at the photograph that showed John as a small child and his mother in a coat and big sunglasses clasping his hand tightly, she felt the urge to know what the woman was thinking as she gazed impassively into the camera, shielded by her glasses. But there was no way of knowing now.

The coat and dress were on the small side, as vintage garments often were, but Delilah had a feeling that they might fit her. On impulse, she jumped up, kicked off her Converse and quickly shed her jumper and jeans, then un-zipped the dress's under-arm fastening and, pushing her arms into the cool silk interior, began to snake her way into it.

She feared breaking the seams but she managed to wiggle herself until her head and arms were free and she could slide the dress down over her hips. When she'd pulled the zip up, the dress was snug but it did fit, just. She wished she could see it but there was no mirror up in the attic. As she'd sus-pected, the dress fell just to the knee and she imagined what kind of shoes might be worn with it. Kitten-heeled winkle-pickers, perhaps. No, that didn't feel right. This dress came from an era of square heels and toes, stacked heels . . . Boots, perhaps? Long black boots that hugged the calves and came up the knee. Laced. Maybe . . . Delilah picked up the coat and felt the weight. Good quality. She slid her arms into it. The sleeves were tight but otherwise it fitted well, falling to the exact length of the dress. Lovely . . . It was old but it still felt stylish, almost fresh. She spun round. Perhaps she could wear this to something, a lunch or a trip to town.

She put her hands into the pockets and at once felt something under the fingers of her right hand. She grasped it and pulled it out. It was the remains of a flower, something that once had been pale – white or pink – though it was now crisp and brown. As she touched it, it crumbled under her fingers, the green-grey stalk falling apart, dropping to the ground and disappearing between a gap in the boards.

As she stared at the dusty remnants, a chill coursed through her body and a strong sense of sadness washed over her. She brushed the flower from her hands as fast as she could, gripped suddenly by a black sensation that seemed to engulf her. She wanted to get the clothes off as fast she could. The idea of wearing them to anything at all seemed absurd. They were freighted with something unpleasant, chilling, something that wanted to drag her down into a dark and fearful place. She struggled out of the coat, letting it drop to the floor despite the thick dust there, and then wrestled for a few moments to get the dress up and over her head, hearing her breath coming in short, almost panicked bursts as she grew increasingly desperate to be free of it. Then it slid up and off, releasing her.

She stared at the abandoned garments, astonished at the depth of feeling that had just possessed her. Shivering in the cool attic air, she realised she was wearing just her underwear. The clothes lay in a black puddle on the floor, the arms of the coat splayed out as though silently requesting an embrace.

'Delilah!' The voice from the bottom of the attic staircase pierced the air.

She jumped violently, then shivered. John. It was all right. 'Up here!' she called back, her voice surprisingly normal.

'Lunch is ready.'

'I'll be right there!' She shivered again, and reached for her clothes. When she was dressed, she picked up the coat and dress, folded them hastily and put them back into the trunk. She slotted the drawers back into place and closed the lid.

I'll come and look at the other things later, she promised herself, though she felt uncertain if she would want to come back alone. Shaking off the last remnant of the nasty black feeling, she headed for the stairs and the normality of lunch with John in the round dining room.

Chapter Three

1965

Alexandra moved through the noisy crowded room like someone who'd walked unexpectedly into a gathering of strangers and was bewildered by what was going on and why all these people were here. She caught a glimpse of herself in a gilt-framed mirror over the fireplace and saw a white face and large, startled-looking blue eyes. She was perfectly turned out, as she was supposed to be, her dark hair smooth and shiny, her face made up, her gown a chiffon confection of the palest blue. But she looked lost.

I'm meant to be enjoying myself, she thought, *but it feels like all this is happening to someone else. Do I dare slip away, go upstairs and be alone for a while? Would anyone miss me?*

The idea was tempting, but her father would be furious if he realised she was gone and she couldn't risk spoiling the unusually sunny mood he'd been in lately. She was basking in his unaccustomed approval and the last thing she wanted was to lose it again. She looked over at Laurence, who was sipping champagne and laughing loudly at someone's joke. Would he notice if she quietly disappeared?

Just then a white-gloved hand landed on her arm, startling her. She looked at it and then up at the owner. It was Mrs Freeman, smiling at her, her teeth brownish yellow behind her thick post-box-red lipstick. She always looked rather masculine, her heavy dark brows and large square chin at odds with her feminine dress and sparkling jewels.

'I haven't offered my congratulations,' Mrs Freeman said. 'Although am I supposed to congratulate the bride-to-be? I believe it's the man who is congratulated, and the lady is commended on her choice. In which case, well done, my dear. You've chosen well.'

Alexandra smiled weakly. 'Thank you.'

'The ring – may I see it? Oh, what a beauty. A fine stone considering it's so small. Family jewel, is it? These charming little pieces often are.'

Alexandra nodded. The two old diamonds in their golden claws glittered ferociously in the light from the chandelier. Between them, the antique ruby looked deep and still as a pool of claret. It still felt odd and heavy on her finger.

'And the wedding?' asked Mrs Freeman. 'When is it to be?'

'June,' said Alexandra, feeling as though she were talking in a dream. Would June ever come? She half hoped not. It was only three months away but it seemed impossibly distant. Perhaps something would happen before then to transform her life and take away the strange, unimaginable future she had agreed to. When she tried to conjure images of what her wedding day might be like, she found she could picture only a misty scene, with people flickering in and out of focus. Laurence was in it, but he kept his back, strong and square in a morning coat, turned on her and when she tried to make him face her, he became a blank.

'Wonderful.' Mrs Freeman smiled again, clasping Alexandra's hands between her own for a moment, the heavy cotton gloves making it feel as though her hands were swaddled in bandages. 'You've blossomed, my dear. It must be happiness. You were such a mousy little thing and now look at you. A touch of lipstick and powder, a decent dress, and you've turned out rather pretty.' She released Alexandra's hands. 'And have the Stirlings come to celebrate with us?' Mrs Freeman looked about, her heavy eyebrows raised as she scanned the room.

Alexandra felt herself colouring. 'No . . . no. My father . . . No,' she finished lamely. Once the Stirlings had been friends of theirs; Nicky Stirling and his cousins had been her childhood playmates, but now she was forbidden to see them and they had been shut out of her father's life. The fact of their absence was glaring.

'Oh, yes, of course,' said Mrs Freeman, who seemed to remember the need for discretion and added awkwardly, 'Well, never mind. I mustn't keep you from your fiancé. He's very handsome, isn't he?'

They both looked to where Laurence was standing in a small circle of men, smiling broadly, laughing and talking. He did look handsome at that particular moment: his blond hair was cut short in the severe military style and it suited his rather small head and features, and his blue eyes were bright with animation. His obvious good humour made him look personable.

'Yes,' she replied mechanically. 'I'm very lucky.'

'Go on then, dear,' urged Mrs Freeman. 'We want to see you together, you know.'

Alexandra obeyed, making her way through the throng, nodding at friends and acquaintances. There was her father, in deep conversation with Laurence's father. She wondered if he was talking about her, and tried to imagine him saying how proud he was of her, but even now that he seemed happy with her at last, she couldn't make it ring true. He'd always been a distant father but after her mother died and it was just the two of them, he had become colder and more remote than ever. She'd been unable to do anything right; even her presence seemed to irritate him. All her life she'd been trying to please him but he'd never seemed satisfied, until now.

The tantalising prize of winning his approval had been dangled in front of her the day he had called her into his study to tell her that he had as good as arranged a husband for her.

'Julian Sykes and I have been talking and we both agree that his boy Laurence could make a very good match for you. He has excellent prospects in the Blues. It's a good regiment and he's keen to find a wife. All successful officers need a good wife to support them. I'd like you to meet him, and if you both get on, there's no reason why it shouldn't turn out very well for all of us.' Her father had given her a cold smile, one of the ones that told her the conversation was at an end, that no opposition would be brooked. He always demanded complete obedience and questions were not tolerated. No matter how often she resolved to stand up to him, Alexandra couldn't help being cowed by his tremendous strength of will and his absolute certainty in his own opinions. She had distant memories of towering rages directed at her mother and she'd do anything to avoid bringing down that awful anger on her own head. The truth was, she wanted desperately to win his love. What harm could it do to meet this man, if that was what her father wished? She could always say no to anything more if she wanted to.

So she let it happen. One day there was tea, with Laurence Sykes sitting awkwardly opposite her and asking polite questions, before the two of them were told to walk around the garden together for half an hour. Another two or three visits just like the first followed, and then there was a trip to London where the two young people, accompanied by Mr and Mrs Sykes and Alexandra's father, dined out in a horrible, formal restaurant with fish-eyed waiters and clinking silver, and then went on to a dance club. Girls in stiff satin dresses with long gloves waltzed awkwardly with young men in tail coats and brilliantined hair. Alexandra knew it was supposed to be fun, a taste of the sophisticated life that awaited her if she married, but it had felt like an enforced jollity that was hollow at its heart.

Laurence was perfectly pleasant and seemed kind enough, but she felt nothing more than friendship for him. He was nice looking, if rather small for a soldier, with his fair hair in that short military haircut, and eyes of washed-out pale blue, like a morning sky after a rain storm. He had regular, almost delicately small features and straight teeth with particularly sharp canines that emerged high in the gum and gave him a rather wolfish look when he smiled. His slim bony hands always had a cigarette clenched in the fingers, and he jiggled his left knee unconsciously when he smoked. He talked to her of everyday things and appeared interested in her uneventful life. She found that once she had a willing listener, she could chatter on for ages about nothing much and rather enjoy the feeling of amiable companionship. If marriage was like that, perhaps it wouldn't be so bad. A couple of times she'd caught him staring at her in a peculiar way, and had smiled at him shyly, almost hopefully, wondering if he might be able to awaken something in her like girls felt in books and poems for men they loved, but he'd quickly glanced away.

Perhaps she was asking too much to feel those things, whatever they were. It might even be better if she didn't. Sometimes she wondered whether there was something wrong with her. Nobody else seemed to struggle with suppressing their emotions the way she did. She was quick to tears or laughter, prone to wanting to dance for joy or slump down with misery, and she lived every word of the books she read. Her aunt told her she wore her heart on her sleeve, which she supposed meant the same thing. She sensed that life might be a good deal easier if she could learn to live it without feeling anything at all.

Her father's enthusiasm for the match grew. It was

revealed in the way Mrs Richards, the seamstress, came to the house to fit dresses, skirts and coats that her father had ordered for her. He arranged for a small amount of pin money to be paid into her post office account 'for you to have a little fun with, for lipsticks and so forth', and he began to talk to her over his newspaper at breakfast, making comments on world affairs that he obviously hoped she would absorb. She felt that she had let things go too far to pull back now, and that the inevitable was approaching.

It's for the best, she told herself stoutly. *It's what he wants for me. Besides, I've got virtually nothing to do but keep house. Am I going to sit in the cold breakfast room, morning after morning, pouring coffee for Father, forever?*

Perhaps marriage, whatever it meant, would be a better fate than that.

When Laurence appeared unexpectedly one afternoon, she knew that the moment had arrived. Her stomach lurched with something that she supposed must be excitement when she was called down to the drawing room to find him there, white faced and trembling, but with bravado in his eyes as though he was determined to prove himself.

The words, sounding well-worn even though she had never heard them before, came out as she stood there, feeling shabby and schoolgirlish in her tartan skirt and old green jumper. They fell in and out of her consciousness like a wireless with the volume turned high and then low and back again. 'The respect and admiration I have for you . . . over recent months . . . ripened to something deeper . . . If you would do me the honour . . . the happiest man in the world . . . become my wife.'

There she stood, listening as she stared at him and wondered who on earth he was. She couldn't help feeling sympathy for him, so pale, his fingertips shuddering. Was the terror in his eyes for fear she might reject him or accept him? Why was he asking if he might share his life with her? Did he love her? She wasn't sure if he had said it or not.

It seemed an age that she stood there staring, unable to speak, feeling that she was at a great fork in the road where two futures awaited, each hidden from view but equally momentous. The day she learned her mother had died had been the only other time she had felt this way: as though, after years of sameness, life had made a sudden decisive turn and everything had changed in an instant.

'Your father,' ventured Laurence at last, to fill the yawning silence, 'has given his permission.'

She remembered her duty. Besides, being proposed to felt a little like being asked to dance. Never refuse – it had been drummed into her. It's bad manners to turn somebody down and hurt their feelings. It doesn't matter what you want, you must do what is asked of you.

One of the forks in the road faded and disappeared. There had really only been one path all along. She took a deep breath.

'Thank you. Yes, of course.'

'You . . . you'll marry me?'

'Yes,' she said distantly, adding, 'please,' in a small voice and then, more uncertainly, 'thank you.'

'No. I must thank you.' A look of intense relief passed over his face and she felt a sudden bond with him. They were both glad it was over. 'You've made me very happy.'

He approached stiffly and she thought for a moment he was going to embrace her, but he lifted her hand and pressed it to his lips.

Her father was delighted when they went together to tell him, and the smile he gave her and the kiss on her cheek filled her with a sense of happiness that warmed her like a cup of hot milk on a cold day. He even embraced her briefly and she clung to him, her chest constricted with emotion, not wanting the precious moment to end.

'Well done, Sykes,' he said heartily to Laurence, before taking her fiancé away to drink a good claret in his study. Alexandra sat in the window seat in the drawing room and tried to recall every sensation of her father's embrace, quietly and deeply happy.

The next few days, with the air full of satisfaction and hope, were the happiest she could remember. Everybody was so delighted at the news of the engagement that Alexandra felt that she had evidently done the right thing and she was glad to have pleased them all so much. But the feelings and emotions they attributed to her and Laurence were so at odds with reality that she couldn't help feeling a shade of apprehension.

'You must long to be alone together!' ladies cooed. 'Oh, young love, so wonderful, so romantic! The first flush of passion – quite the most delicious thing in the world.'

Alexandra stole glances at her fiancé and wondered if he felt these things but she saw no evidence of it. He didn't try to be alone with her – almost the opposite, in fact – and he certainly didn't make her feel that he thought of her romantically. The things that were supposed to come with love – like kisses and embraces – simply didn't feature. Perhaps, she thought, they would come after the ceremony.

Her father wrote to his sister Felicity, who arrived with three suitcases to take over the arrangements and make sure that everything was done properly. It was she who had organised the engagement party.

Now here Alexandra was, in her ice-blue chiffon, receiving the nice comments, the congratulations, and still it felt unreal. She shook hands with Laurence's parents who smiled at her and said they looked forward to welcoming her into their family as a daughter, and greeted his younger sister, Maeve, and his older brother, Robert, whose smile she didn't like, or his pale blue eyes, so like Laurence's. Soon she would know these people intimately.

How strange, she thought. *This is going to happen to me. It's going to be my life.*

But she couldn't shake the feeling that it was all about someone else. It was the same when the wedding presents arrived, endless boxes of glassware, vases, china ornaments, bonbonnières, trinket boxes, lamps and ugly paintings. These were going to furnish her new life in the married quarters in London, where the Royal Horse Guards were based. But it was impossible to imagine that after finally winning her father's approval she was going to leave him forever, so she tried not to think about it at all.

When the wedding was only a week away, Alexandra couldn't ignore the fact of the suitcase in her room filling with clothes as the drawers and wardrobe emptied. At night she covered the suitcase with a blanket, turned her back on the pile of trousseau and tried to pretend none of it was there.

When Aunt Felicity called her into the spare room and asked if she was all right, Alexandra was surprised. She thought she was doing very well at being all right. Everybody was happy with her. Her father had been sunny and well disposed towards her for weeks now. 'Yes, of course. I'm perfectly well, thank you.'

Her aunt looked worried. 'But you're so thin, Alexandra, thinner than ever. Are you sure you're quite ready for this . . . for your marriage, I mean?' She took hold of Alexandra's hand and clutched it in her own.

'Yes . . . I think so.' There didn't seem to be any other answer. What could change? It was all going to happen, it had been decided.

Felicity gazed searchingly at her, still clasping her hand tightly. Her thin mouth, wrinkled around the lips, looked stern but her eyes were worried. 'And . . . I don't suppose anyone has told you about what marriage means, have they? About . . . love and children?'

Aunt Felicity had been married once but her husband had been killed in the war, only a fortnight after the wedding, and she had never married again. Alexandra shook her head.

'Of course they haven't,' muttered Aunt Felicity. 'Who is there to tell you, you poor lamb?' She pulled Alexandra gently over to the bed and they both sat down. 'Now, listen, my dear. I do not presume to know the innermost secrets of your heart, but you have agreed to become Laurence's wife and I assume you would not do that unless you love him. You must understand that marriage makes certain require-ments of women, and when a man and a woman love each other more than anything, this requirement is no burden – indeed, it is a pleasure and a matter of great fulfilment.' Felicity stopped, and sighed shortly, her expression con-cerned and awkward at the same time. Alexandra felt her cheeks burning and stared down at the candlewick bed cover, one finger tracing round and round the raised pattern. 'But,' continued her aunt, 'I believe it can be an ordeal and an onerous duty if there is not a mutual love between a husband and wife. Do you know what I'm talking about, Alexandra?'

Alexandra nodded, thinking that she did understand her aunt's words, just not very much about what they meant in practical terms.

'Good, good.' Her aunt began to colour around the cheekbones and she looked flustered. 'And . . . the way children are made. Do you know about that, my dear?'

Alexandra nodded again. The village woman who had come to look after her when her mother had died had explained it, at the time when she first experienced her monthly course. It had sounded more revolting than anything she could have imagined and she had decided that it must be a pack of lies, until girls at school had whispered about it and she had learned that what she had been told was more or less true. But, just as her aunt had said, the girls had agreed that if your husband was your one true love, it was heaven. Otherwise, it was sheer hell. Therefore, it followed that you would not know if you had married your one true love until the wedding night, when the experience that followed would reveal all. She tried to imagine Laurence doing that with her but again it was impossible. All she could imagine was his cool lips pressed on hers, pressing and pressing and pressing . . .

'Alexandra? Are you all right?'

'Oh!' She looked up into her aunt's worried eyes. 'Yes, yes.'

'Well, I'm glad we had this little talk, aren't you? It's put my mind at rest. But . . .' She hesitated again, troubled. 'You do love Laurence, don't you?'

I may as well get used to saying it, Alexandra thought. *After all, I'm going to be promising to love him forever in a week.* 'Yes, Aunt. Of course.'

'Good.' Her aunt squeezed her hand and smiled. 'Then I'm sure you'll be very happy, my dear. Now, let's go downstairs and have some tea.'

Mrs Richards came up trumps with the wedding dress. Alexandra thought that it looked just like something in a society magazine, the kind that might be worn at a smart London wedding, with its pleasingly full skirt, long tight sleeves and lace train.

'You'll look an angel!' Mrs Richards said, dabbing her eyes, and even Aunt Felicity seemed impressed. It seemed a consolation that her wedding dress would be so pretty.

And then, one morning, Alexandra woke up in her old bedroom, opened her eyes to the dress hanging on the back of the bedroom door, and knew that today she was going to wear it for its proper purpose. When she was dressed and the veil was arranged over her face, she looked at her reflection and saw an almost ghostly white figure, its face concealed, the eyes only just discernible through the net. She could not see her own expression.

Outside the church her father turned to her, smiled and said, 'You look lovely, my dear.' He kissed her cheek and took her hand, placing it on his arm and covering it with his own. Her heart lifted with pleasure. 'Are you ready?'

She nodded. The strains of Handel were pumped out by the wheezing organ, and they set off up the aisle, followed by two tiny attendants, the children of a relation – a little girl in pink organza and a boy in a kilt and a brass-buttoned jacket with a frothy lace cravat – towards Laurence, who waited at the top, his brother beside him. The church was full. Through her veil, everyone seemed misty and half obscured but there they all were: her own family, local people who'd known her all her life and, on the other side, Laurence's family. There was his mother, small and fair and somehow a little monkeyish, a bit like Laurence himself, his sister Maeve, and his father, her own father's friend, who had made this come to pass. They'd all come, putting on dresses and hats, morning coats and polished shoes. Everything that needed to be done had been done. There was no backing out now. She clutched her father tighter, taking comfort from the unfamiliar feeling of his closeness and the firm arm beneath her hand.

As she approached Laurence, she could see beads of sweat on his nose and forehead. His skin was paper white and his chest moved rapidly under his coat. He looked as though he was going to faint. Alexandra felt light-headed and dizzy herself; she had not been able to keep down the toast that Aunt Felicity had made her eat, and now there was a painful knot in her stomach. It occurred to her that both she and Laurence might faint and she had a wild urge to laugh at the mental picture of the bride and groom both unconscious before the altar.

Laurence tried to smile at her as she came level with him but he looked suddenly sickly and swayed for a moment before he seemed to regain control of himself.

'Are you all right?' the vicar asked quietly as the organ sounded the last notes.

Laurence nodded, gulping for breath, and his brother said, 'He's fine. Overcome with happiness, that's all. You can start.'

Alexandra had the sudden feeling that until now they'd been playing a game of getting married and everyone had made a terrible mistake and taken them seriously. *What are we doing?* she thought. *Isn't anyone going to stop us?*

But no one said anything, not even when they were asked if they knew of any just cause or impediment. When bidden, Alexandra took Laurence's hand, repeated the words, listened as he spoke the same to her, and still couldn't shake the strange impression that all this was make-believe, not really happening to her, even as she watched him push the slim gold band onto her fourth finger. Surely at the end of this odd ritual, she would take off the white dress and the veil, give back the flowers, put on her old clothes and go back to her room, still Alexandra Crewe, nineteen years old, living with her father and wondering when her life would begin.

But when she walked out of the church at Laurence's side, into the blustery June sunshine, everything had changed. In half an hour, and to the tune of reedy hymns and an aria sung flat by a girl from the village, she had been transformed into someone called Mrs Laurence Sykes. She was now a wife, a woman of the world, with new duties and tasks ahead of her.

That evening they set off in Laurence's Triumph Herald, her suitcase wedged on the back seat, to go to the seaside for their honeymoon, and they would return not to her home but to married quarters in London.

Her old life was gone forever.

Chapter Four

Present day

Delilah's whole life with John had almost never come to pass. The magazine had booked a fashion shoot at Fort Stirling and she was meant to be directing it, but she decided to send her deputy instead.

'I just don't feel up to it,' she'd said to Grey the day before, sitting at her desk clutching a skinny latte and holding the telephone to her ear with her shoulder while she scrolled through a series of photographs on her computer. 'Rachel's bound to be there, undermining my authority and doing whatever she likes. Milly can take my place.'

'Is this because of Harry?' asked Grey, his voice stern down the telephone line.

She'd sighed and clicked her mouse on another image. It expanded to fill her screen. A fashionable model was pulling a silly face and it was just the wrong side of being cute. She deleted it. 'Maybe.'

'Darling, you've got to pull yourself together. This is the third time you two have broken up. You're ready to let him go and get on with your life. To be honest, I think you were over him a long time ago.'

'Perhaps you're right.' She knew it was true: she couldn't go on being reeled in and cast away. It was emotionally exhausting and her desire for Harry had gradually been eroded by the pain he kept putting her through. Grey had been there plenty of times to mop up tears, fill wine glasses and analyse Harry and his emotions until the early hours, but even he was now urging her to buck up.

'Of course I'm right. And I don't work half as well with Milly. I need you there. This is an expensive shoot – you've got to come, it won't work without you. Especially if Rachel starts playing up.'

She thought for a moment. 'Oh, all right,' she said, knowing he wouldn't back down. 'You win.'

'You're driving as well. Pick me up at seven.' Grey put the phone down.

The next morning, she'd pulled her Volkswagen Beetle up in front of his Notting Hill flat, they'd loaded his camera equipment into the back and then set off down the M3 towards Fort Stirling. It had been midday before they'd arrived, both hot and thirsty and desperate to stretch their legs.

'Wow,' Delilah had said, as they pulled up in front of the house. The drive from the gates to the house had been extraordinary, weaving its way through velvety green parkland past oaks, elms and limes, all venerable with age. It had led to a place that looked part storybook castle and part elegant Regency house, a building that gently flowed from

an ancient round tower on one side through to a battle-
mented Tudor front and an extended wing of wonderful
eighteenth-century symmetry. Despite its collection of ages
and styles, the house felt as melded and comfortable with
itself as a stack of pillows, nestled into a hollow and protected by a phalanx of trees behind. Delilah and Grey
climbed out of the car. 'What *is* this place?'

'It is splendid,' admitted Grey, standing back and taking
it all in. 'I've heard of Fort Stirling, but never been here.
They're not a very social family, the Stirlings. You don't tend
to stumble across them at parties.'

'It's so beautiful.' Delilah waved an arm out towards the
parkland. 'All of it.'

'That's Dorset for you. Well lived-in, softened by centuries
of husbandry into this delightful landscape. Now, we'd
better find Rachel and see if the models have arrived.'

Standing under a grand ornamental porch, they pulled on
a bell handle set beside the huge arched front door, and one
of the set assistants answered.

'Where's the owner?' Delilah asked as they were led
through the vast entrance hall with a black-and-white che-
quered marble floor. The assistant shrugged.

She guessed whoever it was had made themselves scarce.
People with a house like this were paid good money by
magazines and film crews for its use as a setting for fashion
shoots and period dramas and they probably knew well
enough by now to stay in the background and let them get
on with it. After all, they got reimbursed for anything that
wasn't left exactly as found.

Rachel was in a huge room decorated in turquoise and gold. 'Isn't this magnificent?' she bellowed, when she saw Delilah and Grey approaching.

'You haven't gone too mad, have you, Rach?' Delilah asked warily, knowing how the stylist could go completely overboard when not reined in.

'Of course not!' Rachel said indignantly. 'But we're going to make the most of this adorable setting, and the fantastic clothes I've managed to get. Look.' She went over to a rail where tiny model-sized garments hung in a mass of colour and fabric: slippery silks, wispy chiffon, glossy leather and rubber, along with tweeds and knits of every variety. 'Dior, Chanel, Stella McCartney, Givenchy, McQueen, you name it. It's going to be glorious. Wait till I show you the props!'

Delilah sighed, feeling that she could really do without a fight today. It was always the same when Rachel was brought in on a job, and she appeared without fail on the juiciest gigs. The bigger the house, the grander the setting, the bigger the budget, the more likely Rachel was to appear and spoil it. Give her a bog-standard studio shoot in a stuffy little place in Tooting with the clothes of a new designer, and she was nowhere to be seen. It came from being the cousin of the magazine's publisher and a snob into the bargain. She had no compunction in stamping down Delilah's ideas and authority and imposing her own vision, even though Delilah was the magazine's art director.

Rachel was dressed eccentrically as usual in a vintage Edwardian gown, customised with a black-and-white-striped bustle and a long hot-pink tutu beneath, and she tripped along the corridors on platform heels in a rustle of satin. Delilah followed behind, feeling ridiculously normal in her jeans, grey silk T-shirt and plimsolls. She'd learned that it was easy to feel plain and frumpy on a shoot, what with the gorgeous models wafting about in designer gear, so she'd adopted a look that suited her and was both stylish and practical. She might not have a model figure but she was happy with her tall, fairly athletic frame. Grey was always telling her to show off her legs more, but she preferred to wear jeans or black trousers most of the time. 'Wear more colour!' he'd scold. 'That endless black and white, don't you get sick of it?' But she was fond of her monochrome working wardrobe.

In the office, she wore white shirts and dark jackets with her trousers, adding a sharp heel for the fashion edge that the magazine required. On a shoot, she'd dress right down; it was how other people looked that mattered, after all, and she just needed to be comfortable. Today she'd twisted her long, thick fair hair up into a bun and stuck a variety of pens and pencils through it, partly to keep it in place and partly because, when she was working, not being able to find a pen when she needed one drove her mad. She knew Grey would hate it, even though he'd carefully not commented when he climbed into the car that morning. He was always urging her to wear more make-up and get her hair properly styled, but she only laughed. She liked her long hair, even if it did take an hour to blow dry it properly, and too much make-up made her look clownish. Her face was the natural kind, the skin clear with a few freckles over her nose, her lashes naturally dark. Her face was well defined, with strong cheekbones, a sturdy nose and a well-formed, almost Roman mouth. She could never transform the way the models did, their plain, small-featured faces becoming ethereally beautiful under the layers of make-up. She glimpsed three of them now, as they passed the makeshift salon, where a team wielding hair tongs and eyebrow brushes were turning the blank-faced, hollow-cheeked girls into raving beauties.

I think I prefer being me, Delilah thought. Grey always told her she was gorgeous, and while she knew that wasn't quite true, she was also content that she made the best of what she had.

Rachel led them to a large window overlooking a court-yard below, then looked down and said happily, 'There we are!'

Delilah joined her, gazing out over a quadrangle sur-rounded by yet another part of the house. On the patch of emerald-green lawn were a collection of large animals that looked as though they were constructed from painted papier mâché. There was a huge white swan with a golden crown on its head, a large white rabbit in a checked waistcoat standing on its hind legs, a mouse, its head cocked inquisi-tively, carrying a basket, and a twisting green serpent poised to strike. Other smaller creatures stood caught mid-pose as though frozen by the White Witch's wand.

'Rachel!' said Delilah, horrified, pressing her forehead to the glass. 'What have you done? How much did those cost?'

'Peanuts, darling, peanuts! And you did say *fairy tales.* I thought they were completely perfect – don't you? As soon as I saw them, I said yes, yes, yes!' Rachel smiled at her, fluttering her heavily mascara'd eyelashes. Two men appeared on the lawn below and started hauling the mouse towards a door leading into the house.

'But I ordered props,' Delilah protested, still too bewildered to be cross. 'We've got ladders and tons of tulle and all the things we discussed in the office.'

'Oh, honey, but these are marvellous! Aren't they much better than boring old ladders?'

There was a shout on the lawn and they both looked down to see a man standing there, hands on hips, looking crossly at the giant animals and the mouse being dragged indoors.

'Whoops, it's the manager,' said Rachel. 'You deal with him, darling, I'm *so* busy.' She turned on her heel, flashing pink netting, and tripped off down the hall towards the make-up room.

Delilah sighed. She didn't need this. Not today. Not the way she was feeling, which was tired, hollow and all wept out. *I need a holiday*, she told herself. *A good long holiday somewhere hot. I can just tell today is going to be a nightmare.*

Somehow she found her way downstairs, wondering how anyone managed to find their way round this huge house, and was just in time to see the mouse's tail disappearing into a long gallery. Along the corridor came a man in jeans and a soft cotton shirt rolled up at the elbows, his dark hair short but thick and greying at the temples.

'Hey, you, what's going on here? There's a bloody menagerie on the inner lawn and those vandals have just dragged a giant mouse right over the flowerbed! And its tail has left a huge channel all over the grass!'

He was right opposite her now, his expression indignant. She stared back, feeling near the end of her tether.

'I think you'll find we've got permission,' she said brusquely.

'Really?' He looked combative. 'Well, not from me.'

'Not from you, no,' she said, trying to sound superior. 'From the owner.'

'The owner?' He frowned.

'Yes. He's allowed us to do whatever necessary for our shoot.'

'Has he? And he knows about these giant animals, does he? These ludicrous rabbits and hedgehogs and whatever?'

'They're all integral to our artistic vision,' Delilah said loftily, lifting her chin but thinking inside that Rachel definitely owed her for this sturdy defence of all her nonsense. Although, knowing Rachel, Delilah suspected that the pictures would turn out to be wonderful. 'He's perfectly fine with it. I spoke to him myself.'

Just then, there was a movement at the window, and they both turned to see that the enormous rabbit was now being carried past it but its handlers were out of sight, and the effect was of the massive creature slowly making its way across the lawn unaided.

Delilah stared at it and then glanced at the manager, who was turning back to look at her, his expression startled. The moment they caught sight of one another's faces, the comic element of it all struck them simultaneously and they began to laugh.

'I should have expected something like this,' the man said. 'I don't know why I'm shocked. It doesn't quite take the biscuit from the time I let some famous glamour puss get married here and we had glass coaches and white horses and whatever, but almost.' He shook his head and laughed again. 'Giant fairy-tale creatures. How do you all make a living at this?'

'Advertising, mostly,' said Delilah, still giggling at the memory of the enormous rabbit walking by. *I need to laugh*, she realised. *It's been a long time.*

The man put his hand out. 'I'm John Stirling.'

She took it and they shook firmly. 'Hello, I'm Delilah Young.' She smiled, then froze. 'Oh . . . wait. Stirling . . . Are you . . .'

'The owner? Yes, I am. Delighted to make your acquaintance, Miss Young.'

She felt herself blush and go hot. 'Oh God, you must think I'm dreadful, lying to you like that. About talking to you and getting your permission. I'm not normally so brazen . . .'

'Don't worry at all.' He smiled back at her. 'I rather enjoyed it. But let's be clear – my lawn is going to be put back to its proper state, isn't it?'

'Absolutely,' Delilah said, relieved. 'If I have to lay fresh turf myself.'

'I'm sure that won't be necessary,' he said and smiled

again. His eyes, she noticed, were a soft grey and when he smiled, he got a dimple in his left cheek.

'Are we good to go yet, darling?'

Delilah turned to see Grey coming in through the front door, lugging some equipment.

'God, I wish I'd brought an assistant!' he said, panting. His gaze fell on John Stirling. 'Could you possibly make yourself useful and go out and get my reflectors? They're on the drive. And when you've done that, I could murder a cup of tea.'

Delilah opened her mouth to explain, but John Stirling quietened her with a quick look, a conspiratorial smile and a loud, 'No problem.' She watched him head outside to collect the reflectors.

'Come on, missy,' Grey said to her, starting to head up the stairs. 'Let's get this show on the road.'

Perhaps it might have ended there, Delilah reflected, with a pleasant conversation and a smile, and then their lives would have continued on their different paths, Delilah going back to her tiny London flat and her sore heart, pining after Harry. But just as she was loading the car with Grey's equipment to take him and it back to London, John Stirling came out to see her. She was the last of the shoot party. Rachel had roared off in her vintage Jag as soon as the exciting bit was over, leaving everyone else to clear up, while the models had been packed into their car to find a coffee shop that could supply them with the endless soya lattes that appeared to be all that kept them going. Make-up artists, hairdressers, electricians and shoot assistants had all left, and then it was only Delilah and Grey, making sure everything had been left shipshape.

'Are you off?' asked John Stirling, coming up to the car.

Delilah nodded. 'Yes. We're all done. Thank you so much.'

'Not at all. And my new animal collection. I hope no one will be whisking that away from me any time soon.'

'Oh – yes, I should have said. The company will be coming in the morning to take them away.' She smiled at him. 'And you must let me know if anything needs to be put back as it was. I'll sort it out for you.'

'Thank you, Miss Young. Thank you very much.' There had been something in his gaze that drew her to him, a kind of familiarity as though they already knew each other quite well. A spark of something she recognised. *You're like me*, she thought, and then laughed inwardly at the idea. How could the owner of a place like this be anything like her?

In the car, heading back towards the motorway, Grey said, 'Oooh, he likes you!'

'No, he doesn't,' Delilah said stoutly, but feeling a pleasurable sense of awakening excitement nonetheless.

'He does! And did you see? No wedding ring.'

'His type often don't wear them,' replied Delilah, trying to concentrate on the winding country roads.

'But still, he's not. I could tell. He had a lonely air about him, definitely craving female company.'

'I should think the man who owns Fort Stirling is fighting them off!'

'Mmm, don't think so. Grey's inner voice is never wrong, remember? You wait and see, something might be cooking there. I'm serious.'

She'd changed the subject but, back in London, things kept popping into her consciousness to remind her of John Stirling and the day she had spent in his magical home. She picked up a stray back copy of the magazine and saw it contained a feature on that very house. When she opened her post a few days later, she discovered she had an invitation from a friend to stay the weekend in a hotel just near Fort Stirling. Then in a biography she was reading she found a reference to the Stirling family of Northmoor, Dorset. *Weird*, she thought. *But it doesn't mean anything. Just synchronicity, I guess, but still . . .*

In the week since the shoot, the break-up with Harry had somehow lost its sting, as though her day at the old house had set her free, and now she couldn't quite remember why she had cared so much. There were other men out there, after all, other possibilities, other potential lives, all waiting for her to walk out and take whichever path she wanted.

'Delilah?' It was her assistant Roxie, putting her head round Delilah's door.

'Yup?' She glanced over from her screen where she'd been absorbed in a portfolio sent to her by an aspiring photographer.

'You've got a visitor.'

She frowned over the top of her black-rimmed glasses. 'Who? I'm not expecting anyone.'

'His name is John. He's sitting out in reception.'

'John?' she echoed. She was bewildered for a moment, then thought, *Could it be?* She stood up, grateful suddenly that she'd dressed up for a cocktail party she was planning to go to after work and was wearing a navy silk Alberta Ferretti dress with a silver tweed blazer over the top, and her long fair hair was freshly blow-dried into loose waves. She put her glasses on the desk. 'Okay, I'll go out and see him.'

Her stomach swooped pleasantly when she saw John Stirling was sitting there, one leg lazily crossed over the other knee, in dark trousers, a shirt and a very well-cut jacket, flicking through a magazine from the coffee table. He looked up as she came over, and stood up at once, a smile lighting up his expression, making his slightly angular face suddenly handsome. She noticed the dimple in his left cheek again, and the way it was rather winsome and boyish.

'Hello,' he said. 'I hope you don't mind me dropping by. I'm on one of my very rare visits to London and was walking through the square when I suddenly thought . . . why don't I drop by and ask when the house is going to feature?'

She smiled back, awkward but pleased. No one just dropped by like that for such a flimsy reason. There were plenty of ways of finding out which issue Fort Stirling was going to appear in. 'Well, it's lovely to see you. Come into my office.'

'Or . . .' He looked thoughtful. 'We could go out for a spot of lunch if you're free.' He consulted a chunky wristwatch. 'It's almost one.'

Excitement sparkled through her. 'That sounds lovely. I'd really like that.'

'Good. Me too.'

They'd gone out to a nearby French bistro that Delilah knew, and sat outside watching London go by while they ate buttery garlic snails and then bloody chargrilled steaks with hot salty chips and peppery watercress. All the while they talked about nothing and everything. He was a good listener and wanted to know about her home back on the Welsh borders, her family, her job, her life. She told him about lots of things, but not about Harry, and he told her about his life in the country and that he was divorced. They sat there all afternoon, Delilah ringing in to say she wouldn't be back in the office, and then she ditched the cocktail party too and they went to a bar near Regent Street and talked on all evening. By the end of the night, they both knew that something had started.

It had been dizzying and delightful as she began to fall in love. He drove up to see her twice a week until one Friday night they kissed under a street lamp by Embankment tube station, oblivious to the people all around them. He came back to her tiny west London flat and they had frantic, clothes-tearing-off sex in the sitting room, before moving to the bedroom for long, tender hours of delicious lovemaking. She loved his smell, the feel of his skin, the muscled hardness of his back and thighs, and the way their bodies fitted together so perfectly. She was exhilarated at the rightness of it all, and he couldn't take his hands off her or keep his mouth from hers for any length of time. They wanted nothing more than one another, talking and laughing and confiding, and always ending up in bed again. He stayed the entire weekend and the flat, usually her haven, was empty and soulless when he'd gone. When he returned, he had a bag with him.

'I don't need to go back for a while,' he said. 'They're filming something at the house. I've left my cousin Ben in charge. He works for me. He can handle it all.'

'That's wonderful,' Delilah said with a smile, an effervescent excitement bubbling inside her. 'I'm glad you can stay.'

He gazed at her hungrily. 'I can't keep away from you. You're lighting up my life, Delilah. You've changed everything, you don't know how much.'

She felt reborn into happiness, Harry forgotten in her passion for John. He was funny, charming and witty, with a soulful side that intrigued her. He didn't speak much about himself or his family, and gave her only sketchy details of his history when she pressed for them, telling her that his father was ill with encroaching dementia, and that his mother had died years before, though he didn't elaborate. He had no brothers and sisters and he felt the weight of his great inheritance: the house and all that came with it. It was no wonder, she thought, that he had a tendency to spells of silence, when a dark mood descended on him and he seemed to vanish inside himself. When she asked him what was wrong, he would always snap out of it, smile again and tell her that it was nothing. But every few nights he was rocked by bad dreams that made him convulse, twist and cry out in his sleep, and he would wake panting and wild-eyed, in a panic that he could not describe. Then she would hold him and soothe him until it had passed and he fell asleep again.

*

The return to Fort Stirling made Delilah feel as though she was in a fairy tale. John drove her back on a frosty autumn day so that they could spend a weekend there, just the two of them, and the house looked impossibly beautiful against the sparkling icy parkland. When the gloomy afternoon fell, it was cosy inside with the lamps lit and the fire burning. The housekeeper had left a stew bubbling and potatoes baking. They drank wine in the small sitting room at the back of the house and made love in front of the fire.

Lying in his arms afterwards on a pile of cushions and watching the dancing flames, she said with a studied idleness, 'That portrait hanging in the hall – is it her?'

He stiffened slightly. 'Who?'

'Your first wife.' Earlier in the day, when John had gone to fetch something, she'd been looking at the pictures and had noticed the pastel and watercolour painting of a woman. It had a chocolate-box quality: the hair too blonde and smooth, the eyes too big and the mouth too cupid-bowed to be entirely plausible as a true likeness, but there was nevertheless a defiant air about the face. Underneath a small gold plate read *Vanna Ford Stirling*. It was obvious she was American, just from the way she'd kept her surname like that. Delilah had stared at it, curious. John had told her that his first wife was called Vanna. They had been married for four years and had split up amicably over a decade ago. She lived back in the States now, and had remarried. She was probably signing herself Vanna Ford Stirling Smith, or whatever her new name was.

'Vanna?' John relaxed. 'Yes, that's her.'

'Isn't it a bit strange to keep a picture of her hanging up?'

'Not really. Once a Stirling, always a Stirling.'

She paused and said lightly, 'Why did you two split up?'

'Usual reason. We married too young. She fell out of love with this house, and eventually with me. And I couldn't blame her. I can hardly bear this place myself.'

'That can't be true,' Delilah murmured, nuzzling his shoulder. 'It's glorious. And it's your home. You belong here.'

'So they tell me,' he said wryly.

'Do you really not like it?' She couldn't understand it. The house enchanted her. Everywhere she looked, she saw something beautiful, and each time she passed a window she was dazzled by the views across the lawns, parkland and woods.

He thought. 'I like parts of it. But . . .' His gaze slid to her and then away again. 'These old houses are saturated with the past – it's hard to escape it, hard to make the place your own.' He'd squeezed her hand. 'But your enthusiasm is helping me to look at it through fresh eyes. Forget the things I'd rather not remember.' He fixed her with a serious look. 'I don't want you thinking that Vanna means anything to me. She doesn't – not in that way. It was all a long time ago.'

'I won't,' she said, happy that she had nothing to fear from the past. She had not really felt menaced by the spectre of an ex-wife, but it was good to be reassured.

When they went up to bed, there was a beautiful package with her name on it nestling on her pillow. Inside was a ring, an antique aquamarine set with tiny flickering diamonds.

'Will you?' he said, his eyes hopeful and yet trusting. 'If you can bear a miserable old cove like me?'

'Of course, of course I will!' She burst into tears of happiness and hugged him.

The wedding was held as soon as they could arrange it, a small ceremony at a London register office with only close friends and immediate family, mostly Delilah's. John's father, he said, was too ill to attend.

'Don't you have anyone else you'd like to come?'

John shook his head. 'I can't be bothered with all my aunts and uncles and cousins. I like to keep things quiet with just friends. Do you mind?'

'Of course not,' she'd said. 'I've got enough family for both of us. You can have as many of my relations as you'd like and you're very welcome to them.'

Despite the grey skies and squalling winter rain, the day was all she wanted: romantic and stylish, with a lunch at a very expensive hotel after the ceremony. Then they went to Hawaii for three long and delicious weeks of honeymoon. John taught her how to surf and they spent all day on the beach before returning to their luxurious chalet at the hotel for baths, dinner and bed. She really couldn't imagine it was possible to be happier. At night, he told her how much he loved and needed her.

'You're the light of my life,' he whispered. 'I mean that.'

'I love you too,' she replied, overwhelmed with the bliss of being married to a man she loved and who needed her so much. His mordant wit charmed her; even his black moods were interesting and a little romantic. She felt certain she could make him happy and help him forget the misery of his childhood. Together, they could face anything.

But as the end of the honeymoon approached, the atmosphere changed. John stopped smiling and joking, and his periods of silent withdrawal became longer. The mood became heavy and no matter how much she tried to bring peace and good humour to the situation, she couldn't defuse the tension. They had never rowed, not seriously, but she had the sense that something was building and it was beyond her control to stop it.

The night before they left, John seemed keyed up in a way she'd never seen before and, on an impulse, she arranged for them both to have massages in the hotel spa to relax him. Afterwards, back in the chalet as they prepared to go for dinner, she thought he seemed calmer, though his grey eyes were still flinty in the way that signalled he was not at ease. She kept up an easy chatter to divert him while they got ready.

'I can't quite believe that on Monday I'll be back in the office as usual,' she said lightly, putting on her earrings in front of the mirror. The aquamarine in her engagement ring looked even bluer against the tan she'd acquired, and her face was glowing with the effects of sunshine and seawater. She could see John behind her, leaning against the wall, his hands thrust down low in his pockets. He looked strained. 'It's been so wonderful here, I haven't given home a thought. Goodness knows what's waiting for me when I get back. My inbox will be a nightmare.'

John glanced up at her reflection and their eyes met.

Why is he so tense and unhappy? The massage obviously hadn't worked as well as she'd hoped. She felt a rush of love and tenderness for him, wanting to take him in her arms and soothe all the bad feelings away.

He said, 'It doesn't matter really now, does it? You won't be there for long. How long is your notice period? A month?'

She pushed the back of her earring on and shook out her hair. It fell thick and fair over her shoulders. The sun had lightened it several shades, and her freckles had come out. 'What do you mean?'

'You'll be resigning when you get back, won't you? I thought you might do it before we left but you had so much on with the wedding, I didn't bring it up.'

She stared at him, startled. They had talked only vaguely about what would happen when they returned but she had assumed that the arrangement they had before the wedding would go on for a while longer: London in the week in her little flat, Fort Stirling at weekends and holidays, with John going back when there was an urgent need for him to be there. She'd grown accustomed to his being able to do what he wanted, leaving his cousin in charge when necessary so that they could be together. When John had talked about how they would live at the house, she'd pictured them there at some unspecified point in the future, when she felt ready to give up her London life or when circumstances decreed it. They'd agreed before the wedding that Delilah would come off the Pill and they would let things take their course. She was thirty-four and ready for motherhood when it came, but she had the vague impression that it could take a few months for the Pill's effects to wear off and so didn't expect to become pregnant immediately. She turned back from the mirror to face him and said slowly, 'You mean – stop working?'

He frowned. 'Well, how are you going to commute to London every day from Dorset? It's not exactly practical, is it? Where else would you live but with me, for God's sake?'

'But . . .' She stared at him helplessly. It seemed obvious now he said it, but she hadn't properly thought through the implications: that her career would need to be given up at once. 'Why didn't you say something before now?'

He laughed in a joyless way. 'I'm sorry, darling, but I thought you understood. I come as a package with the house. I belong at Fort Stirling. That's just the way it is. It was lovely having time to ourselves but I can't stay away indefinitely. It's just not possible. That place is my life and my work. Besides, my father is there and he needs me.'

'What about my work?' she said slowly. 'Doesn't that matter?'

'Anyone can do your job,' he said. 'But only I can do mine.'

She'd been hurt at the implication and he'd become exasperated because he hadn't meant to imply her job was easy, just that their circumstances were different. They'd begun to squabble and then to shout, and then they were having a proper quarrel.

'So my job and life don't matter?' she'd cried. He seemed like a stranger suddenly, and she hated it.

His eyes flashed with irritation. 'You married me – you must have understood that meant you were marrying the house as well!'

'We never talked about it!'

'Because it was glaringly obvious. You'll have to give up your job if we're going to be together. Besides, when you have a baby, you'll be stopping work anyway.'

'Oh, you've decided that, have you?' She felt furious. Even though she had half thought the same, his assumption enraged her. 'Am I supposed to become a full-time mother just because you say so? How dare you make those decisions on my behalf?'

He stared at her, his eyes steely, and something in him seemed to snap. He shouted, 'I don't have a choice – I've *never* had a choice – and now you've married me, neither do you! The sooner you understand that, the better!' He stormed out into the night, slamming the door behind him and leaving her weeping and frightened because she'd never seen him look at her in that terrible way, or heard such a tone of bitter resignation in his voice.

When he finally came back to bed, she was still awake. She wrapped her arms round him and said she was sorry. She'd thought it over and of course it was stupid of her not to realise that the fort would have to be their home right from the start. She would give up her job.

'I knew in my heart I'd do it eventually,' she said, stroking his back and feeling him relax in her arms. 'I suppose I just hadn't quite admitted it would be sooner rather than later. But you're right, my life is with you now. It's what I want.'

He'd hugged her back and kissed her. 'Thank you. I do love you, darling, and I'm sorry for that horrible row. I should have talked to you about all this, but I'm not very good at it, I'm afraid. I don't like admitting things, even to myself. I know what it means to give up your work. If it's any consolation, there's plenty to do at the house, believe me. It's a whole career in itself.' Smiling down at her, the dimple in his left cheek appearing, he said, 'You never know, we might have a honeymoon baby and then you'll have lots to keep you busy.'

'Maybe,' she'd said, relieved and happy that there was peace between them again. 'We'll see.'

Within a month, her notice was worked out, her flat had been rented and she had taken the first steps towards beginning her new life at Fort Stirling. The vast house was now her home. There was no sign of a baby yet.

Chapter Five
1965

Eastbourne seemed like a strange place for a honeymoon. Alexandra might not know much about such things but she had the vague idea that Paris or Venice were the right kinds of places, or somewhere by the sea in a hot country.

They had the sea, all right, but apart from that, not even a hotel. The little motor car had roared past The Grand on the sea front and Alexandra, who had expected them to stop, was quite disconcerted. Her husband – the word was strange and tasted bad, leaving a bitterness in her mouth – didn't so much as flick a glance at the place but continued frowning at the road ahead, a cigarette clamped between his lips or occasionally between his fingers.

He must know what he's doing, she thought. Her hands were pressed tightly into the seat on either side of her, her fingertips hooked into the grainy leather. They had barely spoken to one another since they had said their vows a few hours earlier. The bells had been pealing as they emerged from the church, her arm resting on the rough wool of his morning coat, and there'd been a swift glance at each other, a kind of half-smile on Laurence's lips, and he murmured, 'Are you all right?' to which she'd answered, 'Yes,' and then added hesitantly, 'darling.' His blue gaze slid away from her and he said nothing more. A moment later, they'd been surrounded by people, hustled into a waiting car and driven home again. She walked into the house feeling a little ridiculous now in her dress with its cumbersome train and the long froth of veil around her shoulders, and was greeted by two staring village girls holding trays of asparagus rolls. They'd bobbed curtsies and said, 'Hello, mum,' in a way that made her realise that everyone saw her differently since the little ritual in the church.

The reception passed in a hubbub of noise and a blur of tightly packed people. There was hardly enough room for the guests in the drawing room and some spilled out onto the terrace, as the village girls passed among them offering trays of food and sherry. Alexandra escaped the bunches of inquisitive ladies and with some muttered excuses slipped into the dining room, where the wedding presents had been laid out on the sideboard, displayed for anyone who cared to look. She went over, her train tucked over one arm, and inspected them. They didn't feel like hers and she wondered if it would be better if she simply left them where they were. The cut-glass vases and crystal looked more at home here than it ever would wherever they were going, not that she had much idea where that was.

'Delightful, aren't they?'

She jumped and turned to see Laurence's brother walking across the room towards her, looking like a comical little bantam with his chest puffed out and his hands clasped behind his back. He had fair hair like Laurence, swept back from his forehead, but unlike Laurence, with his thin, almost gaunt face, Robert was plump and his cheeks were ruddier than his brother's, as though blood had been pumped hard into the little veins and capillaries and got stuck there.

Robert came up and stood close to her, his shoulder almost brushing her as he leaned forward to examine the presents. 'Quite a haul. A respectable amount to start married life with.' He tilted his head so that he was looking up at her from one pale blue eye. 'Don't you think?'

She nodded. His nearness made her uncomfortable. 'They're very nice,' she said politely, although she had no feelings for the pile of glittering glass, silver and china.

'Look at this.' Robert lifted up a large blue and white china vase, something in the style of Chinese porcelain but with department-store sturdiness. 'Quite charming.' He held it out to her. She let the train fall from her arm and took the vase. It was heavier than it looked and she felt her arms sag under its weight.

'Here, give it back.' Robert reached out, his hands closing over hers. He smiled at her. 'I should have known a little thing like you wouldn't be able to manage it.'

She stared back at him, aware of his hot hands on top of hers, and then released her grip. The vase slid awkwardly away. Robert scrabbled for it but it resisted his clammy fingers and fell to the floor with a heavy thump. They both stared at it as it rolled back and forth on the carpet, like a fat baby unable to turn over because of its round belly.

It was unbroken, its solidity too much of a match for the floor.

'No harm done,' Robert said with obvious relief. He bent down to pick it up and when he rose again, his blue eyes were reddened with the effort. He put it back on the sideboard.

Perhaps his trousers are too tight, Alexandra thought. His whole suit seemed to be straining a little as though it had been fitted some years before when his frame was altogether slimmer.

Robert was breathing heavily from his exertion, the air whistling through his nostrils. She noticed tiny dark hairs shuddering within the caverns. He was pushing his face closer to hers, and his expression was changing from politeness to a kind of wolfish hunger. 'You're a pretty little thing, aren't you?' he said, his voice suddenly low. 'You're rather wasted on Laurence. He's never been a ladies' man, never had the eye. Never been able to read those little flirtatious games you like to play.' His rubicund face was approaching, his eyes like those blue and yellow swirly marbles in the jar in her room. 'But I can. You're being very naughty, aren't you? You know exactly what you're doing.'

'I don't understand,' she said, confused.

He was breathing a little faster. 'I like it, and you know it. I know about women. All you want is to excite a man and make him desire you. You're damn well succeeding.' He thrust his face at her and reached out with his large red hands, pawing at her chest.

Horrified and repulsed, she only knew she had to get out.

She whirled around, heading for the dining room door. There was a fearful rent and she felt herself jerk back.

'Christ!' exclaimed Robert. She turned to see he was staring down at the floor, where his black shoes were standing firmly on a remnant of the train. He had torn it clean off. She gasped, picked up her skirts and ran out of the room, leaving him there with the puddle of white silk at his feet.

It had been almost a relief to leave after that. She'd run trembling to her room and slammed the door, leaning against it and biting her lip hard not to cry.

He's a beast, a beast! she thought. The idea that she wanted to excite him, to make him pant and turn red like a fool, was ridiculous and hurtful. Was it because she was married now? Was that why men might think she was teasing them? It was baffling and horrible. She looked around. The sight of her old books and pictures, and the suitcases standing by the door, the whole place looking empty already, was almost too painful.

I mustn't tell Laurence, she thought. *I know that would be very wrong. He might believe Robert, he might think I did want to . . . to . . .* She couldn't quite imagine what anyone might think she wanted to do with Robert. The idea of his face touching hers made her shudder. Pushing it out of her mind, she concentrated on taking off the spoiled dress, a difficult task without help, and putting on her going-away costume: a blue wool dress and matching coat edged in white, with a small white hat and white pointed shoes.

When she'd come down, cold and calm, there'd been general amusement.

'She can't wait, old man!' cried a male voice from the back, amid the laughing. 'You'd better get on your way.'

She'd stood there, awkward in her smart, grown-up clothes, and wondered why they were laughing. Then Laurence came up to her and twenty minutes later she was pressing her lips to her father's cold cheek and then Aunt Felicity's powdery soft one, and they were saying goodbye. She glimpsed Robert Sykes in the crowd that came to wave them off with a cheer, and looked away with a concealed shiver. Then the car roared away from the house and she was alone with her husband at last.

'Mr and Mrs Sykes? Yes, I have the booking here.' The lady, her hair set in lank curls that looked at least a fortnight old, peered through her glasses at the register. 'That's right. Sea view. Room eight. Arthur will show you up.' Then she shrieked loudly, 'Arthur! Arthur! Come and carry some luggage.' Her voice returned to its normal tone as she said with a smile, 'Honeymooners, are you?'

Alexandra looked about. This was nothing more than a cheap seaside boarding house, the kind with pretensions to gentility, with gaudy old master reproductions on the walls, crocheted covers on every surface and carpets that were tacky underfoot. Why had Laurence brought her here? Couldn't he think of anything better than this?

Arthur appeared, a tubby man wearing his braces over his shirt, and took the two larger cases while Laurence brought the smaller bags, and they followed him up the staircase and along a hall to room eight.

When they were left alone in their bedroom, Alexandra noticed that there were two beds separated by a slim night table with a pink china lamp on it. She stared at them. What did this mean? Were they going to be sleeping apart? A shimmer of relief went through her and she let out a long, slow breath. She'd been holding it, she realised, as they'd come through the door.

Into the chamber, she thought, obscurely wondering if she were quoting something. A bridal chamber. And then she wanted to laugh. This was her bridal chamber! A greasy-walled, shabby little room with a view of a patch of shingle and an inky smear of sea. Laurence was standing by the window staring out at it. As her gaze landed on him, he took out a packet of cigarettes and lit one, turning to face her as he exhaled a cloud of grey smoke.

'Are you hungry?'

It was the first thing he'd said to her for a long time. 'I . . . yes . . . Yes, I am.' She realised that she'd barely eaten all day. Her breakfast had been lost down the lavatory and she hadn't had the stomach for asparagus rolls.

'So am I,' Laurence replied. He took a small strand of tobacco off his tongue and then smiled at her. 'I don't think they do dinner here. Let's go and see what we can find.'

They went out into the already darkening evening and found a small restaurant where they ate fish and chips on china plates as they talked politely about the day, and then a dry, dusty-tasting strawberry meringue. After they'd both had a cup of coffee, they walked very slowly back along the road towards their boarding house. Laurence reached out and took her hand, putting it over his arm and holding it in his. His mood seemed to have turned tender.

'You looked very pretty today,' he said in a confiding tone, his gaze sliding over to her.

'Did I?' She was surprised. It hadn't occurred to her to wonder if he had responded to her in that way. She had just hoped that she looked right, rather than pretty.

'The other men were jealous, I could see that.' He sounded pleased about it.

She remembered Robert Sykes' face pressed up close to hers, the sight of the inside of his nostrils, and felt a wave of nausea. She clutched Laurence's arm tighter and looked up at him. He was suddenly handsome to her, with his fair hair carefully combed and his pale face. He seemed clean and neat and honourable, not like his brother in the least. She felt safe with him and a rush of affection for him coursed through her.

My husband, she thought, still wonderingly. *This is my husband*. She smiled back up at him. 'I'm glad I made you proud,' she replied.

'You did. Very.' He lifted her hand to his lips and kissed it. His mouth was cool from the night breeze. 'And here we are.'

She wanted, in this moment of sudden intimacy, to ask him why he had chosen this strange guest house but before she could frame the question, they were walking up the steps and Laurence was saying, 'Let's hope Mrs Addington isn't on the desk,' as he pushed open the front door.

But there she was, watching them as they came in. 'Good evening, Mr Sykes!' she trilled. 'If you and your wife would like a drink, the bar is open to guests.' She nodded to an open door leading off the hallway and Alexandra turned to see a plushly carpeted room set up with a polished counter and easy chairs around small wooden tables. It was empty except for a man holding a newspaper, peering out from around it to see who was in the hall. When his gaze caught hers, he quickly disappeared behind his paper.

'No, thank you,' Laurence said. 'I think we'll go straight up. It's been a busy day.'

'Indeed,' the landlady said with a sugary smile. 'And a very special one, too. Congratulations on behalf of us all, I'm sure.' She watched with a knowing smile as they walked up the stairs.

Alexandra stared at herself in the mirror. She'd come along the hall to the shared bathroom, with her night things over one arm. The idea of changing in front of Laurence was horrifying and she had no wish to see him begin to take off all the things that civilised him and made him a gentleman – his jacket, waistcoat, shirt and cufflinks, his belt and trousers and then ... what would he reveal underneath? She felt appalled at the idea that he would humble himself by undressing in front of her. She wasn't sure if he'd be vulnerable beneath, a kind of helpless child, or reveal an animal maleness, like a bull or a stallion with its shameless, swinging organs – a strong and strident difference that she would have to contend with as best she could. It didn't seem right, not at all.

Her face was pale and her eyes frightened. She combed out her dark hair so that it fell long over her shoulders. She stared at her high-necked nightdress and, after a moment, undid two of the buttons at the top. Then she quickly did them up again.

'I don't know what to do,' she said to herself. Her cheeks looked hollow with fear. What was she doing here, in this strange place with this strange man? And what was about to happen?

There was no help for it. She couldn't stay here forever. Other guests might be waiting. And besides, it would look odd if she were too long. She picked up the pile of her clothes and shoes, her washbag and hairbrush and made her way back along the hall. To her relief, Laurence had already changed into his pyjamas and cleaned his teeth in the room's washbasin. Now he was in one of the beds, a newspaper resting on the blanket.

'Hello,' he said, smiling as she came in. 'I took this one, is that all right?'

'Of course.' She turned back the covers of her bed and slipped between them. They were chilly and she rubbed her feet to warm them up, as she did at home.

'Are you all right?' Laurence was watching her.

'Yes, thank you.' It was disconcerting. Her bedroom had always been a private place before now. The only person who had ever come in was her mother. Alexandra could still remember her mother's weight as she sat on the bed, one hand stroking Alexandra's hair, the other holding her hand as they talked about the events of the day. Then, a gentle kiss, the footsteps, the pause in the doorway as she turned to smile, and the sudden change from a person to a silhouette as the light went out. Since the accident, no one had come to turn out the light – she had to go to the switch herself and scamper back over the cold floor to her bed. There were no bedtime kisses and no gentle words. Until now, perhaps.

She lay down and closed her eyes. Events of the day scudded through her head and before she knew it, she began to sink into sleep. A click made her eyes open wide to blackness; Laurence had turned off the lamp. Her heart began to pound beneath her nightgown, thudding against her chest.

Nothing happened for a while and then she heard him get quietly out of his bed and walk around to hers.

'Alexandra?'

She said nothing but squeezed her eyes shut, lying as still as she could.

'Are you awake?'

Honesty had been drummed into her since girlhood. 'Yes.'

'May I . . . I'd like to . . . join you.' His voice was low, almost pleading.

'Of course.' She did nothing to help him, though, lying stock still, one fist clenched with tension. She felt the blanket and sheet lift, and cold air waft in. He climbed in behind her, squeezing onto the narrow mattress, pressing his body to hers.

She was holding her breath, she realised, and she released

it slowly, pulling in another as quietly as she could. Laurence wrapped one arm around her, tucking his legs up under hers. He began to nuzzle at her neck. She stayed utterly still, her eyes open wide against the darkness, wondering what she was supposed to do.

He was rubbing himself against her body, she realised, and one hand was stroking her behind, following the curve of her buttocks down and then up again, softly at first and then with more force. Then he began to move his hips against her. Something hard prodded her in the buttocks as his stroking grew rougher, and the heavy breathing in her ear where he was pressing his face into her neck louder.

'Help me, can't you?' he muttered.

'What shall I do?'

'Pull up your nightdress.'

She hesitated. So this was it. That thing they had talked about was going to happen to her now. It was hard to imagine that it might possibly be heaven, but there was still time, she supposed, for the bliss to begin. If only she weren't so frightened. Reaching down, she slipped her nightgown up as best she could and lay still again, feeling exposed. Now Laurence's hand was on her bare bottom and he was stroking and pinching her there.

'Do you like it?' he murmured in her ear between his panting breaths. 'Is this nice?'

'Yes,' she said miserably, and he responded by pinching her a little harder and saying, 'Good, good.'

Now his hand moved suddenly around her hip and onto her belly. She gasped but managed to stifle it. No one had touched her here since the doctor had pressed her to check for appendicitis when she was twelve. Aunt Felicity had given her hot-water bottles to press against herself when her period pains came, but had never looked. And now this man's hand was on her – not just any man, her *husband* – and to her horror, it was heading downwards, towards the private place between her legs where no one but she had ever been.

Long thin fingers that felt like knobbly sticks probed her. She bit her teeth down into her lip and concentrated on letting no sounds escape her, though she wanted to say *Stop! Don't do that!* and push him away. But the hard scrabbling on her tender flesh went on, as though he was searching for something underneath her. She realised that the prodding in her buttocks was getting more pronounced and then a moment later, after Laurence had fumbled with his pyjama bottoms, she knew with a hot, appalled certainty what was poking at her.

What am I supposed to do? she wondered, agonised. She had no idea. She had never imagined that this might happen with her facing away from her husband. Now he was sliding his hand between her thighs and trying to press them apart. It felt vaguely ludicrous.

'Can't you help a bit more?' he panted in her ear, and she obediently raised her leg. The hot-tipped prodding thing was at her buttocks, prying between them. She was in a curdle of mortification and confusion, afraid of whatever it was that was supposed to happen next.

'Turn around,' he said.

She wriggled round, hampered by the nightdress twirled around her waist, until she was on her back.

'Move your legs apart and I'll go between them.'

'All right,' she said in a small, fearful voice. She was grateful for the cloak of darkness as she let her legs fall open, revealing the soft heart between them. She couldn't see him at all but she could smell Pears soap and a musty oil scent that might be his hair cream, and she could feel the warmth of his body, though his skin was still cool to touch. He was kneeling between her thighs now and as she glanced down, she saw something long and thin rearing out from his groin, and quickly looked away, her breath coming in fast, frightened pants. Surely this would hurt her, it must.

'I'm going to try now,' he said.

She shut her eyes as he lay down on her. He was not much taller than she was and almost as slim. His cool skin was virtually hairless and he didn't weigh much as he let his body rest on hers. Then she felt it.

'Why . . . can't . . . I . . .' He spoke through clenched teeth. 'What's happening? What's wrong?'

'I don't know,' she replied anxiously. 'What's supposed to happen?'

'Don't be a goose, you must know that! You're supposed to let me in. You'd better guide me.'

Guide you where? she thought, but she put out her hand, moving it in the direction of the insistent prodder. Then she touched it, screamed and pulled her hand back as though it had burnt her.

'What's wrong?' he hissed. 'Why the blazes did you do that? You'll wake everyone up!' He was evidently angry.

'I'm sorry . . . I was startled.'

'Come on, let's try again.'

She put out her hand again, gathered her courage and seized the rod. It was hot and smooth and slender, like its owner.

'Ow, don't pinch it, you clumsy idiot,' he snapped. 'Now, put it in.'

But he might as well have asked her to conjure a coin from his ear. She had no idea where to manoeuvre the thing, or how she was going to take it in. There seemed to be no earthly way that could happen. They carried on for ten fruitless minutes, Laurence getting more agitated and Alexandra more despairing at her stubbornly resistant body. At last, he swore hard under his breath and sighed. She noticed that he was limper now, eventually shrinking away to a small, soft, curled snail of a thing nestled in the coarse hair at the base of his belly. He climbed off her and out of the little bed, saying, 'I give up. It's a waste of time. Just work out what you're doing wrong and we'll try again another time.'

'Yes,' she said meekly, humiliated but deeply relieved now it was over. She knew it must be her fault that it had been such an awful experience. 'I'm sorry, Laurence.'

He grunted as he returned to his own bed. She rolled over, pulling down her nightdress. Sooner than she could have imagined possible, she was asleep.

But the next morning, the knowing look of the landlady and the impertinence of her raised eyebrow and the amused pursing of her lips were almost more than Alexandra could stand. She didn't know what to be more ashamed of: that Mrs Addington thought she had been successfully deflowered, or her own failure to do whatever it was that Laurence had wanted.

Chapter Six

Present day

Even after more than six months of marriage, Delilah found it hard to remember that letters addressed to Mrs Stirling were for her. She picked up the daily stack that had been left out for her in the hall and flicked it as she wandered down the long passage towards the kitchen. The post usually came early and John always sorted it first, removing anything that wasn't for her and spiriting it away into the estate office where he spent so many hours working, a place where she knew he preferred to be alone.

She didn't recognise any of the correspondents, which meant it was probably the usual raft of requests. She was still getting used to being constantly approached for help by worthy causes – some wanted her to attend a smart fund-raiser, others requested free use of the house or grounds, and yet more asked for her to give money or donate objects. She wished she could help them all but sometimes she wished they would leave her alone; if she acceded to all requests, the house would be continually full of people and empty of anything else, as it would have all been given away. Besides, it wasn't in her power to say yes or no without John's permission, and he would only consider ideas that would bring the house as much income for as little effort as possible. That was why photo shoots and filming were fine but he gave short shrift to suggestions that they should do anything for free.

Delilah tore open one of the letters as she went into the kitchen where Janey, their housekeeper, was cleaning the butler sink.

'Morning, Janey. Is there any coffee on the go?'

Janey looked up with a smile. 'Hello there. Yes, there's some just brewed up fresh in the jug. I'll pour you a mug.'

'No, don't worry, I'll get it.' She put the letters down on the scrubbed pine table and went to get herself the coffee. She liked the kitchen, a large and bright room, and Janey kept it welcoming, with vases of flowers, bowls of fruit and the scent of fresh cooking. Delilah relished the feeling of being in a normal home. Nowhere else in the house felt like this.

'How are you today?' she asked, sipping on her coffee.

'Oh, very well. Lovely to see the sun, isn't it?'

Delilah nodded. She got on well with Janey and was glad of her company. It stopped the house being so unbearably empty. Knowing that Janey and Erryl, her husband, were in the lodge down the drive was comforting, and made her feel a little less stranded out here in the middle of the estate. Janey came in most days to manage the house, along with the help of cleaners, while Erryl took care of the grounds and did odd jobs that didn't need a specialist. No doubt in the old days relations between housekeeper and mistress would have been much more formal, but she and Janey had an easy time together. At first, Janey had called her 'Mrs Stirling' but Delilah had coaxed her out of it, although she still preferred to say nothing rather than actually use Delilah's name. Erryl called her 'ma'am' and she didn't seem able to do a thing about it. 'I'm going to take Mungo for a walk in the woods.'

'Just the day for it, it'll be lovely up there. Are you taking some coffee in to Mr Stirling?'

'Oh – er, yes. I'll take it before I go out.' She flushed slightly. She'd hoped Janey might do the honours today. John was in a bad mood because the VAT return was due, and she preferred not to knock on the office door if she could help it.

They talked over domestic details while Delilah drank her coffee and opened her post, putting most of it aside to read more carefully later, then she got up to go, almost reluctant to leave the pleasant normality of the kitchen.

'Right,' she said, standing up. 'I'll take some coffee to John and then get on my way.'

'See you later – enjoy yourself.'

The estate office was down the hall, towards the front of the house. She knocked on the door and went in. John was staring at the computer, one hand on the mouse, frowning with concentration.

'Coffee break,' she announced.

He looked up, startled. 'Hello. Thanks for that. I could do with a breather.' He sat back in his chair and sighed.

'You started early this morning,' she said, putting the mug down on the desk. The room was lined with shelves full of files, and John's desk was scattered with papers of all kinds. 'How is the VAT going?'

He made a face. 'Bloody awful. I don't know what I pay the accountant for. I do everything but fill in the boxes.'

Delilah gestured to a box of papers and receipts. 'Isn't he going to work his way through that?'

'Yes, good point. I can do without that fresh hell. What are you up to?'

'I'm going to take Mungo for a walk, then answer letters.'

He fixed her with an enquiring look. 'Any news?'

She remembered how his eyes used to soften from their usual granite grey to a cloudier colour when he looked at her. These days he seemed to have lost that tenderness towards her, and she longed to see it again. She smiled and said, 'Nothing yet.'

An expression of hope crossed his face. 'Well, that's good, isn't it? How late are you?'

'It's two days now.'

'Are you going to do a test?'

'Maybe not today. If there's still nothing by Saturday, I'll do one.' She'd learned not to do the tests too early: a negative result somehow still held the possibility of hope. It was only when she felt the familiar drag in her belly and found that her period had started that she accepted that, once again, she was not pregnant.

'Okay. Two days is good, isn't it? That's longer than last time.'

She observed the anxious look on his face and wondered when their lives had become so all absorbed by this desire to have a child. It hadn't seemed so desperately important at first, when she'd been busy closing down her London life and making the move here. But gradually the fact of months passing without any sign of a baby began to dominate everything. 'I know, but I'm not usually late all the time. I'm worried it's the stress playing havoc with me. Let's wait and see. You know there's nothing we can do about it,' she said. A fear played at the back of her mind that their failure to conceive was beginning to drive them apart, but she tried to banish that thought. They both wanted this, and it wouldn't help if they began blaming each other.

He gave her a wan smile. 'You're right, I suppose. Best not to think about it.'

'Exactly. Now, I'd better leave you to the joys of accounting. Good luck.'

'Thanks. See you at lunch.' He turned back to his computer screen, frowning. She let herself out quietly.

Delilah called Mungo from his basket and he came scampering excitedly, knowing they were going for a walk. She had never had a dog until now, thinking she did not much like them, but it was hard not to respond to the little cocker spaniel with his glossy black coat, long soft ears and trusting brown eyes. He didn't feel like hers yet, but she was beginning to enjoy him.

'Come on, boy,' she said, taking a cardigan off a hook and opening the boot room door. Outside in the garden, Mungo sniffed around, nosing at the flower beds. She breathed in and took in her surroundings. The air was fresh and clean. The summer was ripening to that jewel-like moment when the gardens glowed with ripe fruit and vegetables, and the sky turned a gold-soaked blue and offered the prospect of long, shimmering green days that would fade slowly into warm evenings with pink-streaked skies. She loved this time of year, with its fresh scents and fluttering breezes. Summer still felt young and undusty. Everything good was still to come.

With Mungo trotting at her heels, she made her way through the formal gardens that lay behind the house, the neatly arranged box hedges in their perfectly symmetrical patterns and the ordered beds. They gave her a sense of calm that came from well-planned detail and good organisation. She caught a movement and looked over to see Ben hard at work among the beds. He was bent low, the brown flesh of his muscled arms glowing in the sunshine. He always wore the same things: shabby brown shorts with gardening gloves stuffed in the pocket, a white T-shirt with smears of brown and green, a tool belt at his waist and sturdy boots. He hadn't seen her and she wondered whether to call out to him. She'd liked Ben as soon as she met him, drawn to him by his simple, unpretentious air and his willingness to help. Now she valued the way he was so even-tempered and always happy to see her and take a few minutes away from the garden to chat.

I could ask him about the gymkhana, she thought. One of her letters was from the pony club requesting the use of a field for their annual competition day. She hadn't wanted to bother John with it when he had so much on, but Ben would probably know what it was all about.

Delilah started over towards him, then paused, wondering why she was hesitating. There was nothing wrong in talking to Ben, but lately she'd noticed she was often thinking of him. Most days she wandered into the garden to seek him out, sometimes with a cup of tea or a glass of water for him. He was such easy company – cheerful, good-humoured and friendly. After the tension of John's mood swings and low spirits, she found Ben's company relaxing. She didn't need to be on full alert for a temper change. It was a relief, even if she knew that it wasn't entirely how things should be.

There's no harm in it, she said to herself. *He's just a friend. He's John's cousin so we're practically related. He works here so I'm bound to see him all the time.*

She watched as Ben straightened up and used his forearm to brush his light brown hair from his sweaty forehead. He noticed her and lifted his arm to wave, a broad smile on his face. She smiled and waved back, wondering if she should go to him after all, then caught herself. That wasn't the plan. She intended to walk Mungo, and she would. Ben was gazing at her, obviously expecting her to come over, so she gestured towards the yew walk to indicate where she was going. He nodded and turned back to his work, and she called to Mungo and headed towards the old gates that led out of the garden and into the woods beyond, glad to be getting away from what she felt obscurely was a source of danger.

Don't be ridiculous, she scolded herself as she entered the cool of the woods, the undergrowth lush and spidery with foliage. *You're imagining things.*

She'd always had a strong and creative imagination, which she supposed was what had led her to the magazine world, but she'd also prided herself on her pragmatism and was easily exasperated by people like Rachel, who lived her entire life like she was in a daft movie. Delilah had managed to reconcile herself to giving up her job by deciding to focus all that creativity and energy on the house and turn it into something vibrant and alive. At first, she'd had complete confidence in her ability to take it on and tame it but now, after six months, she was quailing before the task. Her first winter had been nothing less than an ordeal. She had never been so cold, as freezing weather descended and took the whole house in its icy grip. The place seemed shrouded in almost continual darkness, as though it was actually near the Arctic Circle and locked into six months of night, and the vast rooms that had once been so enchanting were like chilly museum pieces. Her ideas about bringing them all back to life and persuading John to light the fires and turn on the lamps so that they could actually use them seemed ridiculous when she stood in the grey morning light of the drawing room and saw her breath turn to frosty clouds. Under the eyes of the long-dead Stirlings gazing down at her from the wall, she'd felt that attempting to warm the place was beyond her power. Besides, what was the point?

It wasn't as though the two of them could occupy all the rooms at once, and even one was far too large for them. The only one they bothered with was the library, where at weekends the fire was lit and glasses of whisky and ginger wine put out, in accordance with some old family custom. Then, with the huge velvet curtains closed and the lamps on, and Mungo snoozing on the rug, she could pretend for a while that her dream of what it would be like to live in a house like this was coming true. But the reality was that most often she and John ate in the kitchen and then spent their evenings in the snug, which had once been a sitting room for live-in staff and still had a faintly impersonal, almost institutional air. The furniture was old and worn, everything make-do, nothing loved or treasured. There they would sit on the ancient rug-covered, dog-hairy sofa and watch the television together. So much for her dreams of wafting about the turquoise and gold drawing room in a silk tea dress, hosting soirees or entertaining London friends at glamorous parties in her great house. John was not at all keen on the idea of visitors, and after a few awkward weekends, she hadn't repeated the experience.

'Perhaps when you've had the chance to redecorate?' Grey had suggested sympathetically when he had stayed. 'I love the naïve charm of having your guest bathroom half a mile away from the guest bedroom, but I do rather rely on hot water when I finally get there.'

'Sorry, sorry!' she'd said humbly. 'You've been so uncomfortable. I will get that mattress seen to, I promise.'

'It's not just that, though,' he said, and leant in confidingly.

87

'If I'm honest, I've found the whole place a bit spooky. I never thought a house could be too big, but I'm beginning to think that this one is. The emptiness just seems to press down on one, doesn't it?'

That was exactly it, Delilah thought. There was no way to occupy it all and gradually she had come to feel smaller and less effectual as the house loomed over her. The days were manageable. Then she could fling open a door and see whatever lay beyond if she felt like it. But as night fell, the place seemed to swell in size and she felt the tingling of childish terrors. When they went up to bed, she dreaded leaving the snug, even with its hideous furniture, and ascending the narrow back stairs to the upper part of the main house and the great stretch of dark corridor ahead that disappeared into door-lined blackness. They couldn't turn on the light because there was no way to turn it off further down the hall, so it meant a quick walk in the blackness down towards their bedroom at the front of the house and she was always intimidated by the huge empty house all around them. The closed doors hinted at something unpleasant contained behind them and she had to rein in her imagination in case it ran wild and set off a panic. If she was with John, she could hold his hand and feel his warmth and his air of sensible normality. Alone, it was all she could do not to break into a gasping run and dash for the bedroom. Once inside, there was safety. As soon as the light came on, the glow doused her fears and she would laugh at herself for being so stupid.

But it wasn't normal to be afraid like this in her own

home. Her flat in London had been a refuge, a sanctuary. She would close its front door with a sense of relief that now she could shut out the world and nestle down into her own space, refreshing herself in quiet and safety.

If only John would let her start redecorating, making the place more comfortable and more their own. If only they could fill it with people, the way it was meant to be, and conquer the deadening quiet that way. But it seemed that it belonged to the generations of the past more than to them.

She walked through the woods almost without seeing them, lost in her own thoughts and only vaguely aware of Mungo racing away and returning. Then, suddenly, she emerged into bright sunlight, its warmth giving her a burst of pleasurable energy, and she realised she was in a clearing. Her eye was caught by the old tower sitting on the slight hill at its centre. She'd seen it before on walks but had always skirted it. Now, as Mungo bounded up the hill, invigorated by all the open space and breeze-rippled grass, she headed towards it for a closer look. She'd never seen anything like it. Ben had told her it was built in the nineteenth century, which accounted for its Gothic appearance, and that it had been the equivalent of a summer house or garden shed for the owner, just a little place to hang out when there was nothing else to do, but it had been decaying for decades. As she approached, she saw that it was in a frightful state, with fallen masonry everywhere and the inside rotten and full of weeds and brambles. The entrance to the tower had been boarded up and a sign on the front warned that there was no entry permitted owing to the unsafe structure but, peering in at the narrow window, she saw a few abandoned beer cans and other rubbish that showed people had managed to get in at some point recently, though why they would want to, she couldn't imagine. The place was a dangerous old wreck, the interior damp and fetid. It had an unpleasant atmosphere too. She didn't feel any desire to explore it further and when Mungo barked and raced away, she followed him with some relief.

It was almost lunchtime when she got back. Mungo was still energetic and as they approached the house, he raced off round the side of the west wing and over to the soft green lawn they called the quad that sat between the wings of the house. Delilah called for him, exasperated. The dog seemed insatiably attracted to the only bit of the garden he was really forbidden to go on – not counting the kitchen garden, which had a gate that kept him out – because John didn't want him scratching up the velvety smoothness of the grass, or making a mess on it.

She hurried round the corner to the quad but when she got there, Mungo was nowhere to be seen.

'Mungo! Where are you?' She went after him, wondering if he had gone into the rose garden where he liked to lap at the water in the fountain, and she was just heading towards it when she saw a figure in the distance, white-haired and a little hunched. She recognised John's father and stopped. He was shuffling along one of the garden paths, apparently on his own.

John's father lived in the old coach house, now converted

to a comfortable home, where he was cared for by a nurse. Delilah had only met him a few times, and on the last occasion, the old man hadn't been able to grasp that she was John's wife. In fact, he had ignored her altogether and had concentrated instead on asking John the same question about the Van Dyke in the gallery over and over, even though John kept explaining that it was on loan to an exhibition. It was obvious he was in the grip of dementia. Alzheimer's, John said, but at a stage where he could slip in and out of awareness, sometimes appearing quite normal and others definitely confused.

Now he was coming towards her, looking thin and bent over in a shirt and baggy cardigan and loose cord trousers. She wondered, panicked, about what she should do, feeling suddenly as though she didn't belong here at all but could be thrown off the premises at any minute by this old man who didn't know who she was. It was his house after all. He was still the lord. John had responsibility for it all, but he didn't own it yet.

He's my father-in-law, she reminded herself. *We're family now.* She stepped forward, smiling, and said, 'Hello' – then stopped short, wondering what to call him. What was his first name? Her mind was a blank. He'd taken some of the wonderful sixties photographs in the drawing room and they had his signature across the bottom but she couldn't remember it now. Then she should call him Lord Northmoor and yet that seemed far too formal considering they were now related. She was stumped, staring mutely as he approached, before giving up and saying brightly, 'How are you? It's a lovely day, isn't it?'

'Elaine?' he said loudly, his voice rising with a hopeful inflection at the end. 'Elaine, is that you?'

'No, no,' Delilah replied, glad that he was communicating with her. 'I'm not Elaine. I'm Delilah, John's wife.'

'Elaine,' he said in a low voice, the name leaving him on a sigh. 'Where have you been all this time?'

'I . . . I'm sorry. You're mistaken, I'm not Elaine. Can I help you find her? Does she live around here?'

'Oh, Elaine – it's so good to see you.' His eyes, so like John's but faded to a foggy off-white, were full of hope. He must have been handsome once, Delilah thought, but his confusion made him appear older than he probably was. He put out his arms.

She froze. She couldn't accept the embrace when he thought she was someone else – or should she anyway? Would it be worse to refuse? The old man was obviously happy to see this Elaine person.

He was just about to wrap her in his arms when another voice floated out over the garden. 'There you are! What are you doing, wandering off like this?'

Delilah looked over the old man's shoulder and saw his nurse, Anna, coming towards them. She wore a matronly blue dress that buttoned up the front, and her large arms wobbled as she came along the path at a smart pace.

The man said in a quavering voice, 'I'm looking at the garden . . . just looking.'

The nurse reached them. 'Hello, Mrs Stirling! I hope you haven't been startled by his lordship.'

'No, not at all.' Delilah smiled, relieved that a professional was here to deal with the situation. 'I don't think he knows me, though. He seems to think I'm someone called Elaine. Do you know who that is?'

Anna thought for a moment, then shook her head. 'No, I've not heard of an Elaine before. But who knows where his mind is going these days? It could be anywhere in the past seventy years or so.' She took the elderly man's arm and gently turned him in the direction of the old coach house. 'Come on now, let's get you back.'

'Shall I come with you?' Delilah asked, feeling she should offer to help.

'No, don't worry. You get on.'

John's father followed Anna obediently, and appeared to have forgotten about Delilah the moment she was out of sight.

Mungo came bounding up.

'There you are! Come on then, boy, let's get inside.' Delilah patted her thigh to bring him to heel, looked over her shoulder one last time at the old man being led away, and continued back to the house.

Chapter Seven

1965

Alexandra stood in front of the mirror in the hall of the tiny flat she and Laurence shared in the married quarters and ran her fingertips over her hair. It felt unfamiliar and shell-like, beads of lacquer clinging to it like tiny hard rain-drops. At Chez Joel they'd made it shorter, with a jaunty curl and a lift at the roots from the giant black hairdryer that she'd sat under for a hot half hour. The new style made her look older, and so did the make-up. Sophie Tortworth had showed her how to apply panstick, rubbing it in until her face became a solid tan blankness. She'd learned how to rim her lids with the kohl and to spit onto the cake of hard black mascara and then comb it onto her lashes with the little brush until they stuck out spikily around her eyes like fat spiders' legs. The first time he'd seen her efforts, Laurence had laughed, but Sophie told her she looked very glamorous and grown-up, much better than the dowdy girl who'd arrived in married quarters a few months before.

I look like a wife now, she thought. *I look like one of them.*

That was what she hoped. She wanted to belong, if only to stop them questioning her about how she was enjoying married life. It was bewildering to be surrounded by people after her quiet existence, and there was so much entertaining and so many functions to go to. Almost every week there was a dinner in the mess, the men in their bright dress uniforms and the women in stiff silks and glittering with jewellery. Alexandra could sense the competition going on between the wives, as they admired in honeyed tones one another's dresses and shoes, the little evening bags rough with beaded embroidery, the silken ribbons holding back hair in the styles from that month's magazines, and the glimmer of a new rope of pearls or bracelet. So far, though, they'd been nice to her, telling her how young and pretty she was, as though comforting her for her lack of style and the fact she only had one evening dress. At the dinners and lunches and coffee mornings she was expected to attend, she could tell she was being assessed even while they were cooing over her.

Alexandra was glad of Sophie, the wife of a lieutenant colonel, who'd taken a shine to her and decided to polish her up with a little London glamour.

'It's obvious you don't have the first idea!' she'd exclaimed but not in an unfriendly way. Sophie had made the most of unfortunate teeth and a big nose by emphasising her eyes with blue shadow and getting her hair set into a style like a movie star's. 'And it's a shame because you really are very pretty! Such big blue eyes, and that little pixie nose. Darling, I'd have given anything for a nose like that – you're so lucky.

But you don't do anything with yourself. Didn't your mother teach you how to put on lipstick?'

'My mother's dead,' Alexandra had remarked flatly, and then felt guilty seeing Sophie flush and her eyelids flutter with embarrassment. 'But don't worry, it was ages ago.'

Sophie looked relieved. 'Well, then, I'll take you to Boots. It's the only thing for it.'

They bought panstick, eye pencil and mascara, powder and a slippery lipstick of frosted pink grease, and then Sophie had insisted on a haircut.

Now Alexandra looked quite different from the day she and Laurence had arrived, pale and exhausted after their honeymoon. The whole experience in Eastbourne had been traumatic for both of them. They had attempted several times to manage whatever it was they were supposed to do in bed and it always ended in mortifying failure. Laurence started lingering in the bar after dinner while she went up to the room alone. She'd only been able to sleep after he'd come in at last as she lay stock still and hardly breathing, listening to him stumble about the room, swearing gently as he undressed, before falling into bed and a loud, drunken sleep. She was torn between bitter disappointment that she was failing him somehow, and deep relief that they were not going to go through the humiliation of trying again.

In their new flat, they shared a bed but they barely touched. When Laurence came home sober and in good time, they went through the same little bedtime ritual. She turned onto her right shoulder, he onto his left; they murmured a polite goodnight and stayed back to back until morning. But that was happening less and less. He ate in the mess so regularly that she hardly bothered preparing supper now in the tiny galley kitchen, as more often than not she sat waiting as it turned leathery and unappetising in the oven. She'd know then that he'd come back drunk.

Was it so unusual to be like this? She had the vague idea that her parents had been the same: together and yet apart. Real married life wasn't like the stories of romance; it was about existing in a civil and separate manner, keeping up appearances at parties and fulfilling obligation in private. That was why she kept the little flat so tidy: she didn't want Laurence to think she had failed him in all areas. She wanted to be a good wife, even if she wasn't yet able to do that thing with him.

But she knew that they would have to succeed at some point, or what would happen about children?

Alexandra pulled on a cardigan over her summer dress and went out, nodding a hello to the sentries as she left the barracks. She liked seeing them there: it made her feel safe and protected in the middle of this big, strange city. At first London had seemed so vast, she'd been utterly overwhelmed and very homesick. But gradually she was getting to know it, and to conjure up the courage to venture out little distances away from the safety of home. It helped having Hyde Park so close. She crossed the road and went through the iron gate into the park, relishing the sense of freedom. She didn't mind this kind of loneliness, when she could wander and explore in peace. Laurence was out most of the time on his mysterious army duties, and housework seemed to take very little time out of the great stretching days. Despite the social round, there were still these afternoons with nothing to do, when only Alexandra was without children to care for, or shopping to do, or any of the many activities the other wives were so frantic with. That was when she'd started wandering in the park, which she'd begun to love. It was so huge, a vast expanse of green that stretched away into wooded copses with the glitter of water and the golden arch of a bridge beyond. It was busy with people, strolling in the sunshine, children running or roller skating or riding bicycles – it was the holidays now, of course – and tourists with maps probably looking for the Albert Memorial. On the sandy track that ran along the inner circle of the tarmacked road horses came trotting past ridden by smart young ladies in velvet hats, their bottoms rising and falling in the saddle with steady little bumps.

Alexandra crossed the road, getting grit in her sandals from the bridle path, and started ambling across the cool grass, not sure of where she was heading. There was a limit to how far she could go, after all, no matter how much she might want to wander on forever. Her duty would call her back, the inexorable move of the clock hands towards six o'clock when she should be at home, ready in case Laurence returned and expected a drink and dinner on the table by seven.

She walked on, thinking about home and wondering if her father had read the long chatty letters she sent once a week. She had only received two postcards in return, both terse and concerned with things like the planning committee on the parish council. Perhaps her father might visit her one day. Laurence would probably be riding in a parade soon, attending at some royal event, and perhaps she might be able to ask her father along to see it. Surely he would like that. She wanted him to come and see the life he had chosen for her and to make it worthwhile by giving her his approval.

Just ahead of her, a girl in a short dress, sunglasses and a large hat was lying on a wrought-iron bench, twisted in an odd way with her chin lifted and one arm thrown up. A man was standing nearby, similarly outlandish in tight white trousers and a bright pink jacket. His dark hair looked shaggy and long after the short army cuts she was now used to, and he was bent over, with a large black camera pressed to his eye, taking pictures of the girl.

Alexandra stopped nearby, watching as the man squinted through the camera and called instructions to the girl. She obediently bent herself into poses as he clicked away, turning her head and holding it for an instant so that he could capture it, before striking another attitude. The model was pretty but unsmiling, which seemed to Alexandra to be the wrong kind of behaviour when one's picture was being taken. She loitered silently, watching with interest.

'Hey, do you mind? I can do without a lot of gawping if it's all the same!' The man had turned around to face her. He lowered his camera, frowning. 'I'm trying to take some pictures here. It's not a tourist attraction, you know. This is a serious business – for a fashion magazine.'

'I'm sorry, I didn't think I was disturbing you,' Alexandra

said, flushing. He was rude but perhaps her staring had been ruder. 'I'll go now.'

She turned and began to walk swiftly away.

'Wait a moment, no need to run off – wait, will you?' His voice came after her and she stopped, not turning around, blinking at the grass that was almost acid-green in the bright sunshine. She heard him say, 'Turn around – don't I know you?'

Know me? she thought, astonished. *Who would know me? Who do I know? I don't know anyone . . .*

She turned slowly back to face the man by the bench. He was looking at her in a curious way and as she stared at him, his features seemed to transform, rearranging themselves into something familiar.

'Alexandra?' he said in a tone of surprise. 'You're Alexandra Crewe, aren't you?'

She nodded, confused. Then, just as he said his name, it came rushing back with a force that almost knocked her over. How could she not have recognised him at once?

He said, 'Don't you remember me? I'm Nicky Stirling. How incredible!'

And then he was walking towards her, a smile across his face, and she knew him at once, even though she hadn't seen him since he was twelve years old and her mother had not yet died.

'I think this is just the craziest coincidence!' Nicky said, beaming. He seemed so happy to see her, she could scarcely understand why. The model had been sent away and they were in a coffee bar, staring at one another across a Formica table and each taking in how the other had changed from childhood.

'It is,' she said breathlessly. 'It's very strange.' She had an odd dizzy sensation being near him. It was like stepping back into her own past, a place that often seemed obscure and veiled, even to her. But she remembered that she had been happy once, and he had been there then.

'I haven't seen you for years,' he went on, shaking his head. 'But we used to play together, didn't we, when we were kids? Remember?'

Images flashed in her mind – children playing in woods and by streams – and she heard the echo of shouts and laughter over the distance of years. They had been those scrambling, eager children with dirty faces and scuffed boots, climbing and jumping and playing their games of pretend. 'Pretend you're the enemy and you want to get me, and this is my castle and you're trying to get in!' There had been many long summer days in the woods, and in the gardens of Fort Stirling, when cowboys and Indians pursued each other through trees and behind box hedges. There was a little temple in the rose garden that had become their headquarters. She could see Nicky now, tousle-haired, with grubby knees below his shorts, as he issued orders or doled out rations of the food and drink they had stolen from the kitchen. He'd always been the leader. His cousins had played with them – what were their names? – and some village boys and the children of whoever was visiting the big house. Nicky had always been her hero, though, the one she hoped would pick her for his team when they divided up into sides. She was just a child to him, though he never let the girls feel second best. After all, his cousin – the girl; her name was something short – was much tougher and faster than her fat little brother.

Then, during one awful summer, everything had changed. Her mother died, and she'd been forbidden from seeing any of her old friends. Their favourite place, the old folly, had been put out of bounds forever, even though they'd never really been allowed to play there in the first place – it was too dangerous. Then Nicky had gone back to school and after that, they'd never played together again.

The memory of the sudden fissure seemed to strike Nicky at the same time. He began to look awkward and said quickly, 'But that was all ages ago now. We were just silly kids, weren't we? So – how are you? What have you been doing?' His glance fell on the glinting stone in the ring on her left hand. 'I see you're married.'

'That's right.'

'Oh. Congratulations and everything. What's he like?'

She blinked at him. He had lost all the soft pink and white boyishness of his youth; his face was smooth and tanned but tougher, his grey eyes brighter under thick brows, his hair darker. But he still had that energy around him, the mysterious force that drew people to him and made them do as he said. He emanated a vigour that she didn't think she'd ever seen in anyone else. She felt suddenly that everyone she'd met since Nicky had been pale and lifeless in comparison; he was so alive, from his hands with their long, graceful fingers that were constantly moving, to his mobile mouth. The air around him almost seemed to vibrate with energy.

'What's he like?' repeated Nicky.

'Who?' she asked.

'Who?' He stared and then laughed. 'Your husband! What's he like? Who is he? Do I know him?'

'His name is Laurence Sykes. He's in the Royal Horse Guards.'

Nicky shook his head. 'No. Don't know him.'

'I don't think there's any reason why you should.'

'I can't believe it. Little Alexandra Crewe, all grown-up and married.' He smiled at her cheekily. 'Well, you beat me to it. I'm nowhere near all that, I'm afraid.'

'Do you live in London now?'

He nodded. 'Yes. I'm busy disgracing the family name. Pa is furious with me but I've told him I'm going to do what I want while I damn well can. He thinks I've gone totally off my rocker being a photographer. No better than a trades- man as far as he's concerned. He doesn't understand that it's different now, practically respectable.'

'So that's what you do now?'

'Yes.' He looked pleased with himself for a moment, his shoulders hunching in a kind of nonchalantly proud way. 'You know the kind of thing – fashion. Art. Photo essays for literary magazines.'

Alexandra was impressed. 'And . . . foreign wars and things like that?'

'Not exactly. No.'

'Where will I have seen your work? In *The Times*? Or *Vogue*?'

He laughed a touch ruefully. 'Er . . . no, none of those, I'm afraid.'

'Then where?'

He grinned. 'All right, you've caught me out. I'm not doing much proper work, if you must know. I just do a lot of stuff on spec. I get pretty girls to model for me and then try my luck with the pictures in case anyone is interested. Sometimes they are. I got some published in the *Picture Post* recently, lovely shots of a girl by the seaside. And whenever I go to one of those ghastly deb parties, I take pictures of the girls for their parents, and then try and hawk them to *London Life* – what was the old *Tatler* till just recently. They're in the market for that kind of thing. I spent an afternoon in the East End taking pictures of urchins to see if a magazine wanted them, but no one did. But I'm going to break through one of these days, see if I don't.'

'I'm sure you will,' Alexandra said with complete sincerity. Nicky had always been impossibly glamorous as far as she was concerned.

She noticed he was staring at her, his brow furrowed a little as his gaze moved over her face, looking at her in a different kind of way.

'You know, you're rather a looker under that awful make-up you're wearing. You should come and pose for me.'

She flushed, not knowing whether to be flattered or hurt. 'Well—'

'Really, I mean it. I've got a studio set up in my flat. Come and see me there and I'll take your portrait. I'm quite good if I do say so myself.'

'How did you amuse yourself today?' Laurence asked as they sat together in the tiny room that was both their sitting and dining room, eating the meal she'd prepared.

'I met an old friend, actually.'

'Really?' Laurence flicked his cool gaze up at her. His pale blue eyes always had a chilly look about them. 'Who is she?'

'Not she. He.'

Laurence's fork stopped in the movement towards his mouth, hovered and then continued on its way. When he could speak again, he said, 'Who is this "he"?'

'A friend from home. Nicky Stirling.'

'Stirling . . . Yes, I've heard of them. The family from that big house near your village.'

She nodded. 'That's right. We used to play together as children. It was very strange seeing him again; he's changed so much. He's a photographer now. He suggested taking my portrait.'

Laurence put down his fork. 'Did he? That's an odd career for a man like him. He's probably just amusing himself. I don't suppose there's any harm in you sitting for him.' He looked thoughtful and she could see ideas passing through his mind as clearly as a film playing out. He was thinking about how it might enhance his social cachet to have an aristocratic photographer take his wife's picture. They would frame the result and prop it up on the side table, and when visitors came and admired it, Laurence would be able to say casually that it had been taken by an old family friend, Nicky Stirling, the heir to the Northmoor title, had they heard of him?

'You don't mind then?' Alexandra ventured timidly.

'No, of course not. Arrange something. And we must have him to supper to thank him for his interest.'

Alexandra thought of the scrap of paper in her coat pocket with Nicky's strong black handwriting scrawled across it: a number and the words *Telephone me tomorrow morning*.

'All right,' she said, a flutter of excitement winging swiftly inside her. 'I will.'

The next day she had to find a telephone box to make her call, and she felt almost furtive as she left the barracks and walked into Knightsbridge like a spy on a secret mission. There was a public telephone by the station but she had to wait for a man in a mac to finish a very long conversation, and she stood there feeling foolish and faintly guilty. At last the man hung up and pushed his way out of the booth and she stepped inside, wrinkling her nose at the sour smell within. She took out some coins, dropped one into the slot and pressed the button, then dialled the number that she already knew by heart, holding her breath as it connected. The ringing tone sounded a dozen times and she exhaled her disappointment. So that's how it was. He hadn't really meant it. He'd forgotten. A strange and unexpected grief pierced her; it was as though a shutter between her and the past had been raised for moment, letting her glimpse a forgotten world, and now it had slammed down again, leaving her in darkness. She slowly held out the receiver to replace it on its cradle when she heard the tinny sound of a voice emanating from it. 'Hello, hello? Who's that?'

Gasping, she snatched it back to her ear as she reached out and pressed the second button so that her coin rattled downwards and she was connected. 'It's Alexandra. You told me to telephone you so I have.'

A pause. Had he forgotten her entirely? Had she been presumptuous in thinking he really meant her to do as he'd suggested?

'Oh, yes. The beautiful Miss Crewe. I mean . . . Mrs Sykes. I hoped you would call. Are you going to sit for me?'

Her heart was thumping in her chest. 'Yes . . . yes, please. I'd like to very much.'

'Good. Come tomorrow at two. Don't wear that make-up whatever you do.'

She touched her cheek. It was quite bare. She'd already thrown the panstick in the bin. 'I won't.'

'Here's the address. Are you ready?'

Chapter Eight

Present day

John was in a good mood on Saturday morning, released from the burden of the VAT return which had been emailed to the accountant the previous afternoon. When Delilah woke, he was lying next to her propped on one arm, gazing down at her with a tender expression. She smiled happily at him, blinking sleepily, and he bent in to kiss her.

'Mmm, you taste delicious.' He pressed his mouth to her ear. 'I can't resist you . . .'

His lips trailed warm kisses down her neck, setting off a delightful tingle on her skin, then he returned to her mouth, kissing her gently and letting his tongue probe softly until she opened her lips to him.

Delilah savoured the dark taste of her husband. At times like this, she felt the decade or so between them. He wasn't a milk-and-honey boy but a man, and he tasted of musk and old leather, citrus cologne and what she imagined cigar smoke ought to smell like but didn't. She loved the masculinity of his scent and the way it made her feel. Sometimes she recalled Harry, who now seemed bland and flavourless compared to John. She hadn't really known that an almost mystical bond could be felt through sex until she and John had made love, and she'd experienced a deep, animal desire to be connected, and to give in return all the pleasure that was received. There was also his unembarrassed desire to dominate without being dominating, and after years of Harry deferring to her in every way, it had been exciting and invigorating to feel that she didn't have to be in complete control. It was part of what had made her fall so giddily, so addictively in love.

His hand went to the silkiness of her nightdress and he pulled down the straps so that her breasts fell free of it. He slid it off her and discarded it, then took her breasts in his hands and kissed each one softly. She let out a long breath. She hadn't realised how much she wanted this or how much she'd missed this feeling of pure desire. Sex had been mechanical for them lately, performed with the end of pregnancy firmly in mind. But now she was hungry for his mouth and body, and she pulled him to her quickly, wanting to feel the firmness of his chest against hers and run her hands along his broad back and down to his buttocks. He brought his mouth to her neck, kissing and anointing her skin with tiny licks and nips. She murmured appreciatively as he worked his way up to her mouth, and kissed her hard again, his passion stronger now. She could feel his hunger for her and she pressed back against him, relishing the way his hardness dug into her belly, eager to possess her. She dropped her hand downwards and found the soft opening in his pyjama bottoms, reaching in to touch him. He moaned softly as she wrapped her hand around him.

'I can't wait long for you,' he warned.

'I don't want you to.'

He pulled off his pyjamas in a quick movement as she lay back to welcome him, lifting her arms to him and relishing the weight of his body as he rolled onto her. She knew that he loved the feeling of her soft belly and breasts under him and the way she opened herself to him. He sighed with pleasure as he ran his hand over her hips and along the curve of her waist. She curled her legs around his thighs, urging him to find the place and there he was. It was so familiar and yet each time she revelled in the sensation of their bodies being joined, and the delicious fulfilment as he pressed home.

They didn't speak but stared into each other's eyes, reading the emotions there. They could see that they were both at the mercy of their physical passion as it grew stronger and fiercer, both finding excitement in the other's arousal. She pulled him closer and deeper, rising up to meet him, feeling as though she would never be able to have enough of him. But their morning passion was fast and urgent and the end came quickly, as their desire for one another sped them on until they both reached the brink of pleasure.

When they were lying together afterwards, she sighed contentedly, happy that they had made love with such enthusiastic enjoyment after the way it had been recently. 'That was *very* nice.'

'It always is. You always are.' He trailed his finger along the soft flesh of her inner arm and said slowly, 'I'm sorry if I've been a grouch lately. I know I'm not easy to live with sometimes. You're so good to put up with me.'

She grasped at the feeling of connection between them. 'Are you okay? You've been so down, and you seem to be getting more morose, not less.'

John looked away and sighed, rubbing one hand across the dark stubble on his chin. 'I'm sorry, I can't explain it . . . this place. It's hard for me, you know? Sometimes I feel like this house wants to smother me alive. There's no end to the demands it makes on me. And then there's Dad.' His expression saddened. 'He's getting worse. It's taking him away from me. For years, it was just the two of us and now that his memory is going, it's taking the past – my life, I mean – with it. I'm going to spend the morning with him today and I'm dreading it, dreading seeing what else has been lost. There'll only be me left to remember soon. It feels very lonely.'

She felt a surge of sympathy for him and squeezed his arm for comfort. 'Oh, darling – we can build new memories together.'

He smiled wanly. 'I hope so. Fingers crossed.' He paused and said, 'Are you doing your pregnancy test today?'

'Later,' she said, trying to hide the tremor of anxiety she felt at the thought. 'I've run out of kits. I'll need to pick up some more.'

'Okay,' he said, dropping a kiss on her cheek. 'Let me know when the big moment happens, won't you?'

Saturday breakfast was a long, lazy meal served in the round blue dining room in an old-fashioned way that always reminded Delilah of a hotel, with napkin-lined bread baskets,

111

hot dishes with sausages, bacon and scrambled egg, and coffee served in a silver pot. As she poured out some milk, she said, 'Why don't I come over with you this time?'

John looked up from his porridge and the newspaper. Erryl had dropped the papers off early that morning, and then they were left to themselves for the rest of the weekend since Delilah had put a stop to the tradition of Janey coming to do Sunday lunch every week. When it was just the two of them, she was happy to do it herself; if there were visitors to entertain, she appreciated Janey taking the strain of cooking. 'Come where?' he asked.

'To visit your father, of course.'

John's expression became closed, almost anxious. He sighed and took a sip of his coffee, before saying, 'Why?'

'Because I'd like to.'

'I don't understand why you'd want to spend a perfectly nice Saturday morning sitting with an old man you barely know – a man who's never going to know you. He hardly remembers who I am half the time.'

'But I'm part of the family now. I want to show support – both for him and for you.'

John looked over at her, a touch of pleading in his eyes. 'Darling, I'd find it more supportive if you stayed away. It's tedious enough for me, answering the same questions over and over again. I'd find it uncomfortable if you had to endure the same thing, without even the memory of my father as he used to be to sustain you through the boredom.'

She stared back, not sure what to say to that. It seemed odd that there was this kind of division between people who lived so close to one another, with her in the big house and the old man in the coach house next door, and only John allowed to move between the two. She ate a spoonful of her own porridge slowly, savouring the nutty, salty taste softened by a swirl of cold cream. She said, 'I think you're worrying too much. I met your father in the garden the other day and he was perfectly fine.'

'Oh?' John stiffened for a moment and blinked rapidly. Then he sat back in his chair and fixed his gaze on her. He looked so handsome, she thought, in his old cotton shirt, washed to down-like softness, and dark jeans. 'Did you two have a chat? Did he remember you?'

She hesitated before answering, wondering why John seemed just a touch anxious, then said, 'He didn't know me, I'm afraid. But if he saw me more often, perhaps he might get to know that we're married.'

'I shouldn't count on it,' John said, his gaze turning back to the cricket reports in the paper. 'He barely remembered who Vanna was, and that was before he lost his marbles.'

Delilah said nothing, hurt by the mention of Vanna and the inference that if the old man couldn't remember the stylish and fascinating Vanna, he was hardly likely to recall boring Delilah. At least, that was what it sounded like to her. She wanted to laugh it off but somehow felt wounded.

'Did he say anything else?' John asked idly as he turned the page.

'Yes, actually.' It was, Delilah thought, the perfect opportunity to ask about what had been niggling at the back of her mind. 'He seemed to think I was someone called Elaine.

He was quite insistent that I was her, even when I tried to tell him that I wasn't.'

John went quite still and his jaw tightened.

'Do you know who that is?' she asked. 'Does it mean anything to you?'

There was a small pause and he replied, 'No, I'm afraid it doesn't. It must be someone from his distant past. That means more to him than the present these days.' He began to move quickly, putting down his paper, drinking the last of his coffee and pushing back his chair all at once. 'You can see why it's pointless coming to spend a morning with my father. If he thinks you're someone else, then it's only going to confuse him, isn't it? Much better if we do it my way. I'll see you at lunchtime.'

A moment later she heard the kitchen door slam, indicating that he'd gone out that way to take the shortcut to the coach house.

'Bloody man!' she said with exasperation, putting down her spoon. He'd used her question about the mysterious Elaine as a reason to stop her going with him to see his father.

I can't understand it, she thought. *Why wouldn't he want me to go with him? Surely I could make it easier for him.*

She sat back in frustration, wondering why he refused her help. At first, the two of them had been so connected, but all the passionate lovemaking and long hours wrapped in each other's arms talking had not made him share every part of his complicated heart with her. Now she was worried by how much they seemed to be moving apart. Ever since she'd come to the house, John's misery appeared to be increasing. His nightmares came more often and his dark moods were more frequent, as though something inside him was tormenting him with ever greater force. And yet he refused to let her in. How could she help him if he didn't? And what would her life be if the man she loved gradually turned into a stranger tortured by the burden of his inheritance and yet unwilling to change anything?

It must be the house, she thought. *That and his father. It's all I can think.*

It seemed that there was only one way she could ease his pain. John appeared to have placed all his hopes of salvation in a baby, and the longer they went without a sign of one, the worse things were becoming. She stood up, a wave of anxiety flooding through her. Was that the only way she could heal him? And what if her growing fear proved correct? What if they – or she – couldn't have a child?

She shivered and pushed that vision of the future from her mind, and began to lay the breakfast dishes on the mahogany tray.

Delilah missed Janey's solid, amiable presence in the kitchen. She wondered idly if she could take Ben a cup of tea in the garden, then remembered that it was Saturday and he would be in his cottage over at Home Farm, and was disappointed. It occurred to her that she could surprise him with a visit. She could see him now, slouchy in jeans and a T-shirt, out of those gardening things for once, his feet bare and his hair wet from the shower. His grey-green eyes would widen with surprise, then a smile would broaden across his face, and he'd say, 'Delilah! This is an unexpected pleasure. Why don't you come in?' She knew he would be happy to see her. She would do it. She would get in the car, drive the couple of miles over to the farm – it was part of the Fort Stirling estate and not far away – and she would take him something nice from the garden as a pretext . . . She stopped unloading the breakfast tray and stood stock-still in the kitchen.

You don't need to spend time with Ben, she told herself sternly. *That's not where the solution lies.*

She started putting the breakfast things in the dishwasher, making herself think of John instead. He would be in the coach house now, sitting across from his father, trying to follow the vagaries of his mind or attempting to anchor it down with facts about the weather, the house, the estate. She pictured the portrait of John's father, a full-length oil by the staircase that showed a young, vibrant and handsome man. The white-haired old man next door was the same person, just as John was the round-faced boy in his prep school uniform, holding his mother's hand, she expressionless behind a huge pair of Jackie O-style sunglasses, as they stood together next to a sleek-bodied car.

She couldn't remember exactly what John's mother's name was now. Had she ever been told? John had only called her 'my mother' and he spoke of her rarely – in fact, only when Delilah pressed him on it.

Then it burst upon her.

But of course! Elaine must be John's mother! That's why his father thought I was her – his wife from long ago. I don't

116

suppose we look much like each other, considering she was dark and I'm fair, but perhaps that doesn't matter when your mind and memory are impaired.

She left the dishwasher half loaded and hurried along the hall to the library. It was dull and fusty in the mornings, before the sun had moved around to illuminate it through the rows of long, elegant windows. Dust hung in the air around the cabinets of books with their doors of wire mesh protecting the antique tomes inside. The leather-and-gilt volumes weren't of much interest to her; she preferred the shelves on the other side of the room, where there were novels and books on art and history, collections of letters, volumes of the peerage and *Who's Who*, and lots of juicy biographies and revelatory exposés. It was also where the old albums were kept, leather bound and stamped with the Stirling crest on the spines and covers. There were cellar books, books of menus going back to the big house parties of the nineteenth century, and visitors' books. And there were photograph albums bound in green and red calfskin.

Delilah plucked one out, sat down on the library floor and opened it on her crossed legs. It weighed a ton, the black pages alone stiff and heavy, even before the black-and-white prints had been mounted. They weren't family snaps – each one had been taken with a determined sense of subject and framing. Most were inside the house; it was virtually unchanged from today and it was odd to see pictures taken in the library and then to flick her gaze upwards to see the exact same furniture in the identical configuration. Under each large print was a caption written in white ink, neat capitals spelling out who the picture was of. The names meant nothing to Delilah but she loved looking at the frozen moments, people snapped and preserved forever in their youth. The men had hair that touched their collars at the back, and that was either shaggy at the front or swooped back in a thick quiff; they wore tight shirts, shiny drainpipe trousers and Chelsea boots; some were wearing cardigans and dark square-framed glasses, or striped tops with leather jackets, giving them a tough edge. The girls wore tight pencil skirts and blouses, or fitted sweaters, their hair in loose curls or pulled back into long ponytails. They had flicks of black eyeliner on their lids and had darkened their brows with kohl. There were obviously parties going on: she could see bottles, full ashtrays, people dancing to a gramophone on the walnut table by the window – she looked up: the table was still there, the gramophone had now disappeared – or else young men strummed guitars together. How amazing it must have been to be young and have a house like this to play in.

There was no sign of John's father in the photographs, but he must have been behind the camera. A vague memory floated into her mind of John telling her that his father had once been a society photographer in the sixties. And occasionally she saw the delicate pale face, large eyes and soft dark hair of the woman she recognised as John's mother. She seemed to be apart from the others somehow, always in the shadows or seen in the half-light. Only once or twice was she caught full-on by the camera and then it was always unawares, when the tilt of her head or the shape of her mouth was quite heartbreakingly pure. Underneath her image was only the letter 'A' in bold white strokes.

'A,' murmured Delilah. 'What happened to you, A?' She was struck by how young the woman looked. She must be younger than Delilah was now. And yet, within a few years, she was dead, and exactly how she died Delilah didn't know. Whenever she'd thought of it, she supplied some kind of unspecified illness for which treatment back then would have been more primitive: a cancer or a blood disease. But, she realised, she had no way of knowing that was true.

She felt a sudden bond to this other woman who had come here so many years before, to the same place, the same furniture, the same park and gardens. So little had changed, according to the photographs. Had A shivered in the freezing rooms in winter, as well? She'd probably slept in the same four-poster bed, its grandeur muted by the orange hangings that hadn't been replaced since midway through the previous century. Had she run along the corridor, wide-eyed and frightened, desperate for the light of the bedroom to banish the dark emptiness all around, just as Delilah did?

But the pictures seemed to show that the house had been full of people and parties then. Perhaps A hadn't been afraid of the silence and the unoccupied space. *Parties might be the answer*, she thought. *Noise. People. Life.*

She sighed. Well, that was the end of that. Unless the name was spelt most unusually with A, John's mother was definitely not Elaine. She closed the album. Now she was curious to know what John's mother's name was. Surely there must be clues elsewhere.

There were other photograph albums, but on impulse she turned instead to the visitors' books, pulling them out to examine. There were three of them, covering a period from the middle of the nineteenth century, with long lists of names and addresses in faded but exquisite copperplate hands, the roster of guests reading like a society comedy: Lady This and Sir Someone That and the Duke of Wherever. She flicked through the pages, wondering what the house was like when it had been so full of people, bustle, chatter and endless meals. That was what this place had been designed for – not for two people rattling around alone, gradually being squashed by the weight of the past.

The final visitors' book was the saddest. The house parties stopped abruptly after the advent of the Great War, and did not start again for over five years. When they did, the grand country weekends were gone forever. These house parties were smaller and less extravagant, although they picked up towards the end of the twenties. When the Second World War began, the names kept coming for a while, but now there were Colonels, Lieutenants and Captains visiting the house, and then the parties clearly stopped. Delilah remembered John telling her the house had been requisitioned for a while in the war, as a convalescent home for soldiers. The visitors' book had not been brought out again for a long time because it was only in the late fifties that the names began to appear again.

The titles and double or triple-barrelled surnames of the past all but disappeared. Now there were first names alone, or signatures like 'Jimmy J', and instead of addresses guests scrawled comments: 'Great party, Nicky! Like your gaff' or 'Unforgettable time here at the fort – wine, women and rock 'n' roll, oh yeah!'

On they went, the parties stretching into the next decade, and then she saw it: 'We had a marvellous time thanks to the wonderful Nicky and beauteous Alex – see you both very soon! Gareth and Rita.'

So that was John's mother's name. Alex.

She said it out loud, and then glanced up quickly as though afraid she might have summoned a ghost by speaking the name. The library was still and silent around her.

It's a pretty name, she thought. Knowing it made her more real somehow.

She flicked over more pages, looking for further clues, but now she had the name she wanted, there was nothing more to discover. She kept alert for an Elaine but there was none that she could see. And then, abruptly, after eight years, the parties stopped. There were no more names in the book at all. The rest of the creamy pages were empty.

Why did it all stop there? she wondered. She went back to where she had first seen Alex's name. The date was 1966. And then, in 1974, it finished, just like that.

That must have been when she died, she thought. *I suppose Nicky didn't feel like having any more parties after that . . . ever, by the looks of it.*

A sense of melancholy drifted over her. How sad it was that John's mother had died; she'd been so young, and so pretty and with so much to live for. Had she known she was going to die? Leaving a child behind must be a terrible agony . . . She imagined Alex, pale and thin, lying back on the pillow in the four-poster upstairs, having John brought to her so she could say goodbye, and then breathing her last. It gave her a morbid shiver. Had John's mother died in the bed where she slept?

Stop letting your imagination run away with you, she scolded herself. *You've no idea. Perhaps it was an accident. In a way, I hope it was – something quick, without suffering.*

It occurred to her that it was odd she didn't know this fact of how Alex had died. She felt as though they were linked over the years: both marrying Stirlings, both living at this great house. There had been Vanna in between, of course, but Vanna had not managed to cope with this place. Delilah imagined she probably lived now in something modern, light and perfectly decorated, with lots of beige and white, spotless sofas, glass, silver and mirrors. It would be the antidote to this place, with its shabbiness, dust and decay.

A cold feeling ran over her. Vanna had left before time, and so, in a way, had Alex.

Will I be overwhelmed by it too? Is it fate?

A shiver of nasty apprehension shook her shoulders. She was already oppressed by this place, and the way it was governing her marriage.

No, she thought resolutely. *I'm strong enough, I know I am. I can help John through it, and survive it myself. I can make it a success.*

She put the books back carefully, making them look as undisturbed as possible.

*

Over lunch, Delilah felt a dull pull of pain in her abdomen and her spirits sank. She tried to keep up a cheerful exterior, but she knew that another month had gone by unsuccessfully, and when afterwards she was sure, she went to find John and tell him.

'I'm sorry,' she whispered, as he took it in. 'There's always next month.'

'Yes.' He looked away to hide the disappointment in his face. 'There's always next month.'

To break the dismal silence that followed, she said, 'You haven't forgotten that Susie invited me to that exhibition in London, have you? I thought I might go. It'll mean going away for a few days – if you don't need me here.'

John looked back her, expressionless now. 'No, no. You go. I don't need you.'

The way he phrased his answer seemed bleakly pointed and it hurt. 'All right,' she said, trying to smile. She remembered her fear in the library that she might not be up to all this, and reminded herself of her resolve to stay the course. 'If you're sure it's all right. It'll be such a short time away, I'll be back before you know it. I'll ring her now and tell her I'll be up on Monday.'

As she went to find her phone to call Susie, she was depressed to think that the delightful bond they had shared that morning had entirely vanished.

Chapter Nine

1965

The address was a mews house down a tiny cobbled dead-end road just behind a smart Belgravia square. The door was opened to Alexandra's knock by a pretty blonde girl in cropped black trousers and a long black knitted jumper that hung to her thighs. She stared at Alexandra before saying 'Yes?' in a faintly hostile way.

'I'm looking for Nicky Stirling. Is this the right address?'

The girl said nothing and a male voice behind called from the depths, 'Who is it, Polly? Is that her?'

'Just finding out!' the girl threw back over her shoulder. 'What's your name?' she demanded, facing Alexandra again with her cold gaze.

'Alexandra Sykes.'

'You'd better come in then.' She turned and retreated into the house, and Alexandra followed her into the gloom, finding herself in a tiny sitting room, furnished eclectically and full of interesting objects. Beyond she spotted a small kitchen, but was immediately distracted by a pair of long legs in black trousers descending the stairs and the next moment Nicky had appeared, tall and rangy, and he was hurrying over to kiss both her cheeks.

'You came!' He was smiling, his eyes bright. 'You've met Pols, of course. She's my assistant. She helps me.'

'You mean, I do all the work,' Polly responded tartly.

'Some of it. You should be grateful, you little hoyden.' He turned to Alexandra and said confidentially, 'I found her working on the broken biscuit counter in Woolworths. She owes everything to me, don't you, sweetheart?'

'Hardly,' replied Polly.

'Be nice, you devil. You've met Mrs Sykes. She is charm incarnate and she's going to have a picture taken. Make her a cup of tea, will you? Come on, Alex, let's go upstairs.' Nicky headed back up the staircase, Alexandra following behind, feeling shocked at being called Alex. He had used to call her that, she remembered suddenly, and no one had since. She felt that strange buzzing sensation again, the one of being connected almost physically to the past; it was so strong, she had to concentrate on climbing the stairs, in case she toppled over under its force. They gained the first floor where a ladder led up through a hatch in the ceiling.

'This way.' He climbed up and when he'd clambered through the hole, his head reappeared, framed by the hatch. 'Come on, it's easier than it looks. I'll help you.'

She put her handbag strap over the crook of her arm and grasped the ladder. Nicky's hand reached down, his palm broad and open for hers. She climbed up, took his hand and he pulled her into the space beyond. The loft had been boarded and painted black, but bright sunshine poured in through three skylights. A fan whirred in the corner, to counter the stultifying effect of the heat rising from below and the fiery sunlight beating through the glass above. Around about was scattered photographic equipment: tripods, lights, reflective discs, paper backgrounds plain and painted, boxes spilling wires and plugs, and the cameras themselves.

'My studio,' he explained. 'For now, anyway.'

'Why is it black?' she asked, looking around. 'I thought photographers needed light.'

'We do. But these days it's easy to make light' – he nodded towards the great lamps on their tripods – 'and it's much harder to take it away. But when the blinds are down it's pitch dark in here. That way I can get some good effects.'

'It's terrific,' she said. He seemed to know what he was talking about and the set-up looked very professional.

Nicky seemed pleased by her praise. 'Of course I need a better way to get here – I can't exactly ask Laurence Olivier or Dame Edith Evans to climb a ladder to my loft.'

'Have you photographed Laurence Olivier?' she asked, impressed.

'Um – no, not yet, but I'm sure it's just a matter of time. So we're going to take your picture up here. I'll use the white backdrop and keep the blinds open. I want natural light, plenty of it, to show off your rather stunning complexion.' He gazed at her in a way that showed he was now looking at her with an artistic, appraising eye. 'I'm glad you're not wearing that orange stuff. You barely need a scrap of make-up – it's extraordinary. But of course we'll put something on you or you'll be washed out. There's a particular look I want, very fresh and now.' He bent over the hatch. 'Polly! Where are you? Get up here, and bring the kit! And the tea!' He looked back up at Alexandra, smiling and shaking his head. 'What on earth am I supposed to do with that girl?'

She smiled back, suddenly enchanted by him as he stood there, tall and rather skinny, his hair tousled, his shirt open at the neck. His face was too round to be classically handsome and yet he gave the impression of being very good-looking. Perhaps it was the way his grey eyes stared out from under his black brows, their colour intensified by his tan. He had long lashes too, almost like a girl's, although he was anything but feminine. His mouth entranced her: it was wide and generous and expressive and gave the impression that he was voracious for everything in life. She could see the boy she once knew, but changed into a man whose vivacity and energy made him fascinating to her. And he looked so modern with his black leather trousers and suede shoes. They were strange objects to her and yet on him they looked wonderful. He seemed so free and so unencumbered by the kinds of things that imprisoned Laurence: the army regulations, the dress codes, the endless rules and traditions that dictated everything.

'Now,' he said softly. 'What shall we do with you, eh?' He frowned. 'It's very strange, Alex, but you look so . . . just like that little girl. I feel very odd when I'm with you – as though everything that happened since I last saw you is a kind of dream and the only things that are real are you and that time when we were kids.'

'I know,' she whispered. 'That's how I feel too.'

'Isn't it peculiar?' he said conspiratorially. 'I mean, we haven't seen each other for so long, we're virtually strangers. But you seem so familiar.'

She stared back at him, nervous but excited, her fingertips trembling with the anticipation of something, though she had no idea what it might be. An adventure of some sort, perhaps, some knowledge or something she was going to learn . . .

'I've been thinking about it since we met in the park,' he murmured. 'About what happened back then.'

There was a sudden clatter as a tray appeared on the floor by the hatch, pushed through by an unseen hand and followed by Polly's fair head.

'Ah,' exclaimed Nicky, 'here she is with the tea. She's a deft hand with that tray, aren't you? Lots of practice. Now, Pol, I need you to put some war paint on Mrs Sykes – what we discussed earlier.' He turned back to Alexandra. 'I'm just going to sort out some bits and bobs while Polly gets you ready.'

When he went, clambering away down the hatch, it was as though all sense of life had gone with him and she was left bereft in the hot airless space. Polly took a bag from over one shoulder and emptied pots and brushes on to the floor. Then she looked over at Alexandra and said coldly, 'Don't be flattered. This is what he does with all the girls.'

It was like a punch in the stomach but she tried to show nothing on her face of the swirling dark disappointment that was drowning out all the pleasure she'd experienced so far.

When Polly came towards her, gesturing for her to sit down on a collapsible chair, Alexandra was startled by a violent feeling of jealousy, because Polly was close to Nicky and part of his world.

He came up again twenty minutes later. Polly was doing something to the front of her hair with a hairbrush but her face was finished. Nicky approached, saying, 'Let's take a look then.'

Alexandra looked up at him, aware of a slight heaviness on her lids and moisture on her lips. Nicky was staring at her, astonishment in his eyes. He seemed stunned by her transformation, then pulled himself together, looked away and turned to Polly. 'Well done, Polls. A triumph. You got it just right. Exactly as I wanted.'

'Can I see?' Alexandra asked, desperately curious.

He looked back at her, a curiously bashful expression on his face as he took in her changed face again, then smiled and shook his head. 'Oh no. Don't want you getting stiff and awkward. I don't want you deciding who you are when it's me who does that.' He became decisive again, looking at her now with detached appraisal and working out how to get the effect he wanted. 'Right, Alex, come over here. See that large blue cushion on the floor? I want you to sit on that. Polly, I want a key light, that's all. But we'll need the reflectors, one there and the other there.' He gestured and Polly obeyed orders. Nicky started changing his camera settings, saying, 'I want you relaxed. I want you to think about things that make you calm and happy.'

What could such things be? As if he could read her mind, Nicky went on, 'Happy days with your husband, your wedding, Sunday afternoons together . . .' He stopped suddenly and their eyes met. His expression changed, though she couldn't identify what to. Was it sympathy? He said quickly, 'Think of home then. Think of the meadows and the river where we used to play – do you remember?'

She smiled. He lifted the camera to his eye.

'That's right, Alex. Now, don't smile, just dream . . . Move your head to the left, put your chin down . . . yes . . . just like that.' The shutter began clicking and with the sound of his voice, she started to relax, letting herself float somewhere safe as she moved according to his directions, allowing the camera's needs to shape her and his commands to propel her as he wanted.

After the session was finished, they left Polly to deal with the films and Nicky took her out to a nearby cafe on Elizabeth Street.

'I think the pictures are going to be beautiful,' he said as he sipped hot black coffee from a white china cup.

'I'm sure you've done something marvellous,' she replied. The make-up had been wiped away before she'd seen it and she'd glimpsed only her normal self in the reflection that showed in the cafe windows on their way in. 'You were very impressive, the way you know what to do.'

'Thanks, but actually, I mean you.' He smiled at her, then said hesitantly, 'But you seem so very sad.'

'Do I?' She was surprised. She'd been happier today than she could remember being for a long time.

'Yes. Are you very miserable?'

'No! No.' She thought of afternoons wandering through Hyde Park and her plan to explore London when the weather changed. She thought of her enjoyment of solitude and quiet, and the way she could drift through days with her imaginings and dreams. She considered the noisy coffee mornings with Sophie and the other wives, who all seemed so worldly-wise, and the bright chatter they brought into her life. 'I'm perfectly happy.'

'But when I mentioned your husband . . .' He looked worried. 'Your face . . . it was a study of sorrow.'

She pictured Laurence, the stranger to whom she was now eternally bound. They were friendly enough but the memory of those dreadful nights of fumbling failure and mutual humiliation stood between them. It had been almost three months now since they married. That early period must be the hardest time, she thought. It would surely get easier as they learned to love one another the way they were supposed to. Perhaps one day, somehow, children would come and they would have something to love together.

'Well,' Nicky said briskly, 'we don't have to talk about that. It's prying of me, and I'm sorry. I shouldn't have said anything. Tell me about something else. Tell me about your friends. Would any of them fancy having their photographs taken, do you think?'

*

131

At home she wondered what Polly had meant when she said that Nicky was the same with all the girls. How could he be? Could he really have that connection of their shared past with anyone else? Surely it was impossible. As she served Laurence his supper of a grilled pork chop and potatoes, she was lost in a dream world, replaying every moment of her day with Nicky and the delicious surrender she had felt as he had taken her photograph. He had controlled her and she had let him, revelling in the feeling that she was giving him what he wanted. When she'd hit the perfect pose he'd say, 'Yes, that's it,' in a deep, sincere way that gave her a chill of pleasure.

The photographs came a few days later in a brown envelope addressed in a flowing hand to Mrs Laurence Sykes. She opened it and out slipped some large black-and-white portraits and a note that read: *These are the best. Lovely, don't you think?*

She gasped as she looked at them. Were they really her? The girl in the picture had enormous eyes framed by huge curving lashes – the ones that Polly had gummed on before painting swooping black lines over the lids and out at the corners of her eyes – and her pale lips glistened. Her hair was lightly ruffled to create a natural effect, her fringe falling lightly to her eyes, and she gazed up unsmiling at the camera with a look of almost tangible vulnerability. In one picture, she looked away towards some unseen corner of the room. In another she was gazing out just past the lens as though seeing a whole world beyond it. The portraits were full of easy sensuality and grace but also melancholy. They were not like anything she had seen before.

When she showed them to Laurence, he frowned at them and said, 'I see. He's one of these avant-garde types, is he?' A sour look crossed his face as he pushed the pictures away. 'Someone like him can afford to be.' But after a moment he said, 'Still, we should see him. Ask him for supper.'

Alexandra wrote a polite note of thanks and asked Nicky to come and dine. He wrote back saying she was very kind but he wished they'd join him for dinner instead, as he had used the pictures to get an important commission and he owed her instead of the other way round. Laurence was pleased: not only would he establish a friendship with his wife's society connection but he would perhaps meet other similar people and become part of a smart crowd.

But the club where Nicky took them wasn't the grand establishment Laurence had envisaged; it was a bohemian place in a cellar near Notting Hill Gate where people wore strange clothes and listened to raucous music. Nicky fitted right in wearing his leather trousers teamed with the pink jacket she'd first seen him in, but Laurence was evidently ill at ease in his smart suit and tie, his short Guards haircut making him look quite out of place. Alexandra felt stuffy and overdressed in the outfit she'd thought would be suit-able – a pale blue two-piece suit with a diamante brooch – when the other girls were wearing sweaters and mini-skirts, or trendy little dresses that stopped well above their knees. She wanted to be like them, so at ease and comfortable with themselves. They danced and drank and smoked cigarettes with casual sophistication, and the music thumped at an unapologetic volume. The pounding rhythm was obviously meant to make everyone want to dance. A thrill ran through her at the sight of so much youth and freedom and possibility. Along with the fug of smoke and thudding beat from the jukebox, there was the unmistakeable tang of adventure in the air.

Nicky was charming and did his best to put Laurence at his ease, asking him questions and focusing on him almost entirely while Alexandra sipped her drink and observed what was happening around her, but the evening was difficult. Even a few drinks didn't seem to loosen him up. If anything, Laurence became stiffer and more contained as the evening got into full swing around him. When the music became louder and people began to dance in the small space set aside for the purpose, Laurence was visibly uncomfortable. He lit cigarette after cigarette, his left leg twitching, and there was an air of anxiety around him as though he expected trouble of some kind. He didn't seem able to relax while they ate dinner at a small table at the edge of the dance floor, watching the writhing and bopping crowd.

When they'd finished and the music was turned up louder, Nicky leaned over to Alexandra. 'Would you like to dance?'

She wanted to very much, even if the prospect of going among those self-possessed people made her nervous. She'd longed all evening to have a moment alone with Nicky. His presence was magnetic to her, and she'd had to make a constant effort not to stare at him, forcing herself to look elsewhere in case Laurence should notice what a pull Nicky exerted over her. Instead, she'd looked at all the girls with their cool confidence and wondered if any of them had been

Nicky's girlfriend, or if any one in particular was catching his eye. The girl in the mustard-coloured mini-skirt and long boots maybe? Her blonde hair swung enticingly as she bobbed to the music. Or perhaps he liked the striking red-head with her short hair and white lipstick. Surely he must fancy these fashionable women with their style and sophistication? But he wanted to dance with her, and she didn't think she could bear it if she was not allowed.

She looked questioningly at Laurence, who fidgeted and exhaled a stream of smoke before nodding curtly and saying, 'If you like. They all look damn stupid if you ask me.'

Feeling relieved, she stood up quickly, afraid he might change his mind, smoothed out the creases in her blue skirt and followed Nicky to the dance floor.

'So that's your husband,' Nicky said as he turned to face her. He took her in a hold as though they were going to waltz but he then began to move around quite freely without any real purpose. Alexandra tried to mimic his movements but couldn't work out any pattern to what he was doing. She felt that she must look, as Laurence had said, stupid. Her stuffy blue suit and clumsy dancing must be ridiculous to everyone else. No doubt they were all laughing at her.

'Yes, that's him,' she said apologetically. She glanced over to where Laurence sat smoking at their table, his eyes darting about as he observed the crowd around him. 'I'm sorry if he's a little unsmiling. He's in the army; he's used to rather a different world.'

'Oh, don't worry. I know his sort. But . . .' He leaned in

towards her and his nearness made her skin tingle. 'You and he don't seem very close, that's all.'

'We . . . we didn't know each other long before we married.' She was at a loss as to how to explain it. She wanted to tell him that getting married had not been her idea and that she hadn't understood its implications until it was too late, but it didn't seem right to open her heart to him like that.

'I see.' He looked knowing. 'You didn't say you have a baby.'

'I haven't.' She flushed violently. 'It wasn't like that! Not at all.'

'Ah. I'm sorry.' He looked awkward and his large hand squeezed hers. 'I just assumed . . . I shouldn't have. How dreadful. Please forgive me.' He gazed down into her eyes with a puzzled expression. 'I just can't understand how a girl like you . . . and someone like him . . . it doesn't make any sense at all. Perhaps it's why you seem so sad.'

She stared back at him, and at that moment she became deeply aware of his physical presence and the way their bodies were touching: his thighs against hers, her chest brushing his shirt, their arms pressed together and their hands holding. The sensation of his skin on hers was overpowering, almost too much to bear – wonderful and terrifying at the same time. Her heart began to race and she felt almost giddy, the effect of his nearness sending her senses haywire. She longed to press even closer to him, to absorb him somehow. His male strength and the warmth of his body were electrifying, unlike anything she had felt when

Laurence was close to her. At that moment, something changed inside her and she had a sudden and intense realisation that this was something that she was supposed to feel. It was what had been missing with Laurence and it could not be summoned up at will. She would never feel this for her husband. The thought struck her like a revelation, wonderful and yet terrible. At last she knew what was possible and that she was not dead inside, and the knowledge made her simultaneously euphoric and as wretched as if her life was over. But surely the strength of this . . . whatever it was . . . was far too much, much greater than she was supposed to experience. It was making her faint, helpless. Then she looked up into his eyes and saw at once that he was feeling it too, or something like it. He was staring at her with astonishment as though he'd just seen her for the first time. There was none of the photographer's objective appraisal in his grey eyes now. It was more than the surprise he'd shown when he'd seen her made up by Polly. He was looking at her with a profound intensity that sent her stomach whirling and her nerves singing, and their connection almost crackled through their palms.

The music stopped and they pulled apart, both breathless, still staring at one another.

'I must go back,' she stuttered.

'Yes,' he replied, and she knew that he understood everything.

She turned and weaved her way back through the crowd on the dance floor to where Laurence sat.

'I think it's time to go,' he said, grinding out his cigarette and standing up. He looked so out of place, so small and formal in his suit.

'All right,' she said, although she wasn't sure how she was going to survive even a few more hours trapped back in her old life. Old life? It was her only life. Except that she knew that something raw and physical and exciting existed inside her, and that knowledge was going to torture her. Nicky filled every corner of her mind and being. There was nothing but him. How could she exist away from him? Her life with Laurence was a dead one, she knew that now.

As she put on her coat, she felt electricity course down her shoulder and spine and knew that he was there behind her.

'Are you leaving?' Nicky asked. He looked different, his face suddenly a little drawn and his eyes more intense than ever. His easy smile had vanished and he seemed strained.

'Yes, sorry,' Laurence said through tight lips. 'It's late. I must get my wife home.'

Nicky shook his hand and said in a voice that was clearly meant to sound jolly, 'I'm having a party next week at my place. I'll send a card. Please come.'

'Thank you, we will. And thanks too for dinner. Decent of you.'

'It was only right. Alex's portraits have brought me some excellent business.' Nicky glanced at her quickly but turned away as though he was afraid to look at her too long. He gave a brief smile in her direction. 'Goodnight. I hope I'll see you soon. Would you excuse me? I think I've seen a friend I must speak to.'

In the taxi on the way home, Laurence said in a slightly sneering tone, 'Alex?'

'That's what he used to call me when we were children.'

'Oh. How terribly sweet.' He didn't hide the sarcasm. 'God knows if we'll go to his party if it's like that awful club. He's spoiled, that's all too plain. Bet his old dad is a gibbering wreck with a son like that.'

Laurence sighed and Alexandra sensed the wave of injustice he breathed out: how was it, he seemed to be saying, that a man like Nicky was born to treat so lightly the kind of privilege that he, Laurence, would have valued and venerated? It simply wasn't fair.

She leaned her hot forehead against the cool glass of the taxi window, wishing only to be at home in bed, her back safely turned to Laurence, so that she could take out the events of the evening and examine them, replay them, relive them, and feel what she had felt so powerfully in Nicky's arms. She shivered lightly at the memory.

'Cold?' asked Laurence.

'No . . . yes,' she said. He mustn't guess. That was the most important thing.

The next morning she had a letter delivered. Inside was a plain white card that read, 'I must see you. Meet me in the park this afternoon by the Albert Memorial, 3.30. Telephone if you can't come. N.'

Chapter Ten

Present day

On Sunday afternoon John put his head round the door of the snug and said, 'What are you up to?'

Delilah looked up from the laptop balanced precariously on her lap and smiled, glad to see him looking brighter since the disappointment that she wasn't pregnant. 'Just emailing my mother,' she said. Her family were in Wales and ever since she had moved to London in her twenties they had acted as though she had vanished into a far-off land where she could not be reached. Apart from a couple of trips to see her, when they'd been appalled by the journey, the size of the city and the expense of being there, they'd rarely even asked to visit. Her sisters and brother had stayed in Wales, got married and had children; they were all settled and happy where they were. When Delilah had married John, her family had seen it as the rightful continuation of her fairy-tale existence, but did not expect to be included in it. If anything, the distance between them all grew even greater, although Delilah tried to bridge it with regular correspond-ence and invitations to the house that were never taken up.

She didn't like it – she wanted to share all this with her family, show them another version of life they might find interesting – but there was little she could do except keep tapping out the emails and trying to find a time when she and John could visit Wales, though it seemed impossible to get everyone together. 'What are you up to?'

'Not much. I need to stretch my legs and work off some of that lunch. Shall we take Mungo for a walk?'

'Yes, let's,' she said, saving her message and getting up. 'I'd love that.'

Five minutes later they were strolling out of the house, an excited Mungo leaping up and down around them, trying to chivvy them along. He seemed to love walks with the both of them more than solo outings. They went past the old swimming pool, which Delilah thought had a kind of lichened charm. It must have been put in some time in the thirties when its black-and-white tiles and carved stone ornamentation had been the height of fashion. A heating system had been installed but it hadn't worked for years according to John. The water looked inviting, sparkling and blue in the sunshine, but Delilah knew it was icy. John plunged in every morning and swam thirty laps, emerging braced, his skin burning scarlet with cold and exertion. They went along the yew walk and then out of the wrought gates with their stone pillars on either side, each topped with an owl.

'I love those owls,' Delilah said as they went.

'Me too. They're old friends. Guarding the gates of the house with their wise old stares.'

They went towards the woods, whistling for Mungo occasionally when he'd been lost in the undergrowth just a little too long. He always reappeared, jaunty and excited, his thick coat stuck with burrs and twigs. Delilah picked some stems of elderflower and couldn't help imagining a wonderful fashion shoot as they went. Perhaps a Robin Hood theme: girls in tones of green, leather trousers, silken shirts, tiny hats. She saw them darting between trees, standing with a bow and arrow at the ready or with a hunting horn pressed to scarlet lips. Or a Greek vision of dryads and hamadryades and nymphs of water and flowers – a little hackneyed maybe, but she could imagine Rachel bringing something extraordinary to the scene. She remembered how Rachel loved her animal tableaux and playing with size. Perhaps she'd do a *Brambly Hedge* tribute, with the models as those delightfully milkmaid-ish mice in their striped skirts and floral puffs of overskirt, carrying baskets bulging with giant acorns.

I miss work, she thought with nostalgia. Perhaps it was easy to forget the endless boring meetings, the daily deluge of emails, the frustration of getting things done and the panic when it all went wrong, and just recall the excitement and glamour and the feeling of being at the heart of things. But she would be back there next week. She felt a flutter of pleasurable anticipation. She needed some fun for a change.

'What are you thinking?' John asked. He had a switch in his hand and was flicking the tops of plants as he went, taking off leaves and flower heads with it.

'Don't do that!' protested Delilah. 'You're hurting them!'

He gave her a look and laughed. 'Hurting them . . . you're too sensitive. You'll need to toughen up to live around here. You can't be weeping over the fate of flowers.'

'It seems pointless to destroy them for no reason. Anyway, I was just thinking about what fun we could have doing a fashion shoot here. My mind is whirling over it.'

'I suppose I have a lot of reasons to be grateful for the last shoot we had here, but I'm not desperate to repeat the experience.'

'Don't you want the house to be used more? It could bring in a real income if we made more of it. It doesn't have to be weddings, if that's what you're afraid of. There are lots of fun things we could do.'

'The house just about supports itself,' John said. 'I don't think we need all the trouble that would go with opening it up. Besides, you know what I'm like around people. Crowds don't bring out the best in me.'

She tried to read him. He was not being terribly positive but his face had not taken on that shut-off look that meant all discussion was at an end, so she persisted. 'I know it would be a big hassle, but I could take that off your shoulders. I'd like to put our own mark on the place – wouldn't you? You wouldn't believe how many people are interested in the house, how many requests I get for visits and use of the grounds . . .'

'I do believe it,' he said shortly. 'I'm only too well aware of it.'

'We could attract a really glamorous crowd to a place like this. I think it could be exciting.' They came out of the thickness of the woods into the clearing where the strange old folly stood. She pointed over to it. 'I mean, just look at that place – it's falling to pieces! We could do something with that! Think what a marvellous holiday let it could be – we could refit it as a luxurious honeymoon retreat just big enough for two, with a room on each floor. Or it could be an artist's studio or writer's garret.' She felt excitement building at all the ideas that were rushing around her brain. She could see it now as a beautiful, tiny nest, made cosy with every possible comfort.

They had stopped on the slight slope that led to the folly, and it stood black and a little imposing right ahead of them. Even in the bright sunlight, it was rather forbidding, silhouetted against the sky. It really was in a state, practically falling over, with holes in the walls, no roof, and foliage emerging through what was left of the windows. It would take thousands to make it habitable again. She glanced over at John. His face had darkened and his eyes had turned stormy.

'What's wrong?' she asked, panicked by his expression.

'We're not going to do anything to that . . . thing.'

'But why not?' She was mystified. Couldn't he see what wonderful things they could do? 'We could restore it, make it useful again. It's just rotting away there.'

'Good.' He almost spat the word out. 'As far as I'm concerned, the sooner the better. I hate the damn place. If I had my way, it would be pulled down tomorrow but bloody English Heritage or whoever would never allow it. I'd be sued and fined or even sent to prison if I so much as touched it – so as far as I'm concerned, it can fall down on its own.'

'I don't understand.' She spread her hands at him help-lessly.

'It's a death trap. I almost fell off it myself when I was a boy. That place is bad luck, do you understand? I don't want you going near it! Do you promise me?' He came up close to her, dropping his switch on the ground and taking hold of her jacket. 'Promise me, Delilah!'

'All right,' she said, stunned by the force of his reaction. 'I won't go near it. I had no idea you felt so strongly.'

'Well . . .' He let go of her, looking at his hands as though surprised by his own reaction. 'You do now. I just don't want you going there. It's bad luck. It always has been and it always will be. Stay away. Promise me.'

She looked over at the folly again. A chill crept down her back. 'I promise.'

The mood between them was spoiled after that. John shut off from her, in that way he often did. He replied if she asked a question but only in a word or two, and he offered nothing more but settled back into a brooding silence. She avoided the topic of the folly, though she wanted to ask him exactly what had happened there. When they got back to the house, John went into the office and shut the door.

He'll always do this, she thought. *There will always be the work it takes to run this place. Whenever he needs to get away, the house will provide the perfect excuse.*

On impulse, she went to the kitchen, scooped up from the

larder a tin containing a fresh lemon cake that Janey had left them for the weekend, and headed out to her car. A moment later, she was roaring away up the driveway, feeling more liberated as she saw the house disappearing in the rear-view mirror. She knew the way because John had pointed it out when they'd passed – the small grey-stone cottage under a low, mossy tiled roof, set back from the road on the out-skirts of the village.

This is ridiculous, she told herself. *I don't even know if he's there.*

But she didn't turn around.

Parking on the wide kerb at the roadside, she took the cake tin and walked purposefully down the grassy driveway towards the cottage. Plump purple wisteria bunches hung prettily over the front door. There was no answer when she knocked but just as she was about to turn away dis-appointed, she remembered that this was Ben's cottage, after all, and went around to the garden. Sure enough, there he was, digging hard among the raised vegetable beds.

'Ben, hello!' she called, walking towards him over the grass.

He looked up, startled, and then smiled with evident pleasure to see her. He stood up and leant on his shovel. 'Well, hello, yourself. What are you doing here?'

She held up the cake tin. 'Brought you something for tea! Do you fancy a cup and a piece of Janey's lemon cake?'

'You're an angel in human form. I can't think of anything I'd like more right now. Stay there – I'll come to you.'

*

Five minutes later, they were sitting at the kitchen table while the kettle on the range started to heat up with a sizzle and a hiss. Ben was cooling down from his exertions but he still had a glow of sweat on his nose and his hair was damp and rumpled.

He really is quite good-looking, Delilah thought. She could see a resemblance to John in the shape of his eyes and the high bridge to his nose but he had such an open expression. It occurred to her that perhaps John might have looked like this if he hadn't had so much pain in his life.

Does Ben have a girlfriend? Surely he must. Not that it's any of my business. I can hardly ask – it would seem very odd and nosy.

'This is an unexpected pleasure,' Ben said, gazing at her keenly. 'But what brought you over on a Sunday? I thought you'd be with John.'

She felt her cheeks flush slightly. 'Oh, he's busy in the estate office. You know what he's like.'

Ben said slowly, 'Yes. I do.'

'And I wanted to ask you something.'

'Shoot.' He turned his attention to the lemon cake, now on a plate, and cut two thick slices as Delilah spoke.

'I had a letter from the pony club,' she said. 'They want to know if they can hold a gymkhana in the lower field.'

Ben nodded. 'Yes, it's an annual thing – at least it was. I know John's not too keen on letting them use the lower field as it sometimes doubles up as a cricket pitch and all those ponies can churn up the ground. But they could hold it over on the eastern side, if John agrees. We'll need to give the

Whitefield paddock a mow and a clear-up, but I reckon that will do them well enough. I don't mind setting it up.'

Delilah gave him a grateful smile. 'That would be wonderful, Ben, thanks. I'll use all my powers to persuade John. You're a star. I don't know what we'd do without you.'

Ben shrugged and said, over-lightly, 'It's fine. I'm happy to help. John knows that.'

She wondered why he said it in that tone, as though there was some resentment there, something she should know about. John had always seemed perfectly amiable towards his younger cousin although, now she considered it, he gave the impression of doing Ben a favour by letting him manage the Fort Stirling gardens. She said without thinking, 'Ben, why do you look after the gardens at the house? Don't you have enough to do with the farm?'

He brightened at the mention of the gardens. 'Ah, well – I just oversee the farm. I keep an eye on it and direct things when I'm needed, but otherwise I let them get on with it. I'm not really a farmer; I only do it because my dad can't anymore. My real love is the gardens, so I prefer to spend my time there, doing what I really enjoy.'

'Weeding?' she said with a laugh.

He laughed as well. 'I couldn't do all the weeding there, even if I wanted to. Erryl does a lot, and the other gardener who comes up to help from April to November. But I like to manage it, plan and control it. You've no idea of the satisfaction that comes with creating a wonderful garden – getting nature to do just as you want and making plants strong, healthy and beautiful.'

'You're right, I haven't. It's not my world at all. But I love the results. The gardens are so gorgeous. They feel like they have a restorative power, as though they can heal people.'

Ben gave her an eager look. 'Absolutely – that's what I think too. Nature *can* heal. I've got a dream that one day we could open the gardens to people who really need them. We could offer ways for people with problems – like depression or addiction – to get in touch with nature. And there are kids who've only known concrete and inner cities all their lives – we could do some real good for them. If Fort Stirling were mine, that's what I'd do.'

Delilah stared back at him, touched by his passion and a little excited by his inspiration. That was exactly the kind of thing she thought the house had the potential for: its mighty size and grandeur could be channelled into something positive and life-affirming, rather than allowing it to dominate everything to no purpose. 'Have you suggested that to John?'

He gave her a sideways look as though uncertain what to say, then said tentatively, 'John's not exactly keen on allowing people in through the gates. He'd prefer to keep them out if he could.'

'Yes – but I'm working on him.'

A sympathetic expression crossed his face. 'As long as he's not working on you.'

'What do you mean?' she said, startled.

'Oh . . .' He looked away, a little shame-faced. 'I don't know. You came here so bright and happy in the winter. And now . . . well, you don't seem the same, that's all. You look a bit beaten somehow.'

'Do I?' She was astonished that he'd noticed.

He looked back at her and his gaze seemed somehow more penetrating. 'Yes. As though you're finding it all a bit much. I think you're a very good thing for John but I can't help wondering if he's such a good thing for you.' He reddened slightly and looked embarrassed. 'I'm sorry, I'm talking out of turn. I don't mean to imply anything about John – I've nothing against him. I'm just worried about you.'

It was most odd the way such a tiny amount of sympathy could affect her. She felt suddenly shaky and needy, on the brink of blurting out everything: the way John had changed and the pain he seemed to suffer, her misery at not getting pregnant, and the effect the house was having on her, grinding her down so that she felt a little smaller every day. If she told him, what would happen? She had a sudden longing for as much kindness as he could give her. When she spoke, her voice sounded reedy and trembling. 'I'm doing my best. But it isn't easy.'

He nodded. 'I bet you thought you'd be able to sort the place out, but the house isn't a place that's easily changed.' A concerned expression crossed Ben's face. 'I admire you for taking it on, that's for sure.'

She felt a stinging behind her eyes and told herself to get a grip. The kettle began to whistle on the stove top and when Ben got up to make the tea she took the opportunity to regain control. To hide her emotions, she said loudly with a laugh, 'I'm learning how eternal everything is. I can't so much as rehang a curtain or move a photograph frame. You know that old folly? I told John we should do it up and repair it, and he nearly had a fit. He told me the whole place was bad luck.'

Ben brought over the teapot and mugs. He was a good advertisement for gardening as a way of keeping fit, she thought as her eyes drifted over his strong physique. 'Oh yes, the folly.' He poured out the tea. 'We used to play there when we were kids, but on pain of a hiding if we got caught. They boarded it up eventually and I think it was going to be knocked down. Then John got a letter from the heritage people saying the thing had been listed and he couldn't touch it. I can't say I'm fond of it myself. It's kind of creepy.'

'I know what you mean, but that's because it's such a wreck. I think it's rather elegant and it could be amazing if it was restored.'

Ben looked doubtful. 'I can't imagine what you'd do with it. It's so odd – too small to be a house, not much use as anything at all.'

'That was why it was a folly, I suppose. Something that cost a lot for little effect.'

Ben passed her a mug of tea and pushed a plate with some cake on it towards her. 'There were some rumours about the old place.'

'Really?' She was interested. 'What?'

'Not very nice ones. Apparently there were a couple of deaths up there.'

'Deaths? What do you mean? Accidents?'

'No – suicides, I think. People jumping off. Goodbye, cruel world and all that.'

'Suicides,' echoed Delilah. 'Do you know who?'

Ben shook his head. 'No, sorry. Honestly, my parents didn't talk about things like that to me. It was probably just rumour, or something that happened outside living memory. I shouldn't think it's been possible to climb high enough up the folly to jump for decades at least.'

'But still,' Delilah said, 'it explains why there are bad connotations with it, doesn't it?'

She remembered John's stormy expression and the fear she'd seen in his eyes as he looked at the old place. He implied that he'd come closer than most to plummeting off the folly. Perhaps that, coupled with the rumours of strange deaths, were what caused his intense dislike.

'It's a grim old thing. I can see why John doesn't like it,' Ben said, taking a big bite of lemon cake. 'This cake is the business, by the way. You must tell Janey she's a marvel.'

She smiled. He looked so nice and normal munching away across the table from her. The kitchen, so much smaller than the vast flagged one at home, was cosy and comforting. She wondered what the rest of the cottage was like. Perhaps she and John would have been happier in a place like this, a home that was the right size for two.

'I'd better go in a minute,' she said. 'John doesn't know I'm here.'

He looked straight at her and for a guilty moment she felt as though they were engaged in a conspiracy. She and Ben had already as good as agreed that John was difficult, and that he was making her miserable. Now she had admitted that she'd come here without telling her husband, as though it was an act of disloyalty towards him, instead of the desire to see a friend. She felt a blush climb over her cheeks and hoped that Ben had not noticed it.

He continued to gaze at her intensely and then said in a low voice, 'Well, we'd better make sure you get home soon. I don't want to get you into trouble. But have your tea first before you go, won't you?'

Driving back over the brow of the hill towards the house, Delilah felt a sense of dread at going back there. Once she'd imagined that this place was the setting for the finale of her very own fairy tale; now she felt the story was running in reverse, taking her in quite the wrong direction. Fort Stirling looked almost sinister, sitting in its giant hollow, its windows dark, waiting for her to return so that it could beckon her back into its dark interior.

The kitchen was deserted when she went in, John nowhere to be seen. He was still shut away in the estate office and didn't emerge until she had already gone up to bed and was asleep.

When she left for the early train to London the next day, John was dead to the world, the covers up around his ears, so she wasn't able to say goodbye.

Chapter Eleven

1965

Prince Albert gazed out from his memorial towards the circular hall that also bore his name, his black form sitting beneath its Gothic canopy as though he were in his own private cathedral, still fretting over affairs of state. Around him were the symbols of how much he had to worry about – agriculture, manufacture, commerce and engineering – and the great nations of the world represented by semi-clothed goddesses holding tridents aloft.

Alexandra walked towards the memorial, excited and apprehensive, tingling with nerves at what she was doing. Had last night really happened? It seemed like a dream but she had only to think herself back onto that crowded dance floor and imagine Nicky's body close to hers for all the fearsome deliciousness to flood back. She hadn't imagined any of it, and Nicky's note was further proof, if she needed it.

She was afraid of what might happen but nonetheless she had dressed carefully for the meeting. Her usual conservative clothes seemed hopelessly stuffy after what she'd seen in the club, and the warm day outside called for something easy and fresh. In her wardrobe was a pale pink short-sleeved dress that buttoned at the top and had a belt at the waist from which the skirt flared out. She had no memory of buying it – perhaps Sophie had lent it to her – but it was just right. She slipped it on and put on her sandals. She stroked mascara over her eyelashes to get the sooty look Polly had given her for the photographs and put on frosted pink lipstick. Then she hurried out of the barracks and headed west towards the Kensington end of the park. At every step, her conscience told her she must turn back, and warned her that seeing Nicky was a reckless thing to do, knowing how he made her feel. *I mustn't*, she told herself, but there was no earthly way she could stop. She was being pulled towards him as irresistibly as if he held a rope that was tied about her waist and was reeling her in to him.

What about Laurence? asked the voice in her head. But she refused to listen. How could she turn away from something that made her feel so alive, and condemn herself to a living death with her husband? She knew that was what she ought to do. She knew that if she saw Nicky, something frightful might happen. But she also knew that whatever it was would be wonderful too, and she was powerless to resist.

Then, suddenly, she saw him sitting on a bench near the memorial, hunched over and looking almost as lost in thought as the effigy of the prince. He wore a white linen jacket instead of his bright pink one, blue trousers instead of the black leather, and a striped scarf at his neck. He was staring at the ground in front of him, his hands clasped. The sight of him provoked a turmoil of excitement in her belly that radiated out over her skin, prickling like hundreds of tiny needles. Nervous butterflies swirled inside her. It was not too late to turn back. He didn't know she was there.

'Hello!' she called, heedless of what her conscience was saying. The sight of him was like sweetness to her soul.

He looked up and a smile illuminated his face. As she neared him, she wondered what it was he had that Laurence lacked so entirely. Nicky was handsome but Laurence wasn't ugly. It was something about the light in his eyes, his spirit and vivacity that made him so different from all the other men in the world. Nicky seemed touched by a magic that gave him a glowing aura and it pulled her towards him with an irresistible force. As a child, she'd always admired him with a kind of giddy hero-worship, but that had been nothing like this. They were grown-up now and she knew beyond all doubt that this was a grown-up emotion.

'You're here.' He stood up and kissed her cheek, then took her hands in his and gazed down at her. She felt breathless and weak as he touched her. 'We need to talk about last night.'

'Yes,' she said simply. Now that she saw him, the fearful nervousness she had been feeling on the way here vanished and she knew that she would surrender to him completely if he wanted her to. It was something she had no control over. She ought to feel guilty because she was married but it would make no difference at all to what happened.

'I know it's ridiculous.' He laughed nervously. 'We hardly know each other . . .'

'Yes, we do,' she corrected. 'We always have.'

'You're right. I feel as though we've always been connected. When I'm with you, nothing else seems quite real.'

They stared at one another, knowing they stood on the brink and that in one more moment it would be impossible to turn back. Something would be said and then they would have to make choices.

Except that Alexandra knew that she had no choice at all.

'I can't stop thinking about you,' he said softly. His hands tightened around hers. 'You're filling every corner of my mind. All I can think about is being close to you.'

'It's the same for me.' She smiled back. She was filled with a sense of delicious calm, the kind she once used to feel on Sunday afternoons when her father went to his study and she did jigsaws on the floor of the drawing room while her mother sat and sewed or read aloud. It was the feeling of being at home, where she belonged. 'I just want to be with you.'

'This is madness,' Nicky said, shaking his head. She loved the way his hair was so tousled. She wanted to reach up and touch it. 'Shall we go to my place? Somewhere we can be alone.'

'Is Polly there?'

'No. And if she was, I could send her away.'

Alexandra felt a sensation of distaste; it was perfectly all right as long it was just the two of them in their private world. Anyone else knowing would make it wrong. 'I don't want her to see us together,' she whispered.

'She won't. No one will.' He closed his eyes for a moment

and inhaled through his nose. 'My God, you're driving me wild. Let's go.'

They took a taxi from just outside the Albert Hall, and only a few minutes later they were in the mews. It was deserted and no one saw them as Nicky opened the front door and led her inside. The place was empty.

'You see? She'll be gone for ages. I sent her off for supplies and she has to get up to Islington.' Nicky took her hand and pulled her gently round to face him.

She had no idea where Islington was but at this moment she was unable to care about that, or about Polly either. The feelings racing through her were so overwhelming, there could be a hurricane outside and she wouldn't notice. It was like she had been given some kind of potion that had brought her almost unbearably to life. Every cell in her body seemed to be vibrating, crying out for closeness to Nicky.

His eyes searched her face tenderly. 'Are you sure you want to do this? Your husband—'

'Shh.' She pressed a finger to his lips. 'Don't talk about that. I don't want to think about anything but this.'

He kissed the finger on his lips and she gasped at the warm softness of his mouth. Nicky took her hand in his and put his other hand behind her head. 'You're exquisite,' he said under his breath. 'The closer I am to you, the more perfect you are.'

She was trembling, possessed by a fierce longing for his touch. She hungered for his mouth on hers, his hands on her skin. This was desire, strong and demanding, and more than she could possibly conquer, even if she wanted to. She stared up at him and her lips parted involuntarily. He looked down at them and his expression changed to something she was almost frightened of: in his eyes was the same hard need she was experiencing herself.

He reached for her and then his mouth was on hers. At last she was being given exactly what she had been craving; the touch of his skin, the taste of his lips, and his delicious scent ignited something new and exciting inside her. Her blood sang as he kissed her. She'd always resisted Laurence's hard, pressing mouth but now she desired Nicky and wanted him in every way. Without thinking, she opened her mouth under his and felt the soft warm wetness of his tongue. She said, 'Oh,' but it came out as a tiny noise, almost a moan, that seemed to inflame him and he pulled her closer to him. She lifted her hands to his head, losing her fingertips in his hair, opening to his thrusting tongue as he took possession of her mouth, relishing his sweet taste. It was more glorious than she could have imagined. So this – *this* – was what they were talking about, what the fuss was about. She had begun to think it was all a stupid lie designed to cover the flat nastiness of physical love. But this one kiss was the most beautiful thing that had ever happened to her and the longer it went on, the more she wanted it, her whole body respond-ing like an instrument under the hands of a skilled musician. Excitement rose all over her but particularly in the heat of her stomach and in the places where Laurence had scrabbled and scratched with so little effect. That part seemed to be awakening along with the rest of her, tingling, heating up, making her aware of its presence.

They kissed for long minutes until Alexandra felt almost drunk on the pleasure of his mouth and tongue. *It should be repellent*, she thought, *this exploration of another's mouth*, but with Nicky, it was bliss. The sensation of their mutual pleasure in the kiss was like the stoking of a fire inside her that flared up and burst into flame, demanding ever more fuel.

He pulled away at last; his eyes were both tender and glazed with hard lust. 'Alexandra,' he said, almost with wonder.

'Yes . . .' She gazed hungrily at his mouth, wondering when she would be allowed to have it back again.

'You're incredible . . . this is incredible . . .' He seemed bewildered by what they had just shared. She felt elated: did this mean that what seemed so extraordinary to her was also out of the ordinary for someone like Nicky, who had, she assumed, kissed hundreds of girls?

'Yes,' she said, leaning against him, revelling in the feeling of his arms around her. She felt as though she had come home. 'It is incredible.'

Alexandra knew now what walking on air meant. She returned from Belgravia in a kind of floating trance, taking her time, wishing the journey home could take longer so that she could savour this wonderful joyous feeling. She smiled at everyone she passed, wondering if she was glowing as much on the outside as she was within. She had left him – Nicky, her . . . her . . . not lover, not yet . . . *yet*. She chided herself, laughing but afraid at the same time, both of whether she dared and of how much she wanted it. At home she would have to conceal this delight and the magical thing she had discovered. She wanted to stop people and say, 'Kissing! Isn't it marvellous? Oh, I adore it!' Instead she beamed at them as though she loved them, the pallid people who weren't Nicky and weren't lucky enough to be the woman he had just kissed.

At home, she must stifle it all, damp down the raging fires, so she let the happiness free while she could. By the time Laurence returned home, she was almost normal, muted but polite. He didn't seem to notice anything at all as he sawed at the piece of beef she had overcooked and later, as they read together in bed, he remarked that she seemed in a good mood, but that was all.

Polly knew, of course. When she opened the door to Alexandra the next day, it was in her eyes: a kind of accusation mixed with weary acceptance. Nicky said it was better that Polly knew; she was around the place so much and they would never be able to coordinate Alexandra's visits with her absences. But he tried to send her out as much as possible so that the two of them could be together, or else they met in the park, as far away from the barracks entrance as possible, finding patches of long grass where they could lie on rugs together, far off the pathways in case one of the army wives came by.

They talked, remembering every moment of the past they

had spent together, wondering at the unknown reasons they'd been kept apart as children, marvelling at all the hours they'd already passed in one another's company without feeling like this when it was so inevitable, and they kissed – long, delicious kisses that made them both oblivious to the outside world. Once they were roused by the shrill whistles and laughter of some passing boys, and another time an old man shouted that they were disgusting, making a vile public exhibition of themselves. Alexandra was mortified but it took very little to make her forget and kiss again; Nicky was like a drug – the more she took, the more she needed.

The kisses were amazing but they felt the pull of more than one another's mouths. Nicky's hands caressed her arms, her sides and strayed to her bottom and bosom, his fingers gentle but eager. She yearned for his skin, to unbutton his shirt and slip her hand inside to touch the warmth within. And she had felt him swelling against her thigh and it sent shivers of delight through her. She knew that it would be so different with Nicky, that he wouldn't blame her for not knowing what to do. She was even certain that with him, she would know what to do. And she was sure that it would only be a matter of time before they couldn't resist going to bed. But still, the remembrance of her wedding vows played through her mind, and he had not yet asked her to break them.

They spent two blissful weeks of summer days together before Laurence noticed anything.

After dinner one evening he looked at her over the top of his paper and said, 'Have you been to the hairdresser today?'

She looked up, startled, and shook her head. 'No . . .' She was sewing, an activity that let her sink delightfully into her imagination.

He frowned. 'A new lipstick?'

She shook her head again.

Bending a corner of the newspaper down so that he could see her better, he inspected her. 'You're different, but I can't quite say why.'

'I . . . I had a nice walk in the park today,' she improvised. 'Perhaps I caught the sun.' But the truth was she had spent two hours curled up with Nicky on the sofa in his tiny sitting room, murmuring and kissing, before he had gone off to work photographing a society luncheon for *Sketch*.

'Perhaps that's what it is. It suits you.' He flicked the corner of the paper back up again, and she let out an inward sigh of relief. She was safe. There was no way he would link her happiness to Nicky; he appeared to have forgotten all about him and hadn't even noticed that the promised invitation to a party had never arrived.

But when they went to bed that night, he put his hand on her hip as she lay with her back to him and whispered into the gloom, 'I think we should try to . . . you know.'

She froze, everything in her repelled by his touch. He revolted her now and she couldn't imagine how she had ever let him come near her. *But*, she told herself, *I have to behave normally.* She turned over onto her back and whispered, 'All right.'

I hate it and I hate you, said a voice in her head as he edged himself closer to her and then manoeuvred himself on top of her. He smelt sour to her, of cigarettes with something bitter mixed in, and his paltry weight, after Nicky's height and heft, made him seem pathetic. As he approached her mouth with his hard, unloving lips, she couldn't stop herself turning her head so that they landed on her cheek. One hand went to her left breast and clutched it, squeezing it hard. He rubbed his groin against her nightdress but she could feel nothing through the cotton of his pyjamas, no prodding, no stiffness. She was glad. The thought of that thing sent a wave of nausea through her.

'Look at me,' he murmured, and she turned her face so that she was gazing into his cool blue eyes. 'You look very pretty at the moment. I didn't realise how pretty you are.'

She stayed stock-still, letting him look at her, but the jeering voice in her head was saying, *Not for you, though. Only for him.*

He lowered his mouth onto hers and she closed her eyes, not moving or responding, as he pressed down. Then, to her horror, she felt the tiny wet point of his tongue slide out and push between her lips. It made everything in her cry out in protest. Her mouth belonged to Nicky. Laurence's tongue was loathsome. She would be sick, she would scream, she would—

He persisted for a moment and then suddenly pulled his tongue away, muttering, 'I'm sorry, I don't know . . .'

She lay still again, not moving or speaking. She knew that he was not in the least aroused by her. He was trying but there was nothing about his body to show that he desired her, and they couldn't continue without that.

This is all wrong, said a voice in her head. The voice was firm, decided, and she knew it spoke the truth. This marriage was a stupid mistake, a dead thing created by other people, like some Frankenstein's monster, and forced upon them. It was an utter failure. Laurence didn't love her and she offered him as little as he offered her.

He sighed. 'We'll try again another time,' he said in a small voice, and she felt simultaneously sorry for him, and deeply scornful. Then he climbed off her and they resumed their normal positions, back to back, not touching at all.

Chapter Twelve

Present day

London was a shock after so long at Fort Stirling. Delilah was overwhelmed by the city with all its people and the way they seemed to crowd in on each other and on her.

This used to be my life, she reminded herself. *I used to travel every day pressed up against strangers and not think anything of it.*

She remembered her morning commutes, the takeaway coffees, the dash into work with all the thousands of others, the crowded cafes and busy parks, the bars thronged with people in the evening, and then getting the train home late to her tiny flat.

The country had re-sensitised her to the city: its size, density and frantic pace. It was half terrifying and half exciting; being here felt like being a part of things again. But it was so hot and dusty that she couldn't help thinking of the cool parkland and delicious gardens of home.

I'll be back there soon enough, she told herself. Now that she was away from the house, she felt an odd mixture of relief to be free of it and a yearning to be back. What a strange place it was – it seemed to hold the promise of heaven and hell simultaneously. Most of all, she wished she and John had been able to make up after that silly bad feeling about the folly. If he'd come to London with her, they might have been able to recapture some of the bliss they'd shared before they married. But she knew he wouldn't have agreed to it. Not with the way things were now.

'Ah, hello, darling.' Grey kissed her on both cheeks, his neat little beard scratchy on her face. 'Gorgeous to see you. I'm surprised you could bear to leave that beautiful castle of yours. Or did the plumbing finally defeat you?'

'Hello,' Delilah said, kissing him back with a smile. The room was humming already, full of people holding drinks and talking while discreetly watching the new arrivals. She'd felt daunted as she came in – it had been so long since she'd been among the fashion crowd – but she'd spotted Grey in his tangerine shantung suit at once, and made for him. 'Actually, I couldn't wait to come. It was very nice of Susie to invite me.'

'She's a sweetheart, isn't she? She's over there, holding court. I can't believe how wonderful this exhibition is. It's the couture collection of some crazy society woman with more money than anyone needs. It's going to be sold for charity after it's been displayed. Susie's curating it, and then selling it at her auction house, the cunning little vixen. You must see some of the incredible Dior. But it's the early Alexander McQueen I love.' He looked her up and down. 'You look very nice. Lovely to see you glammed up instead of doing your country mouse routine. How's life?'

'Fine, thanks.' She smiled but Grey gave her a knowing look. 'You know . . . surviving.'

'That bad, eh? You'd better tell me about it later when we have some dinner.' He put a comforting hand on her arm. 'Fun first, all right?'

Delilah nodded. 'Fun first. I could do with some.'

It was a taste of her old life: a smart gathering full of well-known faces – actors, models, journalists and designers – with press photographers and gossip columnists prowling among them. Waiters offered them pomegranate and ginger martinis to sip as they made their way round the exhibits, strolling between the glass cases with their faceless mannequins dressed in exquisite clothes.

'Oh my goodness,' Delilah said excitedly, 'look at that original St Laurent Le Smoking jacket. How amazing! It's beautiful.'

'But that *incredible* Lacroix . . .'

'Oh, that collection of Chanel – I want all of it!'

'Go to Susie's auction and buy it, of course. Perhaps she'll give you a little discount as it's you.' Grey glanced over her shoulder. 'And here's the woman herself.'

Susie came up, beautifully dressed in designer clothes and with glossy blonde hair, and hugged Delilah with a cry of excitement. 'Angel! It's been too long! You vanished to the country and not so much as a wedding jig did I dance.'

'I know.' Delilah felt a little sheepish. 'It was all rather whirlwind and exciting.'

'Is it utter, utter, *utter* bliss?'

Delilah paused for a moment and then said, 'Completely.' It was what people wanted to hear after all.

'I'm so happy for you, darling, we all are.' Susie gripped Delilah's hand to show her sincerity, then said, 'I've got to mingle but look – here's Rachel to say hello.'

'Delilah!' Rachel, a shimmering vision in black platform shoes, gold trousers, a Chinese silk tunic top and crimson lipstick, tottered up and put smacking kisses on both cheeks. 'Wonderful to see you. How is the gorgeous John? And *when* are you going to have a party at that fabulous house of yours? Don't you know it's a duty when you've got that much square footage at your disposal?'

Once she was in Rachel's orbit, more people approached, and soon she was lost in conversation, telling everyone how marvellous life was and how they must come down and visit very soon. When, hours later, the staff were discreetly hurrying people on their way, Rachel said, 'If you're at a loose end, Delilah, Grey and I are doing a shoot in New York next week. The art director's just been taken ill and I hear they're looking for a freelance replacement. Are you interested?'

Delilah paused, tempted. The prospect of using her creative skills again was enticing and for a moment she hungered intensely for the feeling of being at the heart of a shoot, part of a team that buzzed with energy and excitement as it created miniature works of fashion art. But the thought of how John might greet the idea of her going to New York made her hold back. 'It sounds good,' she said eventually, keeping her options open. 'Why don't you send me an email with the details?'

'Will do,' beamed Rachel, who had become noticeably friendlier. 'It would be so fantastic to have you with us! We miss your talents!'

'I just might,' said Delilah, enjoying basking in Rachel's goodwill.

As they walked along the dark Brompton Road, Grey said, 'You're not seriously going to do it, are you? John would hate it, wouldn't he?'

'There's no harm in thinking about it. Of course John wouldn't like it but . . .' She gave him a meaningful look.

'Ah, I see. Let's go into Gennario's and have some pasta and you can *spill*.'

Over truffle ravioli and Pinot Grigio, she told Grey about how things had taken a turn for the worse. 'I can't open my mouth without saying the wrong thing. He's always been prone to black moods, but it used to be sunshine for the most part and the occasional stormy spell. Now it's the other way around. My head tells me it's because of what he's going through at the moment, losing his father to dementia and managing the estate all alone. But I can't help feeling hurt by it, and as though I'm making it worse instead of better – when all I want is to help him.' Delilah played miserably with the ravioli, sliding it around in its pungent buttery sauce. 'And we haven't had any luck getting pregnant, which is intensifying everything. We're both so anxious about it that we can't relax and enjoy ourselves. I feel that John thinks a baby will help him get over whatever it is that's torturing him so badly, and that's why it's become so incredibly important.'

'Honey, I'm sure you'll get preggers before too long. It's really been a short time, hasn't it?' Grey said sympathetically. 'And it can't be easy for John watching his father disintegrate before his eyes.'

Delilah nodded. 'He said it's as though he's losing the only person who remembers his childhood.'

'His mother died when he was a boy, didn't she?'

'That's right.'

'What happened?'

'I don't know. He hardly talks of her.' Delilah remembered the photographs in the album, recalling the delicate features, huge eyes and air of vulnerability. 'I know her name was Alex, and she died when he was a small boy. I think he was at prep school at the time. There's a picture of him in his uniform holding her hand. It's heartbreaking, really.'

'Poor guy. He's not had it easy, has he?'

'No. But I can't seem to help him. I was so sure I could make him better,' she said sadly. Her eyes filled with tears. 'I feel so powerless to fight off whatever's tormenting him.'

'I'm so sorry,' Grey said, his tone heartfelt. He thought for a moment and said, 'You know what? Perhaps John's afraid to love you completely. He might fear in some way that you're going to leave him, like his mother did.'

She stared at him across the tea light flickering in a glass holder between them, struck by this new idea. 'Do you think so?'

'It's a possibility. If you could find out what happened to his mother, perhaps you'd be able to understand how to help him.'

'Really?' She thought. 'I suppose that makes sense. I want to know what happened to her myself. I've been thinking of her a lot lately – how she coped with the burden of Fort Stirling. Whenever I get another stack of letters requesting this, that and the other, I wonder if she got the same and how she managed it all.' She frowned. 'But how I'll find out, I don't know. I hate asking John: anything about his child-hood sends him into the worst black mood you can imagine. And I can't ask his father – it wouldn't be right, even if he could remember. Janey's only been there a few years. There's Ben . . . I suppose I could ask him, though his head's mostly full of facts about plants and growing seasons.'

'Who's Ben? The gardener?'

'No – John's cousin. He was away when you stayed. And he is also a gardener.'

'John has a cousin who lives at the house?'

'No, he's in a cottage nearby. He's really lovely.'

Grey flicked a glance at her. 'Is he now?'

She felt suddenly awkward. Grey had always had a dis-concerting ability to pick up on things she thought she'd concealed. 'Yes. And he's family.'

'Oh, well . . . in that case, out of bounds.' He gave her one of his intense looks. 'But you obviously get on with him. How old is he?'

'My age.'

'So younger than John. Good-looking?'

'I don't fancy him, if that's what you're implying,' she said crossly, flushing now.

Grey made a pacifying gesture with his hand and sipped his wine. 'Now, now, I didn't mean to imply you did. I'm glad you've got a friend there, that's all. As for John's mother – why don't you just look her up on the internet?'

'I tried that. She's listed on the occasional database of the peerage, but it says "d.1974". That means died, doesn't it?'

'I think so.' Grey frowned thoughtfully.

'It doesn't say how. Most history websites just concentrate on the title holders – that means the men, of course.'

'A mystery for you to get your teeth into. You should go down to the local church and ask the vicar if he's got records of the burials. That's what they do on the telly.'

'Oh.' She blinked at such a simple idea. 'Can I do that?'

'Nothing to stop you!' Grey put down his fork and smacked his lips. 'That was delicious. But I can't resist the tiramisu. It's amazing here. You must have some.'

'For a treat.' Delilah ate the last bit of ravioli on her fork, and sat back, thinking. 'There is one other thing. John absolutely hates the folly up on the hill, and Ben told me that there have been suicides from the top.'

Grey's eyebrows lifted. 'How interesting.' He leaned in towards her, his eyes bright. 'Well, that's it then. That's your answer. His mother must have jumped from the top and killed herself.'

As she heard him speak, a sense of cold horror engulfed her. She saw it at once, and it was terrible. A dark winter's day and the young woman, Alex, shivering in the clothes she wore in the photographs – a short-sleeved collared jumper, a light A-line skirt – climbing the rotten stairs in the folly, her hair whipped up around her as the wind came racing in through the broken stonework to buffet her. At the top, on that jagged edge, she was pausing, sobbing, desperate, her eyes full of yearning for an end to her suffering. And then, closing her eyes, tottering on the brink, she was stepping forward into the void, her fingers splayed out as she plummeted.

'Are you all right?'

She fought down the sick terror swirling around her stomach. 'Yes . . . yes. I'm fine.'

'You look as though you're going to be ill.'

'I just . . . it's so awful . . . Do you really think that's what happened?'

'It sounds likely, doesn't it?'

Bleakness washed over her. 'What could have been that bad? She had so much . . .'

Grey shrugged. 'We all know these days that depression doesn't bother itself with class, money or celebrity – anyone can suffer. Perhaps she was bipolar and no one knew.'

'That makes sense,' Delilah said, but a heavy weight pressed on her. The cruelty of it was so random, the pain it caused so huge and the waste so enormous.

Grey lifted his hand to summon the waiter. 'But we can't know for sure. It might have been something else entirely. And besides, it was all a long time ago now. It explains why John is prone to feeling blue, though, doesn't it?'

Delilah tried to shake off the morbidity that had engulfed

her. 'Yes, it's only rumour. It might not be true.' The image was so strong, though, that she couldn't dislodge it from her mind; she was certain they'd somehow stumbled on the truth. 'I'm sure he would tell me something like that, anyway. Something so serious and dreadful.'

Grey fixed her with a penetrating look. 'Would he, darling? I must say, he doesn't look like the confiding type to me. More like the suffer-in-silence kind of man.'

She thought of John's stormy moods, the closed door of the office, the nightmares he could never explain. 'Maybe you're right,' she said. 'He hasn't told me so far. He might never tell me. I'll just have to find out on my own.'

'Be careful, Delilah.' Grey held up a finger as if in warning. 'Childhood trauma is a tricky thing. You mustn't go dabbling in it.'

'But if what we think is true, then I have to find out, don't you see?' She pushed away her plate and leaned towards him. 'I'll never understand him unless I do. Besides . . . I want to know. It seems wrong that his mother's life and death have been consigned to secrecy. Why shouldn't she be remembered? It seems like the house just swallows up its women and makes them disappear.' A prickle of fear ran over her fingertips as she said it.

'But sometimes things are secret for a reason. I don't want to encourage you to rush in where angels fear to tread, that's all.'

She returned his gaze with an earnest one. 'Don't worry, I'm not going to cause any trouble. I promise.'

*

She stayed the night in Grey's guest room and lay awake for a while, thinking about John and wondering if he was missing her. This sustained period of coldness between them was horrible. She wanted to ring him and tell him how much she missed him; she craved some reassurance from him that he missed her too, despite the cold way he had said he didn't need her, and that he still loved her. She desperately wanted him to tell her that he didn't blame her for the failure so far to get pregnant. *After all*, she thought, *I love him. That counts for everything.*

She dreamed of the house that night: she was running through its many rooms looking for John, but it was hard to see anything other than shapes and shadows in the grey semi-darkness. But the house had grown into something truly enormous and now there were rooms upon rooms, doors stretching away down endless corridors, more than she could ever hope to open. But the strangest thing was the wind. A tornado seemed to be whirling through the house, a rush of air that was so strong it picked her up off her feet and flew her through the rooms. It pushed her harder and harder, and then suddenly she was flying out over the garden, caught in the fierce current that carried her over the woods, her arms spinning and her legs paddling in mid-air as she swayed and tumbled.

'Wait! Stop!' she was shouting. 'I have to find John!'

Then she realised that she was going over the folly and that, looking down, she could see the young Alex standing on its top. The white face was upturned to her, watching bewildered as she tumbled overhead, and the instant Delilah saw her, she remembered everything that would happen, and shouted, 'Oh, please – please! Don't jump! You mustn't jump!' but her voice was torn from her and carried away in the current of air. Even from so high above, she could see Alex's wide eyes and slender white arms, the puzzlement on her face at the sight of Delilah. 'Don't jump! You mustn't!'

A horrible noise sounded in her head and she woke, breathless from her dream, to find that her mobile phone was ringing. She scooped it up from where it was charging on the bedside table next to her. John's name was flashing on the screen and she pressed to accept the call, wide awake at once.

'John? Are you all right?'

'Delilah . . .' He sounded tired and mournful. The slight slur in his voice made her think he'd been drinking.

'Yes, darling. I'm here. Is everything okay?'

He sighed down the phone and then after a long pause said, 'I miss you.'

'I miss you too, darling,' she said, her heart full of tenderness for him. He was drunk and wanting her, and she wished hard that she could be there to touch him and comfort him.

'I hate it that you're not here. It's the first time we've been separated and I bloody hate it.'

'So do I. I can't wait to be home with you.'

'I'm rattling around here on my own. I'd forgotten how bloody awful it is. I need you. It's lonely here. No – not lonely. They're all here. The ghosts. God, they're all here.'

'John, are you all right?' She remembered her dream. Was

the ghost of his mother one of those who were tormenting him? Who were the others?

'Yes. I'm fine. I'm not going crazy. I'm just being suffocated by this place, as usual. If I could burn it down, I would. But I'm too much of a coward for that.'

'John . . .' She was suddenly afraid that in the grip of morbid drunkenness he might cause himself some harm or do something stupid that he'd regret. 'Don't stay up any longer. I want you to go to bed and sleep. Hug my pillow and pretend I'm there, and when you wake up, I will be. I'm going to come as soon as I can. Do you promise me you'll go straight to sleep?'

He exhaled another long sigh. 'Yes. No Macallan left anyway.'

'Good. Just go up to bed and I'll be home as soon as I can.'

'Okay. Night, darling.' He sounded docile and almost overcome with sleep. He rang off before she could say any more.

She put her phone down. The first train back didn't leave until five thirty in the morning so there was no way to get back before then. She lay down on her pillows and tried to be calm. John had sounded as though he was going to take himself off to bed, just as she'd asked him to. He would be perfectly all right, and would probably sleep well beyond the time it would take Delilah to get home. It was the dream that had left her agitated and unhappy. She couldn't stop thinking about the sight of Alex at the top of the folly, poised to jump, and the feeling that she had to stop it somehow.

She set the alarm on her phone for four thirty and tried to get back to sleep but she only dozed fitfully until it went off and she could get up.

The journey seemed to take forever but the consolation was the glorious sight of the sun rising and watching the day turn from the pale blue and pink of the early morning to rich gold and cerulean, as the suburbs of London disappeared and lush countryside began. Delilah felt as though she could breathe again, and realised to her surprise that perhaps she was not a Londoner any more and never would be again. Fort Stirling had spoiled her for all that. Erryl was waiting for her when she finally arrived at her destination.

'Morning, ma'am,' he said, coming forward to take her bags as she emerged from the station.

'Morning, Erryl. Thanks for collecting me.'

'No problem. Happy to.'

'Is everything all right at home?'

'Seems to be. Janey went up first thing. She said everything seemed just as normal. Mr Stirling's still asleep.'

'Good. I'd like to be there when he wakes up.'

They climbed into the car and Erryl drove them smoothly out of the station car park and along the country lanes bordered with hedges and spreading trees in their thick summery foliage of juicy green.

As they went through the village, Delilah's eye was caught by the church and the leafy graveyard over its walls.

I'll go and see if I can find her grave, she thought. *After all, it can't hurt to look.*

179

The effect of her dream was wearing off now, but she still felt a residue of panic and sadness. Perhaps if she could see the grave, it would bring home that these things actually happened decades ago. There was nothing she could do about it all now.

The village was quiet in the early morning, and storybook pretty in its summer bloom. The houses were the sort that cost a fortune now: beautiful old properties with white-painted windows and immaculate front gardens. There was one she had always noticed as having particular charm with its old curved stone porch above a pale green front door, climbing roses bringing a delicate beauty to the old brick-work, and she wondered who lived there. There was a divide between the village and the big house that John had made no effort to bridge. *I'll have to do something about that*, she thought. *I'll let the pony club have their gymkhana for a start.*

For the first time in a while, it was a relief to see the stone pillars that flanked the gateway to the drive. The car took the brink of the hill and they saw the house lying below, peaceful and serene in its hollow. As soon as Erryl pulled the car up to a halt in front of the house, she ran in, leaving him to bring in her bags. She took the staircase two steps at a time, then hurried along the corridor to John's room at the front of the house. It was still shrouded in darkness despite the sunshine without, the heavy curtains blocking the windows. As she came in, breathless, she saw John shift in the bed and open his eyes.

'Delilah?' he said croakily.

'Yes, darling, I'm back! I'm here.'

He held out his arms and she rushed to him, jumping onto the bed and into his embrace. He was bare-chested, warm and delicious-smelling as he pulled her tightly to him.

'Christ, I've missed you,' he murmured into her hair.

'Me too. But I'm back home now. We're together.'

'I've been horrible to you lately. I'm so sorry.' He pulled away, holding her at arm's length so that he could gaze at her earnestly. 'Do you forgive me?'

Her heart melted at the sight of his pleading grey eyes, and the vulnerability of his mouth. 'Of course I do. I want us to be happy, just as we normally are. I can't be happy without you.'

He hugged her tight again. 'And it turns out I can't be happy without you either.'

'How do you feel?' she asked, running her hand along the firmness of his upper arm.

'Hmm.' He grimaced slightly. 'A bit rough. I had a dram or two too much last night.'

'I was worried about you. You said there were ghosts here. You talked about burning them out.'

'Did I?' He laughed a little sheepishly. 'I'm full of hot air; don't listen to me. I'd never hurt the house. And of course a place like this is haunted – what did you expect? It's been occupied since Norman times. We've got plenty of tormented characters pacing the battlements or floating down corridors.'

'Really? You've never mentioned them before.'

'To be honest, I haven't seen anything myself. I've heard

the odd crash in the night but that's about it. Now . . . don't let's talk about ghosts and ghouls . . . I've missed you.' He began to kiss her tenderly. There was still a hint of whisky on his breath but it was soon lost as they kissed deeply and passionately.

'You're wearing too many clothes,' he murmured, and together they took off her jacket, silk T-shirt and slipped off her white cotton trousers. When she was just in her underwear – a white lace bra and matching knickers – he gazed at her appreciatively. 'That's much better, but still . . . why don't you come here and let me help you?'

She smiled and went to him, hungry for the comfort of making love and needing to feel close to him again.

Afterwards, John fell back into a slumber and she watched him for a while, luxuriating in their reconciliation.

But it won't last, said a voice in her head. *You know it won't.*

A twist of fear turned inside her. She saw their future suddenly: a downward spiral marked by moments like this when they turned to one another in their mutual desperation and need for comfort, only to be forced apart again.

Am I really going to lose him? She couldn't bear the thought, and she stretched out a hand and ran her fingers lightly along his skin so as to feel his warmth but not wake him.

I won't let it happen, she vowed. *I'll find out what troubles him so much. I'll fix it. I know I can do it.*

She thought of Grey telling her to be careful what she stirred up, to be wary of where she rushed in.

But I can't leave things the way they are. It will destroy us, I know it will.

When the email came from Rachel asking Delilah if she wanted the New York commission, she replied saying she'd decided it wasn't for her this time. Maybe another job.

She pressed send, certain she was doing the right thing. This wasn't the time to run away from what was frightening her. She would stay and face it, and whatever it brought her.

Chapter Thirteen

1965

'She's not here. I told you.' Nicky stepped back and let her inside.

'Where is she?' Alexandra went in, glancing anxiously about. The last two times she had visited, Polly had been here and that had meant she had been unable to relax and enjoy her precious time with Nicky.

'Away,' he replied briefly. 'She's not even in London.'

Alexandra breathed out happily, feeling the tension leave her. Not even in London? Then there was nothing to be afraid of and she was happy because today meant so much to her . . .

'I'm so happy to see you,' Nicky said, holding both her hands and smiling down at her. 'I miss you so much when we're not together.'

'Me too,' she said. Then she hugged him impulsively, pressing her face against his warm chest.

'What's this?' he laughed. 'Are you all right?'

She nodded, not knowing how to say what she had resolved to.

'Alex, I mean it . . .' He put his thumb and forefinger on her chin and turned her face to his with a concerned look in his eyes. 'Are you all right? Has Laurence said anything?'

She shook her head, still mute.

'You're worrying me. There's something on your mind, I can tell. What is it, darling?'

He had started calling her that, and she loved it even though she was sure he called lots of people darling. She'd heard him call Polly darling a few times and it had stung, despite knowing there was nothing to it.

'I . . . I want us to go to bed together,' she said, letting it all come out in a rush once she'd decided to say it.

His expression changed from anxiety to something else: surprise and pleasure mixed together. 'Darling . . . are you sure?'

She nodded. 'Completely. It would mean everything to me.'

'Oh . . .' He took a deep breath, as though understanding the solemnity of it, the seriousness with which she was offering herself to him. 'My darling, I can't think of anything I want more than for us to be . . . close – as close as possible.'

'I want it now,' she said quietly. 'Now . . . please.'

He started to laugh and then caught himself. 'I'm sorry. It's not funny, it's wonderful and you're my gorgeous, precious—' He stopped talking to kiss her, his arms taking her into a hard embrace.

She opened her mouth to him, lifting her chin and letting her head fall back so that he would know that she intended to yield entirely to him. She had decided this when she'd realised how much she abhorred being close to her husband and how afraid she was that one day he would find whatever it was he needed to desire her, and he would learn how to make her body accept him, and then she would belong to him. That prospect outraged her. She wanted to rob him of that victory and make sure it could never be his. Her celebration of what she felt for Nicky and the love that utterly possessed her would mean taking her first step with him. He would have her virginity. Then, no matter what, Laurence could never claim the right to her, not really. She knew it might not make sense to others, but it did to her and she was determined to do it.

Nicky seemed to be letting go of something that had restrained him up until now, kissing her with a new kind of passion. She wondered for a fearful moment what she had unleashed. He was not like Laurence, inexperienced, cold and half-hearted. He had done this before and he knew what she could offer him. She longed to know what that was, afraid that her ignorance might cause her to fail him somehow, and yet she was also sure that her body would take over and tell her instinctively what to do. She already knew that during her kissing sessions with Nicky, she had experienced physical changes. Now she would surely learn their purpose. The excitement began to overshadow any apprehension she was feeling.

'Darling,' he murmured. 'Shall we go upstairs?'

She nodded and they climbed the narrow staircase to Nicky's bedroom with its bedhead upholstered in canary-yellow velvet and covered by an eiderdown of speckled blue like a Delft tile. They had been here before but now she approached the bed almost reverently. So, this was where it would happen. Nicky closed the curtains, sinking the room into daytime gloom.

I'm wicked, she told herself, remembering how the girls at school talked of being with their husbands and the magical moment when the mysteries of love would be revealed. *I'm very bad, beyond redemption. I'm going to bed with a man who isn't my husband.*

She looked down at her wedding band and engagement ring, then slipped them off and put them in her pocket, as Nicky turned to her and kissed her again.

It was mysterious and solemn at the same time as it felt utterly right and unbearably beautiful. Alexandra hadn't expected that. She knew that her love for Nicky would make it less dreadful than it had been with Laurence, but she hadn't anticipated that it would be so moving. From the moment he slowly undressed her, kissing each newly revealed part of her with reverence, she felt close to tears at the same time as she bit her lip with pleasure. He kissed her breasts as he unfastened her bra, marvelling over their beauty and then taking each rosy nipple in his mouth, making her gasp with surprise and then sigh with delight. When she was standing in just her knickers, her summer dress on the floor at her feet, he whispered that she was beautiful beyond measure and that he wanted her. He began to undress himself, taking off his shirt. The longed-for sight of his body made her a little frightened but also exhilarated.

It was so utterly different from her own, the strong muscled arms and the hard chest scattered with dark hair in contrast to her own soft flesh and breasts. He smelled musky and delicious and she wanted to bite his skin, gnaw into the brown warmth of his neck and pull her nails down the broad expanse of his back. He slipped off his trousers and she saw the terrifying bulge beneath, still contained but showing a rigid outline. She was scared but her body reacted by sending signals of delight throbbing through her. Whatever was going to happen, she was evidently preparing for it.

They climbed into the bed, slipping between the cool sheets, before they took off their underwear between long kisses. The taste of his mouth, the delight of the expanse of his skin pressed against hers, the almost unbearable delight of the nips and sucks he gave her neck and nipples had stoked her need. She wanted him to do everything to her and when he was finally completely naked against her own soft flesh, she wasn't afraid at all. The part of him that had seemed so fearsome was now pressed against her, hot, velvety soft and yet hard with desire for her. His fingers stroked her softly, caressing her stomach and then trailing downwards. In the place where Laurence discovered only confusion and obstacle, Nicky's gentle touch found surrender and warmth, and she felt the first shiverings of pleasure as he touched and teased her. They didn't speak but kissed and looked into one another's eyes as his hand found her open and ready for him. She knew now what was going to happen, there was no more mystery, and she let her thighs fall open as he took his place between them. She put her hand down and touched him. His eyes filled with love as she stroked him softly, running her thumb over the soft tip, and then guiding him to the place that seemed most natural.

'Alex,' he said throatily as he hesitated a moment.

'Please . . .' she said. 'I want it so very much.'

'You're so . . . irresistible.' He dropped his head and kissed her, then began to gently press forward, bit by bit, and she felt with astonishment that she was able to take him inside her quite easily, but after only a short way, he hit an obstacle. He frowned, bemused.

Disappointment flooded her. So it wasn't Laurence. It was *her*, after all. It was she who was the failure and now she was going to let Nicky down too, after she had promised him so much. She wanted to hide her face and run away.

'Alex, darling . . .'

'I'm sorry, so sorry,' she burst out.

He looked tentative, then he said, 'Has Laurence made love to you? He has, hasn't he? I mean, after five months of marriage . . .' Then he saw her stricken face and stopped. He took a slow breath. 'Oh my God. I see. Darling, you could have said, you could have told me . . .'

'But I don't know what I'm doing wrong,' she muttered, trying to keep a check on the hot tears that had sprung to her eyes.

'Wrong? You've done nothing wrong – what do you mean?'

'But I can't . . . he can't . . .'

'And you think it's your fault? Oh—' His eyes filled with

189

tenderness. 'My sweetheart, please don't think that. My beauty . . .' He kissed at the two tears that had slid out from under her lids. 'Darling, if you want me to, I'm going to carry on but you must know that you're a virgin and this first time may hurt you a little – do you understand? But once it's over, it will be much better, I promise.'

She gazed up at him, and sniffed. 'All right. I understand.'

He was still partly inside her, and he kissed her passionately until her arms wrapped around his back and she was urging him to press onwards, to do whatever was necessary to make them one at last. Her whole body cried out to have him, her back was arched to him, her legs entwined in his strong muscled ones. His back shuddered slightly with the effort of holding back and then as she whispered encouragement, he put more force behind his thrust and the next moment she gasped as a sharp pain stabbed her and he was deep inside her. They were pressed closely together, his breath in her ear loud and urgent. The pain was over almost at once and she said, 'Oh, keep going, please,' and so he did, and at last she understood it all.

The other wives noticed. Perhaps it was naïve to think that they wouldn't, but Alexandra was still astonished when they began to ask her if there was some good news to share – a baby, perhaps? They said with meaningful smiles that married life must be going well. She glowed, they said, and they wanted her secret, but none of them guessed it. She had been married for far too short a time for them to guess that there was a lover making her eyes sparkle and her step spring with happiness.

One day, as she and Nicky lay in the long grass by a tree in the park, there had been a terrible and terrifying moment when she'd heard the voices of women and children as a small group approached. One of the small boys came running over and the next moment Alexandra found herself looking up into the solemn eyes of the four-year-old son of one of the army wives she knew. She gasped and lay still while Nicky said, 'Now then, young chap, you run along back to Mother,' unaware of how close they were to discovery. The woman's voice came floating over from the path, calling the boy back, and after a moment he turned and ran off. Alexandra was breathless and appalled at the close shave, and after that they went further afield. She knew that soon they would have to decide what to do next. She could only assume that at some point they would resolve to part, but that seemed so impossible at the moment that she preferred not to think about it at all. When they were together, nothing else mattered, and the lovemaking was so intoxicating that she could not have enough of it.

'If only I'd known what it could be like, I'd never have married Laurence,' she told Nicky as she lay in his arms after the storm of passion had passed for a while.

'Perhaps you could have married me instead,' he said casually.

The words hit her like punches. Really? Could a life with love really have been in her reach? But they hadn't met since they were children. In all the years since, when they might have grown to know what they felt, they hadn't laid eyes on one another.

'My father would never have allowed it,' she said. 'He'd have stopped it.'

'I wish I knew why,' Nicky said, frowning. 'What did he have against us?'

'It wasn't just your family. There were other friends he made me give up. He seemed to think I was better off by myself.'

'Bloody odd behaviour,' Nicky said. 'Very rude of the old man, as well. And it makes things awkward in a small place. It doesn't look right.'

Alexandra suspected that very few people had spurned the friendship of the Stirlings. 'I shouldn't think you cared much, really, did you?'

'Don't be silly.' He kissed her swiftly. 'Of course I did. We were friends. I was fond of you. But' – he nuzzled against her – 'not as fond as I am now.'

Alexandra smiled happily at the tickling caress but a thought struck her. 'If my father knew about this, he'd be so furious, I hardly dare think about it.' A sick feeling vibrated through her at the image of her father's anger.

'I shouldn't think mine would exactly be over the moon either,' Nicky replied. 'But it's our lives, isn't it? Aren't we the ones that matter? Not some crusty old men who've had their chances and simply want us to be as miserable as they were. Let's just be happy and to hell with what they all think.'

This seemed outrageous subversion. Everyone knew that

duty and obedience were virtues and that pleasing oneself was wicked and indulgent.

Nicky kissed her nose. 'The expression on your face at the moment is one of the reasons I love you. Let me get my camera; I want to capture it right this instant.'

She lay, trying to keep her face still to preserve her expression for Nicky, but exulting inside with pleasure at the way he had said, so naturally, that he loved her.

Life with Laurence was tolerable now that Nicky was the centre of her universe. The fact that Laurence was her husband was something she tried not to think about and his presence couldn't dim her bright happiness. She was being so appalling, so sinful, and yet it was so wonderful. The only way to cope with it was not to think about it at all.

She stood at the stove in the early evening, humming to herself as she stirred the cream sauce that she intended to pour over the piece of fish roasting in the oven. Potatoes boiled away in their starchy bubble bath, making clouds of steam.

She felt his presence before she saw it, and she turned to see Laurence standing in the doorway, holding something out to her, his face alive with fury.

'What the hell is this?' he hissed.

Her stomach did a sick flip and she felt a nasty prickle down her neck and in her fingertips. He was holding out a magazine that she had bought that day, but not yet read. There on the page, under the headline 'London's newest star photographer', was a print of a photograph that Nicky had taken of her a few weeks ago. It was captioned 'The Bath' and she wasn't named but it was obvious who she was to anyone who knew her. Her hair was pinned casually upwards, strands escaping at her neck, and she was gazing out over the side of a bath, her neck and shoulders bare with the suggestion that she was nude in bathwater behind the high cast-iron sides. She was smiling, her gaze tender, and the portrait was intimate and suggestive. It was a clever photograph that trod a fine line of decency: the nudity was concealed but absolutely there.

Laurence thrust the open pages towards her, his eyes blazing. 'Explain this,' he said, a note of hopelessness in his voice alongside the anger.

'I . . . I . . .' She couldn't begin to understand what the photograph was doing in this magazine. What was Nicky thinking of sending it to be published?

Laurence stared down at the image on the page. 'It's indecent!' he said in a harsh voice. 'Disgusting! Look at you! How could you humiliate me like this?'

Her world was shaking on its axis. She knew that the photograph itself was just the start of it and any second now he would realise that too.

'For God's sake, Alexandra!' he snarled. 'Look at me! Talk to me. What were you thinking? Anyone could see this, anyone, and they'd know . . . they'd know . . .' He couldn't say what they would know. His white face was covered in crimson blotches, his neck scarlet.

'I'm sorry,' she said in a quiet voice. She needed to be calm.

He stared at her, agonised, his pale blue eyes wide and glassy. '*He* took it,' he said in a strained voice. She knew at once that he'd guessed the full extent of the betrayal.

'Yes,' she said in a voice that sounded almost firm.

'Christ!'

She'd never heard such a word from him before and it shocked her. He was shaking now, the magazine trembling in his fingers. He seemed unable to speak any further but instead threw the magazine at her feet where it landed splayed and creased. Her own face gazed up at her with its knowing smile and sideways look. Then he turned and strode out of the flat, slamming the door behind him.

She waited a few minutes but there was no sign that he was coming back, so she stopped cooking, leaving the pots and pans on the stove top and turning off the oven. She picked up the magazine and deposited it in the bin. She wondered if she should find a telephone so she could tell Nicky what had happened and ask him why on earth he'd decided to have the picture printed when a fearful thought struck her – perhaps Laurence had gone to find Nicky so that he could fight him. But Laurence had no idea where Nicky lived and besides, Nicky was probably out.

Alexandra tried to relax but she was on edge with a kind of horrified excitement. It was terrible that Laurence knew her greatest secret but there was also a sort of nervous anticipation, as though she was waiting for the next instalment in a thriller. What would he say? What would happen? Surely he would demand that she give up Nicky . . . and she was certain she couldn't do that. So what on earth would they do? She felt a wave of relief that surely the deception was now at an end, followed by panic at what would happen next.

The hours ticked by and she finally went to bed, although she couldn't sleep as she played scenarios through her mind. Would Laurence want a divorce? Or would he forgive her and ask her to relinquish Nicky?

Just after one o'clock in the morning she heard the front door open and the sound of someone moving heavily about in the sitting room. He must have been drinking in the mess. There wouldn't be any sense out of him tonight – just a whisky or two was enough to slur his speech and make him lose his train of thought. She closed her eyes and willed herself to sleep.

Footsteps approached the bedroom and then the door was flung wide, letting light from the sitting room pierce the darkness.

'Get up,' said Laurence in a tone of voice she had not heard before.

She turned around, blinking in the glare. 'What?'

'Get up!' he snarled.

She sat up and rubbed her eyes. 'Laurence, it's late. You're drunk. I know you're upset—'

'Upset?' he drawled. 'Why on earth should I be upset? My wife, my wife of less than a year, is fucking someone else.'

She drew in a breath at the word he'd used. A ripple of fear shot down her spine.

'Tell me, *darling*,' he said, slurring slightly, 'what made you able to do it with him, huh? You're a cold fucking fish to me. I thought you were frigid with your bloody shut-off body. But you've been with him, haven't you? Don't lie, I can see it in your face. I should have realised it before with the way you've been acting, the way you've been around me. Your little childhood friend has got some damn privileges, hasn't he?'

Alexandra was still, listening to him with mounting fear as her mind began to race over what he might mean to do.

'I should have listened to what they told me about you and your family before I agreed to take you on. Bad blood in it. You seemed so bloody pure but you were just waiting for the right scent to put you in heat.' He swayed forwards. Instinctively she cowered back, a movement that seemed to infuriate him. 'I'm your fucking husband!' he cried, a tormented expression on his face. 'How *dare* you . . . how dare you be like this, you thankless bitch.'

'Please, can't we talk about this in the morning?' Her voice quavered with fright. The language he was using was harsh and showed how unanchored he was. She'd never dreamed Laurence could utter words like that.

He was approaching the bed. 'Do you know what the worst part of this sordid business is? The whole world is going to know I'm a cuckold, with your shameless parading of your behaviour in the press. And what they don't know . . .' He laughed bitterly '. . . what they don't know is that I've not even had a taste of the favours you're so happy to give out. So . . .' He reached a hand to her nightdress and began to tug at the neck. 'Come on, I want my share. I demand my rights.'

His touch was leaden and cold, and there was nothing about him that seemed truly hungry for her. She tried to push him away.

'Laurence, no . . . stop it.'

'I won't stop it,' he snapped, his breathing coming faster now. 'You don't have any right to tell me to stop it. You're mine, don't you understand that? You belong to me!'

Real fear began to possess her as she realised that he was serious. He was drunk and strong. He was trying to assert something. 'Please, get off me, this isn't right . . .'

'Rich, coming from an adulteress. I might have known that as soon as a nob like him made a play, you'd drop your knickers like a whore.' With a sudden tug he ripped the nightdress, tearing it straight downwards over her chest so that her breasts were exposed. She gasped and tried to pull away, but he grabbed her before she had time to move, seizing her arms in both hands, his fingers digging into her soft flesh.

'No!' she cried but he yanked her downwards and kneed her thighs apart. *Oh God, he's going to do it*, she thought, appalled and revolted. Her mind raced despite the fear and she wondered if now that she had made love to Nicky, her body would be able to accept him, even if he was rough and unwanted. Everything in her wanted to reject him, but he was stronger and he wrestled her easily down to his will. She was prone and vulnerable. When he released one of her arms so that he could fumble with the flies of his trousers, she tried to push him away with her free hand but she was helpless. She felt feeble and weak, and that infuriated her.

'Stop it!' she shrieked. 'What kind of a man are you?'

He froze, panting. He had undone his trousers and they hung open. She saw at once that he wasn't going to be able to do to her what he wanted. He couldn't make her belong to him after all. She looked into his face and saw the expression of desperation there.

'Stop it, Laurence,' she said pleadingly, trying to keep her voice gentle. 'Let's talk about this.'

He flicked his gaze up to her and sighed. For a moment she thought he was going to calm down but his eyes fell on her exposed body and his expression changed. The sight of her nakedness seemed to infuriate him and, grimacing, he drew back his hand and slapped her hard across the face, sending her head twisting under the blow. The force of it made her temple hit the headboard and she tasted blood in her mouth. The pain sent her mind spinning and for a dazed moment, she had no idea what had happened until, with a moan, she turned to see that Laurence had pulled back his arm again.

Despite the shock, she knew what she had to do. Laurence had loosened the grip on her arm and she twisted out of his grasp, slithering away before he knew what was happening. He roared his frustration as she dashed to the bedroom door in three strides, heading out into the hall knowing only that she had to escape. She ran to the front door, hearing Laurence crash to the floor as he made to follow her. He was drunk and his loose clothes were inhibiting him but he'd be after her in a moment, maddened now. She could only guess what he might be capable of in this state. Terror propelled her to the coat stand where she hauled down her summer mac and put it on over her torn nightdress, then pushed her feet into her sandals. He was up and at the door.

'Come back here!' he yelled, and she screamed in fright, grabbing at the door catch and frantically trying to open it. She turned and saw him coming at her, his eyes burning with anger, and on instinct she grabbed the coat stand and threw it in his path. The unexpected obstacle baffled his drunken brain and he fell over it, hitting the ground with a heavy thud.

Alexandra turned back to the front door, opened it and ran outside, pulling the door shut behind her. She had no keys. She could not go back in any case, not without risking a beating. Scrabbling in her mac pocket, she found a scarf and dabbed at her throbbing temple. It came away scarlet with blood. Tears rushed to her eyes as the first real pain flooded over her, and she felt suddenly nauseous with dizziness. Her tongue tasted metallic from the blood in her mouth.

I have to get away, she thought, *before he gets up and comes after me*. She stuffed the scarf back in her pocket, buttoned the coat and headed out of the barracks.

At the gates, the sentries eyed her curiously and said, 'Ma'am? Are you all right?'

She mumbled that she was fine and kept her head down, hoping that her wounds weren't too evident. Her face already felt puffy and swollen and it throbbed with pain. She was past the soldiers before they had time to ask more questions and they weren't interested enough to pursue her once she was out of earshot. She walked on at a hurried pace, glad it was a warm night. The tears of shock and hurt began to sting her eyes.

'Alex! What are you doing here?' Nicky looked closer. 'Oh my God, what's happened? Quick, come inside.'

She sobbed in his arms and carried on weeping as he bathed her temple with warm water. He gave her a tooth mug with salt water to gargle for her torn cheek and wrapped her in his rough wool dressing gown that smelled so comfortingly of him.

'He knows!' she said through her tears.

'But how?' Nicky looked baffled. 'How on earth did he cotton on?'

'You put that photograph in the magazine – the one of me in the bath.'

He frowned. 'What are you talking about? I wouldn't do that. It would be madness.'

'Then how—'

Nicky's face cleared and he said in a grim voice, 'Polly. That's the only person it could have been. I fear she's rather territorial.'

Alexandra stared at him, horrified. 'Would she really do that?'

'I'm afraid so. I've been thinking for a while that her possessiveness is getting out of control and now I know for sure. I'll give her a rocket and show her the door when

I see her.' He reached out and stroked her hair. 'I'm sorry, darling. I had no inkling she could do something like this.'

'I can't go back,' she whispered, her eyes feeling as swollen as her face. 'He knows about us – what we've done. He wants to kill me.'

'He's an animal,' Nicky said shortly. 'Of course you can't go back.' He pulled her into an embrace and she sank into the strength of his arms. His lips pressed into the top of her head. 'He had to find out some time. I just wish it hadn't been this way. But you're with me now. I'll look after you, do you hear?'

She nodded, closing her eyes. She was safe at last. She had come home to Nicky.

Chapter Fourteen

Present day

Delilah found her post in the hall, already sorted for her, as usual. She picked up the pile of letters that had grown large in her absence even though she'd been away such a short time. Taking them through to the snug, she saw several were from as far away as the States and Australia. She knew the form. They'd be asking questions about the house, enquiring after paintings or objects inside, or claiming that they were distant Stirling relations and wanted more information about the family tree. It was surprising that so many people evidently expected her to devote such a lot of her time to their pet causes, whether it was writing them an essay on the Fort Stirling china collection or the armaments that hung in the Great Hall, or supplying them with endless photographs of whatever they wished to see, from vases to curtain fabrics. They seemed to think that their quest to draw up the Stirling family tree was just what she'd been waiting for in order to fill her empty hours.

She felt more sympathy for the people who wrote politely asking if they might tour the house, or come to examine a particular painting, or even to see the gardens. She liked the requests from young women to get married in the house. They appealed to her sense of occasion and she always had visions of white wedding dresses, flowers and silver trays of champagne, although she was sure that the reality would be a horrible scramble behind the scenes to get everything done. She turned down all the requests politely.

She had said yes to the pony club, though, and the date of their gymkhana was approaching. She made a mental note to mention it to John while he was still in a good mood. Feeling reckless, she fired off a quick email to Susie, inviting her down to stay and have a look at the clothes she'd found in the attic.

There was a knock on the door and Ben put his head round. 'Not disturbing you, am I?'

She looked up, happy to see him, then remembered how Grey had given her that look when she'd talked about Ben. It was silly – there was nothing between them. 'No, you're not. Come in. I'm just going through all the letters and thinking about how to involve the locals in the house more. I've said yes to the pony club but what about opening the gardens up during the summer? I'm sure lots of people would like that.'

Ben came in. He was dressed in his usual gardening shorts, his legs brown and muscled. She glanced down and then quickly looked away. His unabashed physicality was quite overwhelming when he stood close to her.

'I think that used to happen, actually,' he said, sitting down on the sofa arm, his heavy boots incongruous on the carpet. 'The housekeeper before Janey told me that she used to do teas for visitors to the gardens. But nobody's visited them since I've worked here. I wouldn't mind. I'd love more people to see what we do.'

'It could be lovely,' Delilah said, suddenly enthused. 'We could do gorgeous homemade teas and put some things out for children to play with.' She could see it now: little wrought-iron tables with gingham cloths, vintage teapots, plates of cakes and scones, glass dishes overflowing with jam and cream, and happy children running about.

'Yeah,' Ben said with a laugh, 'but you can bet there would be plenty of regulations and licences and goodness knows what. And you'd have to print up leaflets and tickets, register for VAT and all the rest. Health and safety regs. Provide proper facilities. Get environmental health to grade the kitchen.'

'Oh,' Delilah said, deflated. 'I suppose you're right. Nothing's simple, is it?'

'I don't mean to pour cold water on it,' he said quickly. 'I just think you should consider how much work it will be. But I'm all for it – you know I'd help. And once it was up and running, it would be great. What I would do with this place if I could!' He smiled broadly at her, then his expression became suddenly more serious. 'Delilah, can I ask you something?'

'Yes – of course.' As he looked at her, she felt the odd tingle of excitement mixed with fear that had begun to kindle inside her whenever Ben was near. Was Grey right? Was she attracted to him? *But I love John*, she told herself sternly. *I don't want to be attracted to anyone else. It would be a disaster all round.*

But what you want doesn't come into it, said a voice in her mind. *You can't help what you feel . . . Ben is so sweet and easy to be with. Can't you imagine how much brighter your life would be with him?*

His voice broke into her thoughts. 'Tell me to get lost if you want, but are you all right? I noticed that you disappeared for a bit. I wondered where you were.' His tone became softer. 'I'm worried about you if I'm honest. You seemed a bit wound up when you were round at the cottage the other day.'

'You don't have to be worried,' she said, touched at his concern. 'I only went to a party in London. It's true, I was a bit low when I came round, but I'm fine now.'

He said quietly, 'You looked more than low. You looked desperate. Are you sure you're all right?'

She nodded, unable to speak all of a sudden.

'You do know you can come to me any time if you need to talk about anything, don't you? I'm always here and happy to listen.'

She found her voice and said hesitantly, 'Of course I do. I appreciate it.'

'Okay, then.' He smiled shyly and stood up. 'I'd better be getting back to work then.'

As he turned to go, she remembered what she had wanted to ask him. 'Oh, Ben!'

'Yes?' He turned back, eyebrows raised expectantly.

'I know this is a funny question, but I was wondering if you knew how John's mother died.'

The words hung there between them, sounding very odd now that she had spoken them out loud. The question of why she hadn't asked John seemed to hover over them.

'Well . . .' Ben looked surprised. 'I . . . I'm sorry but I really have no idea. All I know is that something very bad happened. But people just don't talk about it.'

'Really? That's very strange, isn't it? Why the conspiracy of silence?'

'I can't say. It was a long time ago now. I do know that my parents weren't very keen on John's mother – at least, she was never spoken of with any affection. They obviously didn't think she was a good thing. And whatever happened to her didn't make them think any better of her. They didn't talk much about her but I always got that impression, although I couldn't say exactly how.'

'Oh. I see.' She hadn't expected Ben to know the answers but even so, she was disappointed to reach a dead end so fast.

'Sorry. I'm afraid we haven't been all that close as a family.'

'No, I can see that. Still, my own family isn't exactly tight-knit. Not if you move away from our town, at any rate. Thanks.'

'You're welcome.' As he headed out, he said over his shoulder, 'Don't forget what I said. You can come to me at any time.'

*

All morning, Delilah thought over what Ben had said about Alex. It seemed awful that John's father's family might not have liked his wife. Of course, mothers-in-law often had problems with their sons' wives, but for the extended family to think badly of her . . . what reason would they have had? In her photographs she looked respectable enough – almost a beauty even, with large candid blue eyes that seemed to display a kind heart and a sensitive nature. Perhaps, if she had killed herself, hard-hearted people might dislike or despise her for being weak. As Grey said, there was less understanding in those days of what might drive someone to suicide. Had Alex been mentally ill? Depressed? Addicted to something that unbalanced her mind?

She felt suddenly that it was important to know – not just to unlock whatever it was that was tormenting John, but for her own sake. Was there something about this place that could drive a young mother to feel she could not go on? Delilah had an unpleasant sense of foreboding as if that could be her fate too. She went to the drawing room and picked up the photograph of John holding his mother's hand, Alex unreadable behind the large sunglasses. She ran a finger over the half-hidden face and along the white coat.

'Why did you do it?' she murmured, only half aware she was speaking out loud. 'What made you do it?'

After lunch, when Janey mentioned that they'd run out of milk and she was going to take some out of the freezer, Delilah said, 'Don't worry, I need to pop into the village anyway. I'll get some at the shop.'

'All right,' Janey said. 'That means we won't have to wait for it to defrost before we can make some tea. Thanks. You'd better hurry, though. They close at three thirty.'

She took her car and set off down to the village. She made it in plenty of time to pick up a couple of pints of the local milk, and then turned determinedly towards the church, an ancient grey-stone building dominated by a square Norman tower and set back from the road behind an old gate and feathery hedges.

Crunching up the gravel path towards the old building, she wondered why she hadn't come here before. It was beautiful and the silence of the picturesque old graveyard was only broken by the chirrup of birds or the whirr of grasshoppers. She went to the arched wooden door with its bands of iron aged to a dull rusty patina, lifted the large ring handle and pushed it open. It creaked heavily beneath her weight and opened to reveal a dimly lit interior. First there was a kind of porch with hymn books stacked on a shelf and a parish noticeboard with posters announcing the church fête. Beyond that lay the main body of the church and she walked in, savouring the distinctive smell of old cold stone, leather and candlewax. It was cool inside and the lights were off, creating a murky shade. Shafts of coloured sunlight fell through the stained glass windows and illuminated the many wall decorations. She began to look at the ones nearest: there were dedications to the men lost in the world wars, a memorial to six boys from a local Scout troop who'd drowned near the Isle of Wight at the turn of the last century, and a gilded board that listed the vicars of the parish since the first in 1082.

People had come here to be baptised and married for more than a thousand years, she thought, awed. And to be buried. Or remembered, at least.

As soon as she'd seen the first Stirling memorial, she saw one after another, dating back over the previous three centuries: black marble with gold Latin inscriptions, white with elegant black script, the S written like an F to make the words seem curiously lisp-like at first reading. There were white stone angels praying for the souls of dead Stirlings, a tomb with a crusader knight and his lady, a weeping goddess letting petals drop from her hands to show her despair at the loss of children. These were expensive funerary tributes, wealth buying a better standard of grief than the gentlemen and ladies round about who had only small engraved plaques, and the peasants who would have been lucky to have a marked grave at all.

Delilah wandered about, reading the inscriptions and imagining the people who were now long dead and gone. She felt connected to them by her Stirling name despite having only recently become one of them herself. 'Hello, can I help you?'

The voice came out of the shadows and made her jump. She turned to see a friendly man in a dog collar walking towards her from the front of the church.

'Oh! You startled me,' she said with a gasp and a half-laugh.

'Sorry. I was in the vestry. I heard you come in and

thought I'd see how you're doing. Would you like some information about the church?'

'No, thank you – I mean – I'm not a tourist, but you could help me . . .'

The vicar came up and stood beside her. He had a pleasant open face with a grey-streaked beard and tiny, crinkled eyes behind a pair of small round spectacles. 'Happy to help. Are you a local then?'

'Well, yes – and no.'

'Goodness, I'm getting more intrigued to know exactly what you are.' He smiled.

'I'm sorry – my name is Delilah Stirling. I married John Stirling last year. I'm from the fort.'

The vicar raised his eyebrows. 'Ah, how wonderful to meet you! I hoped our paths would cross at some point. It's very exciting to have a newcomer at the house and we'd hoped we could welcome you to the parish.'

She felt suddenly ashamed that she hadn't thought to introduce herself before. There was no tradition of church-going in her family, nor any sense of obligation to the community, but of course it was different in these old-fashioned little English villages where everything still revolved around the village hall. 'I should have come before,' she said, colouring.

'Oh, don't worry about that. Mr Stirling doesn't often make an appearance at church but I knew we'd meet in time. Now, are you enjoying having a look at St Stephen's? It's extremely old, as you've probably gathered.'

'Yes, it's beautiful.'

'And very connected to the Stirling family as you've no doubt noticed.' He began to point out all the funeral monuments that she'd already examined. She listened for a while and then, as soon as he paused for breath, said quickly, 'Yes, but where are they buried?'

'The Stirlings?' He gestured up towards the nave. 'There's a vault where the members of the main family are buried. The minor members have to be content with the churchyard, I'm afraid.'

'Where's the vault?'

'It's below the church with access from behind the vestry. Would you like to go down there?'

'Yes, please.'

He led her to the front of the church, chatting about the various features they were passing, then between a pair of brass gates and through a red curtain into the vestry where there were old oak cupboards fastened with padlocks and a rail holding crisp white choir vestments. Set into the wall was a small arched oak door like the one outside, with a ring handle. The vicar opened it, saying, 'Follow me. It's rather twisty and narrow, I'm afraid. I don't mind that kind of thing myself but I know some do.'

He led the way down a very tight spiral staircase of cold stone. A chill air came up from below and Delilah shivered as she followed him into the darkness. It was only a short descent before the vicar stepped out onto level ground, reached for a switch and the underground chamber was immediately illuminated with a dull yellow light from one dusty bulb suspended from the ceiling.

Before them was a room half of which was divided by iron bars, and behind the bars were large stone boxes with carved inscriptions.

'The family tomb!' the vicar announced cheerfully, waving at it.

Delilah had a strange, shivery sensation and thought: *I'm a Stirling now. Will I end up here in this cold, dark little room, locked away behind bars with the other skeletons?* She said, 'Are people still buried in here?'

'If they want to be. People seem to prefer cremation these days. But we have space for a few more Stirlings if anyone would like to spend eternity in the bosom of their ancestors.'

Delilah looked around. 'How do you get the coffins down the spiral staircase?'

'We don't. There's a trapdoor over there that leads to the churchyard. The coffins are lowered in for interment.'

She walked over to the iron bars and peered through to examine the nearest tombs. There were three Viscounts Northmoor crammed in next to each other, one with his wife and four children along with him, and some other family members, but the inscriptions were awkward to read as most ran around the edge of the tomb and so disappeared out of sight.

'Looking for anyone in particular?' the vicar asked, coming up behind her.

'Yes – I'm looking for the last Lady Northmoor.'

'Oh, yes, she's in there. She died young, poor lady. I noticed her in particular when I had a look around.'

'Oh!' Delilah was filled with an unexpected sadness that

Alex was here after all. She knew that John's mother had died, but here was the incontrovertible evidence of it.

'Yes, she's over on the far right. Her husband's in there with her now. He wanted to be buried with her. He married again, I think, after his wife died, but I never found out what happened to that Lady Northmoor. He seemed to like his first one best.'

Delilah frowned. 'Oh no, that can't be right. John's father isn't dead.'

'You mean Lord Northmoor up at the house? No, of course not, he's very much alive, I'm glad to say. Which Lady Northmoor are you talking about? The lady we have here is the current lord's mother. She died in 1948, I think.'

'No, no – I mean the last Lady Northmoor, John's mother. I think she died in 1974.'

The vicar looked doubtful. 'I haven't heard of her, I'm afraid, and 1974 was well before my time. Father Ronald was the vicar here then. He's very old now. He lives in Rawlston, about two miles from here, in the home there.'

'Surely there are records?'

'Yes, I can check the parish records – they're usually very thorough. I'd have to dig out the year you mentioned.'

Delilah hesitated, feeling she was on the brink of setting something in motion that might roll out of her control, but she took the step anyway. 'There's also a possibility that Lady Northmoor killed herself.'

He looked surprised. 'Really? I really hadn't heard of that. How awful. Then I'm afraid it's unlikely she was buried in the family vault, or even in the churchyard itself, come to that. There was still rather a stern attitude towards suicides even just a few decades ago. They couldn't be buried in hallowed ground.' He shook his head. 'I'm glad to say there is a little more compassion for those desperate souls these days.'

'So she's definitely not here – or in the churchyard?'

'I don't think so but I'll check the records. And you could always ask Father Ronald what he remembers. I believe he likes visitors and has a good recall of the past.'

They turned and made their way back towards the staircase.

'Thank you, Vicar,' she said. She felt a strange relief that they hadn't found Alex in the cold darkness of the underground chamber. 'I really appreciate your help.'

'You're very welcome. I shall look at those records for you when I get the chance.'

They left the dankness of the vault and climbed the spiral staircase to the warm day outside.

Chapter Fifteen

1965

Alexandra did not return to the barracks but wrote to Laurence explaining that after what had happened, she could not come back. She said that their marriage had been a mistake and they would both be happier apart. She hoped he would understand and asked if he would send her things to a hotel in Victoria where she rented a room although she did not stay there. A few days later, she called at the hotel reception and found that a letter had arrived for her.

Alexandra
> *You have humiliated me and disgraced yourself. I am giving you a month to come to your senses and return. I've told everyone that you are visiting your father for the time being. Please be so kind as to keep away from the barracks unless you intend to stay. I will see you in four weeks' time. I don't intend to make your life any easier by sending your things. You can return or lose them.*
>   *Your husband*
> *Laurence*

216

The thought of going back to him made her shiver in horror. She could only see his face as she had left, twisted in fury. He'd been out of control and violent. She never could return. What would life be like for them? No, it was impossible.

The mention of her father made her feel ill. All the time since she'd been with Nicky, she had shut out of her mind the knowledge that her father would be appalled beyond measure at what she was doing: he would consider it wicked. Alexandra leaving her husband would be something he could not countenance, and she dreaded to think what he would say when he found out. But now she had experienced this other way to live, not even her father's love could draw her back, despite knowing how difficult it was to win and how hard to retain. The struggle for his approval seemed so tough and thankless compared to the easy and natural delight of Nicky's love for her. All she hoped was to delay for as long as possible the evil day when he would know her for the dissolute woman she was, and that perhaps he might understand that she couldn't live a lifetime without knowing real love. It was most likely a futile hope but she clung on to it anyway.

In the meantime, there was the bliss of being with Nicky all the time. She'd been afraid she was asking too much of him to take her on like this – another man's runaway wife, who'd arrived almost naked with nothing to offer him but her love. To her joy, that seemed to be enough for Nicky. He'd never shown her anything but absolute devotion and he appeared as determined as she was that she would never go back to Laurence. He'd made sure she had everything she needed when Laurence refused to send her belongings.

I won't think about the future or about what Father will say, she told herself firmly. *I'm with Nicky now and I don't care what might happen – I'll face that when it comes. For now, he loves me and we're together.*

The month passed and Alexandra began to believe that somehow it was going to be all right. She had escaped with no one noticing and they were going to be left alone. Every day she woke with Nicky in his cosy bedroom and was flooded with happiness and relief that she had escaped her old life into this bright, happy new one, filled with love and laughter. Polly was no longer at the house. When she'd arrived for work the day after Alexandra had arrived, Nicky had summoned her for a private interview, his face like thunder. Alex had heard raised voices, Polly's sobs and shrieks, and then the front door had been slammed and that was the last they had seen of her. Alexandra liked to help Nicky now, when he was in the roof-top studio, learning the names of lenses and lights and what they did. When he was out on an assignment, she stayed in the mews house cooking or reading, or went out wandering.

One day she found herself walking near Pall Mall and saw from the barriers that lined the road and the great ceremonial flags hanging at intervals from tall poles that a royal procession was taking place. She approached the barriers where people stood three or four deep, a mixture of Londoners and tourists, and heard the distant tinny rhythm of the marching band and the clip-clop of the accompanying horses carrying the royal guard.

'What's happening?' she asked a man standing near her.

'A prime minister on a state visit,' he replied. 'Don't know who.'

She watched curiously for a moment as the procession approached and just as the magnificent beasts, glossy and superbly trained, began to pass her, each with an immaculately turned-out rider clad in black brass-buttoned tunics with white gloves and breeches, wearing a polished brass helmet with its plume of red horsehair, it suddenly burst on her what this meant. This was Laurence's own regiment, the Blues, whose duty it was to provide the royal guard. She had seen them many times in training but they had a new magnificence in their ceremonial uniforms. Alexandra drew a short shocked breath and looked up at the faces of the soldiers as they passed. She wanted to turn away but couldn't prevent herself scanning each one. Then, as she knew she would, she saw Laurence, his thin face framed by the thick gold chin strap of his helmet, and it was inevitable that he should somehow sense her presence and turn his eyes to the right so that his light blue gaze locked with hers. She saw that he recognised her immediately and while he appeared outwardly impassive, he paled and his hands twitched as they held the black reins. His gaze burned into her for no more than an instant and then moved on to stare straight ahead, a perfectly controlled soldier in the perfectly formed ranks of horsemen.

The rest of the crowd murmured and began to clap and

cheer as the royal carriage came into view. Alexandra turned and walked away as fast as she could, her heart sprinting in her chest. That was her husband. Much as she wanted to forget him, he still existed and the wedding ring on her finger proved that they were still legally bound together. But the month was almost up. What then?

She wanted to talk to Nicky about it, but when she got back, the house was empty with only a note left folded on the kitchen table to show he'd been there. She pulled it open in panic, fearing that he had left her or was ordering her to leave, but it was a quickly scrawled message to tell her that he had been called home and would let her know about it as soon as he could. He was sorry he'd missed her.

There was no news until the next day and Alexandra existed in a horrible emptiness. This was what life without Nicky would be and she knew she couldn't stand it. When he telephoned in the evening, her whole being thrilled to the sound of his voice.

'Are you all right, Nicky? What is it? What's happened?'

'It's my father. I'm sorry to say he's died.'

'Oh, Nicky!' Her heart swelled with tenderness and sympathy. 'I'm so sorry.'

'Thank you, darling. It wasn't a shock, if that's any comfort. The funeral is on Friday.'

'Do you want me there? I'd like to be with you.'

There was a pause and Nicky said, 'I don't think it would be wise. Not yet.'

'No . . . no, of course not.' She imagined herself appearing at Nicky's side, to the shock of the village and probably to the consternation of his family. And it was inevitable her father would hear of it too. She wasn't ready for that.

Nicky went on: 'It would be no fun for you here, I'm busy with inheritance matters as well. Besides taking on the house, I have to persuade my stepmother to leave. We're just agreeing where she'll go but I think I've managed to make Bournemouth sound most attractive. Listen, darling, I have to go. I'll call again and I'll be back just as soon as I can.'

That night she stared into space, thinking fearfully of what the inheritance meant. Their life in the little mews house was so beautiful. She didn't want a new chapter to open, for a different existence to come along and spoil everything. How would they keep this sense of blissful togetherness if Nicky was going to be taken away from her by the great house and all that went with it?

When Nicky came back two days later, she fell into his arms and they went to bed at once, hungry for one another after so long apart. Afterwards, she held him tightly, stroking his hair and listening as he talked about what had happened.

'It was all so odd,' he murmured, his cheek pressed against her breast, an arm over her waist. 'I wasn't close to my father but the funeral was a wretched experience. They put him in the family vault alongside my ma, and it was rather awful standing down there in the dark watching my father join my mother and thinking: *Well, that's me next.*'

'Not for years and years,' whispered Alexandra, unable to contemplate that horror.

'No.' He gazed up at her, his eyes almost beseeching. 'But

it made me realise that I don't want to be without you. Life is for living. We should be together.'

Happiness bubbled up inside her. 'That's what I want too, more than anything.' Her joy faded. 'But there's Laurence. He wants an answer. The month is up.'

A stormy look passed over Nicky's face. 'He's a cad. He can't possibly expect you to go back to him after what he did to you. We won't dignify the whole sorry mess with an answer. You never wanted to marry him in the first place. Fort Stirling is mine now – let's go back there and be happy. Let him try and get you if he wants. You'll come with me, won't you, Alex? You'll have to be brave. People will know about us, and fast. Your father is bound to find out.'

She was silent, clutching onto the warm strength of his arms. Could she do it? She'd go home not as the respectable bride who had left, but as the wicked woman who had deserted her husband barely six months after the wedding and set up home with another man. Here in the depths of London she was anonymous. There she would be talked about, discussed, speculated about.

Nicky's hand fell on hers and closed over it, warm and comforting. 'I don't want to go back without you,' he said softly.

'Of course I'll come,' she replied stoutly. She shut the thought of her father from her mind. 'I want to be with you, wherever you are.'

Besides, she added silently, *where else could I go?*

*

'Are you happy to be home?' Nicky asked, shouting over the noise of the car engine as they sped through the country lanes, the wind ruffling their hair.

Alexandra smiled and nodded, not wanting to open her mouth because the wind would whip tendrils of hair into it. The little convertible sports car roared around bends and tore up hills as though there was a horde of barbarians giving chase.

But no one is chasing us, she thought, exhilarated. *We're free. At least for now.*

She was glad that they didn't have to go through the village – she wasn't ready for that – but they approached from the west instead, rounding the woods and climbing the hill until the estate opened out in front of them. Suddenly there was the house: a hotchpotch of styles that melded into a thing of beauty with its graceful chimneys, glittering glass windows and ornate stonework. Around it the soft green parkland billowed out like a cushion and was dotted with trees, their edges already touched with autumn russet.

Fort Stirling was glorious, breathtaking in a way she'd never noticed before. As a child she'd simply accepted it as a big house where she would sometimes play but now she saw what a magnificent piece of history it was, a stone edifice softened to a velvety texture that belied its ancient purpose as the stronghold of the Stirling family. Generations had lived here, defending it, building wealth, cultivating land, reinforcing the family's importance. And all this was Nicky's now. The young man beside her, with his thatch of dark hair, the grey eyes she loved so much, the hands that drove her wild with longing and made her sigh with pleasure – it all belonged to him.

Unaware she was looking at him, he whooped as they sailed down the hill towards the house, the wind tufting his hair. She felt wonderfully carefree. Who could touch them in a place like this? It was a fort, wasn't it? They could lock themselves away and protect themselves against the outside world. It would be just the two of them, needing nothing and no one but each other.

By the time they pulled up in a shower of gravel in front of the ornate front door, a small collection of people had gathered to greet them. When Nicky climbed out of the car, a portly lady in a navy dress came forward and curtsied to him.

'Welcome home, my lord,' she said in a rich Dorset accent.

'Hello, Mrs Spencer, how are you? How is the old place?'

'We're happy to have you back,' she said fervently. 'All of us.' She cast an enquiring look at Alexandra.

'This is . . . Miss Crewe,' Nicky said, seeing the direction of her glance. 'She'll be staying with us. Thomas, our luggage is jammed in the back. Do see if you can extract it.'

A young man in dark trousers, shirt and a waistcoat darted forward, mumbling, 'Yes, my lord.'

Alexandra glanced at Nicky. Of course he was 'my lord' now. He had inherited the title, which made him the new Viscount Northmoor. Nicky Northmoor had quite a ring to it.

But the realisation of his new status made her afraid. How could Nicky live indefinitely with a married woman?

She wondered suddenly if Laurence would divorce her but she did not see how that would improve matters. A divorced woman was just as bad in most people's eyes.

'Come on, Alex, let's go in.' Nicky strode ahead of her, barely acknowledging the bows and curtsies of the gardener and the two maids. Alexandra followed on behind him, smiling shyly at the staff as they gazed at her curiously, and then she was going up the stone steps and through the front door, into the great hall beyond.

Nicky showed her around the house, through the huge salons and drawing rooms, into the grand dining room where a polished mahogany table stretched away with twenty chairs on either side, and into the small circular one with its more manageable round table and the pretty turquoise wallpaper printed with fruit and flowers. 'French wallpaper,' Nicky remarked. 'Very old and special apparently.' He grinned at her. 'I don't really understand such things. Perhaps you do.'

'Not really,' she replied, thinking of the very ordinary wallpaper they had at home. 'But I'll try.'

As they wandered through the halls and galleries, she understood how Nicky had been drawn to photography. He had grown up around beautiful things that demanded to be recorded. On every wall and from every window there was something to look at: huge old oil paintings, elegant portraits, the vista of the park or the terrace or the quad that lay between the wings of the house. Objects of beauty were everywhere: vases, statues, collections of fine porcelain.

There was costly furniture: huge gilt mirrors, marble-topped tables and inlaid cabinets. And yet for all its magnificent contents, the house felt empty. Even though the staff lived here, the place seemed deserted.

Upstairs, she remembered the way to the nursery where she had once played, but Nicky led her to a white and gold guest bedroom with twin beds and embroidered curtains. It looked impressive at first glance but on closer inspection was shabby and a little dusty. Her suitcase had been placed near an ancient basin in the corner, part shielded by a pink satin curtain, where a spider scuttled about near the plughole.

'Don't worry,' Nicky said, as she looked around it. 'You're not going to be here anyway.'

'I'm not?'

He shook his head and then whisked her up into his arms. 'Of course not! You're going to be with me, naturally.'

'Stay in your room?' she said, scandalised. 'But what will the servants think?'

He laughed, a big booming sound that she felt against her chest. 'You'd rather stay in here and creep along to me after lights out, would you? Come on, Alex, we can do whatever we like! Don't forget, I'm the lord of the manor around here, and I can have whoever I like in my room, even if she is a scarlet woman.' He kissed her neck fondly but she stiffened and pressed him away.

Her eyes filled with tears. 'Don't say that,' she whispered, hurt.

'What? Scarlet woman? Don't be silly, darling, I was joking.'

226

'But it's what people will think. You know they will.'

'Who cares what they think?' he said stoutly. 'I don't and neither should you. Now come on, I want to show you my four-poster. In particular the very comfortable mattress . . .'

Alexandra wondered if she was imagining the disapproving looks from Mrs Spencer and the stifled giggles of the maids when she passed them sweeping carpets in the hallways. She wished she could be like Nicky, sublimely unaware of all that; but then, for them, he was their adored master, the new lord, and she was just his girlfriend, living with him in sin. Her wedding ring was well hidden at the bottom of her washbag but that was no guarantee the staff didn't know exactly who she was.

Nicky had to spend the morning shut away in the library with some men who'd come to see him on business. Alexandra found a desk in the small drawing room that she had noticed the day before. On the top sat a letter rack that held sheets of yellowing notepaper engraved with the fort's address. She took one and sat down at the desk. The blotter was unused but a film of dust needed brushing away. She picked up a pen from the crystal inkwell and dipped it in the ink. The pen had a scratchy nib and sat awkwardly in her hand, but she wrote as best she could.

Dear Father
I suppose you're wondering why you haven't heard from me for a while. The truth is that I haven't been able to make my marriage to Laurence a success and

*I've left him. I'm very sorry. He gave me a month to
come back to him but I'm afraid that expired a little
while ago and I'm not going to return. I've fallen in love
with Nicky Stirling and we are now living at the fort, so,
you see, I'm actually very close to you. I know this is
not what you had wished for me but I hope you will be
happy that I am happy, and please believe me when I say
that my marriage was never going to work whether I
had met Nicky again or not.*

*I will come down and see you tomorrow. I hope you
are well.*

Your loving daughter
Alexandra

She blotted it, folded it and tucked it into one of the
yellow envelopes turned crisp with age. The gum on the flap
was brown and useless so she slipped it closed instead and
wrote her father's name and address on the front. Then, getting up, she went to the hall and put it on the silver tray by
the door where she had seen Nicky leave letters. At that
moment she saw Thomas emerging from the butler's pantry
down the hall.

'Thomas!' she called. 'There's a letter here. Can you see
that it's delivered today, please? By hand, not by post.'

'Yes, miss,' he returned briefly and disappeared down the
hall. She watched him, picking up the smallest hint of impertinence in his manner. She had a feeling that if the servants
had not already connected her with Mr Crewe of the Old
Grange, then they would before the day was out.

Chapter Sixteen

Present day

'This way.'

Delilah led Susie up the creaky wooden stairs to the attics over the east wing, switching on the light bulb as she reached the top. She coughed slightly in the thick dusty air.

'Goodness!' Susie reached the top of the stairs and looked around, blinking in the murky light. She glanced at the piles of old packing cases, boxes spilling their contents and furniture stacked up high to the eaves. 'What a treasure trove! Have you explored it?'

'No, just the odd trunk. I don't like it up here very much.'

'So dusty – it's not very pleasant to breathe, is it?'

'No. You do get used to it, but still, it's not very nice.'

Susie put her hands on her hips, her eyes falling on things of interest. 'But you could spend hours up here rootling around it all.'

'You know these old families – they never throw anything away. I'm sure there are some valuable things up here. But what I was interested in was the clothes.'

'Ooh, yes.' Susie rubbed her hands together. 'Bring it on!'

Susie had replied eagerly to her invitation to visit. She was always on the lookout for new treasures for her auction house, and as she specialised in vintage couture, she was the perfect person, Delilah felt, to help her take a look through the clothes in the attic and see what was up there.

'This is the tin trunk I mentioned in my email.' Delilah lifted it open a good deal more easily than she had the first time. Inside lay the drawer of gloves, stockings and ties and all the other wrapped oddments.

'Oh,' Susie said happily. 'Look at these! How gorgeous! I must get my hands on them.'

'You're like a child in a sweet shop.' Delilah smiled.

'I can't wait to get stuck in.'

'There are some more cases and trunks that I haven't looked inside yet. I'm hopeful of some really good finds. But I don't want to open them up here in the dust and dirt.' She closed the steamer trunk and pushed the catches back into place. 'Shall we take one or two downstairs and open them there?'

'Good idea. Let's.'

They enlisted Erryl's help to get three trunks of clothes down from the attic and into the old guest room at the front of the house, a room that must once have been very grand with its white and gold curtains and gold carpet but was now bedraggled. The curtains were falling to pieces in places, their embroidery hanging out in dull straggles, and the carpet was stained and threadbare. The twin beds looked grubby and as though they had not been slept in for decades.

'Golly, look at this place!' Susie said, gazing about. 'It's like a room that time forgot.'

'Oh, time's remembered it all right,' Delilah said ruefully, looking at the thick dust on the plaster mouldings and the ceiling rose. 'It's people that forgot it. I'll ask Janey why no one's been keeping this room clean.'

'Must be hell doing the housework in a place like this,' Susie remarked, then she grinned at Delilah. 'Although not so bad if you've got servants.'

'Staff!' said Delilah in a mock scandalised tone. 'We don't say servants.'

'Staff then. Still sounds pretty bloody grand if you ask me.'

'Point taken. But this place would be impossible to look after alone. I'm not sure this room is much better than the attic, but come on, let's take a look.'

They knelt down on the dusty carpet and opened one of the cases that Delilah had not yet looked into. A strong smell of camphor and fusty clothes came out. Inside they discovered some antique furs, slightly moth-eaten despite the camphor balls, but otherwise in fine condition.

'These would be worth a lot if you wanted to sell,' Susie said, stroking a russet fox fur admiringly, her fingers sinking into the lush pelt. 'I have lots of clients who'd adore this. They wouldn't touch new fur but don't feel so bad about wearing vintage.'

Delilah shook her head. 'No. I don't think John would allow it. But I'll talk to him. There's not much point in it all rotting upstairs. But I wondered about setting up some kind of exhibition – you know, the clothes of Fort Stirling. With outfits next to old photos, if I can find enough matches. Or else a kind of imagined country house weekend tableaux.'

'I like it!' Susie's eyes glinted with enthusiasm. 'And *then* I could sell the clothes.'

Delilah laughed. 'Maybe. Let's see what else we've got.'

They spent a few very happy hours going through the trunks, finding treasures that included a hand-beaded twenties flapper dress from a prestigious Paris fashion house, and a couple of original Chanel pieces from the thirties. There were skirts, cashmere cardigans, silk and rayon blouses, little strapped shoes and felt hats, and tweed suits. Some of the knits and silks had suffered damage but the mothballs had been effective on the whole.

'Damn moths, how I hate them!' exclaimed Susie, rubbing at some of the grainy strands left by moth cocoons. 'I have to treat everything before it comes on the premises – I don't dare infect the stock. Come on, let's look in the other trunk.'

With sighs of delight, they found some ballgowns: chiffon, silk, organdie and heavy satin thickly embroidered with seed pearls. A black velvet gown with a long train seemed particularly grand and designed to go with diamonds. Tucked away in the corner of the trunk was a smart leather box with a handle on the top for easy carrying. Delilah opened it and found that inside was a tarnished coronet, a circle of silver gilt with sixteen grubby silver balls around a puff of dark crimson velvet topped by a round golden ornament, and with a tiny strip of threadbare ermine around the bottom rim.

'Oh my goodness!' Susie laughed. 'An actual coronet! What's it doing there?'

Delilah examined it with interest. 'I wonder if this is the same as the one in some of the portraits downstairs. Some of the viscountesses were painted in full robes with their little crowns on.'

'Put it on!'

Delilah flushed. It seemed rather presumptuous to put on something she was not entitled to. 'I'm not sure . . .'

'Come on, what does it matter? We're just dressing up. Go on,' urged Susie, flapping her hand at Delilah as though trying to float the coronet up onto her head.

Delilah lifted the little coronet almost tentatively. It was lighter than she'd expected.

'Go on,' Susie said. 'You might have to wear it for real one of these days. If there's a coronation, you might be summoned to the Abbey in your finery.'

Delilah thought instantly of a large black-and-white photograph of John's grandparents in their ceremonial robes, dressed for the coronation of George VI. They stood side by side on a covered dais, their heads held stiffly under their coronets. John's grandmother wore a stiff gown of white satin. Over the top she wore her stately red-velvet robes edged with gold thread and ermine, worn like an overdress with little cap sleeves and fastened at the front over her bodice. An ermine-edged cloak hung from her shoulders and fell into a long train at her feet, and she wore a many-stranded pearl choker with a large cameo pinned to it. She looked magnificent if rather frightening. *This must be the coronet from that photograph*, thought Delilah. *Another link to the women of Fort Stirling, although Alex probably never wore it. She'd have been too young for the last coronation.*

Delilah perched it on her head. 'There,' she said, flushing.

Susie did a mock curtsey, which looked rather odd in her sitting position. 'Oh, your ladyship!'

'Don't.' She whisked it off and put it on the floor. 'The robes must be somewhere. I'll show you the picture of them downstairs.'

'If they're in the attic, I bet the moths have got the velvet,' Susie said mournfully. 'That's exactly the kind of thing they do, the evil critters. The more valuable the fabric, the more they like it.'

'Let's look at the other trunk. I want to show you the clothes I discovered.' As she reached for the other trunk, she felt a strange buzzing sensation and the thought floated into her head: *But these are* her *clothes.* When Delilah had first seen them, she hadn't known what she did now. She hadn't seen so many images of Alex, or known that she'd killed herself, or looked for her body. She hadn't dreamed of her on the top of the folly, ready to leap to her death . . .

'Love the trunk – a real vintage steamer,' Susie was saying, but Delilah barely heard her. Instead she was only aware of the rushing in her head and the curious buzzing in her ears. She stared as Susie reached across her to lift out the top drawer and reveal the clothes beneath. Folded just below were the black dress and matching coat she had tried on in the attic and she watched, almost frozen, as Susie lifted them out, exclaiming at the quality and shaking them out to examine more closely.

'Don't,' Delilah said, snapping back to herself. She put her hand out towards the dress.

'What?'

'Leave it. Not that. Put it back.'

Susie looked at the dress. 'What's special about it? I mean, it's a beautifully made dress and coat set but—'

'I don't know. I tried it on and it made me feel . . . strange. Unpleasant.' She remembered it now – the horrible sensation she'd felt as she'd pulled that dried flower from the coat pocket.

Susie looked at her, eyebrows raised quizzically. 'Are you getting sensitive to the spooky in a place like this? I'm not surprised with so many dead people's possessions around you. Come on, it's just a dress like all the rest of the stuff. You didn't mind about that.'

'I can't explain it. I don't like it being touched. We should put it back.'

Susie climbed to her feet, lifting the dress with her, leaving the coat on the floor. 'Okay, I'll put it back – let me just look at it.' She held the dress up against herself, admiring the way it fell to just above her knee. 'It's gorgeous! If you don't like it, can I try it on?'

Delilah felt a rush of panic, as though she had to protect Alex in some way. 'No, Susie, please – put it back!'

The door opened and John put his head round it, saying, 'Hello. Erryl told me he'd carted a ton of stuff for you two— oh.' He had seen the dress that Susie was holding and he stopped abruptly, staring at it. 'What's that?' he said in a changed voice.

'Just a dress we found in a trunk,' Susie said. 'What do you think? Does it suit me?'

Delilah stared, agonised. Of all the terrible luck, that they should be looking at his dead mother's things as he appeared. He would probably not have seen these clothes since he was a boy, since his mother had worn them.

His smile vanished and he came slowly into the room, his gaze fixed on the dress. He'd gone pale. 'No,' he said in an odd, almost robotic voice. 'No, it doesn't suit you.' He walked past Susie, who stood there still holding up the dress, her expression surprised, and reached the trunk. He looked down into it: lying on the top were folded jumpers with distinctive patterns, skirts and a striped pussy-cat-bow blouse. He turned his gaze to Delilah, who was kneeling by the trunk and staring up at him, horrified. He seemed to have been slowed by what he was seeing, as though reduced to half speed. 'Were these upstairs with the rest?'

She nodded slowly. 'I'm sorry,' she whispered.

He stared back at the clothes, whiter than ever, his mouth set in a hard line. He seemed to be seeing them not as they were now, folded on beds of tissue paper, but as they once had been, worn by a living, breathing woman. He turned back to Delilah and said in a curt voice: 'Burn them.'

'What?' she replied, taken aback.

'You heard me. Burn the lot.'

'There's no need for that, John!' Susie interjected, smiling. 'If you don't want the clothes, I'd be delighted to take them off your hands and sell them. My commission is thirty-five per cent and—'

'I said *burn them*.' His eyes were frozen granite and his voice harsh. 'I don't want to see these things in the house again.'

He turned and strode out without another word, leaving Delilah and Susie staring at one another in shocked silence.

It was much later that night. Delilah lay in bed, pressed up against John, her front to his back so that her body nestled into his and her arms wrapped tightly around his middle. He wasn't moving but she knew he wasn't asleep. From the faint flutter she could feel as he breathed in and out, she knew that he was agitated. She was trying to transmit warmth and comfort through her body, to calm him down and reassure him that he was safe and loved.

He's afraid of something, she thought. All she could imagine was that his boyhood trauma, the loss of his mother, had been awakened by the sight of her clothing. It had been appallingly insensitive of her. She should have waited until she knew John was out of the house before bringing his mother's things downstairs. She was furious with Susie for displaying that particular dress as John walked in. If she had only put it down when Delilah had told her to, he might not have seen what they had been looking at and all this might have been avoided. As it was, she had to explain to Susie that it was best if they put a stop to the clothes show for now, and returned to it another day. Susie had stayed for lunch as they'd planned but the sparkle had gone out of the day. Delilah was distracted and unable to do much more than think about John and where he was, and what mood he was in. It wasn't long before Susie made her excuses.

'I'll come back before too long,' she said, kissing Delilah goodbye at the front door. 'I might come by train next time – it's a hell of a drive. But it's been lovely to see you. I wouldn't have missed that coronet for anything. Let me know if you find the robes.'

'I will. Have a safe journey back.' Delilah kissed her friend's cheeks, hoping Susie did not realise how relieved she was to see her go.

Susie pulled back to look Delilah right in the eye. 'Now, promise me,' she said sternly, 'that you're not going to go burning that stuff. John will calm down, I guarantee it, and he'll see the sense of selling it off. It would be a crime to destroy those lovely things. Some of those gloves were real kid as well. I'd love to know what else is there. Do say I can come back and have a rootle.'

'Of course you can,' Delilah said. 'Whenever you want. Well – perhaps give it a few weeks at least to let things die down.'

'All right. Bye, sweetie.'

As soon as Susie had closed the door of her car and started up the engine, Delilah raced to find John but he had not been in the estate office or watching the afternoon sport on the telly in the small sitting room, or in their bedroom. She'd wandered all over the house calling for him, when, in a sudden moment of inspiration, she climbed the dusty attic stairs and found the hatch to the roof open. Putting her head out, she saw him sitting on the gently sloping eaves a little way along, his feet on the broad lead ledge that edged the guttering. The Victorian faux battlements that had been added to the east wing bordered the outside of the gutter and made it perfectly safe to sit there. She pulled herself up and scrambled out.

'John?'

Stepping carefully to avoid dislodging any slates, she went towards him, walking at an angle. He turned to look at her and then gazed back out at the view.

'Are you all right?' she said a little breathlessly as she reached him.

There was a long silence. She could hear the summer breeze whistling around the chimney tops. It was windier up here than she'd expected and her fair hair was lifted up to flick around her face and into her mouth. She pulled it away and tried to tuck it behind one ear but the wind wouldn't leave it alone. She stared at her husband, at his thin angular face with the dusting of dark stubble that showed he hadn't shaved today. His grey eyes were stormy and distant as he stared out over the stretch of green parkland below, the dark mass of the woods and the edge of the distant village just glimpsed behind the curve of the hill.

'Those were your mother's things, weren't they?' she said.

He nodded, still not looking at her.

'I'm so sorry, darling. I wish that hadn't happened. I wish you hadn't seen those clothes.'

'It doesn't matter,' he said shortly. 'They're just things.'

'They connect you to the past.'

'I suppose so.'

'The past that hurt you.' She pulled her errant hair out of her mouth again, where the wind insisted on driving it. She felt that here was a moment when she could ask simply, 'What happened?' and he would answer her. She was desperate to know and yet something wouldn't let her speak. It felt wrong to demand that he open his private grief to satisfy her curiosity. He would offer it when he was ready. If he didn't wish to tell her, was it really her right to pry and demand answers?

'Will you come down?' she asked.

After a minute he said, 'Soon. Not just yet.' He turned to look at her, and his gaze softened. He put his hand out to hers and said, 'You go in. I'll join you.'

She had left him there, climbing back down into the almost unbearable stuffiness of the attics, while he sat in the buffeting wind staring out over the great expanse beyond.

Much later, when he came to bed, he lay with his back to her, and she moved to hug him tightly and kiss the back of his neck.

'I love you,' she whispered, and rubbed her cheek against him.

He murmured something and she hugged him more tightly, wanting to let some of her loving energy flow into him through a kind of osmosis. She could almost feel his sadness and longed to make it better if she could. Her hand caressed his skin, travelling over his hip and stomach.

'Did you hear me?' he asked, turning towards her.

'No. What did you say?'

'I said – you won't forget that I want those things burnt, will you?'

Her hand stopped on his chest. Then she exhaled softly into the darkness, stroked her fingers over him again and said, 'I won't forget.'

Chapter Seventeen

1965

Alexandra set out for the village but was only halfway there before she wished she'd brought one of the old bicycles she'd seen propped against the wall in the garage. The walk from the house to the gate was at least a mile and then there was the hill to climb and the descent into the village. As she approached its outskirts, she felt a flutter of nerves. She was bound to meet someone she knew and what was her story? How did Miss Crewe – or rather, Mrs Sykes now – come to be walking down the street alone when she was last seen being whisked away on honeymoon by her new husband?

But she saw almost no one, just a boy in long shorts loping along on an errand of some kind. As she reached the Old Grange, she was glad that no one had spoiled her quiet approach. She would once have gone to let herself in the back, where Emily would have been bustling about in the kitchen, but now she walked up to the white front door where dark red roses were still blooming against the mellow stone, and rapped the brass knocker smartly.

She waited but there was no answer so she knocked again more loudly. Just as she was considering whether to take the side path to the back, the door opened. Emily stood there, her expression agonised.

'Oh, miss!' she exclaimed in a whisper. 'Miss Alexandra, it's lovely to see you—'

'Hello, Emily, how are you?' she said merrily. Emily had worked at the house for as long as she could remember and was like a friend to her. 'Is my father ready for me? Shall I go to the study? Can you bring us some tea?'

'Oh . . .' Emily's brown eyes looked even more pained and she glanced over her shoulder in consternation before turning back to Alexandra. 'He can't—'

'Is he busy? I'll come in and wait.' She stepped forward to make her way inside but Emily kept the door half closed and barred her way.

'You don't understand, miss. I can't let you in . . . He's forbidden it.' A pleading look crossed her face and she whispered, 'I'm so sorry, miss, he won't have it any other way and I daren't disobey.'

There was a horrible pause, then Alexandra said brightly, 'Of course not.' She was surprised she sounded so calm considering the torrent of horrible emotions she was battling inside.

'He said you would call and I wasn't to let you in under any circumstances.' Tears filled the maid's eyes. 'It's a terrible thing, miss, terrible . . .'

'Don't be silly, Emily, I'm sure he has his reasons and of course you must obey your instructions.' She smiled bravely even though tears were pricking her own eyes. She blinked hard. 'It's so nice to see you, though. Are you well?'

'Yes, miss,' whispered Emily, her mouth turning down at the corners and one hand clutching her apron.

'Good. I'll come back soon and we'll be able to have a good gossip, won't we? I want to hear all the news. I'm sure there's been lots going on while I've been away.'

Emily's gaze slid away from hers. 'Oh, miss,' she said sadly, '*you're* all the news at the moment. What you've done. Where you are.'

Alexandra stared at her, a clammy sickness crawling over her. 'I see. Well . . . you know how people talk, Emily. But I wouldn't want you to think badly of me.'

Emily stared at the stone doorstep and whispered, 'No, miss, I couldn't do that, no matter what they all say.' She jerked up, evidently hearing something from inside that Alexandra could not. 'I must go.'

'Yes. Goodbye, Emily. Goodbye.' Alexandra turned and hurried down the path, not wanting to see the front door of her old home closed in her face.

The walk home was very different: difficult and drenched with misery. She knew, when Mrs Hobson the post mistress saw her and crossed the road to avoid her, keeping her eyes firmly in front, that Emily had not been mistaken. The news of her scandalous return must have been keeping them all occupied for days. No doubt it had begun to spread as soon as she had arrived back and the servants had carried the delicious gossip into the village. She had been a fool to think otherwise. They must be saying horrible things, dreadful, unkind things . . . But she could live with that if she had to – being with Nicky was worth the price of being discussed over cups of tea in houses all over the county. It was the rejection by her father that was making her heart ache and she couldn't stop herself sobbing as she walked blindly back along the lane.

In the house, all was quiet, but as she went in her eye was drawn at once to a letter that sat in the silver tray on the console table. She recognised her father's handwriting. He had addressed his letter to Mrs Laurence Sykes, care of Fort Stirling. She plucked it up, her hands trembling as she opened it and took out the letter inside.

Alexandra

You have disappointed me more than I can express and disgraced yourself as well as our family. Until you come to your senses and return to your husband, I cannot regard you as my daughter. I prayed that you had not inherited your mother's wanton spirit but I can see now that was a forlorn hope. I have had no option but to tell your husband exactly what I know of your whereabouts and I intend to assist him in every way possible. I can only be grateful that there are as yet no children to be hurt by your immense and destructive selfishness. If you think I am to be mollified by the fact that you are the concubine of Lord Northmoor, you are quite mistaken. I am deeply mortified and ashamed, as you should be.

Gerald Crewe

She read it over several times, the paper shaking in her unsteady fingers, her heart pounding in her chest. A horrible whirring in her head made her think suddenly that she was going to faint and she reached out to the marble-topped console for support. She gasped for air to loosen her constricted chest.

So that's it, she thought. *He hates me. I've lost my father forever.*

Everything seemed to be pressing down on her and darkness descended. She fell to her knees.

'Miss, are you all right?' One of the maids had come running and now put a hand on her shoulder. 'What's wrong? I'll fetch his lordship.'

Alexandra was dimly aware through her panic of the girl rushing away and returning with Nicky, and then she was being carried into the drawing room and laid down on the sofa there, as hands undid her coat and took it from her. A glass of water was brought and they tried to make her drink it but she was in the grip of something she didn't understand: a breathless agonised darkness from which she could not escape.

She heard Nicky tell Thomas to help him, and they carried her upstairs to bed. Nicky sent them all away and sat beside her, holding her hand and soothing her until gradually the panic began to lessen and she could breathe again. The tears began to fall then but after a while the crying passed, leaving her strangely calm.

'I read that beastly letter,' Nicky said, stroking the back of her hand. His voice was grim with suppressed fury. 'What kind of a man is your father?'

'He doesn't mean to be cruel,' she said weakly. 'He only wants what's best for me, I suppose.'

'How can you say that, Alex? Look at the way he's written to you! He's a monster of selfishness – he forced you into that marriage and now he's going to punish you because you couldn't stand it!' Nicky's eyes flashed with anger on her behalf.

'He wasn't always like this,' Alexandra protested. 'It was only after my mother died. I think the grief of losing her made him that way. He didn't seem to be happy after that. I never understood why, though.'

Nicky hunched over her hand, holding it harder in the gloom of the bedroom, avoiding her gaze.

'What?' she asked, suddenly alert to his mood. 'What is it?'

He looked up, his eyes sorrowful. 'What did they tell you about your mother?'

'Well . . .' She was puzzled. She made an effort to remember. It was so long since she'd thought about it. Most of the time, she'd tried to forget. 'There was a terrible atmosphere in the house for weeks beforehand, and I knew that she wasn't herself. Then my father woke me early one morning and told me that Mother had died in the night. He said she'd fallen ill very suddenly and died before the doctor could come. He told me to stay in my room while everything was dealt with.'

'Did you see her?' Nicky asked softly. His thumb stroked the back of her hand.

Alexandra shook her head. 'No,' she replied in a small voice. 'I wanted to, but I didn't dare ask.'

'Did you go to the funeral?'

'Father said I was too young and that it would upset me. My aunt came and took me away to the seaside for a long time. Perhaps it was only a week or two but it seemed a very long time to me then. When I got home, everything was difficult and horrible. It wasn't long after that Father stopped me seeing my old friends. That was when we were forbidden from seeing each other, don't you remember?'

Nicky carried on rubbing his thumb over her hand and said nothing.

'Do you know something?' she asked apprehensively. When he glanced up, the expression in his eyes frightened her. 'Tell me, Nicky!'

'Darling, what did they say she died of?'

'Aunt Felicity said it was a brain fever that came on very suddenly in the night.' She blinked at him, fear growing inside her.

'Well . . . ' Pity crossed his face. 'Alex, I'm so sorry . . . I must tell you what I heard. Perhaps it was only rumour but they said she killed herself. They said she threw herself from the folly in the woods. That was why we weren't allowed to play there anymore. I always thought our families kept apart afterwards because my parents thought it was all very shameful. Perhaps your father felt the same.'

The silence in the room became freighted with something awful: horror and grief combined. Alexandra's limbs were numb, her skin cold. 'Why didn't you tell me before?' she said through stiff lips.

Nicky looked contrite. 'I'm sorry. I guessed you didn't know when we talked about the past and I didn't want to hurt you.' Anger seemed to reinvigorate him. 'But if it's true, my guess is that your father drove her to it! He's nothing less than a monster.'

'Don't say that!' she cried. 'Can't you see he was all I had for all those years after my mother died?' She fell back on the pillows and turned her face to the wall, struggling to understand what he had said. It made a macabre and awful sense. There had been no grave to visit, no love around her mother's memory, no shared stories of her. Alexandra could only remember anger and coldness, and a sense of everyone being punished for whatever had happened. Life had shut down, and never been the same again.

The folly. That awful, broken tower. She shivered. Pictures began to form in her mind, terrible images of her mother falling from its jagged top and lying broken on the ground at the bottom. *It can't be true*. But somehow she knew that it was, and all these years she had been the only one not to know the truth.

'Are you all right?' Nicky whispered. He inspected her carefully as if looking for signs of grief but her eyes were dry.

'Yes,' she said, her voice blank. It was too much to take in all at once.

'Can I get you something?'

She shook her head.

'I'm sorry to tell you something so awful but I thought you should know if it would help you cope with what that man has done to you. Can't you see you're better off without him?'

She nodded but stayed silent, staring at the wall and the pattern of the paper, trying and trying to understand.

Alexandra stayed in bed all day, staring dumbly at the wall as she attempted to make sense of what Nicky had told her. In a few short hours, she'd lost her father and everything she had believed about her mother had changed. She struggled to absorb it and was unable to find the energy for anything else, even when Nicky came and sat with her and tried to distract her.

By evening, a strange calm and sense of determination descended on her. She got out of bed and went downstairs to the dining room where Nicky was having supper.

'Darling!' He got up and rushed over to her, concern on his face. 'Are you recovered? Should you be down here? You've had a nervous shock.'

'I'm quite well,' she said. 'Really.'

He eyed her with anxiety. 'I'm worried about you.'

'I don't want you to be,' Alexandra said urgently. 'I don't want anything to change for us. I can't alter the past. I did my crying over losing my mother a long time ago, and I can't bring her back. My father has made it plain how he feels about me. I've lost enough of my life to him and I don't want to lose any more.' She went over to him and clutched his arm. 'I mean it, Nicky. You're my world now. You're all that's real and true. I don't want to think about the terrible things that happened – just about how we can be happy.'

He looked at her with uncertainty mixed with relief. 'I'm glad to hear that. I really am. But . . . are you sure you're all right?'

'Perfectly,' she said fervently. 'I want us to be happy. The past is the past. The future is what I want to think about now.'

'Good,' said Nicky. He smiled. 'I'm very glad, darling.'

She sat down at her place and reached for her napkin, outwardly as calm and serene as if the last two days had never happened.

Alexandra heard the noise of the van long before she saw it. She'd been reading in the drawing room – at least, she'd been staring at a page for an hour while her mind took her to the dark places she couldn't help visiting ever since Nicky had told her the truth about her mother. She'd wanted to shut it all away but instead visions of the tower were haunting her, floating into her head when she least expected it, or coming to her dreams and filling her with cold terror. She was on the point of getting up to leave the chilly drawing room and find Nicky when she heard the roar of an engine. She got up and went to the window at the front and saw the van bowling down the hill towards the house. Was it a tradesman or a worker come to deliver or fix something?

As the van came to a halt in front of the house, she heard the shouts from inside and then people spilled out onto the gravel, a gaggle of young men and women. Just then Nicky came past, drawn by the noise.

'Who are they?' she asked, frowning, puzzled by the sudden invasion.

'Don't you recognise them?' Nicky's face had lit up with happy excitement. 'It's Sandy and the gang from the club! He's got at least half a dozen of them – Patsy, Alfie, David . . . Look!'

As Nicky opened the front door and hurried out to them, Alexandra stared again through the window. Now he had said that, she did recognise one or two faces from smoky, drink-soaked evenings in the Notting Hill club, where they went to spend their evenings talking and dancing when they weren't closeted away in the mews house. And there was Sandy himself, the de facto leader, his hair thinning prematurely and his cheeks flushed, coming over to give Nicky a hug and a slap on the shoulder. Patsy, the sex kitten in her pencil skirt and tight jumper, followed, wrapping her arms around Nicky's neck with a shriek of delight. Alexandra had never felt at ease around Patsy, with her hedonistic eagerness to take anything she was offered, whether to swallow, smoke or snort, and then be as wild as possible. She'd always looked at Nicky through half-closed smoky eyelids in a way that made Alexandra's heart sink.

'I wasn't expecting you!' Nicky was saying with a laugh as they all milled round him.

'I said we'd drop by some time, didn't I?' demanded Sandy. He pulled out a cigarette and lit it. 'And today's your lucky day, mate. Me and the kids are going to make the place *sing*. We brought the record player. Are you in the mood for a party?'

Nicky turned to look for Alex, and she waved to him from the window, smiling. She could tell he wanted her approval. Perhaps it was good for them to have visitors. The house had been too gloomy recently, the atmosphere of bereavement lying heavy on it – Nicky's and her own.

They all crowded into the hall and she was suddenly surrounded by life and noise. It was startling but not unpleasant. She felt even more sure that they needed this injection of vivacity.

'Hello, Sandy,' she said as he came up to kiss her.

'Hi, Alex, said Sandy in his soft drawling voice. He'd added an American intonation to his Scottish accent for sophistication, and the effect was rather odd. 'How's tricks, baby?'

'Very good, thank you.'

Nicky was beaming. 'Isn't it great to see everyone? Let's get the party started! Patsy says she can make us whisky sours!'

'That sounds fun,' Alexandra said with a smile. She could see that Nicky was excited. He obviously needed to live a little.

Perhaps I do too. Perhaps we've been alone, just the two of us, for a little too long.

They were young, she reminded herself. Parties and drinking would help her to forget all those dark troubles, and concentrate on youth and love and everything she and Nicky had at their disposal to enjoy themselves.

Nicky led the way into the library, animated and excited to be with his London crowd again, and she followed.

Chapter Eighteen

Present day

The summer would be a hot one if it continued like this. They woke to bright blue mornings that deepened to blazing warmth and then melted slowly into long, soft evenings rich with scents from the garden. Outside the kitchen, the lavender border buzzed with bees and sent its sweet fragrance into the air. By the fruit canes, white cabbage butterflies fluttered crazily about as if intoxicated by the treasure of dropping berries. The bricks of the walled garden baked in the heat and radiated an earthy warmth, and everywhere lush greenery crept and crawled and grew.

Delilah could see summer in her own reflection: her skin had tanned despite her efforts to shield herself from the sun, and there was a pinky-gold glow to her face along with the freckles across her nose. These days her hair was longer, and she pulled it back into a loose ponytail which, with her summer dresses and sandshoes, made her look younger.

A new kind of quiet had descended on the house. She hadn't seen Ben for a few days as he was busy designing an irrigation system that would run at first off the mains but later from a reservoir of stored rain water – like a giant water butt, he described it – and he spent hours in the workshop with lengths of rubber hose and widgets and hundreds of scraps of paper with scribbled drawings on them. Erryl grumbled that he was having to handle the garden almost singlehanded with Ben so occupied, but it was John who climbed on the mower and rode up and down the lawns and along the borders of the parkland, keeping everything neat. Sheep, cows and horses kept everything else in check, razoring down the grass in the surrounding fields and paddocks. John became a familiar sight, in his shabby cargo shorts and hiking boots, naked from the waist up, his skin burnished by the sun and an old straw hat on his head, as he steered the ride-on mower up and down. Mungo would lie nearby in the shade of a tree, too hot to do anything but let his tongue loll out and watch his master playing his odd game of driving back and forth on the grass. On the compost heap, the collection of grass clippings grew into a mountain, dry and straw-like on top but with a scent of fermenting vegetation and fertile decay within.

Delilah preferred to be outside now, surrounded by all the life and light and vigour of the garden, and she took her laptop out to the summer house, away from the chilly depths of the house where the silence hung ever more heavily. She was beginning to dread being there, especially alone. The house seemed to hunger for life inside it so badly that it felt as though it wanted to drain hers out of her and absorb it into its walls.

She sat in the summer house, looking out at the lushness

of the garden in full bloom. Perhaps it was a good thing there was the gymkhana next weekend. If John could see what pleasure this place could bring people, and that peace and quiet would always return in the end, perhaps he would be more positive about her idea for clothes exhibitions and doing teas for people visiting the garden.

Not that she had dared tell him about those plans. Ever since Susie's visit, he'd become distant again, brushing away her attempts to apologise and acting as though she wasn't even there most of the time. Even telling him about the gymkhana had failed to get his attention. He'd just said grimly that as she'd gone ahead without consulting him, there was not much he could do about it, and it had added to the icy atmosphere between them.

Susie's thank you email had ended with: *Tell me you haven't burnt those wonderful clothes! I will never forgive you if you have!*

Delilah was torn. On the one hand, she didn't see how she would be able to consign all those beautiful things, the only real tangible link John had left with his mother, to the flames – not only because of their intrinsic value but because if he ever regretted his decision, there would be no undoing it. But she also didn't want to be drawn into a conspiracy of disobedience with Susie. Those things belonged to John and she had no right to go against his wishes.

She put her laptop to sleep and went out to find Erryl who was mending a bit of fallen stone wall, and asked him when he usually lit a garden fire.

'Bonfire season is the autumn with all the leaves to get

rid of,' Erryl said, stretching his back and shoulders as he straightened up. 'There don't tend to be many in the summer unless there's a party. Mr Stirling used to have an annual summer get-together for his birthday and it was a proper knees-up. We'd have a fire then.'

'Did he?' *Of course*, she thought, *his birthday's in August. Perfect for an outdoor party.*

'Oh, yes. People would bring tents and pitch them in the big field and there'd be a bonfire set up there. But the day would start down here at the house and end with a big barbecue, before they went up to the field for the bonfire – dancing, music . . . right into the night it went.'

'It sounds fun. When was this?'

'During Mr Stirling's first marriage.' Erryl looked at her askance, evidently embarrassed. 'Sorry, ma'am. That's how it was, though.'

'Don't worry, I don't mind. I'm interested! Did they end when Vanna left?'

'No, they went on for a few more years. But gradually they got smaller. Then Mr Stirling stopped bothering.'

Delilah thought for a moment and then said, 'But Janey said you'd only been here a few years. How do you know?'

Erryl laughed shyly. 'Ah – Janey's only been here a few years. I've been here longer. I was in the lodge as a bachelor for twenty years if you must know, since the old lord was living in the big house.'

'Then . . .' A thought occurred to her, bringing a tremor of excitement with it. She said eagerly, 'Did you know Alex – I mean, John's mother?'

'No, no. She was before my time. But I could sense that she was gone, if you know what I mean.' He shook his head. 'It was all terrible, raw, even though she'd been gone years. The old lord used to drink a lot, if you'll excuse me saying, and I knew exactly why he did it: he was drowning his sorrows. I've seen it before. There's those that drink because they can't stop, and those that drink to forget. He was one of the forgetters.'

'So you don't know what happened to Lady Northmoor? How she died?'

Erryl shook his head again. 'Whatever it was, it was a bad business. That much I do know. I never knew a place or a man so sad.'

Erryl had solved the problem of the clothes, for now at least. There was no way to burn them. With no bonfires until the autumn, how could she? She wasn't exactly going against John's wishes, but still, she knew she ought to put the trunk somewhere safe. She didn't want John to stumble on it somehow, become enraged and do something rash. But where?

Come on, she said to herself. *This is a house with over a hundred rooms! I should be able to find somewhere to put a trunk.*

In the still of the afternoon, she decided to go to bits of the house she'd not yet become familiar with. She knew the downstairs fairly well – the grand hall, the state reception rooms that were left untouched most of the time except by cleaners, and the library and the salons. Despite the tour she'd had when she first arrived, she knew very little about the rest of the house except for the main bedrooms and the attics. Over the back of the building were the servants' bedrooms, little white-painted rooms still with iron bedsteads and shabby old furniture, and over the east wing was the old nursery floor. She found herself going there first, opening the old oak door that shut it firmly off from the grown-up part of house, so that there was a definite divide between the civilised adults and the children, as though they were in training for the time when they would be allowed to cross that divide and behave appropriately on the other side.

The nursery wing had evidently not been altered for many years, and its layout was reminiscent of an Edwardian attitude to childrearing. There was a bedroom that was probably meant for Nanny, a large and imposing room with flowered wallpaper and pictures on the walls of country landscapes and flowers. Two smaller bedrooms, bare but with religious tracts hanging on the walls, were most likely meant for nursery maids. And then a bathroom and a small nursery kitchen where meals could be prepared without the need for bothering the cook downstairs, who was no doubt run ragged preparing those extraordinary dinner parties Delilah had read about in the visitors' book. The little kitchen was a period piece in itself, with pantry cupboards, an iron sink and an ancient cooker with two gas rings and a small oven. Delilah resisted the urge to look in the cupboards and moved on.

Next was the night nursery: a large room with two beds in it, two armchairs in front of a fireplace and a bookcase with some children's books still in it. Bedside tables with lamps on top, chests of drawers and a wardrobe completed the room.

Delilah gazed around, imagining John up here as a boy, tucked into one of those beds, falling asleep as the fire flickered and Nanny sat in one of the armchairs mending holes in socks. Would that have been how it was? Would he have felt safe and secure up here, so far from his parents, a tiny island of smallness in this vast house? And how would Alex have felt, with her son shut away behind that thick heavy door?

She could picture Alex walking through the door and into the nursery, her face bright with the anticipation of seeing John. 'Hello, Nanny,' she'd say, 'is my boy around?' and John would come racing into her arms. This part of the house was probably the warmest and most welcoming of all. Perhaps Alex spent as much time here as she could, away from the huge cold state rooms below, luxuriating in the cosiness of the nursery and the pleasure of being close to John.

But then she left him . . .

The cosiness she'd imagined vanished and she was standing in the cold gloom once more. Would the nursery ever come alive again? she wondered. Would a child of hers ever play up here, or snuggle down under blankets with the curtains pulled tight against the night outside? It felt odd, almost painful, to imagine it. The place seemed to intensify her sense of emptiness within as well as without. She left it quickly.

Next door was the day nursery. A playroom, estate agents would call it now. It was large and light with windows that looked out over the park, and a huge rocking horse stood by the windows, his legs stretched out in a gallop but his real horsehair mane lying flat against his painted neck. Bookshelves stretched from the floor to the ceiling on either side of the fireplace, still full of books – worn paperbacks and hardbacks of all kinds. There was a big cupboard at the back of the room where she assumed that toys had been stored, so she walked over and opened it. She expected to see mountains of vintage toys but was startled to find that it was empty, its broad shelves bare but for lining paper, some desiccated moth corpses and the occasional dead fly lying on its back with bent legs.

Where are all the toys? she wondered.

Perhaps they'd been taken to the attics. But how strange to leave the books and the rocking horse and everything else, and take the toys away.

Then it occurred to her that this cupboard would be the perfect place to put the trunk of Alex's clothes. It would be a tight fit but it should just be able to slide beneath the bottom shelf and sit there snugly until needed. She was pleased. She'd found an excellent hiding place – not *hiding,* that sounded too deceitful – a *storage* place for the trunk which meant that John would not be distressed by accidentally stumbling on it. The question now was how she would get the trunk here. It was hardly something she could do on her own and she couldn't ask John. It felt wrong to get Erryl to participate in something that was in effect going against his master's orders.

There was only one person she could ask.

*

'I'm delighted to help. Where do you want me?' Ben smiled at her keenly, washing his hands in the kitchen sink. The water churned and bubbled around his large square palms.

Delilah gave him a grateful look. 'Thanks so much, you're very kind. I don't want to drag you away from your irrigation masterpiece for long. I just need some help taking an old trunk up from one of the guest rooms to the nursery. It's easier than the attics and we might need the guest room.'

'Really?' Ben looked surprised. There were plenty of guest rooms in usable condition.

'That is – I'm thinking of redecorating it. So I don't want it turned into a store room as well.'

He shrugged. 'Fair enough. Lead on.'

They went into the main house together and she led the way to the white and gold room where the trunk had been left since Susie's visit.

'You're right, it could do with a freshen up,' Ben said, wrinkling his nose in distaste as they went in. 'I bet you'd make it brilliant, though.'

'Thanks,' she said, feeling a little uncomfortable about her lie. She would have to embark on cleaning it now, just to feel at ease with her conscience. 'The trunk's all closed up. We only have to carry it over to the east wing.'

'No problemo.' Ben marched over, stretched his arms wide to grasp a handle on either side and picked up the whole trunk by himself. His biceps bulged with the effort.

'I was going to take one side,' Delilah exclaimed, laughing. 'You're not supposed to do it all.'

'It's fine. Just tell me where to take it.'

She led him along the main corridor. He staggered slightly with the awkwardness of holding the trunk but the weight was obviously no problem and he followed her through the oak door and into the nursery wing.

'I remember this bit of the house,' he said as they entered. 'I got sent up here to play a few times with my sisters. We didn't like it much. There was nothing to play with.'

'Do you mean in here?' Delilah opened the door to the day nursery where the horse was still frozen mid-gallop, his wooden teeth clamped down over his brass bit.

'Yep.' Ben followed her in. 'Where do you want this?'

'Over here.' She went over to the cupboard and opened the door. 'I thought it could sit nicely under this shelf.'

He settled the trunk down with evident relief and pushed it backwards under the shelf. When he'd pushed it back as far as it would go, it was still proud of the shelf which meant that the door wouldn't shut.

'Oh, it doesn't fit,' Delilah said, disappointed. She'd thought the space was perfect.

'Hold on. It doesn't fit because there's something stopping it from reaching the back wall. Let's see.' Ben pulled the trunk out again, got down on his knees and bent over so that he could peer under the shelf. 'Here we are. I was right. There's something there.'

He reached out a long arm and pulled out an object. Delilah saw a flash of pink and cream and gold.

'What is it?' she asked.

'A doll,' he said, holding it up. 'A Barbie doll, by the look of it.'

263

'Is it Barbie?' Delilah asked, frowning. 'It looks more like a Sindy. She's got a round face and rather a sweet look.'

'Not my area of expertise, I'm afraid.' Ben shrugged apologetically. 'You'll know more than me.'

She took the doll from him and inspected it. It was a classic pink plastic figure, with a mass of dusty gold nylon hair, painted round eyes and a rosy pout, cheeks that had been slightly greyed with dirt, and limbs that moved at the shoulders and hips but nowhere else. This one was supposed to be a ballet dancer, as she wore a shiny pink leotard and a netting tutu with streamers of dust on it, and on her feet were moulded ballet slippers that could not be taken off.

'I wonder what it was doing there,' Delilah said. 'Would someone have given John a toy like this?'

'Doubt it. He got bikes and Meccano, I should think. I don't think he was the kind of boy to want dolls.'

'No.' She frowned, turning the doll over as she examined it. 'I don't either. But this doll is too new to belong to the generation before, isn't it? I mean – she's relatively new. When were Barbies made? Or Sindys, come to that?'

'Dunno. The fifties? The sixties?'

A thought occurred to her. 'But could it belong to one of your sisters? You said you used to play up here.'

Ben nodded, his expression thoughtful. 'That's right. I suppose it's possible. But I don't remember either of them having a ballerina doll like that. My parents were terrible old fogeys. The girls got rag dolls and handmade dolls' houses and that sort of thing. They didn't much like plastic. But it's possible. It could have been a gift.'

'Yes,' Delilah said. 'That would explain it.'

'I'll ask the girls when I think of it. We speak on the phone occasionally but they're both so busy with their London lives, they don't visit much.'

'That would be great, thanks.' She turned her attention from the doll. 'Shall we see if the trunk fits now?'

Ben pushed it back and it slid nicely into place, exactly filling the available space.

'Thanks so much, Ben, I really appreciate it,' she said happily. 'I couldn't have done it without you.'

She looked down and caught an expression of tenderness on his face. 'You're very welcome,' he said softly, and she smiled back. They were so comfortable together.

'Shall we go downstairs?'

'Sure.' He got to his feet. 'I need to get back to work.'

They headed back towards the main part of the house, Delilah still clutching the doll in her hand. She would put her somewhere safe, and then do some research.

Chapter Nineteen

1965

Sandy and his friends stayed for almost a week and the night before their promised departure, there was another party. In fact, Alexandra thought with exhaustion, there seemed to have been endless little parties since they'd arrived. The easy rhythm of her life with Nicky had changed into one of extremely late nights and days that began at lunchtime with groans and demands for strong coffee. By late afternoon people had recovered sufficiently to begin again, perhaps with a tour of the cellars to select the wines for that evening. Then Patsy would begin making her cocktails and someone else would start the gramophone up or tune the radio to whatever station they could pick up from abroad, searching for decent music to listen to. After that, they were on their way to another drunken evening of smoking and dancing until the early hours.

But she found it kept her mind off the darkness swirling at the back of it, and all the pain she was stubbornly trying to ignore. Late nights, glasses of wine and, afterwards, the warmth and comfort of Nicky's arms helped her to disconnect from the disruptive, disturbing voices in her head.

Mrs Spencer, who had not so far shown much interest in Alexandra and only treated her with the minimum of politeness, took her aside to say, 'Miss Crewe, can you please tell his lordship that all these late nights are not fair on the staff? Without a regular dinner hour, they don't know whether they're coming or going, and his friends are asking for anything they fancy whenever they feel like it! Last night, one of the young men woke up Tilly and told her to make him a sandwich – and it was after midnight! We can't be expected to put up with that.'

'No, Mrs Spencer. I will certainly tell him how you all feel,' she said dutifully, and obediently relayed the news to Nicky who looked a little shamefaced.

'The guys don't understand,' he said, 'they think it's like some kind of hotel. I'll explain. But they're leaving tomorrow. This will be our last big night, and then we'll all recuperate for a bit.'

Alexandra knew that while she'd welcomed the life that had been breathed into the house, she wouldn't be sorry to have Nicky to herself again so that they could settle into their old routine. Perhaps she could even open her heart to him about what she was suffering. She was sure that he had no idea. She'd succeeded in making him believe that the revelation about her mother's death was something she had simply accepted and filed away, just as she'd managed to pretend that she didn't care much about her father's rejection. She hoped she would be able to keep it that way, and eventually it would all become as easy to bear as she made it look.

The last night party followed the familiar pattern, except that Nicky had decreed a big dinner in the dining room with the family silver brought out to give the art crowd a little taste of how things were done at the fort on special occasions. The table gleamed in the light from curved silver candelabra and the crystal sparkled as the cellar's best wines were poured into it.

'This is impressive, Nicky, old man,' Sandy said, taking a gulp of his claret. 'You've treated us very well, hasn't he, chaps?'

There was a general chorus of appreciation, and Alexandra noticed that Patsy had seated herself next to Nicky and was fluttering her heavily made-up eyelids at him. She felt a small stab of jealousy but it was nothing she couldn't control. All week Patsy had been her usual flirtatious self, but she had appeared to respect that Alexandra was Nicky's girl now. Perhaps, on the last night, she was willing to chance her arm with the owner of Fort Stirling, but Alexandra was not afraid, even if she didn't like Patsy's style very much. She knew that Nicky loved her.

It's odd, she thought, *here I am with this unconventional crowd, with the girls who drink and the men who love their rock and roll music, and yet I'm the most unconventional of them all. I'm the ruined woman, not even divorced and living with another man.*

They finished dinner and went through to the library where the gramophone was already pumping out the American hits that the girls loved – Ray Charles, Roy Orbison and the rest – while the boys discussed blues music.

Alexandra watched them while one of the girls, already drunk, talked to her earnestly about something entirely incomprehensible, another couple kissed on the sofa and Nicky went around with his camera trying to frame shots and rearrange the lights to the best advantage.

'My lord?' It was Thomas, pale and apprehensive as he ventured into the party.

'What is it?' Nicky said, trying to take a glass shade off a curved reading light.

'There is someone who insists on seeing you. I've shown him into the small salon.'

'Oh – who?'

'He wouldn't say.'

'Well, tell him to go away. We're busy.' Nicky's voice was already thickened by the Tennessee bourbon that Patsy had been using to make Manhattans.

Thomas bowed and left, but he was back a few moments later.

'I'm afraid he won't go. He insists on seeing you.'

Alexandra got up. She was the least affected by alcohol as she didn't have a taste for whisky and could only manage a little wine with dinner. 'I'll sort it out, Nicky,' she said, and followed Thomas down the hall.

'He's very persistent and I can't order him away – he's . . . he's a gentleman,' Thomas explained apologetically.

'I see. Don't worry, it's fine, Thomas. I can handle it now.'

Thomas led the way to the door of the salon and opened

it. Alexandra stepped inside and gasped with fright. Standing in front of the fireplace was Laurence, his hands in his pockets as he stared at the oil landscape that hung above the mantel. He turned and his expression changed from hostility into something even more hateful.

'So it's true,' he said, his blue eyes like ice. 'You *are* here. Your father wrote to tell me where I might find you. Is your lover such a coward he can't even face me? Get your things at once. You're coming back with me. You've had your fun but I can't go on forever making excuses for your absence. I'll be damned if you'll make me a disgrace. You can stop all this now and come back where you belong.'

'Thomas, can you get Lord Northmoor for me?' Alexandra asked faintly. 'Please tell him it's urgent.'

'Yes, miss.' Thomas turned and hurried away down the hall.

'You've been living it up, haven't you?' Sardonic amusement danced in his eyes, but the throbbing in his throat betrayed his anxiety. 'Quite a place, this. No wonder you wanted to run away – it makes our flat look like the butler's pantry. I suppose you're sorry you married me, when you could have had all of this respectably, instead of as his mistress.'

'Laurence,' she said miserably, 'I'm sorry you've come. You shouldn't have.'

'No, I'm sure you'd much rather I left you in peace, but you're my wife, dammit. Get your coat now, you're coming with me. You don't seem to understand that you're legally and morally mine.'

'No, I'm not,' she whispered. 'I never will be.'

'The law says differently. I've come to fetch you and I'm not going without you. Your father agrees. If you ever want to be reconciled with him, you must come now.'

She could only stare at him in horrified disbelief. The idea that she might actually go with him seemed incomprehensible. Walk away from everything that was true and good and real in her life, and turn instead to a dead, sterile existence where she would surely be suffocated? She would rather die.

'No,' she said in a strangled voice. 'Never.'

He took a menacing step towards her. 'Didn't you hear what I said? You're still my wife and you're obliged to do as I say. You belong to me.'

A kind of madness whirled through her brain born of fear and desperation. She felt her face distort and her voice came out in a harsh scream. 'No! It's all over! I don't know what kind of lie you've been spinning but you're going to have to go back and tell them the truth – I've gone and I'm never coming back. Even if Nicky threw me out, you would be the last person I'd turn to because I'd rather starve on the streets than be your wife!'

As she stood panting at him, her eyes blazing in fury, Laurence's expression became despairing. He stepped towards her, his eyes beseeching.

'Please, I beg you, Alexandra. You don't understand what this means. I need you. You must come back with me—'

At that moment, she felt Nicky at her shoulder.

'Get out of my house, Sykes,' he commanded, his face stony and his fists clenched.

Laurence turned even whiter, and Alexandra could see he was trembling. He was afraid. She was surprised by the wash of pity she felt.

'I don't know how you can look me in the eye,' he said, a touch of nobility about his thin face and set shoulders. 'You've acted like a cad, taking another man's wife. They'll throw you out of White's for it, you'll see. I had hoped to protect us all from the inevitable scandal but you're evidently too shameless for that.'

'You're the one who hit your wife,' Nicky said coldly. 'As far as I can see, you've got no claim on her now. And we're happy.'

'For now,' Laurence said in a jeering tone. He turned to Alexandra. 'And when he's tired of you, you'll be good for nothing and no one. What will you do then?'

'Get out!' roared Nicky.

Sandy appeared behind them. 'Is there a problem, Nicky?' he asked, his voice slurred.

'No,' Nicky said, his eyes fixed on Laurence. 'Sykes here is just leaving. Aren't you?'

'I'm going,' Laurence said stiffly. 'I can see it was a mistake to come.'

'Who is this ghastly weed?' drawled Sandy.

'No one of any importance,' Nicky replied contemptuously. Alexandra put a hand on his arm.

'Please don't,' she whispered. They had won and he was going. There seemed little point in humiliating him as well.

Laurence tried to leave but the other men pointedly wouldn't move out of his way and he was forced to press between them. Thomas stood in the hall, his eyes wide at the drama he was witnessing, and he held the front door open to the darkness beyond. As Laurence passed Alexandra he stopped, looked her in the eye and said quietly, 'You don't know what you've done.' Then he marched out into the hall with his chin up, as though he was in one of his regiment's parades, and walked out the door.

Sandy turned to Nicky. 'Is he causing trouble?'

'He came to threaten us and attempt to ruin our lives,' Nicky returned.

'We can't have that, Nick, you're the best of bloody men! And Alexandra is a priceless jewel amongst women!' Sandy swayed slightly, his cheeks flushed with indignation at the insult to his friends. 'Let's give the shit a send-off he won't forget.'

'Nicky, no!' Alexandra pleaded. 'Let him go!'

But it was too late. Sandy had already spotted a box full of empty bottles that had been taken from the library and put in the hall to be carried out to the garages. He went to it, picked up two empty wine bottles and carried them to the front door. Alexandra hurried after him, and saw that Laurence was getting into his car, the little Triumph Herald that he had used to take her on their honeymoon.

Before she could stop him, Sandy yelled, 'Good riddance to you!' and lobbed the bottle at the car. It spun through the air, glinting in the light from the hall, and bounced off the roof, leaving a dent as it shattered on the gravel. Laurence looked round, shocked.

'Don't!' cried Alexandra, putting out a hand to stop

Sandy throwing the other one but it was too late. It whirled through the air and smashed into the side of Laurence's head, knocking him sideways so that he groaned and staggered, evidently stunned. He put one hand to his cheek where a deep red mark was already forming.

'Laurence!' Alexandra ran down the front steps towards him. 'Are you all right?'

He was frowning, rubbing at his face and staring at the bottle as it rolled, still intact, on the ground at his feet. As she approached, he looked up, his eyes dazed, and said roughly, 'Stay the hell away from me. You've brought me enough bad luck already. I hope you're happy that you've destroyed me.'

She stopped short and gazed at him. An awful sadness at what had happened between them welled up in her. 'I'm sorry, Laurence. Really I am.'

'Not as sorry as I am,' he muttered. 'Now, if you can call your beasts off, I'm going to leave.'

But the crowd of partygoers had come out to witness the fun and they wanted to join in. With a chorus of shouts and laughs they began to lob more bottles from the top of the steps, not, it seemed, with the intention of hitting Laurence or his car, but for the pleasure of seeing them shatter into sparkling shards on the gravel. She could hear Nicky trying to stop them, trying to explain that it would be difficult to clear away the broken glass, but no one was listening.

Laurence rubbed at his cheek again, then climbed into the front seat of his car. The next moment the Herald was heading for the drive, swerving erratically to avoid the shards on the ground. Alexandra jumped as a bottle landed close by her and smashed into pieces. She turned and ran back, one arm shielding herself in case of a direct hit. Nicky saw what was happening and yelled at the others to stop throwing the bottles, snatching the missiles from their hands in his fury. They gave up their sport, and retreated into the house, laughing. As Alexandra reached the top of the steps, Nicky waited for her with his arms open.

'Don't worry, darling, we've seen him off for good,' he said comfortingly, folding her into his embrace.

Alexandra hugged him, taking solace from the warmth of his body, but she wished that it had not ended with Laurence being treated like that. She felt no justice at the blow he had suffered, only a nasty creeping sense of shame.

It was two days later, as they were at breakfast in the round dining room, when Thomas came in, went quietly to Nicky and whispered in his ear. Nicky got up at once, putting his napkin on his chair, saying, 'Will you excuse me, darling?'

Alexandra looked up briefly from the book she'd been studying while she nibbled on toast and marmalade. The house seemed so blissfully quiet and civilised now that Sandy and his friends had gone, and she was appreciating the tranquil hours. Music and drink had not been enough to heal her heartache, and she hoped that quiet might now help instead. But she had the sense of gathering trouble; after what had happened when Laurence was here, she was expecting legal papers at any moment announcing his intention to divorce her. She could imagine the scandal. No doubt

Nicky's involvement would mean the press would take an interest, and she could imagine what view her father would take of that. It was hard to believe that he would ever forgive her for dragging the family name through such disgrace. But what choice did she have? She longed to be free of her marriage and she was sure Laurence did too. It had filled her with sadness to see him here, begging her to return, when he must know as well as she did that only a life of misery awaited them if they stayed together.

When Nicky came back, she sensed a change in the atmosphere immediately. 'Is everything all right, darling?'

He sat in the chair beside her, instead of the one opposite that he normally took, and put a hand on hers, his grey eyes serious.

'What is it?' she said with a short laugh. 'You're worrying me.'

'Darling, I've got some very sad news.'

She sat bolt upright with a gasp. 'It's Father, isn't it? Oh no, I can't bear it! Something's happened to him.' She screwed her eyes shut, her fists clenching hard so that her fingernails dug into her palm. She couldn't cope with the idea that she would lose him without their making peace.

'No, no, it's not that – your father's fine as far as I know.' Nicky bit his lip and then said, 'But you're right, something has happened. It's Laurence. I'm afraid there was an accident when he was on his way back to London from here. For some reason he took a wrong turn – he must have got lost in the darkness. He . . . the car . . .'

'Is he all right?' she said, stricken. In her mind, she could see him as he left, dazed and stumbling slightly as he climbed into the driver's seat, the missiles still falling around him.

Nicky's hand tightened around hers. 'Alex, he went off Dursford Bridge and into the reservoir. They only found the car yesterday. I'm afraid that Laurence was still inside it.'

She pulled in a hot, painful breath. The world seemed to darken around her.

Nicky was talking very fast suddenly about how there had been complaints about the bridge in recent years and how it was possible for someone who didn't know the place well to be confused by the sharp turn just before the bridge itself and take it at the wrong angle, and how the railings had been earmarked for replacement, but Alexandra barely heard him. Instead she only saw the little car swerving as Laurence drove away. He'd been hit on the head by a bottle. He was dazed. Perhaps he'd been in a state of semi-consciousness. He should never have been driving, not in that condition.

She turned and gazed at Nicky in horror. '*We* did it,' she whispered. She felt numb and yet twisted up inside at the same time.

'No, we didn't!' Nicky looked astonished. 'What are you talking about? It was an awful accident but that's all! Of course we had nothing to do with it.'

'He was hit on the head. Sandy hit him with the bottle. He was almost knocked unconscious.'

'He was fine,' Nicky said robustly. 'It only grazed him. It was wrong of Sandy to chuck the bottles but it was just a lark.'

Alexandra said nothing. It had not seemed to her in the least like a lark to pelt a man with glass. She felt the drag of confusion and guilt. *Poor Laurence*, she thought, seeing him panicked and bewildered as the ice-cold water rose into the little car, sucking him down into its blackness. She saw him wrestling with the door and remembered how it used to jam from time to time, and Laurence would use a special trick to get it open. Perhaps, in the shock, he forgot the trick, or couldn't force the door against the weight of the water, and then he would have felt it at his chest, his neck, then over his mouth and nose until . . .

She gasped again, making a tiny squeak that could not begin to convey her horror at what she was witnessing inside her head.

Nicky leaned forward to her and said quietly, 'It's too awful, darling, and of course I wish it hadn't happened. But it wasn't our fault. You know that, don't you?'

She looked away, not able to say honestly that she did.

The inquest declared it an accidental death through careless driving. The injury on the dead man's cheek was noted but it was assumed that it had been acquired during the course of the accident. It was noted that Laurence Sykes had been in the vicinity of the reservoir after a visit to Fort Stirling but only Thomas was called upon to give evidence and he testified that the deceased had drunk nothing and stayed only a short time. There had been no further questions, and Thomas offered nothing more. The coroner seemed satisfied with the verdict and the case was closed.

It did not stop gossip, though. Alexandra knew that Thomas had seen the goings-on before Laurence had left and she dreaded to think what people might be saying. She feared that everyone would be thinking what she herself thought: that the accident was no doubt a result of what Laurence Sykes had suffered at the hands of his vicious, immoral wife and the man who had cruelly cuckolded him.

The letter came from the solicitor, sent to her father's address and then forwarded to her with a curt, dark hand on the front of the envelope. Inside she was informed that, as his wife, she was entitled to all of Laurence's possessions and what was in his bank account at the time of his death. The circumstances of his death meant that the army regretted she would not be eligible for a widow's pension. She was informed that the funeral would be held the following week, and it told her the place and time.

'Should I go?' she said, holding out the letter to Nicky.

'Of course not,' he said, frowning. 'I think it would be in extremely poor taste. You must send some flowers but no more than that.'

'You're right. I'll return all the money to his family, of course,' she said. 'I can hardly keep it, or his things. It wouldn't be right.'

They gazed at each other. Alexandra didn't know what to feel. Only a short time past she had loathed Laurence and hoped never to see him again. She could hardly rend her garments and tear her hair now that he was dead. But she couldn't shake the guilt she felt.

Perhaps I did hate him, she thought, *but I never wanted him dead. I didn't mean for him to die.*

Nicky lifted one of her hands and kissed it. 'You realise this means that you're free now? We can be properly happy together.'

She looked at him with frightened eyes and said, 'Do you think there's something wrong with me, Nicky?'

'Of course not,' he said, looking astonished. 'What do you mean?'

'My mother . . . and now Laurence . . . I feel as if I'm bad luck somehow.'

'That's ridiculous. Of course you're not. I've never heard anything so stupid.' He pulled her close and kissed her. 'You're good luck to me. The best I can imagine.' He held her for a moment and she took comfort from his warm strength. If he loved her, she could face whatever she had to. He was the best thing in her life, and their love was her salvation.

'Alex,' he said suddenly, 'let's go away. This place has become so gloomy, and we're too close to your wicked old dad and the gossiping village. After what happened to Laurence, I feel we need to seize the day and live life while we can. Why don't we get away from it all? Let's go to Africa. Or India. I want to take my camera and see some heat and dust and some *reality*. I want to discover what the whole thing is about, what we're *here* for. Don't you?'

She considered it. The more she thought about it, the better the idea appeared. 'Yes,' she said wholeheartedly. She wanted to escape it all, just as he did. Her home was with

Nicky – wherever he was she could be happy. They could leave the misery and despair of this place and find new, untainted ones where they would be free. 'Yes, it's a marvellous idea.'

'And then,' he said, clasping her hands, 'when we get back, and this unpleasant business is forgotten, we'll get married and be happy ever after – won't we?'

'Yes,' she said fervently. She didn't tell him she was afraid that happiness won this way must surely come with its own price.

PART TWO

Chapter Twenty

1967

'Your ladyship! Oh, what a joy to see you!'

Quite a different welcome, Alexandra thought wryly, to the one she received on her first visit to the house over a year ago. Nevertheless, she was glad. She was respectable at last.

'Hello, Mrs Spencer,' she said, smiling at the small welcoming party. The servants were beaming, happy to put the old days behind them now that there was all this new excitement.

The housekeeper dashed forward, eager to get close. 'Is this the little angel? Oh, may I see?'

Alexandra lowered the bundle she had pressed to her shoulder and carefully folded away the knitted blanket to reveal the small face inside. Its eyes were tightly shut, the little cupid's bow lips parted and the round cheeks flushed with sleep. He was the most beautiful thing she could possibly imagine, so it was only to be expected when Mrs Spencer went into raptures over the perfection of the baby.

'So, what do you think of my son?' Nicky said, coming up behind Alexandra. 'He's a little champ, isn't he?'

Mrs Spencer gave him a solemn but joyful look. 'Oh, my lord, he's the most wonderful baby. You must be so proud.'

'I am.' He took off his sunglasses. 'This is John Valentine Stirling – my son and heir.' He smiled down proudly at the baby and put his arm around Alexandra. 'Haven't I grown up, Mrs Spencer? I'm a husband and father now.'

'You certainly have, my lord,' the housekeeper said. 'We heard the news about your wedding – what a shame you decided to get married abroad; we'd have loved a wedding here, you know. It's been many years since we've celebrated a proper Stirling wedding!'

'We'll see what we can do,' Nicky said. 'I'm sure we can arrange a party to celebrate everything: the wedding, John's arrival and our homecoming.'

'Darling,' Alexandra said anxiously, 'let's get the baby inside. I don't want him catching a chill.'

They'd been accustomed to a hot climate for so many months now that England seemed abysmally cold, even though it was summer here. They had left on their adventure as soon as it could be arranged, though it took a few months – Alexandra needed a passport, for one thing – and it wasn't until the spring that they had finally got on their way. As the coast of England disappeared into the distance, she'd stood on board the deck of the boat taking them to France on the first leg of their journey, and had felt her spirits lift. Abroad, she could forget what had happened in the past, and think only of that day, or even of the present hour. Life was just about her and Nicky, and whatever new sights and sounds the day brought her. She felt released from what had gone before, and her past life seemed like a half-remembered dream. The sense of liberation she felt was intoxicating. On the ship, Nicky had slipped a gold band around her ring finger and said, 'Easier for us if everyone thinks we're already married.'

She'd looked at it, marvelling. It wasn't even a real wedding ring and yet it meant a hundred times more than her ring from Laurence ever had.

They took their time making their way to India, stopping wherever took their fancy or taking sudden detours when they felt like it; Nicky's money gave them the freedom to do whatever they wanted. As they left Europe behind, she took in new sights: deserts and mosques, camels and monkeys, long rattling trains that crossed vast distances crammed with people, with even more riding on the roof and the platforms between the carriages. She learned to live with the heat and the dry dust, how to bargain for tea and fruit, and to wear a headscarf when it was required. Most of all, she loved being with Nicky every minute, the two of them against the world. Everyone accepted without question that she was his wife, and she revelled in the way she could be with him without feeling guilty or sordid.

When they finally reached India, they followed their whim to whichever adventure seemed most appealing. They travelled in battered vans or on crowded trains; sometimes they even rode elephants as they explored the ancient cities or gazed out across the limitless landscape. Everything was strange and new: the colours, the smells, the food, and the punishing, never-ending heat.

It was in the hills above Darjeeling that they realised that Alexandra was expecting a baby. After a burst of excitement and worry about how to get home, they decided to continue with their journey. They were free of the censorious eyes of the world here; Alexandra could grow bigger without gossip, and they could do things at their own pace. Neither of them thought to wonder what they would do if there were problems with the pregnancy, sharing a simple blind faith that their baby would arrive safely when it was ready, and until then they had six months to do as they pleased.

Alexandra's belly grew bigger and bigger and the only causes of anxiety were a nasty night of food poisoning and a dose of flu. The baby always kicked reassuringly afterwards and Alexandra bloomed, happy in a way she had never known before. She was astonished at how pregnancy made her feel: she was in awe of her body's power to build a tiny human being inside her without her needing to do anything. She felt obscurely that she ought to be frightened of what was happening but she could only welcome it. Nicky's child was being created inside her and she felt like a precious vessel containing something holy. One day when they were visiting a temple, she was surrounded by women who touched her belly in awe and murmured what she thought must be blessings. She felt like a goddess herself, being worshipped and adored.

But there was the problem of getting married. Even Nicky's carefree attitude to convention was challenged by the thought that he would father a child without being married. He had the future of Fort Stirling to consider and it would be no good to have a child out of wedlock, particularly if it were a son who then couldn't inherit. Even in India, there was no escaping the Fort entirely. They discussed marriage from time to time, and how they would manage it before the baby came, but always put it off for just a little while longer.

When they arrived on the crystal white beaches of Goa, with fringes of palm trees and huts on the sand within the sound of the waves, Alexandra knew from her tightly swollen belly that they couldn't delay much longer.

Nicky was sitting cross-legged at the entrance to their hut, smoking. He had discarded English clothes almost entirely since they'd arrived, and wore baggy white cotton trousers and an embroidered waistcoat over a torso now burnt dark brown. He was watching the rhythm of the waves as they rolled into the shore, while he expelled clouds of sweet, fragrant smoke. He bought the tobacco from a man who wandered up and down the beaches looking for tourists and it always seemed to calm him down.

'Nicky?' She lay on a soft mattress in the gloom of the hut, one hand on her belly, where she could feel the kicks and twitches of the baby.

'Hmm?'

'The baby will be here soon. The doctor I saw in Arambol told me that it was only six weeks at the most. The baby is a good size already, he told me. It might even come early.'

Nicky took a long drag on his cigarette and blew out a stream of smoke but said nothing. It was always a little harder to get through to him when he was smoking.

'I'm scared,' she said softly.

He turned to look at her, his face tender. 'Don't be scared. Your body will know what to do. It's a miracle like that, the way you carry inside yourself the power to transmit life. It'll be fine, you won't need to do a thing, your instinct will take over.'

Alexandra was silent for a moment, wondering if it would really be so easy. It was not how she had ever heard child-birth spoken of, even in the veiled, indirect way ladies had used. Then she said, 'But I don't want to have this baby before we're married. I couldn't bear that.'

Nicky moved round on his haunches to face her properly. 'I feel the same – and you're right, we mustn't risk it. I've got to make sure this little one has a name or there'll be no end of trouble. I'll sort everything out tomorrow and we'll do it as soon as we can.'

'Thank you, darling.' Alexandra lay back on the mattress, satisfied. This would be so different from the kind of wedding she had been brought up to expect – but then, she had had that and what good had it been to her? Whatever this was, it would join her to the man she loved and create a family for her baby to be born into. That was all that mattered.

Nicky was as good as his word. After all the months of in-action, they were married a few days later in two separate ceremonies. The first was a dreamy and beautiful occasion. A crowd of the people they had met in Goa, as well as local people, arrived to witness the wedding. Nicky waited on the beach in his baggy Indian trousers, a white collarless shirt and a white spangled waistcoat, next to a local shaman who was to conduct the marriage. Alexandra walked over hot white sand to join him, wearing a red and gold sari that flowed elegantly over her vast bump, and flowers in her hair. She didn't understand much of the ceremony but at times their hands were joined together and incantations were muttered, fragrant spices burned in the fire that had been set on the beach, and prayers offered to spirits of the earth and sky. At the end, she and Nicky sat together on an exquisitely embroidered rug while local men played sitars and drums as girls in sparkling veils and haram pants danced, and the wedding feast lasted long into the velvety night. The beach looked so beautiful, illuminated by the bonfires burning along it, with music sounding and people drinking and dancing in celebration, that Alexandra felt she was living in a dream of happiness. But she knew that this ceremony was just theatre. It was the other that really mattered.

The next day, they travelled to a nearby town and paid a short visit to a white-clad Indian man, an attorney at law, who took a sheaf of rupees and in return had them sign some official-looking documents, then gave them a signed and stamped certificate. They were married.

She held Nicky's hand, more moved than she had been the day before, silently and deeply thankful that they were united at last.

'So, my darling,' Nicky said, staring at their certificate as they returned to the beach in a bicycle rickshaw, sheltered from the sun by a tatty plastic canopy. 'Now you're officially a Stirling.' He kissed her. 'Not that we needed some piece of paper to tell us that.'

That night, Alexandra made sure that she slipped the marriage certificate carefully into the safest place in their possessions, along with their money and passports.

Two weeks later, with the help of two village women who, despite having no English, provided support and comfort through a long and painful night, Alexandra gave birth to a healthy son. The rapture and delight she and Nicky felt in the baby was all encompassing. Even their travelling seemed to lose its excitement in the thrill of his existence. The outside world shrank and disappeared as they became absorbed in the baby, awake or asleep or at the breast, in his blue eyes, soft skin and tiny fingers and toes. Alexandra, overwhelmed with love, wanted to settle with her little chick and concentrate entirely on him. Within a few weeks, Nicky suggested that they went home, and Alexandra eagerly agreed. She had been dreaming of forests and rain and the particular green of Dorset, and longed to be there with her baby. Little John needed to be home, in the place he truly belonged.

They packed their things and Alexandra wrapped John to her chest in the papoose style she had learned from the local women, and he nestled there all the way back to England. The journey took weeks as they rattled back on trains and in buses, leaving India behind and travelling through Pakistan and Iran. It was a more anxious thing to travel now they had the baby to consider, and Alexandra fretted over the heat and the sand and the state of the buses. But as long as she could look down and see his face pressed to her heart, and she could feel his small fingers curled around her large one, or was able to put him to the breast when he cried, she could bear it.

When they left Turkey and sailed around the coast of Greece to Italy where they boarded a train northwards, she felt suddenly wistful for the freedom of their lives abroad, and the colour and warmth of India. But that was over now. As they were back in Europe, Alexandra unwound the soft cotton papoose and began to carry John in a blanket instead. In Paris, they discarded their travelling clothes and bought new ones. Nicky put a suit back on, and she bought skirts and blouses and summer dresses with belts and buttons, quite unlike the flowing robes she'd grown accustomed to. By the time they arrived at Portsmouth, they looked like a proper English family again, with the baby in a blue romper and a white cotton hat. Only the depth of their tans showed that they had been living a different kind of life altogether, but even those were already beginning to fade.

Back at Fort Stirling, the past, with its awkwardness, seemed to be erased. With the new generation of Stirlings in the house, any unusual arrangements prior to the wedding were forgotten. It was understood that irregularities had been made right, and soon a stream of visitors were making their way to the house to call on the new viscountess and coo over the baby, who was turning into the most handsome child ever seen – at least, in Alexandra's eyes. Nicky, too, was a devoted father and now that he was head of the family, he seemed to be able to relinquish his old party crowd and his dreams of a photography career to concentrate on running the estate and taking part in the life of the county.

Alexandra was soon absorbed in the new demands that were made on her: besides caring for John whenever she could – the nanny that Nicky had insisted on was very territorial and clearly resented Alexandra's presence in the nursery except at given times – she was called upon to do all manner of civic duties, from opening fêtes and judging winners at the garden shows, to handing out prizes at local schools and visiting hospitals. No one had much cared who she was before, but now she was Lady Northmoor of Fort Stirling, she seemed to embody some kind of authority. When she admired a Victoria sponge at the Women's Institute, it immediately became something better than it had been. If she considered pansies prettier than snowdrops, or crochet superior to needlepoint, then everyone agreed that was absolutely the case. Perhaps, she thought, she ought to draw confidence from all of this, but instead she felt a kind of mild panic that she was inadvertently leading everyone in the wrong direction, like a reluctant Pied Piper.

What mattered more was that she seemed to be accepted by the extended family as well. The various aunts, uncles and cousins arriving to inspect the new arrival and welcome Alexandra into the family treated her with friendly kindness, and she apparently passed whatever tests were being set her.

Nicky's cousin, George Stirling, lived only a few miles away and yet John was already toddling around by the time he paid his visit. He had been the fat boy she remembered from their childhood games, so Alex had looked forward to seeing him again, but his visit was marked by a puzzling awkwardness and a distinct lack of friendliness. He had grown into a stout man and looked older than his years, with reddened cheeks that hinted at a blood pressure higher than was good for him. He'd smiled and been outwardly polite, hoping she might come and meet his fiancée soon, and that they would all become friends, but his stony gaze had quite chilled Alexandra. He had shown no interest in John at all.

'Don't bother about old George,' Nicky had said airily when his cousin had left. 'He's never had much charm and what there was got kicked out of him at school. Poor kid was bullied to bits. No doubt his nose is a bit out of joint now John is here, as George was the heir apparent, but he'll get used to the idea. He's got Home Farm to himself, after all.'

She hoped that when she met the fiancée, things would improve.

The following month, Alexandra sat for her portrait and when it hung in the hall of Fort Stirling, alongside those of other viscountesses going back hundreds of years, she began to believe that everything was going to be all right.

While Alexandra had been in India, the memory of her father had faded to a shadow and she had done her best to forget him. Now his presence began to loom large in her mind and the knowledge that he was a few miles away in the Old Grange, implacably opposed to her new life, haunted her. She had found happiness now, at last, and she wanted him to share in it, and to be glad for her. A fortnight after their return, she wrote to her father telling him about John, enclosing a clipping of his birth announcement from *The Times* and a photograph of the baby, and asking if she might bring his grandson to see him. A few days later she received a terse note in response.

> *You may believe that your elevation to Lady Northmoor has scrubbed out your sins, but I do not. You carry the weight of a man's death on your conscience. The child is no grandson of mine – there is bad blood in him, the same as your own, and that is that.*
> GC

She read it over and over, curiously calm, as though her father had destroyed her ability to weep over him. Did this scrap of paper mark the final chapter in her relationship with him? It must. He was adamant that there would be no forgiveness, and she had never known him change his mind about anything.

'Forget him,' said Nicky, furious and scornful when she showed him the note. 'Let the old fellow rot in his own bitterness. Can't you see what he's like? He's a tyrant. Look what he did to your mother. He'll hound you the same way if you let him! You're better off keeping away. And if he dies a lonely death, he'll only have himself to blame.'

Alexandra knew it was not that easy. She held John close to her, hugging him as tightly as she could without hurting him. She showed nothing outwardly, but inside a fear was growing that she had somehow stained him with something of her own wrongdoing. But there didn't seem any way to put it right.

Chapter Twenty-One

Present day

The doll was hidden under a pile of jumpers in Delilah's chest of drawers, where there was no danger of John seeing it. When she went out for a morning walk with Mungo, Ben came loping over to tell her that he'd spoken to his older sister the previous evening and asked her about it. She couldn't remember ever having a doll like that.

'It's one of those things, I suppose,' Delilah said, half an eye on Mungo, who was sniffing around the flower beds. 'There are probably lots of mysteries in the house, when you think about how many people have lived there over the years.'

'You're right. By the way, I asked my sis about that folly too.'

Delilah said quickly, 'Yes? What did she say?'

'She said people definitely jumped off it – and at least one woman, she thinks, but she doesn't remember it being our aunt. But like I said, the family just didn't talk about her, and once we went away to school, we didn't hear any gossip.' He looked at her keenly. 'Why don't you ask John?'

She flushed and looked away. 'I . . . I should, I know. But it's such a sensitive subject for him, as you can understand. I don't want to ask something like that if I've got it wrong.'

Ben nodded. 'I know. He's not easy, is he?'

She gazed at the gravel path, not wanting to be drawn into disloyalty, even if Ben was right. He seemed to sense her discomfort because he said quickly, 'And that's not surprising, considering what the poor bloke has been through.'

A thought occurred to her and she said, 'Ben – do you and John get along? I've almost never seen you together.'

'Of course,' he said sturdily, though she caught the slight hint of awkwardness below. 'I suppose there's an age difference between us that doesn't help' – he caught himself, obviously remembering that it was the same difference as between John and Delilah – 'but . . . well, I guess we're just very different.'

They certainly were, Delilah thought, as she walked with Mungo out of the gardens and into the woods. Sometimes it seemed to her that they had polarised the house between them: John had become its gloom and darkness and despair, while Ben had taken on the beauty and light and growth it was capable of. Was it any wonder she was being drawn towards that sunny, life-enhancing side of things and away from the misery?

A terrible thought crossed her mind before she could stop it. Perhaps it was John's fault that there was no baby, not hers. And there was Ben, conjuring up new life all the time with his gardener's skill, making the earth fertile and the plants bloom and multiply . . .

She had the sudden vision of Ben taking her to bed, planting a child in her, his vigorous seed taking root . . . then she caught herself with horrified guilt.

I mustn't think that way, she told herself, appalled at what her imagination could create for her. And yet, the tiny glimpse in her mind's eye of his strong brown body on hers had been thrilling, and made her a little dizzy.

No. It's impossible. She shook her head hard as if to dislodge the treacherous image. Mungo had run off ahead and as she emerged from the wood and out into the clearing she could see him up by the folly, nosing around among the overgrowth and the fallen masonry.

The air was full of the buzzing of insects and the two-note coo of a pigeon floated into the still afternoon. Delilah looked over at the broken tower, sticking up craggily against the blue sky. It brought a bitter taste to her mouth. The last time she had been here, she hadn't guessed what significance it held. Now she knew why it caused such horror in John, and she was aghast that she'd even suggested they renovate it as a place for honeymooners. What a horrible, crass idea! Now she couldn't bring herself to go near it. She was glad it was boarded up and wished, like John, it could be pulled down altogether, its grim skeleton shattered by a bulldozer and shovelled away.

'Mungo!' she called, and turned back for home.

John refused to come out and see the gymkhana. He said he would spend the day at the coach house with his father until all the pony club brats, as he called them, had gone home with their ghastly rosettes and even ghastlier mummies.

'Dad hasn't been well lately. I don't want him upset by all the noise and traffic. I'll keep him calm,' he said.

Delilah at once felt guilty: it hadn't occurred to her that the day might be disruptive for John's father. 'There shouldn't be much noise from that distance and Ben's arranged the parking well away from the house. I haven't seen your father for ages. Can I come and say hello to him?'

'No,' snapped John. When he saw the hurt expression on her face, he said, 'I told you – he's not well. If he doesn't recognise you, you'll only make the situation worse.'

She gazed at him, stricken, and whispered, 'Are you going to shut me out forever?'

But he was already stalking away and didn't hear her.

During the afternoon, Delilah went up to the field to see what was going on and was soon chatting to some of the locals, watching the competition and visiting the tea tent to see what was on offer – thinking privately that she would make much better teas herself if she ever got the chance. She was about to head back to the house when the pony club president, Mr Harris, introduced himself, shaking her hand vigorously.

'Mrs Stirling, thank you so much for allowing us to use the paddock. It's been a marvellous venue and a splendid time has been had by all.'

'You're very welcome,' she replied. 'It's been fun. I've loved watching the children on their ponies.'

'We wondered if you might do us the honour of awarding our silver cup to the best all-rounder. It's just about to be announced.'

'Oh.' Delilah looked around, flushing with embarrassment. Lots of the mothers had come in smart summer dresses and designer sunglasses. Here she was, just in her jeans and a cheap floaty top, her hair messy, and wearing a pair of old sandals. 'Well, I'm not sure . . . I'm hardly prepared. And I'm a bit of a stranger to horses myself.'

Mr Harris grinned, his sandy eyebrows beetling. 'Now, that doesn't matter a bit. Please do come, we'd be so honoured.'

It would have been ungracious to refuse, so she said, 'All right, if you're sure you want me.'

She accompanied him up to the judges' platform and took her place as it was announced over the tinny loudspeaker system that she would be presenting the prize. Feeling very out of place next to the judges in their smart navy blazers, she took the little silver trophy in hand and said, 'Well done,' as she handed it over to a neatly turned-out young girl rider in jodhpurs, jacket and a riding hat.

There was a round of applause that felt very much like the final huzzah of the day, and then the crowds began to disperse, heading towards the makeshift car park in the next field, or towards the rows of horse boxes, leading tired ponies by the head while children trailed after.

Now that Delilah had been publicly identified, she was at once surrounded by people keen to introduce themselves, and she guessed by their enthusiasm that she had been the object of curiosity for a while, but everyone was so pleasant and friendly that she rather enjoyed the attention. She talked politely until she felt it really was time to leave, so she excused herself and headed back to the house, trying not to catch anyone's eye.

'Mrs Stirling!' came a breathless voice from behind her.

She turned and saw a plump lady in a vivid flowery dress hurrying towards her across the hummocky grass of the outer field. 'Yes?'

'I'm so sorry to keep you but I felt I simply must introduce myself. My name is Grace Urquhart.'

'How do you do,' Delilah replied politely, her heart sinking. She had the feeling that a long and difficult-to-escape conversation was about to ensue.

Grace Urquhart reached her, panting and rather flushed from her dash across the field in unsuitable shoes. She caught her breath, flapping her hands in front of her face, and said, 'Oh, my, this heat! I'm dying from it!' Beads of sweat stood out all over her nose and forehead and she blinked rapidly.

'It is warm, but it's been perfect weather for the gymkhana,' Delilah said, giving her time to cool down.

'Yes, yes, indeed . . . Oooh, I'm sorry. That's better, I'm getting my breath. Now, I wanted to talk to you because my maiden name isn't, of course, Urquhart . . .' She took a deep breath and her expression became almost triumphant. 'It's Sykes!'

Delilah waited for more explanation but when none came, she said a neutral, 'Oh.'

The woman frowned. 'Doesn't that mean anything to you?'

'I'm afraid not.'

'But your husband's mother was married to my husband's second cousin once removed. I've been doing the Sykes family tree. There's a big landowning family up in Yorkshire we're distantly connected to but it was very exciting to discover that we've got a connection down here, so close to home.'

Delilah shook her head, puzzled. 'I'm sorry, what did you say?'

'Your husband's mother was married twice – once to Lord Stirling, of course, but before that to Lieutenant Laurence Sykes in the Blues and Royals. Or just the Blues they were then, I think.' Grace Urquhart's mouth turned down into an expression of sadness. 'Of course, it didn't end well, as I'm sure you know.'

Delilah's heart was beating quickly and her breath came in shorter bursts. 'I'm terribly sorry, I don't know. You see, I've not been a Stirling long, and I've not yet learned all the ins and outs of the family. What happened?'

'I don't know all that much myself but Laurence Sykes died in a car accident, going off a bridge and into a reservoir. The Dursford Reservoir, just a few miles away. A nasty accident, apparently, poor man. But . . .'

'But?' prompted Delilah.

Grace coloured slightly. 'Well, I don't like to say if you've not heard it before.'

'Please do, Mrs Urquhart,' she said in what she hoped

was a commanding tone and, sure enough, the other woman seemed to take this as an order.

'There's a rumour in my husband's family that the death wasn't exactly an accident. They think he may have' – she leaned forward confidentially and said in a loud stage whisper – 'done it on purpose!'

'On purpose?' Delilah echoed, surprised.

Grace nodded and said, 'Yes. Because he'd been up at the house, you see, and Lady Northmoor was already there, living with Lord Northmoor, although she wasn't Lady Northmoor then, of course, she was still Mrs Sykes. And what are we to think when a woman is living with another man and her husband drives off a perfectly sound bridge to his death?'

'What indeed?' said Delilah, trying to absorb and make sense of what Grace Urquhart was saying to her. 'How fascinating. Thank you so much for letting me know. I must get back to the house now, but would you mind leaving me your number? That way I can reach you if I have any questions.'

'Of course not,' Mrs Urquhart said, pleased, the sting of Delilah's departure softened by the idea that they would keep in touch. 'Please call me any time. I'd be delighted to help if I possibly can.'

'Is the grim fiesta over?' John asked, going to the fridge and pulling a beer from its cool depths. He popped it open and took a long drink.

'If you mean the gymkhana, then yes,' Delilah said. She had the laptop open on the kitchen table and was doing an internet search at the same time as preparing supper. 'You should have come up, you know. Everyone would have loved to see you.' She gave him a look. 'Haven't you ever heard of *noblesse oblige*?'

He grimaced. 'Heard of it? It's been the bane of my bloody life. I wouldn't be suffering with this damn place if it wasn't.'

'All right, but doing a little more of it wouldn't hurt. I think you could forge local relationships, that's all. People want to feel a connection to the house, they want to belong to it.'

'They wouldn't if they knew what it really meant,' he said, looking irritated. 'They just see the beauty. They don't understand it's a front. It's like the make-up on the face of a raddled old harridan, designed to lure you in and then suck the life out of you.'

Delilah stared at him, startled by the bitterness in his voice. He was utterly sincere. Despite what he'd said before, she'd assumed that a part of him must love the house in a way she never could. After all, his roots were there.

She remembered her encounter with Grace Urquhart and said carefully, 'I heard an interesting thing today. A woman told me that before your mother married your father, she was married to someone called Laurence Sykes. Did you know that?'

John went very still and his eyes widened with surprise. 'What?'

'Yes – she was married twice. And the first husband drowned in the Dursford Reservoir after a car accident.'

He stood by the fridge, the beer in his hand, not moving. He said in a cold voice, 'Can that be true? I had no idea.'

'The woman who talked to me seemed very convincing. She's a Sykes, and has been doing the family tree thing that's such a craze now. Do you think it's likely?'

'Who knows? And to be honest, who cares? They're all dead now. Only my father is left and he can't tell us.'

'Perhaps we should ask him,' she suggested. 'He might find it easier to remember the distant past.'

'I don't see the point,' John said shortly. 'We wouldn't know if he was telling the truth or not.'

'All right. Well, do you mind if I do a bit of investigation myself? I've been looking on the net but I can't find much. The records don't seem to be on there. I think it's going to take quite a bit of poking about.'

John looked suddenly cross. 'Why? What's the bloody point? So my mother was married twice, so what? It won't change anything! I can't see why you're so interested. I don't like you digging away like this. For Christ's sake, Delilah, I didn't marry you to go back to the past, I married you to get away from it!'

His words hung heavy in the air. She stared at him, stricken, as he breathed heavily under knitted brows.

'I just want to understand you better,' she said. 'I want to help you. I thought that if I knew more about the past, I might be able to do that.'

'Don't waste your time,' he said irritably. 'I need you to help me face the future, don't you understand that? I mean, for fuck's sake . . .' He walked over to the kitchen table and slammed his palm down on it, making Delilah jump and her laptop judder. Then he muttered, 'Oh God. Maybe I'm making a mess of the whole thing. It's probably better if we don't have a baby.'

The words hit her like a hard punch to the stomach. 'What?' she whispered.

He shrugged. 'Maybe the fates are telling me that a man like me ought not to have children.'

She stared at him, half frightened now, discomfited by the way he was almost echoing her own thoughts of earlier. She saw a flash of herself and Ben in bed, and quickly banished it. 'What do you mean?'

'Can't you tell?' Irritation seemed to surge through him. He twitched angrily. 'For one thing, this house is bloody well killing me, so why I ought to inflict that on some poor innocent child is completely beyond me! And for another—' He broke off, took up his beer and gulped another mouthful.

'What?' she pressed. A tumult of emotions was rushing through her: fear, astonishment, surprise and horror. Was he really having second thoughts about wanting children? 'What's the other thing?'

When he spoke it was in a low, determined voice. 'This family is miserable. We're destined to suffer. My father is probably happier than he's ever been now he's forgotten the past. He used to be something else – drunk most of the time, permanently despairing and the loneliest man you've ever seen.'

'But that's not you,' Delilah replied, her lips dry. 'We can change the pattern of the past. We've got each other now.

There's no need for you to suffer like your parents. And I'm not going to die like your mother did.'

John stared at her, frozen, his face a study of horror. Then he said in a cold voice, 'What did you say?'

A wave of fear went over her. 'I-I-I said I wasn't going to die like your mother. You don't have to worry about me leaving you.'

John's expression became agonised. 'You don't know anything about it!' he said, his voice raw.

She leapt to her feet, pushing herself away from the table. 'But I want to know! I want to understand you! Why do you keep so much of yourself closed off from me when all I want is for us to be close to each other, to help one another?'

'It's nothing to do with you! I'm trying to escape it all, not drag you into it too!' He slammed down his beer bottle on the kitchen table, and it spouted a little fountain of foam. 'I thought you would be my fresh start, but I can see now that you're going to be cursed by all this just like I am.'

'That's not fair! You have to give me a chance. I have no idea what I'm up against because you won't tell me anything!' She was panting now, furious. 'You won't let me in, John! I can't just be here for the bits you choose, I have to live this life completely with you, or it just won't work. I can't help you if you don't let me!' Her rage was growing with her sense of impotence and thwarted hope. 'You don't let me build a relationship with your father, you won't talk about your mother, or what happened here to make this house such a miserable bloody place! How am I supposed to live like this?'

His eyes had turned dark and fierce. 'What are you going to do now?' he said. A muscle twitched in his jaw, revealing the strain he felt. 'Are you going to leave me?'

'I don't want to leave you, you stupid man! I love you! I don't want you to drive me away!' She felt tears of rage, frustration and despair building up behind her eyes. 'I want *you* and I want us to be a family. But I can only do that if you let me help you.'

'I can't promise you that,' he said flatly.

'Clearly.' She raised her eyes to him, his image beginning to blur. She tried to stop the tears; she wanted very much to stay strong in front of him. 'I just wish you'd open up to me. Not because I want to leave you but because I want to understand what you think and feel.'

John said in his strange, cold voice, 'But just by being here, you're stirring things up. Making things worse.'

She recoiled, gasping with the hurt of his words. 'What? How can you say that?' She felt a sob rising in her throat, turned and stumbled for the door. All she had done for almost a year was try to make John happy. Had she only succeeded in making him more miserable? She didn't believe it – she *knew* they'd been happy together once. Surely they could be again. But then, what did he mean?

He mustn't see me crying and weak, she thought, almost blinded by the hot water in her eyes. The sobs were coming now, pushed out of her lungs in horrible, convulsive waves, as she opened the back door, longing for the fresh air beyond and the release of the outside from the stifling atmosphere in the house. She saw the darkening blue of the sky, a flash of green and then dashed straight into something hard and warm with an 'Ouff!'

'Delilah? Are you all right?'

She had run into Ben, she realised, dazed. He had taken her by the arms to stop her falling back after they'd collided, and was staring down into her tear-streaked face.

'What's wrong?'

'Nothing. I'm fine,' she said, in the teary quaver of someone on the brink of breaking down.

'No, you're not! Come here.' He wrapped her in his arms, pulling her tightly against his broad chest. She smelt the musky aroma of his skin with the tang of sweat. The tears fell again and he murmured, 'There, there, you're okay now,' which made a sound deep in his chest that buzzed against her ear. After a moment, she got control of her crying and pulled away, sniffing.

'I'm sorry,' she said, feeling foolish.

'That's perfectly all right.' He smiled down at her and she saw again the family resemblance to John in his grey-and-green-specked eyes and the slight hook in his long nose. 'We all have moments from time to time, don't we?'

Delilah glanced back towards the house where she saw a movement at the kitchen door. When she pulled away from Ben and turned to look properly, there was nothing there.

'Come and see the camellia bushes,' Ben said. 'They smell incredible at this time of evening. 'If that can't cheer you up, then nothing will.'

She nodded and they walked off down the path together.

Chapter Twenty-Two

1969

'So, are you happy here?' Vera, in a neat tweed suit and high heels, kept up a smart pace as she marched down the gallery, and Alexandra had to hurry to keep up with her.

'Yes, very,' Alexandra said, a little breathless. She'd received a letter on thick ivory paper engraved with an address in the Highlands of Scotland but hadn't a clue who Vera Harrington might be until Nicky had looked at her oddly and said, 'How could you have forgotten Vera?'

Immediately she remembered. Vera was Nicky's older cousin, George Stirling's sister, and had grown up at Home Farm where George still lived. As a girl, she had been tomboyish and fearless, with astonishing cheekbones, a pointed chin, and a passion for horses. Nicky said she had married a horse trainer and gone to live in Scotland. Vera had written to say that she was sorry it had taken such an age to call, but that she would be visiting her brother and could she come to Fort Stirling while she was there. Alexandra had replied that she would be delighted to see her again, and a date had been arranged.

Alexandra had half expected Vera to be like her brother, red-faced and windblown, but she was very elegant, her tweed suit expertly cut and more Parisian than game fair. Her hair was neat and she wore make-up. She had also been a great deal more friendly, hugging Nicky, greeting Alexandra with a kiss, and admiring John, who was now a sturdy two year old with bright fair hair and a mischievous smile. 'Just like his father,' Vera had said with a smile, as John raced about the drawing room, stealing biscuits off the china plate on the table. It had been her suggestion that she and Alexandra go for a walk through the house together.

Vera looked about the gallery fondly and said, 'I used to love riding my bicycle up and down here. It was wonderful for that when it was raining outside. Nicky's father didn't seem to mind. He only cared about cricket balls going through the old glass in the hall downstairs.' She paused and then gave Alexandra a sharp look. 'I'm glad you seem so blissful. I remember you as such a quiet little thing. I would never have guessed that you and my loud, opinionated cousin would be so suited. But of course we didn't know each other well, did we? I remember how we played a little down at the old folly, before I considered myself too grown-up for games like that.' She peered more closely at Alexandra. 'Are you all right? You've gone quite white.'

Alexandra started and tried to shake off the sick feeling that had possessed her suddenly. 'Yes, I'm sorry. But you mentioned the folly. Something awful happened there last week.'

'Oh?'

'John. He ran away from me and got himself up that rotten old staircase. He . . . he nearly fell off. It was dreadfully careless of me to let him get away like that.' She closed her eyes, feeling almost as though she might faint. The memory of that terrible moment filled her with nauseous panic. She had trembled for the rest of the day and sobbed into her pillow at the dreadful pictures that had filled her dreams that night. The image of her mother had come often into her mind, no matter how hard she tried to banish it.

Vera eyed her sympathetically. 'You mustn't blame yourself. Little boys can be very fast and determined. Everything turned out all right, so that's over and done with, isn't it?'

Alexandra nodded, though she couldn't explain that the terror lived on, as though she was permanently standing with John just out of reach, on the brink of toppling away from her to his death. The image was haunting her constantly, popping into her mind at unexpected moments. Sometimes she saw John, and other times a woman in a white nightdress, blown about by the wind. Either way, it was horrifying.

'You shouldn't dwell on it,' Vera said briskly. 'Nothing good comes of fretting like that. You have so many blessings, and you obviously make Nicky very happy. He's quite grown up since I last saw him.'

Alexandra tried to focus on John as he had been just a few minutes ago, when he'd gone back up with Nanny. She longed to be with him, in the cosy surroundings of the nursery sitting room. Despite the mischief, he was such lovely fun at the moment: chatting, smiling and laughing, obviously overjoyed to see her. He was growing fast but he was still such a baby. She loved to hear him say 'Mama' in his pretty cooing voice. It made her heart swell and overflow with love.

Vera stopped and turned to look at her with a strong, direct gaze. She put her hands into the pockets of her tweed jacket. 'Now, I want to ask you something. I've heard that you and Nicky didn't have the most conventional of courtships.'

Alexandra flushed. No one had spoken of it since they'd returned – at least, not to her face. 'That's right,' she said haltingly. 'I . . . was married when Nicky and I met in London. We hadn't seen each other for years and it was . . . well, it just seemed that it was meant to be. I wish I hadn't been married – it was a dreadful mistake.'

'I'd heard something along those lines.' Vera smiled at her, her slim lips curving in a half-moon of a smile. 'Please don't think me impertinent—'

'I don't,' Alexandra said quickly. Vera's manner was so straightforward it was impossible to take offence at it.

'You must understand that inheritance is a tricky thing in our world. It has to be absolutely above board. Nicky has no brothers and sisters, and we must make sure that everything is done properly. There are plenty of people who might consider themselves to have a stake in this house otherwise. Now – Nicky is young and it's always been assumed he would marry and provide plenty of heirs, so no one is feeling done out of anything. But I just wanted to make sure that you understand that. Can I ask . . .' Vera looked uncomfortable just for a moment, and then continued in her plain-speaking way '. . . I know your husband died very tragically. Was he dead before you and Nicky married?'

Alexandra felt a wash of relief that she could answer truthfully. 'Yes. I was a widow when we married.'

'Good.' Vera smiled brightly. 'Then that's all right! I must say, in a perfect world, you and Nicky would have married here where we could witness it – but I'm sure you have your marriage certificate safely tucked away, don't you?'

Alexandra thought of the piece of paper that she had stowed in a locked wooden box in her dressing room. John's birth certificate was there too. They had had him registered at the county register office not long after they'd come back. The registrar had asked to see the marriage certificate but they did not have it, not realising it would be needed. In his loftiest, most aristocratic tones, Nicky had declared that he was sure it wasn't necessary, and the registrar humbly agreed and registered the birth without it.

'Yes,' Alexandra replied. 'It's been done properly.'

'Good!' Vera looked satisfied. 'Then I shall make it my job to quash any silly whispers that might be circulating, and I shall be able to say I've heard it from your own mouth. None too soon – for if I'm not mistaken, you're expecting again, aren't you, dear?'

Alexandra's mouth dropped open in astonishment. She was not even sure herself yet. How had Vera been able to tell?

'I've got three of my own,' Vera said, reading her expression. 'And I breed horses. I have a feel for when a mare is in foal, if you don't mind my making such a comparison.'

'No, of course not.' Alexandra laughed despite herself.

Vera gazed at her earnestly, then took her hand. 'I'm very glad about what you've said. Your little boy is adorable, and I like you very much. Now . . .' She began to walk on again and Alexandra walked beside her. 'I shall no doubt see you at George's wedding in September. Has he mentioned that he wants to hold the reception here?'

'I think Nicky said something about it. Of course we'd be delighted to have it here. That's exactly what the house is designed for. I sometimes feel that we three are simply rattling in it.'

'Three will soon be four.' Vera squeezed her hand. 'And I'm sure there will be many more after that if you're so inclined. Now, let's go and find Nicky. I'm dying to see him.'

Alexandra stood still for a moment. As Vera turned to her questioningly, she said firmly, 'I'm going to do everything I can to make sure that Nicky and our children are safe and cared for. I'll do whatever is necessary.'

Vera looked at her, and appeared to understand why she felt the need to say such a thing. 'I'm very glad to hear it,' she replied. 'Very glad indeed. And by the way, why don't you ask Nicky to have that dreadful old folly knocked down? I think it would be much safer that way.'

In the high summer, Alexandra gave birth to a girl. Nicky wanted to call her Guinevere but Alexandra thought it too unlucky so they decided on Elaine instead.

'Isn't Elaine unlucky?' asked Nicky, entranced by his beautiful daughter as she lay in the cradle next to their bed. Alexandra had recovered well from the straightforward birth but the doctor had prescribed bed rest for a week while she regained her strength and established her breastfeeding. Now she lay tucked up against a pile of snowy pillows, feeling happy and content.

'I don't think so.' Alexandra gazed down proudly, also enraptured by the tiny being she had somehow produced. The luxury of her bedroom at home was far removed from the seaside Goan hut, and she felt very spoiled but also a little nostalgic for the first carefree, sunny days of John's life. 'Who was Elaine again?'

'Elaine of Astolat. The Lady of Shalott.' He said with a flourish: '"'The curse is come upon me!' cried the Lady of Shalott."'

Alexandra looked at him, her eyes wide and horrified. 'Is that right? A curse?'

'Well . . . You know, I think there are lots of Elaines in Arthur. I'll look it up.'

But once the little girl with her mop of dark hair and her navy blue eyes had been called Elaine, they couldn't think of any other name that would suit her better.

John came in to meet the baby, his hand held in Nanny's big one as he was brought into the bedroom.

'Come here, darling,' Alexandra said with her arms out. She'd been careful to make sure that Elaine was in the cradle when John arrived. 'Do you want to meet your sister?'

John nodded, his blue eyes, now tinged grey like his

father's, round as saucers. He ran forward to his mother's embrace and then, from his vantage point beside her on the bed, he stared down into the cradle where Elaine lay, gazing upwards, her small limbs moving jerkily.

'Is she a dolly?'

'No, darling, she's a real live baby.'

'Is she going to live with us? For all the time?'

'Yes – forever and ever. She's your sister and she's going to be your friend. Isn't that lovely?'

He nodded obediently, then climbed down and took a closer look. He put out one chubby hand and brought it close to the baby's face. Alexandra held her breath, fighting the impulse to tell him not to touch and to be careful, and then John put his fingers gently on the soft cheek and said, 'Hello, baby.'

Elaine's small fists waved in the air as if in reply, and Alexandra found her eyes filling with tears. Somehow life had brought her to this place – to a man she loved and two beautiful children. For the first time she began to wonder if the fears that flourished somewhere in the dark recesses of her mind were unfounded.

She and Nicky had never been closer. Their life with two small children was entirely absorbing, and they stopped looking for anything else to fill it. They both found the children a source of intense interest, huge amusement and constant concern. If they weren't laughing at a silly dance that John liked to do for them, or the expression on Elaine's face when she tasted pumpkin, they were in anxious debate about whether to call a doctor to attend to John's fever, or what to do for the baby's teething. Nanny had little truck with any of it, hustling them out of the nursery at any opportunity and telling them briskly that nature was the best doctor and not to fret.

Alexandra treasured the way that Nicky adored the children. It was so different from her own experience of a distant, disapproving father who seemed to consider parenthood a disagreeable duty which consisted of teaching children about the misery of existence. Nicky wanted to share life's joys with John, as he grew into a sturdy little chap with a placid temperament that seemed programmed for happiness. He had no fear of trotting up to the office door, pushing it open and running in to Nicky, certain of kisses and smiles. 'You've got to learn about this place, John,' Nicky would say, pulling the little boy on to his lap to show him what he was doing. 'You're going to be running it one of these days, just like me, and my father before me.'

John loved to play at his father's feet while Nicky worked on estate business, or held a meeting with his agent or saw the tenants. There was always Nanny on hand to take him away if there were grizzles or sniffles.

Nanny would have whisked Elaine away too, if she could, keeping her in the nursery domain where she could be run like a little engine on Nanny's routine, but Alexandra resisted as much as she could. She insisted on feeding the baby herself, even when Nanny sniffed that Elaine was three months old and ought to be weaned. Nanny knew how things were done in big houses, how the children were brought up, and it was difficult to make her change her ways. Alexandra felt as though she and Nanny were locked in a tussle over the children, but she was determined to win it. Nicky saw nothing strange in Nanny taking the children so much, as that had been his own experience, and only laughed when Alexandra complained.

'You're so funny, darling,' he'd say fondly. 'Nanny does an excellent job. And why is she here, if you're going to look after the children?'

Alexandra said she hadn't wanted Nanny in the first place, but Nicky couldn't see any other way of doing things.

She adored John, but something about having a daughter drew Alexandra ever deeper into motherhood. She had a deep yearning to connect with the little girl, and memories of her own mother began to come unexpectedly into her mind. She thought she'd forgotten everything but those years of strain and tension that led up to her mother's death, but other recollections started to return. She found herself humming songs to the baby that she had not realised she knew. She kissed the baby's soft cheek and remembered a presence and a warm, comforting aroma that meant safety and love. She brushed the baby's cheek with her lashes in a butterfly kiss and felt that delicate tickling flutter on her own skin across a distance of many years.

The thoughts she had tried to lock away, ever since the day Nicky had told her what he knew of her mother's death, began to resurface and she started to wonder exactly what had happened to that loving presence and why it had left her life so violently and suddenly. She was shocked by the startling ways she was recalling her loss: a violent thrust of pain in her stomach when her children smiled at her and lifted their arms to her, or a sudden desire to weep when she kissed them.

She needed to know more.

'Your father will never tell you,' Nicky said, when she told him how she felt.

'I know. But there is someone else who might help me.'

Nicky looked surprised. 'Really?'

'I told you that my aunt Felicity came to look after me when my mother died – she told me it was brain fever that killed her. She often came to stay to mind me during the school holidays until I was old enough to look after myself, or I went to stay at her cottage. We were never exactly close but she was kind to me in her way. I think she was fond of me.'

'And you think she can help?'

Alexandra nodded. She held Elaine clasped to her chest where she had fallen asleep. Her dark hair was longer now, and she had a definite look of Alex in the shape of her eyes and the bow of her lips. 'She's the only one left who can.'

'Then you must invite her to stay,' Nicky declared.

'No, no. I don't want her overwhelmed and besides, she's getting on. I'll go to her. I'll take the baby.'

She wanted to act while she still had the conviction it was the right thing to do, so she sat down and wrote the same afternoon.

*

'Come in, my dear, come in.'

Aunt Felicity looked much older than Alexandra had remembered: her hair was still thick but now completely iron-grey, and her face had the soft crinkled texture of scrunched crêpe paper. She gazed down through her glasses at Elaine, who was clutching at Alexandra's hand and trying to balance on two tiny feet. She had recently refused to be put in her pram any longer, insisting on walking despite the fact that she was barely able to yet. 'Now, who is this lovely little thing?'

'My daughter, Elaine,' Alexandra said proudly.

'Of course. You wrote to me with news of her arrival. She's beautiful. Such lovely hair. Let's get you both inside.'

She followed her in, feeling how strange it was to be back in Aunt Felicity's cottage after so long away. Alexandra had last been here as a girl and now she was twice married and a mother, but nothing inside had changed a bit. They sat and drank tea, talking politely of everyday things and watching Elaine play. At last Aunt Felicity fixed her with a steady gaze.

'Now, Alexandra, tell me why you've come to visit me after so long. Naturally I've heard that your life has been quite eventful since I saw you last. It must be five years since your marriage – your first marriage, I mean.'

Alexandra flushed slightly, reaching to stop Elaine from pulling some volumes out of a small bookcase before she answered. 'Yes. You're right. I should have visited before now.'

'Think nothing of it,' Aunt Felicity replied. 'I'm quite happy in my own company and I can't pretend that I am close to my brother. He is not an easy man, as you know. I haven't been to the Old Grange for quite a while.' Her usually composed features slipped into sadness for a moment and she said, 'Gerald was not a natural father, I know that. You had to bear a lot. I often prayed for you, if it's any comfort.'

Alexandra was astonished to hear her aunt talk so frankly. They had never had such openness between them before and she hastened to grasp it. 'He always seemed so angry with me, but I never knew why. Now, after what happened with Laurence and Nicky, he wants nothing to do with me.'

'I knew that marriage was a mistake,' said her aunt, shaking her head sadly. 'I should have done more to stop it. I didn't perhaps realise to what extent your father had arranged it. You must be patient, Alexandra. Eventually he will come to accept that what happened was for the best, in terms of your leaving Laurence. You are happy now with your beautiful children.'

'But Laurence is dead and I think Father blames me for it.'

'He is angry that things didn't work out as he wanted and he is no doubt sorry for whatever part he played in it. But I'm sure he doesn't blame you for the accident.'

'But it means I can't ask him what I need to know,' Alexandra persisted, worried that at any moment her aunt would stop being so candid. 'And that's why I've come to you. Because I thought you might be able to tell me about my mother.' The words began to come out in a rush. 'You see, I find I'm thinking of her more and more but I have so few memories of her. I don't really know what happened.'

Aunt Felicity sat back in her armchair, her expression serious. 'I can guess that Gerald has never spoken to you about it. I can't say I'm surprised. My brother is not an emotional man. That is to say, he has never understood sentiment and I think it is probably fair to say that he certainly never understood women. He's not really a man who should have married but once he did, he had very fixed ideas about what a marriage should be. I'm afraid that your mother was not a woman who could easily live with what he demanded.'

Alexandra stared back, desperate to absorb every vital word. Here she was, at last, on the brink of a revelation. Someone was going to tell her something, finally, that would explain the darkness of her childhood and the mysteries that had always surrounded it. If Nicky was right, and her mother had done that awful thing, then perhaps Felicity could tell her why.

Aunt Felicity said, with a touch of her old stiffness, 'You're very like your mother, Alexandra. Tender-hearted with paper-thin skin. All your emotions, your heart, are close to the surface. You are so easy to hurt, Alexandra, just like she was. Those raw feelings of yours . . . sometimes I think they're a curse rather than a blessing. You experience life in such a heightened way that it's almost too much for you at times. Your father doesn't understand such things. He thinks you can learn to control your emotions, and should be forced to be tougher and stronger. He doesn't realise how easy it is to break someone who has so little protection, so little between them and the outside world. The truth is, he sees it as feminine weakness and he hates it.'

'Is that how he felt about my mother?' whispered Alexandra. Elaine had sat down on her plump nappied bottom and was playing with some wooden carved figures she'd found on a low table. She babbled to herself as she thumped them on the floor.

Aunt Felicity watched her as she spoke. 'Yes, I think so. He was infuriated by her. He couldn't love her in the way she needed him to, and I'm afraid it made her very ill. I don't know if I could say that it killed her but her unhappiness made her very vulnerable. I'm afraid that she did not have the strength to fight when the illness came.'

Alexandra stared straight into her aunt's eyes and said bluntly, 'Nicky told me that he heard she killed herself.'

Felicity drew in a sharp breath and the look in her eyes told Alexandra that she was right. Her aunt said quickly, 'Her mind was disturbed, Alexandra, you must believe that.'

'You said she had a brain fever.' It came out in an accusing tone. 'How can I believe anything you tell me?'

'I meant it metaphorically, to make it easier for you to accept. She was not herself. She was in the grip of something terrible. Nothing else would have made her do it.'

'She jumped from the old folly, didn't she?'

Her aunt looked away, unable to meet Alexandra's gaze.

Alexandra felt tears prick her eyes. She reached down and scooped up Elaine, pulling her soft, sweet-smelling warmth onto her lap, resting her cheek against the little girl's silky hair. 'Why?' she asked, in a whisper. 'Why did she do it?'

'That I can't say.'

'Can't – or won't?'

'Can't. I don't know, Alexandra. No one does. I don't believe your father knows why either. But she caused him great shame and he found that very difficult to forgive. It was hidden from you, to protect you from that shame.'

'Did he drive her to it?' asked Alexandra, her voice raw with the need to know the truth.

Felicity closed her eyes for a moment and when she opened them again, her old coolness was back. 'I would not presume to judge,' she said, 'and neither should you. You must forget it and hope that one day you and your father will be reconciled. That's the only way. Now, let's talk of something else.'

Chapter Twenty-Three

Present day

Whenever Delilah thought about her husband, it was with a rush of misery. After their row, he had slept the night on the sofa in the snug and had avoided her ever since. What was happening to them? Were they falling apart?

She wondered if he had seen her in Ben's arms. It had only been for a moment but she could feel it now if she closed her eyes and conjured up the sensation of his strong embrace, the warmth of his chest and the sweet aroma that came from him. Then he had let her go. He'd asked her why she was crying and they'd spent a pleasant half an hour chatting about the camellias before she'd gone back into the house, but she sensed that there was a growing alliance between them against John. What was awful was that now she wanted it.

For the first time, she wondered if her marriage had been a mistake. John had been so awful to her lately and it seemed that despite all her efforts and all her love, her marriage was crumbling. The thought filled her with a deep sadness.

Can I still save it? she wondered. *Do I have the strength? Can I fix him?*

But, more than that, she wondered if she still wanted to.

Outside, the weather was murkier than it had been for the last few days, with heavy whitish-grey clouds pressing down on them, and Delilah had to get away for a while to clear her head. She drove to town, ostensibly to do some shopping and have a coffee somewhere, but she asked in a cafe for directions to the local library and went there instead.

Inside, she asked how to go about doing local research. A friendly lady in rimless spectacles showed her to the computers and the reference section.

'If you're looking for local papers further back than the last ten years, I'm afraid we haven't yet got all the records on the computer,' she said apologetically, taking Delilah to the microfiche system and a stack of folders that contained copies of local newspapers. 'We will be doing it eventually but it takes time, so this is all we've got till then.'

'Of course. Please don't worry. I'm sure I'll manage.'

Left to herself, Delilah took the folder marked with the year she was interested in, and started looking through the old newspaper editions. Each had been photographed and then turned into a kind of negative that only became visible when put on a light box. It was slow work and she began to wonder if she was wasting her time. After all, she didn't know for sure whether what she wanted would even have been in the local paper. She was tempted to start picking out films at random to illuminate but she resisted. If she did that, no doubt she'd skip the one she wanted. So she kept ploughing on, one after the other, scanning the headlines for anything that seemed relevant to her search. The hands of the clock were ticking around to library closing time when she suddenly found what she had been looking for.

'Bingo!' she said as she read the headline. She increased the size so that she could read more easily. *Inquest hears of tragic death in Dursford Reservoir*.

The article reported that, just as Mrs Urquhart had said, a Lieutenant Laurence Sykes had driven off Dursford Bridge in his car and drowned in the reservoir. His car had not appeared to have a fault and his blood had been free of alcohol or any other dangerous substances. He had been briefly at Fort Stirling that evening, visiting his estranged wife, Mrs Alexandra Sykes, but the footman there reported that the lieutenant had been normal when he'd left. A verdict of death through careless driving was recorded.

Delilah sat back, rubbing her eyes. She felt as though she had been staring at the light box for hours and the outline of her vision was blurred.

But she had wasted her time. There was hardly any mention of Alex. It was exactly as Grace Urquhart had said – but had she ever doubted her? What reason would anyone have to make up that story?

It had been so strange that another piece of the jigsaw puzzle should fall into her lap like that, filling out her image of Alex a little further, helping her see a flesh-and-blood person instead of the flatness of the photographs. Alex looked so young in the pictures Delilah had found, it seemed extraordinary that she'd been married twice. She must have been practically a child when she married Laurence Sykes. What had happened to make her run off with John's father? Unless she had been the kind of woman to marry for the house and the title. She wouldn't have been the first.

But Delilah couldn't think it of her. Not when she recalled her wide blue eyes with their childlike vulnerability. 'The beauteous Alex' was how she'd been described in the visitors' book, and Delilah felt it was true – she'd been a gentle spirit. So why had she taken such a terrible step? The first husband had died tragically, but years before Alexandra, so Delilah couldn't see that the two events could be connected.

Her imagination began supplying stories for Alex: her husband was unfaithful, he had hundreds of affairs under her nose and she couldn't stand it . . . Or some of the guests brought hallucinogenic drugs to their parties and persuaded Alex to try some, and under the influence she attempted to fly from the top of the folly . . . Or . . .

None of them quite worked. None were convincing.

She felt restless, her curiosity unassuaged, and turned back to the microfiche with the sudden thought that there might be a local report of Alexandra's wedding. She decided to start looking from the month after Laurence Sykes' death – surely they would not have married sooner than that – but throughout the next few months there was nothing about the Stirlings at all. She realised that the library was closing in a few minutes so she broke her rule and skipped forward a year. Then, at last, she saw something. It was a tiny piece but it said that Lady Northmoor had attended a coffee morning in aid of the village hall, accompanied by her one-year-old son, the Hon. John Stirling, who had charmed everyone. There was a grainy picture that was almost impossible to make out but it seemed to be a woman holding a baby.

'How annoying,' she said out loud. She wanted to see Alex with little John.

'I'm so sorry but we're closing.' The librarian was back, a sympathetic but firm expression on her face. 'You'll have to finish there today.'

'Okay. Thanks. It's been really useful,' she said, switching off the light box and returning the film to the folder. 'I'll be back.'

'Good. We're happy to help.'

It was only in the car on the way home that it occurred to her that she should not have spent her time looking for the evidence of Laurence Sykes' existence. She should have skipped forward in time and looked at 1974, to search for anything she could find about Alexandra's death. She felt cross with herself. She'd let her encounter with Grace Urquhart divert her from discovering what she really wanted to know.

I'll come back as soon as I can and look again, she promised herself.

When she got home, she felt hot and sticky. A headache pounded behind her eyes, brought on from peering into the white light and reading blurred text. She went upstairs and got changed into her bikini, slipped a loose Indian tunic over the top, scooped up a towel and strolled down to the pool. Its unheated waters usually looked icy and uninviting but today the cool sparkle of turquoise looked refreshing. She took off the tunic and plunged in, relishing the shock of cold that juddered her body and made her heart pound. She swam strong and hard for several lengths, revelling in the feeling of being shut off from the world in her own private place, concentrating on pushing through the water and breathing at the right time. After twenty minutes' hard swimming, she came to halt, holding on to the grainy concrete edge of the old pool and wiping water out of her eyes.

'You're a good swimmer.'

She looked up. Ben was there, smiling down at her.

'Oh – thanks! I'm all right, a bit out of practice.' She felt vulnerable in the water, barely dressed, while he stood there looking. 'I'm going to get out now, I think.'

She swam to the shallow end and climbed up the steps. Ben had come round and was waiting for her, holding out her towel. As she emerged, dripping, from the water, he opened the towel to wrap round her and said, 'Let me.' The next moment he'd enveloped her in it and his strong arms were closing around her. She could feel his body close to hers, and the sensation of her naked wet flesh so near him sent a tingling bolt right through her. He began to rub gently, drying her arms and back. It gave her a feeling of uncomfortable pleasure, a physical enjoyment that her mind could not bear.

'Ben,' she said in a half whisper that seemed to break over his name.

'I'm right here,' he said softly.

He was, she knew that. It was part of the problem. Easy, attractive, pleasant . . . he was always there to remind her how life could be away from the storms and difficulties of her marriage. But she wasn't ready to give up on John yet, even if the desire to surrender to Ben's arms was growing with every moment. The atmosphere between them had changed to something unmistakeable: the way he was so close to her, the way he was touching her. This was no act of pure friendship. There was nothing cousinly in it. A crackling tension surrounded them. She didn't know what to say, but only felt dimly that she needed to cling on to reason and not give in to what her body was telling her she wanted.

'Delilah—' he said in a low voice.

She put up a hand to stop him. 'Don't,' she said pleadingly.

'You must have guessed—'

'Ben, I mean it,' she said, more strongly. 'Please don't say anything – not yet. Not something we might both regret.' She looked up and saw the expression in his eyes. It made something inside her tighten and a line of electricity course down her spine and into her fingertips.

He looked agonised, as though it was taking all his strength to obey her command not to speak.

'I have to go now,' she said breathlessly, and pulled out of his arms.

He put out a hand to her, his fingers landing on her upper arm, and she stopped, her back to him. 'Wait, Delilah, I have to tell you how I feel, ask you if there's any chance that we might—'

'Ben, please, no . . . I can't . . . Not yet. Please understand.'

She began to pad quickly away across the hot terrace, leaving a trail of dark splashes behind her.

'I'll wait for you,' he called after her. 'As long it takes. Until you're ready.'

She didn't reply but hurried to the back door, her towel pulled close around her and her head down to hide the confusion on her face. In the kitchen, Janey was cooking but Delilah did not stop to talk to her. She needed to be alone.

Chapter Twenty-Four

1974

'Mummy, Mummy, watch me!'

Alexandra looked up, half paying attention. Elaine was on her bicycle, cycling over the uneven paving stones of the terrace. She was approaching it with gusto, pedalling hard despite the way she wobbled. Her dark blue eyes stared intently at the ground, her tongue sticking out with the effort of keeping upright.

'Be careful, darling. Don't forget the brakes,' she called as Elaine careered towards the stone balustrade, looking as though she would slam straight into it. Alexandra knew she wouldn't. Elaine was fearless whether she was climbing trees or swinging on ropes, and somehow always managed to emerge unscathed from her intrepid adventures. She had only recently learned to ride the pink bike she'd been given for her birthday and had refused her stabilisers from the start, determined to ride like a big girl. She was already riding well but the fact that her feet didn't quite reach the ground meant that her stopping was a little erratic.

Alexandra turned back to the letter she was reading. It

was from John and she found the whole thing pierced her heart.

I am feeling very miserable and I wish I was at home with
you and Daddy. Please can I come home, please, please?
I will be good, I promise.

She could hardly bear to read the messy print on the paper he'd torn out of an exercise book. She hadn't wanted him to go away to school but Nicky had insisted. It was what was done – he had done it, his friends had done it, and now the sons of his friends were doing it and so John would do it too. The school wasn't far and she would see him twice every half-term and for all of the holidays.

'But he's only seven!' she had pleaded. 'I'm not ready for him to go yet, he's just a baby.'

'He'll have a marvellous time,' Nicky had said, shrugging. 'There'll be hundreds of other boys just like him, games to play, tuck to eat, plenty to keep him busy. It's a little hard at first but I know very well that you soon get used to it. It'll make him grow up a bit – he'll only get babyish if he stays here with you and Elaine.'

She had tried to make him put it off even for a year but he was immoveable. He might be a loving father but he knew how things were done and this was John's fate.

Seeing her little boy in his school uniform, looking desperately small and frightened beside his huge trunk, had been almost too much to endure. When they had left him in his new boarding house and driven away down the drive, his huge tear-filled eyes staring after them, she hadn't been able to stop herself breaking down and sobbing all the way home. It went against something inside her to be separated from John like this. Thinking of him wrenched something within her with enormous pain, not only because she missed him but because she felt she had let him down somehow and not protected him when she should have.

Nicky tolerated her mood for the first few days but he quickly grew impatient as it showed no signs of abating. Eventually he lost his temper.

'I've had enough of this stupid moping!' he yelled. 'We all make sacrifices, we all suffer! We just have to grit our teeth and get on with it. Do you think I wanted to give up everything I had and come here? I didn't have a choice, I just did it.'

'What did you give up?' she asked, incredulous.

'My career in photography,' he shot back.

'But . . . you got *this*.' She waved an arm at the house and towards the window where the green parkland stretched away. 'And you've got me and the children. Aren't we enough?'

He gave her a scornful look. 'You don't understand,' he said. 'There was more to my life than this once.'

'Then why do you have to make John suffer in the same way you did? Why can't he be free of it all?'

'Because he can't,' Nicky replied. 'It was his bad luck to be born to it, just as it was mine, and that means he has to do what I did. That's all there is to it.'

*

It was their first real rift since they'd been married and Alex-andra was made quite desperate by the sense that she and Nicky were growing apart. They'd been so happy since the children had come along – at least, she thought they had. Had he really been yearning for the city life, and all the girls, and his old studio in London? Had their happiness been an illusion? It seemed particularly terrible that they were at odds over one of the people they treasured most in the world.

Elaine wouldn't be sent away, Alex was determined about that. At least there was no tradition that girls had to leave home so young. She would go to the local school with all the other children, leave in the morning and come home to her mother in the afternoon. If at some later date she wanted to go to boarding school, that would be considered, but not when she was so little. She kept Elaine close to her, as though the little girl could numb the pain of being away from John, but she always felt his absence keenly.

Gradually the chill between her and Nicky began to ease off and they moved back towards each other, both having missed the intimate companionship they usually shared. He started to make love to her more than he had for a while, seeking her out in the darkness, his hand creeping warm and smooth to her soft breast and then his lips finding hers. She surrendered to it gratefully, taking comfort from his body and the strength of his embrace. She knew that he was trying to give her another baby. Perhaps that would help – if there were another and another and another to replace the ones he sent away. But there was no sign of a baby yet.

When John came home for the holidays, she raced out to

meet the car that had collected him, her arms open wide. He came running to her, his cap flying off onto the gravel, and jumped into her embrace. She kissed him, laughing joyfully, but he felt different: bonier and longer somehow. The texture of his hair was just a little coarser under her lips and in his eyes there was something else besides excitement and joy at seeing her again. There was a look of experience she had never seen before and, more than that, she thought she saw reproach. But when she asked if he was unhappy, he said airily, 'Oh no, I like school very much. I can't wait to go back actually.'

She ought to have been glad and yet she wondered what he'd endured alone to get through the misery those plaintive little letters had been drenched with.

'Nanny, where's Elaine?'

Alexandra came striding into the hallway where she had heard Elaine's voice only a few minutes before.

'She's gone out to ride her bike, ma'am,' Nanny said, pulling on her coat. 'She hurried off when I said she could, went round to the garages to get it. I'm just going out after her.'

'Make sure she keeps warm, won't you?' Alexandra reached for her own coat. 'I'm driving into the village. I don't know how long I'll be. Perhaps I'll be back for lunch. Will you make sure Elaine has the chicken? I'm sure she's not quite over that cold yet and I do want her to get her strength back.' She stopped and looked at Nanny. 'In fact, I'm not sure she should be out at all. A quiet day in the nursery might be better.'

'Now, ma'am,' said Nanny soothingly, pulling on a pair of gloves, 'a bit of fresh air will do her good. I'll keep her well wrapped up – she's in her purple coat. Some exercise for an hour or so, and then we'll go back in for lunch and she can play with that new doll of hers she's so crazy about.'

'Oh, yes. That. All right. But if she seems too cold, do bring her in.' She looked about her in distraction for the car keys, found a set in the Chinese bowl on the side table and hurried outside. As she went, she checked her pocket for the letter that had come that morning from Aunt Felicity.

Dear Alexandra

    I know your father would not want me to write but I feel I must. I cannot believe he really means what he says when he claims that he does not wish to see you again although that is what he has said over the years whenever I've talked to him on the subject. You are his only daughter and I had hoped he would eventually relent but I am afraid that he is now gravely ill and time is running out. My dear, write to him, request a meeting. Ask if you can make your peace before the end comes. Surely by now he must see that your life has been a success, with your happy marriage and your children. I hope that the old anger will fade with the nearness of the fate we all face.

    Please let me know what you decide to do.

    Your loving aunt

        Felicity

She had read it and barely stopped to think. Her father was ill, dying, and she must go to him. He must want her and need her now, as the end approached. For seven years they had lived in close proximity and never once had she laid eyes on him or heard from him since his last letter. Her Christmas cards were returned unopened. He had never been to the house, attended the christenings of his grandchildren, or even seen them. Invitations were not replied to – perhaps they burned away to ashes in the grate moments after they were received.

She felt that in some way she deserved this punishment of being cast out. She had sinned after all, deserting her husband and living with another man. But after seven years, had she not proved herself again? She was respectable now, a wife and mother, the chatelaine of Fort Stirling. Surely if she could just see him again, speak to him for a moment, his heart would melt and they would be reconciled. Besides, how could she live with herself knowing that her father was a couple of miles away dying in his bed and she had not been there? Her conscience would not allow it.

She got quickly into the car and roared off across the gravel, heading for the village. Five minutes later, she pulled the car to a halt in front of the Old Grange. Her loud knock on the door was answered by a maid she didn't know.

'Yes, m'm?' the girl asked, looking blankly at Alexandra.

She was struck by the awfulness of not being recognised at her own father's house. She had expected Emily to answer her knock. 'I'm here to see . . . Mr Crewe,' she said, trying to sound commanding.

'I'm afraid Mr Crewe is indisposed and not receiving visitors,' the girl said, reciting her sentence in a sing-song way as it had been taught to her. 'But may I say who's called?'

'I'm Lady Northmoor,' she said crisply.

'Oh.' The girl's eyes stretched wide and she bobbed a curtsey. 'Yes, your ladyship.'

'I'd like to come in. I know Mr Crewe. He won't mind.'

The girl stared at her, obviously caught between the obligation to obey a real lady and the instructions that had been laid down for her.

'Now, don't be so frightened. I'll explain the situation if anyone complains. Please let me in.' Alexandra stepped forward and the girl was too timid to stand in her way. The next moment she was in the hallway, surrounded by the familiar blue flowery wallpaper, looking into the round mirror over the hall table with everything just the same.

'Mr Crewe's in bed, your ladyship,' the girl ventured. 'And the doctor's with him at the moment.'

'I see. Well, I'll wait for the doctor. You can take my coat.' She slipped off her coat and handed it to the girl. Just then she heard a door close on the upstairs landing and the familiar figure of the village doctor came into view. He seemed lost in thought as he came downstairs but looked up to see Alexandra standing in the hall as he reached the ground floor. He knew her well from his visits to the house to see the children.

'Oh, Lady Northmoor! I'm glad to see you here. I was just about to write to you as it happens.'

She hurried forward, her expression imploring. 'How is he, Doctor Simpson?'

'Not well, I'm afraid. He's very ill, in fact.'

'What's wrong with him?'

'He's been suffering aches and pains for a while now but we couldn't ascertain the cause. He began to lose weight very rapidly and I suspected that cancer of some sort might be to blame – in a site that meant it remained well hidden until it had progressed too far for any change of treatment.'

Alexandra gasped. Cancer. That meant little chance of recovery. It was a death sentence, she knew that. 'How long has he got?'

The doctor looked grave. 'Not very long at all, I'm afraid, which is why I was on the point of writing to you. I know you and your father are estranged but now . . .'

'Of course, of course.' She bit her lip, fighting back the desire to start explaining everything to the doctor. 'I'd like to see him.'

'He was awake when I left him. He should be capable of speaking to you, though he's in some pain. I've given him morphine but the effects are diminishing as the disease takes its toll. I'm very sorry to have to tell you such bleak news but I see little hope of anything but a short time remaining to him.'

'I see.' She tried not to show that her mouth was trembling or that she felt dizzy and overwhelmed. She realised that she had assumed her father would one day send for her. Now it was obvious that day would never come. She must go to him without being summoned. 'I'm going up to him now.'

'Good.' The doctor smiled. 'I'm sure he will like that.'

You know nothing about it, she thought, as she ascended the stairs.

The last time she had been in this house was her wedding day. She'd run up these stairs in her torn dress, away from Laurence's brother and into her room, panicked and wondering what she had done. That girl was long gone now.

She walked along the hall to the door of her father's room and knocked quietly, gathering her strength. She was afraid but she had to face her fears and do what she knew to be right. A female voice said, 'Come in,' and she entered to see Emily standing at her father's bedside.

The bed was covered in blankets despite the warmth of the room and on the pillows her father's head rested, looking quite different to her last memory of him: he was shrunken and grey, his hair wispy and his cheeks hollow. His eyes were open but only just, flickering slightly with the rise and fall of his chest and the thick rattling breath that came from him. The sight filled her with desperate sadness and pity.

Emily said quietly, 'It's good to see you, miss. I'm only sorry it's in these circumstances is all.'

'Thank you, Emily.' She managed to force a smile. 'I'm glad to see you too. How are you?'

'Oh, don't worry about me. I know it's your father you've come for.' She beckoned Alexandra closer.

She walked tentatively towards the bed. 'Is he asleep?'

'No, I don't think so. He's tired out, though. He's not talking all that much now. Conserving his strength, I should think.' Emily looked down mournfully at the old head on the pillow.

'May I have a few minutes alone with him?'

'Of course. I'll wait outside. You can call if you need me.' Emily went to the door and left quickly.

Alexandra walked to the bedside. There was a chair there, and she sat down on it. Her father's hand, now thin and wasted with the veins raised on his purplish skin, lay on the blanket. She put her own hand out and rested it lightly on his. It felt icy under her touch, as though he was failing inch by slow inch from his fingertips back. He didn't respond but lay there, his battle for breath taking all his concentration.

She leaned forward. 'Father? It's me, Alexandra.'

There was no discernible change.

'I've come to see you, Father. Aunt Felicity wrote to tell me that you're very ill. I want us to make our peace. I'm so sorry that I disappointed you but I hope you can forgive me now.'

She waited for a response, watching the greyish face with the cracked thread veins running all over it, the purplish-grey circles under the eyes. Where had his eyebrows gone? Once they were thick and dark but now they were sparse, white and wiry. His nostrils had sunk into his nose so that it looked different now – pointed and thin. His lips were a hectic red and cracked too. She could see he was dying. So this was age and illness. This was a body collapsing in on itself, failing at last. From the first new moments of life, the howling baby with kicking limbs, all its future self a blue-print inside, through the strength and vigour of childhood

346

with its imperative to grow and become, to manhood and then to the inevitable crumbling of age, as everything begins to wither and stop, it all led to this, the end of the journey.

And what do we leave? she wondered. Only the memory of ourselves in the minds of those living. And our children, if we have them.

'Father,' she whispered. 'I'm here.'

His eyelids lifted slowly and he was staring at her, his eyes clouded and the pupils huge so that the whole iris looked black. He dragged in a breath and then spoke. 'You shouldn't have come.'

'But I wanted to, Father!' She smiled and squeezed his hand gently. 'You're so ill. I had to see you, tell you how sorry I am that we've been apart all these years when we could have been sharing so much. The children . . .'

'Your children mean nothing to me.' His voice was harsh and bitter.

She recoiled and then tried to calm herself. He was sick and perhaps not entirely himself. It would take patience and kindness but her persistence would surely triumph so that they could be reunited before he died. They would weep together and he would beg forgiveness which she would grant. Then they could both be at peace.

'Father, please. Isn't it time to forgive me? I know I was wrong and what I did was terrible, but I was very young and things have turned out well, haven't they?'

'They could not have been worse,' he spat out on his next rattle.

'But I'm married to Nicky, we're happy—'

'I gave you a chance,' he said, fixing her with his strangely distant but penetrating stare. 'I decided to forget the truth. I shut the Stirlings out of our life and brought you up as well as I could. I found you a husband who would take care of you and keep you away from them. But there wasn't any way to stop you. Something wicked in you made you seek him out.'

'Wicked? What do you mean?'

'Wicked. Disgusting. Sinful.'

'Because I left my husband for Nicky? Because I was unfaithful?'

'That was bad enough but it was far worse than that.'

She felt a terrible sense of foreboding. Her next word came out in a whisper. 'Why?'

He blinked slowly at her, the lids moving across his eyeballs as if there was not quite enough moisture for them to slide easily. 'You are like your mother, it seems. She was also unable to resist the Stirling family. She was unfaithful to me with Northmoor. They thought I would be too stupid to find out, or else too grateful for the honour done to me to mind. They reckoned without my pride. When I knew for sure, I put a stop to it but it had been going on for years. *Years.* I believe your deluded mother actually thought he might marry her. That was ridiculous, of course. But what broke everything to pieces was my discovery about you.'

She stared at him, a clammy horror crawling over her skin. 'Me?' How could she have been involved? What did she have to do with it all?

'You're not my daughter.' He said it almost with relish, as

if this was a last pleasure he would savour before he died. He said it as though he'd tried to do the right thing and keep silent but she had insisted and now he wasn't going to deny himself this last triumph, although exactly who he was triumphing over was unclear. 'You're the child of old Northmoor himself. That's right. Your husband's father. You married your half-brother.'

It felt as though a dead weight plummeted through her, taking her breath with it. A nasty sick sensation coursed through her, making her palms tingle and her stomach clench. She replayed his words several times in rapid succession, each time absorbing and then rejecting what she'd heard. 'No.'

'Yes. Yes!' A smile seemed to crack his face, making his deathly pallor even more gruesome. 'I tried to stop it but you wouldn't listen. So I let you wallow in your filth and bring those poor children into the world. Why should I care if the Stirling line poisons itself? You're all tainted now, aren't you? You've got your mother's blood. You've got her madness in you.'

She got to her feet. Her pity for him was gone. Death had not softened him or allowed him to find forgiveness or charity. She thought suddenly of all the many hours they had spent sitting together in church in their pew near the front. All those wasted hours where nothing he had heard about loving kindness had ever meant a thing to him. Instead he'd dealt this blow, this deathly blow to her, destroying her life in an instant and enjoying it too. 'You must hate me very much,' she said in a shaky whisper.

'You can't help it,' he said. 'I never hated you, I simply washed my hands of you. I hated *her*.'

She knew suddenly that this was her last chance. She would never see this man again. 'What did you do to her? What happened?'

'I knew what she intended to do, and I allowed it. I planted the idea of the folly in her mind. I led her to see that it was for the best.' He smiled a ghastly smile that filled her with such horror it was all she could do not to scream. 'I knew that eventually she would be unable to resist. And you remind me of her so much.'

Appalled, she turned and ran out, bumping heedlessly past Emily outside on the landing, hurrying down the stairs and out of the house as fast as she could, as though pursued by demons.

She climbed into her seat and felt the hysteria whirling up in her. No! No, she would not believe it. How could she and Nicky be brother and sister? It was too terrible, too awful to contemplate. It could not be true, but if it were . . . violent sickness twisted her stomach and she retched into her shaking hand.

There was a knock on the window. A face was there, a big white moon under a brown hat, staring in, concerned. 'Lady Northmoor? Are you all right?'

She stared back with frightened eyes. It was one of the local ladies, but she had forgotten her name. 'Yes, yes!' she stammered, then turned the key and pulled away into the road, driving at manic speed to get away from her father forever.

She flew the car up the hill towards Fort Stirling, hardly seeing the route. She was shaking, breathless, her head spinning. What would she say to Nicky? How could she tell him? They'd been living in the most terrible sin for years – oh God, she was going to be sick again – and she'd done those things her father had said: poisoned her family, tainted them.

Her breath came in shallow gasps as she thought of the children. What did it mean for them? The shame for them, the horror for them all . . .

The car mounted the brow of the hill, to take the gentle curve downwards to the house. It was a blur at first – a purple coat and a pink bicycle, that had toiled so hard up the long hill and was now preparing to return – but as Alexandra sailed towards it, the small fuzzy shape in front of her resolved: the little bike wobbled, the small face with dark hair whipped up by the wind became clearer, and the big eyes turned towards her, wide and trusting. Down the hill, Nanny was puffing up towards them.

There was no time to think or to move. For an instant, Alexandra was staring straight into her daughter's eyes before the car, unstoppable, ploughed forward and took the bicycle under its wheels, and its little rider with it.

Chapter Twenty-Five

Present day

Janey called Delilah to the phone mid-morning and when she picked up the handset in the hall, she was surprised to hear the vicar on the other end. He hoped he was not disturbing her.

'No, not at all,' she said. John was out all day on estate business. He had thawed enough towards her to return to their bed, but he was still remote and closed off. She had been staying inside the house, not wanting to bump into Ben. The encounter by the pool kept replaying through her mind and every time she felt a twist of heat inside her, but she wasn't sure what it meant. Sometimes it felt like guilt, or shame, and sometimes like something else that she couldn't yet admit to herself.

'I'm sorry it's taken so long to get back to you,' the vicar said in his friendly way. 'You asked me to find out about where Lady Northmoor was buried, didn't you? I mean, your husband's mother.'

'Yes, that's right.' She sat down on the chair by the telephone table, her attention caught. 'Have you found her?'

'No, I'm afraid I've drawn a blank there. I can't find any mention of her being buried. But you said 1974, didn't you? There is a different death recorded. The name is Elaine Stirling.'

Delilah gasped and went very still.

'Hello?' asked the vicar after a moment. 'Are you there?'

'Yes.' She sounded breathy with the strange excitement that now flooded her. So this was the mysterious Elaine, the one that the old viscount had mistaken her for. Who was she? Had she been a mistress of his? But the surname was the same. 'What does the record say?'

'Well, these things are very sparse, you know. It's not a medical certificate – there's no cause of death or anything like that. But it tells me that she is buried in the churchyard and I wondered if you'd like to come and see the grave.'

'Yes – I would, thank you. I can come right now, if that suits you.'

The vicar was waiting for her in the churchyard, gazing sombrely at the mouldering, lichened gravestones nearest the church. Hearing her footsteps approaching, he looked up with a smile.

'Ah, there you are. You got here jolly fast.'

'Yes – I'm keen to take a look.'

'According to the plan of the graveyard, Elaine Stirling is buried in the far corner, under the large yew tree. Let's go and take a look.'

She followed him as he led the way through the tilting gravestones. 'We don't use this graveyard any more,' he explained as they went. 'I'm glad – it's hard to care for these places: grass to cut, graves to maintain and so on. But there were burials here into the seventies – though most recently it tended to be ashes rather than coffins. There's a big crematorium and graveyard over at Holly Park – that's where most people go these days.'

The grass, she noticed, was particularly lush and green, and she wondered if it was anything to do with the rich source of rot that must have seeped into the soil. Just as she was banishing that picture from her mind, she realised that the vicar had stopped and was kneeling down to look in the long grass around the yew tree. He pulled away some growth and, after a moment, said, 'Hello, I think this might be it.'

Delilah crouched down beside him, aware of the tickling grass on her bare skin, and peered into the cool green gloom beneath the yew tree. There was a small stone set into the ground topped with a tiny marble urn with a sieve-like covering with holes for flower stems. On the gravestone was engraved writing and she leaned closer to read it.

'Elaine Stirling,' she read. '1969–1974. Oh my goodness, she was only five! Oh no, that's awful. Look, there's a line of poetry here. "In one of the stars I shall be living."' Her eyes filled with tears and her throat felt tight. Was there anything sadder than the death of a child? 'What happened to her?'

The vicar looked solemn as he gazed at the tiny grave. 'Poor child. And poor parents. How odd that she should die in 1974, the same year you thought Lady Northmoor died.'

She lifted her head to him, staring but hardly seeing him.

'Wait. You're right. Lady Northmoor died the same year.'

'You said there was a possibility that she killed herself. Well, here is a likely motive, don't you think? Her daughter died at only five years old. Who knows what she suffered?'

Delilah half heard him but there were thoughts whirling around her head as well. Suddenly she saw the doll she had tucked away in her drawer at home, the pink ballet-dancing doll hidden in the playroom all this time. The child was born two years after John. She was dead when he was seven. She had to be his sister. There was surely no one else she could be.

Oh my God – Alex lost a child. She lost her daughter. So that's it. That's why she did it.

The realisation came over her and she felt absolute certainty. But there was still a puzzle.

How could Alex leave John? How can anyone compound the loss of one by leaving the other? It didn't make sense, unless she was ill or out of her mind with grief.

She clambered to her feet. 'Thank you, Vicar, I must go now.'

'Are you all right? You look rather pale. I'm sorry, I forgot that this little girl must be a family member.'

Something occurred to her. 'I don't want to take up too much of your time, but won't the christenings be recorded? Is it possible to look at the records of those?'

'Yes . . . it shouldn't be too difficult. Come and we'll do it now. I don't think you look as though you could wait.'

As she drove home Delilah tried to absorb the things she had learned. She knew now that Elaine Stirling was the second child of Nicky and Alexandra – her christening was in the record – and that she had died at the age of five. After that, there was nothing. No record of Alexandra's burial and no further events in the family until John's wedding to Vanna in 1997.

John had a sister he's never mentioned, she thought. *There are no photographs in the house. Nothing. It's as though she never existed. Why would he hide such a thing from me? I don't understand it.*

She had a sudden recollection of John saying that his family did not breed many girls. How could he say that when he knew that there'd been a daughter – his own sister?

But, she reminded herself, there was no saying how childhood trauma might express itself. If the family had gone through the horror of losing the little girl and then the mother in just a few months, perhaps they had coped by wiping out all the memories of the child and never speaking of either her or Alexandra. It was the only explanation she could think of.

'Alex,' she whispered out loud. Her mind filled with an image of the other woman, distraught, weeping, wailing, perhaps screaming and tearing her hair. She was running, in hysterical tears, towards the folly. She was in the grip of madness. 'Why did you do it? But my God, you must have suffered.'

At home she scanned the family photographs again, looking for new clues, trying to seek out the little girl she now knew had existed. Would she see things she had missed before? She walked through the bedrooms upstairs and stood for a long time in the nursery, gazing at the rocking horse and imagining a child riding it happily and playing with her doll on the rug by the fire. She could see nothing. The years must have erased her absolutely. Perhaps the doll had been the only thing left to find. Except there was still the attic, with its mass of jumble. Something in there might prove that there had once been another child here.

She shook her head, frustrated. What proof did she need? She had the proof – it was in the churchyard under the yew tree and it was printed in the church records. What she did not know was why. She was afraid to ask John. She did not even know if she dared to tell him of her discovery. He hated and feared the past, and she was frightened of how he might react.

John returned that evening, calmer after a long day, tired out and less agitated than he had been recently. They chatted a little over dinner and Delilah tried to keep the conversation light, but her mind was so full of what she had discovered, she could hardly think of anything else. She had planned to wait and see how things were between them before she spoke of it all, but now she realised that it would be impossible to keep back what she knew. Besides, she didn't want there to be more secrets, and she couldn't start by keeping them herself.

'John,' she said tentatively, putting down her fork. She caught his eye, then quailed a little, looking down and stroking the wood of the table. Girding herself mentally, she went on. 'I found something out today and I really want to ask you about it.'

'Oh?' An apprehensive air enveloped him at once. 'What?'

'You remember how your father once asked me if I was called Elaine? Well, there's such an odd coincidence. The vicar mentioned a grave to me and we went to look at it in the churchyard. It's got the name Elaine carved on it. Elaine Stirling. But she died when she was only five years old. Do you know who she was?'

John stared down at his hands, blinking. Then he looked up at her again, clearing his throat. 'Yes. That's my sister. She died in an accident.'

'I'm so sorry. I had no idea. You've never mentioned her,' she said carefully, trying to keep any note of accusation out of her voice. 'Not even when I told you that your father called me Elaine.'

He took a deep breath and released it slowly. 'You're right,' he said. He stared over her shoulder at something on the counter behind. 'I should have said something. But . . . it's hard to explain. Elaine has never been talked about. Ever. You can't understand what her death did to us. I went away to prep school one term and when I got back they were gone: Elaine. And my mother. Just like that. I'd left my family alive and happy and when I returned, there was only my father left. And we were not to talk about the others. It was as though they'd never existed. I had no idea why it had happened – and I missed them so terribly.'

She put a hand out to him, full of pity for what he'd been through. 'That's so awful, John. I'm sorry.'

'I do find it hard to speak about.' He managed a wry smile as he met her gaze for a moment. 'I suppose you've noticed that.'

'Can you talk to me about it, just a little? I'd like to know what happened.'

He seemed to pull on some inner reserve of strength and took a deep breath. 'All right. I know you deserve that. I do remember Elaine, but in odd little flashes: a baby in a pram, a child on a swing, us running down the hall together. I remember her crying one day – I think I'd pushed her off the rocking horse. I have a mental picture of her sitting on the hall floor with some dolls around her, and us opening our stockings in the nursery at Christmas. That's about it. She was sweet, but I suspect most five-year-olds are: angelic, you know, with soft hair and big eyes.' He paused and his lips tightened, then he went on. 'She was killed in a car accident – a hit and run, some rogue driver speeding along the country roads – and not long afterwards, in an agony of grief, I suppose . . . my mother . . . she . . .' He broke off, closing his eyes and biting his lip.

'She killed herself,' ventured Delilah quietly.

His eyes opened. 'You know about that?'

'A few things fit together, that's all. It makes sense.'

John twisted his fingers around each other, watching them intently as he did so. He seemed suddenly lost in his own thoughts and murmured in a low, strained voice, 'I can't understand how she could leave me. She must have loved Elaine very much. I wasn't enough to keep her here.'

'I'm so sorry,' Delilah said, her voice still soft and

comforting. 'I should have guessed there was something strange about that folly when you reacted to it in that way.'

'The folly . . .' He closed his eyes again and shook his head. 'That wretched folly. So that's how you worked it out.'

She nodded.

He stared back down at the table. 'I ought to have told you.'

'It's all out in the open now, though, isn't it?' She felt a sudden surge of hope. They could mend it all now, and start afresh. The old John would come back, the man she'd fallen in love with. 'I mean – I know about Elaine and about how your mother died. You don't have to hide anything from me anymore. There's no need to be afraid.' She got up and went over to him, wrapping her arms around his shoulders. 'You poor boy. You've had a terrible time. I want to help you. I can make it better, I promise.'

He let her hug him, but he was unable to relax into her arms. She longed for him to turn and hug her back and tell her that it was going to be all right now, and that he wanted her to help him let go of the past and all the pain that went with it. But he remained as stiff as ever.

Chapter Twenty-Six

1974

Alexandra hadn't known it was possible to suffer such misery and to continue living. If anything could destroy her, it would be this.

She lay in bed for many days. People came, they moved around the room, whispering and sometimes talking to her. They tried to make her eat and drink. They forced her out to the bathroom and back. She let them do what they wanted. What did any of it matter now?

One day she had walked out of her house. She had had a son, a daughter, a husband. She had had a life. She'd been happy although it was only now she could see how happy. When she'd come back into that house again, everything had changed.

An awful silent scream filled her head as it did hundreds of times a day when she thought of that moment. It took all her strength to endure that terrible wail, the one no one else could hear, as it ripped through her, breaking her heart afresh every time. It thrust a picture into her mind that she feared and dreaded, one that she did not think she could bear to see again but which was constantly torturing her by whatever demons insisted on pressing it before' her eyes. 'Look at this,' they seemed to be saying. 'Look, look, look. You can't escape what you've done, look again.'

She saw over and over that instant when she'd flown over the hill, far too fast, in the grip of her terror and confusion, and seen her . . . Elaine.

'Here she is, your angel,' hissed the demons. 'She's on her little pink bike trying so hard to ride it even though her feet don't touch the ground. But here you are, in your car, shut in your deadly metal box, taking it towards her with all its crushing weight and unstoppable turning wheels. Look at the way she's wobbling, her hair whipped up in her face by the wind, her eyes wide open. Look, she's staring at you, trusting you to help her, to protect her. But you can't stop, can you?'

Then she would see the small pink and purple shape vanish beneath her bonnet, feel it beneath the wheels, hear the sickening crunch of the bicycle as it was crushed under them, then feel the lift and fall of the car as it rolled over the obstacle. Then, always, she would see Nanny, her horrified expression with her mouth open, her eyes stretched, her hands out in a desperate, helpless gesture to stop the car.

Then she would scream herself in agony, to drown out the demons and make them stop their torment, but she knew that they were inside her. She was going to spend the rest of her existence torturing herself and it was all she deserved. She had been stupid to think she could ever be happy or provide happiness. She was born under a curse, and, like the Lady of Shalott, love had brought it down on her head.

Everything was over now, she knew that. Her marriage, her motherhood . . . it was all at an end. She had no idea how she could carry on existing. Nicky came to see her, but she turned away and would not look at him or talk to him. He wept and asked her to speak. He tried to talk about their daughter and absolve her of blame, but it was no good. He didn't understand that it wasn't in his power. The sin was deeper and darker than he could ever imagine. Besides, her love for him, which had been her rock and which had always given her courage to go on, was a wicked thing now. He could no longer help her, nor she him. They must part just when they needed each other like never before.

But she couldn't tell him this. It had to be a burden she carried alone. So she refused to speak or look at him and when the nurses whispered to him that she would eventually relent, she did not say that she never would or could.

There was no day or night, just an endless ongoing despair, but they opened the curtains and revealed that it was day outside. They brought out a suit, a matching coat and dress in black wool, and made her bathe and put it on. Who were these people? They seemed to know her but she had no idea who they were. Then she was taken to the car and driven to the church. Nicky was there – she knew it was him even though he looked like a grotesque version of himself, with his faced lined and etched by grief, his eyes full of agony. They went together into the church and she heard hymns, prayers and poems and then they stood in the churchyard by the yew tree at the back, near a hole in the ground that made her dizzy with horror. They brought the little white box and as it passed her, she reached out a hand and took one of the white flowers on the top. Then she watched as they put the box into the hole – so far down in the dirty darkness – and began to cover it. She said nothing out loud but that was because she was being deafened, shaken and possessed by the vast and frightful noise within her, the howl of the Furies pursuing her. They shrieked her child's name at her, pelting her with it, demanding to know why she had decided to consign her daughter to the world of the dead, to stamp out her life and toss her into this hole.

Somewhere she knew she was going mad. But she had no strength to resist it, and anyway, what was the point of resisting? What could there be beyond this suffering but more suffering? A life of endless suffering? What was the point of anything at all?

They took her home again and put her back into the bed, leaving her alone with the voices and the torment. But she knew they would be back.

One night, a strange calm descended on her. She woke from a sleep that she knew had been torrid and full of the awful images that would never leave her. The voices were quiet at last. She had the sense of a revelation, and even though she didn't know what it was, it was like the blessing of a cool drink with a fevered thirst. She had longed for some peace so that she could think again and here it was at last. With it came a delicious numbness that enabled her at last to move and act. The pain was shut somewhere far away, as though it was confined inside a house and she had managed to climb out on the roof and get away from it, just for a while. Although, of course, she could always decide not to go back in at all.

She climbed out of bed where she now slept alone – perhaps Nicky was in the gold room down the hall – and walked over to the window. Pulling back the heavy curtain, she saw that it was a clear night, the moon like a huge gilded pendant suspended in the sky, the stars arching overhead in their constellations. She must go outside. She had a sense of things ordained, a ritual that she must carry out. It was almost as though she could hear a long-forgotten but familiar voice calling her name, summoning her, and she had no choice but to follow. She went to the bedroom door and opened it. The house was in darkness, a lamp here and there casting a shallow golden glow. She walked out into the hall.

This feeling was rather pleasant, she decided as she went downstairs. The floating sensation that made it feel as if she were so light that only holding onto the banister as she went down kept her from rising up into the air. She felt so empty, as if she were made of nothing. When she reached the large hallway beneath, she saw that the door to the estate office was open and a light shone inside. She looked in. There he was, the man she loved but could no longer live with as a wife. He was slumped on his desk, asleep on one folded arm, a half-empty bottle of whisky by his side. So that was how he was managing. He hadn't learned, as she had, that it was possible to be like this – far above every-thing and looking down upon it, untouched by the grief and despair. Of course, there was a price to pay for this freedom. It meant that certain things must be done. And they would be done.

She left the office and went to the front door. It was bolted and locked and she was too weak to use the great keys or pull back the iron bolts. She drifted instead to the back of the house. On her way, she passed a small pair of boots and remembered the boy. Where was the boy? When had she last seen him? She had no memory of that at all. He had been at school and she had not seen him since. Was he in the house? Did he ever come back from school? Had anyone told him what had happened? She felt a stab of con-cern for him, and then relaxed. What she was doing now was the best possible thing, the last act of her motherly love for him. She was setting him free to live a life without the fear and pain that she would inevitably bring him, saving him by leaving him. After all, if she could kill her precious girl, what might she do to him?

She let herself outside and began to walk. She knew exactly where she was going. There were the gates, open as usual, despite her instructions. There was the path. Once, a long time ago, someone had told her to tell Nicky to knock the folly down. She never had. It had seemed far too power-ful for that. Now she realised why it had that power over her and why she was unable to resist its siren call. It had seemed like a craggy thing, a cold, dank place of danger and destruction. But now she saw it for what it was: a gateway.

Through it, she could see the past. Through it, she would find her future. Like her mother had. Perhaps hers was the sweet voice she could hear, summoning her and promising her peace.

It was strange to be in the woods and not be afraid. Nothing could hurt her now and that gave her an almost gleeful sense of freedom. What on earth had she been so scared of all that time? It had turned out that the thing she had to be most afraid of was herself. There had been no monsters. She had been the instrument of destruction, and now she could see very plainly that she was what must be removed. Whatever dark knowledge she held would end with her.

She kept going through the darkness, careless of the undergrowth and the stony path until she came out into the clearing where the folly stood on the hill. Staring at it, she sighed. She had seen all this before and she knew her part as well as anything she had ever done in her life. It was all inevitable. There was no fear; she simply craved an end to the pain, and if there was any way to see Elaine again, to hold her in her arms and press her face into her hair, breath in her sweet scent and feel her soft skin, then this was surely it. She yearned for that more than anything, and that made all of this so easy. If there was no meeting to be had, if all there was after death was nothing, then that made it easier still.

At the entrance she paused and looked up, and then made her way inside, stepping over the dangerous spikes and fallen masonry, picking her way delicately to the broken stairs and there she found her footing, confident on the slippery boards, climbing lightly upwards towards the glowing blue night sky above. She reached the top floor of the tower and went to stand at the broken wall, looking out over the nightscape below. One more step and she would be free. A single step forward, a plummet and blackness. Peace. Sleep. Those voices would never come back.

She prepared herself, remembering that she knew exactly how this should be done. Her nightdress fluttered around her in the night breeze. She was ready.

Chapter Twenty-Seven

Present day

The night had been disturbed by John's bad dreams. Delilah woke several times to hear him panting in panic, a stifled moaning in his throat that meant he must be howling in his dreams. Her arms around him calmed him, sending him back to sleep until the next one, but she had only managed fitful rest herself. It worried her that he was still tormented by nightmares when things were now out in the open, but perhaps talking about the past had brought it all back, agitating whatever was inside his head.

Over breakfast, John was pallid and red-eyed, barely able to speak. She wondered if she looked just as bad. Eventually he glanced up from his toast and said, 'Delilah, I've been thinking. I need to get away from here for a few days. An old school friend of mine – one of the few I can still tolerate – has asked me if I want to go fishing with him. You haven't met Ralph but he's a good sort, and I think I should go. Dad's much better and estate business can wait for a while.'

'All right. It sounds fun. You need some time away from here, something to enjoy.' She smiled at him and hoped she was concealing the sting of hurt she felt. After a moment she said, 'But if you go away, you'll be missing my fertile time this month.'

He shrugged lightly. 'It's not as though we're exactly hard at it, is it? Missing one month won't matter.'

She tried not to wince. 'All right. If that's what you want.'

'I do. I think we should have a break from each other for a bit. It will be good for us.'

'When will you go?' she asked miserably. A break from her? So her hopes had been misplaced, it seemed. It wasn't a new beginning after all.

'I'll go after breakfast.'

She was startled by the suddenness. 'And when will you be back?'

'I don't know. I'll be away four days or so, I should think. We'll go up to Scotland and make a trip of it. Up in the hills with no computers, or email or phone signals. Proper peace.'

'Sounds very nice.'

He put the last piece of toast in his mouth and got up, wiping his hands and tossing his napkin on the table. 'I'll go and pack now then. I should think you'll enjoy a bit of time without me here.'

She was suddenly aware of the danger in being here alone with Ben because of the feelings that were growing between them and wanted to jump up and shout, 'Don't be so stupid, you mustn't leave me – not now!' Instead she said as breezily as she could, 'I'll keep busy, I expect.'

'Good. I'll come and say goodbye before I go.'

*

John left within half an hour, the car racing up the drive and away as though pursued by something. Delilah watched him go, depression sinking down on her. She was still staring at the empty drive when she saw a flash of red and the Royal Mail van came trundling over the horizon and down towards the house, later than usual. She went out of the front door and down the steps to meet it.

'Hello,' said the postman cheerily as he pulled to a stop in front of the house, leaving the engine running. 'Apologies for my tardiness – got held up at the depot today.' He climbed out of the van with a stack of letters bound with an elastic band and handed it over to her. He glanced at the top of the pile. 'Looks like there's one for you there,' he said.

'Thank you,' Delilah said, looking down at the long stiff white envelope, franked and stamped with the name of a company she didn't recognise.

'No worries.' The postman got back in the van and said, 'Give my regards to his lordship. Have a good day!' He drove off over the crunching gravel.

Delilah did not watch him go. Her attention was on the envelope and the name on the front. It was addressed to Lady Northmoor.

'Lady Northmoor?' she said out loud. There had been no Lady Northmoor at Fort Stirling for years. She pulled it out from under the elastic band and turned it over. There were no clues on the back and the flap remained resolutely stuck down. It was a fresh letter – it had certainly not been stuck in the postal system for forty years, like those postcards the newspapers sometimes reported had arrived at their destination decades after being sent. The black type on the front was strong and confident. This letter knew who it wanted to reach.

Delilah walked slowly inside, staring at the letter in her hand. She knew that Lord Northmoor had signed power of attorney over to John and that John was now in charge of everything. She should hand this letter over to him and ask him what it meant. But she could see him now, whisking it away, his face taking on that shut-off expression as he told her briefly that it was nothing for her to worry about, he would solve it. More secrets.

Before she could change her mind, she slid her finger under the gummed-down flap of the envelope and pulled it open. There! It was torn. There was no going back now. *Besides*, she told herself, *I suppose I'm closer to being Lady Northmoor than anyone else. There's a chance it was actually meant for me.*

She removed the crisply folded white paper within and opened it out. At once she noticed that the address of the intended recipient at the top of the letter did not match the one on the envelope. This one was a place in Greece, on the island of Patmos. The letter read:

> *Dear Lady Northmoor*
>   *This is to confirm that your annual allowance has been raised by 2 per cent to a total of £52,450. Further to instructions from your lawyer, this amount will be transferred in monthly instalments to your nominated account in Greece, with a guarantee against possible*

bank closures or currency difficulties in the eurozone.

Please do not hesitate to contact us if you have any
queries whatsoever.

It was signed off with humble best wishes by a partner of
the legal company but pp'd by a junior hand.

Delilah read it over twice, amazed. What on earth could
it mean? Except . . . was that really possible?

Her heart began pounding and dizziness swooped through
her. She leant against the wall heavily, knocking a small oil
painting of a dog askance on the wall but hardly noticing,
putting out her hand to support herself.

'Oh my God,' she breathed, hardly able to believe the
implications. 'I must be seeing things. It can't be true!'

She read the letter again, trying to see if it could apply to
herself in any way, but there was no way it could be meant
for her.

Money. An allowance. To a Lady Northmoor living in
Greece. She remembered the vault in St Stephen's where
John's grandmother lay interred. There had only been one
Lady Northmoor since. John's mother.

Can Alex be alive?

There was no other conclusion she could draw. She felt a
rush of almost joyful excitement. Alex hadn't been destroyed
by the house after all, she had *survived*. It was incredible. It
felt like waking from a nightmare to find reality was safe and
comforting in comparison. The horror that she'd thought
had taken place on top of the folly had not happened. Tears
prickled her eyes for a moment. *Alive.*

But then bewilderment came with a torrent of questions tumbling into her mind. *Alex didn't jump? She just . . . went away? To Greece? How is that possible?*

Her hands shook, and her breath came in panting gasps as adrenaline raced through her, leaving her fingertips tingling and her scalp prickling. She sank down onto a small chair, her legs unable to support her under the onslaught of emotion, staring at the letter and absorbing the implication. How and why had all this happened? Why had such a dreadful lie been allowed to take root and grow and become the truth? Who had allowed all this?

Then one awful thought pushed out all the others: *Should I tell John? Thank God he's not here . . .*

She closed her eyes, grateful she didn't have to make the decision immediately, not while she was still overwhelmed by what she had read. Before she said anything to anyone, she would have to be absolutely certain there was no mistake . . . She wondered again if she'd misread or misunderstood, but there was only one way the letter could be taken.

But I need proof, she thought, trying to gather herself. *I need more than this.*

She thought for a moment and then went to the hall table, picking up the telephone handset there with clumsy, shaking fingers. Her nervousness made her misdial the solicitors' number twice before she managed to get it to ring.

A receptionist answered.

'May I speak to Gordon Evans?' she asked, reading the typed name at the bottom of the letter.

'He's in a meeting right now. Can I put you through to someone else who can help?'

'Yes, please.' She was transferred to the tinny sound of a piano sonata, listening to her own breath down the handset until a voice spoke.

'Hello, Sarah Hargreaves speaking. How can I help you?'

Delilah looked down at the paper in her hand. 'I've received a letter today which I opened in error. It's from your company to Lady Northmoor.'

There was a pause and the woman on the other end said, 'Yes. We have recently written to Lady Northmoor. We send our correspondence to her address in Greece.'

'Well, I'm afraid in this case you've sent it to Fort Stirling, where there's been no Lady Northmoor for forty years. I'm Mrs Stirling.'

The pause was briefer this time and when the woman spoke again it was with a kind of anxious embarrassment. 'Oh my goodness, I'm so sorry. That must have been my error. Oh dear – I do apologise. Could I ask you to please destroy that letter? And would you mind not mentioning this to anyone? I could get into serious trouble.'

'I understand,' Delilah said, her voice stronger as she began to regain her equilibrium. 'But I'll need a little information in return.'

She walked out into the garden hardly seeing the riot of colour and the teeming life around her. It all seemed invisible, taking second place to the whirl inside her mind.

This letter had come in error – Sarah Hargreaves, embarrassed and rather panicked, had confirmed that. She had also confirmed that the Lady Northmoor currently living on Patmos was indeed Alexandra Stirling. It was almost too much to take in.

John can't know. I'm sure of it. She tried to recall everything that John had said about his mother, and she was certain that he had said his mother had died. No one would lie about such a thing, surely? And how could he be tormented by nightmares and so oppressed by misery if the horror of his mother's suicide was a fantasy?

Delilah shook her head in disbelief. What would Alexandra be like? She wouldn't be that sweet-faced girl in the photographs now, but an old woman. The portrait, like John's father's, had stayed the same but the subject would have withered and changed. Delilah tried to picture her with grey hair, lined skin and a slight stoop. An old lady. She remembered the solicitor's letter. An old lady who enjoyed a generous allowance.

Delilah sat down on one of the stone benches, its rough surface still warm from the afternoon sun. The excitement and bewilderment of the discovery leeched out of her and anger began to boil up in its place, as fierce as it was unexpected.

An image filled her head. It was Alex, passing her days in comfort in the sun, while her only son was left to cope with his loneliness and grief, believing his mother had killed herself.

Fury engulfed her. What kind of a mother would do that?

Of course it was tragic to lose her daughter in whatever circumstances had happened, but to abandon a small boy and his father and simply walk away? That was unforgiveable, wasn't it? It was coldly, horribly selfish. There was no excuse.

She stood up and began to pace round and round the central flowerbed, seeing nothing as a torrent of thoughts crashed into her mind. She felt absurdly betrayed, not just on John's behalf but on her own. She had pitied Alex, felt for her, empathised with her. She had almost lived the other woman's loneliness, the sense of being daunted by this place and everything that came with it. She had experienced something of her terror and been horrified by the final act, the pity and horror of what Alex had done.

Except that she hadn't done it.

'I just don't understand!' she said out loud, coming to a halt and staring out over the woods towards the old folly, hidden from view by the trees.

She wanted, above all, to make sense of all this and how her life had come to be so bound up with what happened here. Ever since she'd come to Fort Stirling, she'd been looking for answers to explain why she was in this house, trapped in its vast solitudes, powerless to change it, inside a marriage that was poisoned by the past.

She could see clearly now that to get the final answers, she would have to leave. They lay elsewhere, with the only person alive who could answer them.

PART THREE

Chapter Twenty-Eight

Present day

The huge ferry made its way through shimmering heat across the bright blue waters of the Aegean Sea. There were crowds everywhere, mostly keeping inside or under the ferry's wide awning on the top deck, though a few hardy souls – tourists, for the most part – stood out in the blazing sunshine looking ahead eagerly to where they were going.

Delilah had spent some of the seven-hour journey dozing in the air-conditioned interior, recovering from her early start, and then breakfasting on black coffee and yoghurt in the restaurant. She had arrived at daybreak, stepping out into suffocating heat at Athens airport, and from there caught a taxi to Piraeus where she'd boarded the ferry. They'd already stopped at various island ports, the great hulking vessel sailing with surprising nimbleness between islands and outcrops of land into small harbours, where it manoeuvred itself up against slender docks to disgorge passengers and take on new ones. Now, as they approached the island of Patmos, Delilah had climbed to the top deck and found a seat that faced out over the railings where she could marvel at the extraordinary vivid blue of the sea as the ferry churned through it. The breeze that came up, tangy and salty, to lash her hair and beat her cheeks was pleasant after the artificial chill inside.

She longed to arrive, and yet she was also apprehensive about what exactly she planned to do.

'I'm just going away for a few days,' she had told Janey. 'While John's on his fishing trip.'

'That sounds lovely,' Janey said, wiping up some dishes. 'Are you going somewhere nice?'

She hadn't wanted to lie but telling the truth would be dangerous, if Janey should mention it later. 'I have a friend, Helen, who lives in Italy,' she said, letting the implication do its work. Helen did live in Italy but Delilah was not going there.

'Italy – how beautiful,' sighed Janey. 'I'm envious. We had a lovely holiday there once.'

'I'm only going for a short trip. I'll probably be back before John is.'

'Enjoy yourself. It'll be good for you to get away from here.'

Janey had not known how true her words were, Delilah thought. The feeling that she ought to get away had almost been as strong as the compulsion to seek out the truth. Her body was refusing to forget the way Ben had made her feel when they'd stood so close, the atmosphere charged with electricity, and she needed some space in which to consider how she really felt about him. She was letting her reaction to

Ben put her marriage at risk. Should she fight the attraction between them? Or was her marriage foundering anyway?

'This is absolute bloody madness,' Grey had said down the phone, when she told him of her intention to go to Greece – at least one person ought to know where she really was. 'What on earth are you doing? Can you really be sure this woman is who you think she is?'

'The lawyer was clear. It's her.'

'Well, why do you have to go there? Can't you just telephone her or something?'

'I think that's an even worse idea,' she replied. 'I can just imagine how quickly she'd hang up on me.'

'Delilah,' Grey said in a worried voice, 'you should just leave all this as it is. You'll do no good meddling in it. I don't want to see you getting hurt. I know what you're like – you want to sort everything out, make everyone happy – but it could backfire.'

'I can't leave it,' she'd replied obstinately. He didn't understand – no one else could. He hadn't seen those pictures in the albums, or lived in this house with all its ghosts and echoes of the past. He hadn't known, as Delilah had, and as Alex had, what it meant to become a Stirling and belong to this huge old place. Alex understood. Finding her seemed more than simply a way to get to the bottom of a mystery; it was also forging a link that might make sense of her own life. That was why she had to go.

'What about John?' Grey persisted. 'Shouldn't you at least ask his opinion on tracking down his dead mother?'

'I can't spring a shock like that on him without seeing her

first, and knowing a bit more about why she did it. She needs to know how she's made him suffer, and explain how she could go and leave him like that, with him thinking she killed herself.'

'You don't think you're going to be able to reconcile them, do you? Tell me you're not thinking about trying something so foolish.'

'Of course not,' Delilah said, even though she had wondered if she might be able to do just that if it seemed that it might help John. 'I'm doing this because I have to know – for myself as much as for John.'

'All right.' He sighed. 'I can tell there's no stopping you. I just hope it doesn't make this whole thing worse, that's all. Keep in touch, darling. I'll come out and join you if you need me.'

She acted before she could change her mind, booking a flight, a ferry and a hotel in minutes – not cheap at such late notice in the summer, but still possible. She had left the following day, with a sense that she was at last taking control after a long time of being at the mercy of other people and places.

Now here she was, a salty rime forming on her lips, feeling the slow rocking of the ferry as it cut through the water on its way to the port of Skala, and soon she would have to decide exactly what she was going to do when she got there.

It was late afternoon by the time they arrived at last; the island stretched across the blue sea like a pair of open arms beckoning them into its bosom. As they approached, the embrace of the island grew tighter so that they seemed to be

384

surrounded by rocky hillside dotted with houses set among groves of olive trees. A mass of glittering white gradually resolved itself into the harbour town, and now she could see that the island was not one thick land mass but a delicate lace of narrow connections and small bays. In the distance, high on the horizon, a jagged edge of dark rock became the castellated border of an ancient building of brown stone that contrasted with the whites and pinks and pale yellows of the flat-roofed houses below. Around the bay were hundreds of boats, from tiny sailing vessels to vast white yachts, moored along the seafront or against rickety wooden jetties poking out into the water.

As the ferry slowed and the engine roared, throwing up white spumes of seawater, she saw that around the port were all the marks of the tourism trade: apartment blocks, hotels, tavernas, restaurants with hundreds of tables and chairs set out along the seafront, racks of mopeds and rows of taxis for hire. She felt a rush of holiday excitement despite herself. She had not known what to expect, thinking of the horror stories of Greek towns overwhelmed with drunken tourists, but this place did not seem like that. The travellers around here were mostly families and there was also a good number of nuns in their sensible plain frocks and dark head coverings. She felt a sudden yearning for John, wishing that he were here to share this new experience, to witness the beauty of the island and to set about exploring it with her.

But I'm not here for that, she reminded herself. *I've come for something else altogether.*

She gazed around at the island while down below the port

workers set about mooring the great ferry against the wharf, and prepared for disembarking the passengers. Behind a gate waited a horde of fresh travellers, ready to take the return journey overnight back to Piraeus.

Is she here? Delilah wondered. *Is Alexandra somewhere close by?* She imagined the dark-haired woman from the photographs – of course she wouldn't look like that – walking through the streets above the town, unaware that the ferry, its arrival and departure so familiar as to be almost invisible, this time had brought a messenger from the life she had left behind.

Tomorrow, she thought, *I'll set about finding her.*

Once the passengers had got out through the port gates, shunted in a different direction to the crowds waiting their turn to board, they dispersed, heading off towards hotels or hailing taxis or looking for bus stops. Delilah consulted her map. She had booked a hotel room in Chora, the main village of the island that lay to the south-west of Skala, higher up and near to the castle on the horizon, which the map told her was actually a monastery. The village had looked only a few minutes' walk from the port but now she could see that it would be quite a hike up a steep hill with her luggage, so she headed for a rank of shabby looking cars with taxi signs on their roofs.

'Chora?' she asked of the driver of the first available car. He leaned out of his open window, his eyes unreadable under his sunglasses. 'How much?'

'Chora – eight euro.'

'Fine. Thanks.' She opened the back door and climbed in, hauling her small suitcase after her. The driver started the car and, with a roar from the rattling engine, they set off through the narrow roads of Skala, expertly avoiding the milling crowds of wandering tourists searching for their holiday accommodation. Most of the buildings were whitewashed, brightened with baskets of flowers or hung with vines, and every other one was a restaurant or a taverna, with tables lining the street or set out under canopies of woven flax. Mopeds and bicycles seemed to be the preferred form of transport and the driver took their buzzing approach in his stride, skimming past bare legs and billowing shirts without so much as a squeeze on the brakes.

They left Skala, ascending the curving asphalt road lined with scrub and eucalyptus trees towards the white village above that shone where the evening sun caught it. The monastery sat strong and dark on the skyline, looking like a Byzantine fort, and at its base white boxes of large villas and houses emerged from pine forests and olive groves. Beneath the grander residences was a tumble of whitewashed roofs, bell towers and walls that marked the heart of the village.

The driver pulled to a halt by a high wall with a tangle of greenery falling over the top. 'We stop here.'

'I'm staying at Hotel Joannis,' she said, looking out of the taxi window at the narrow path curving away into the village. 'Is it close by?'

He gestured up the hill. 'You will find it up there. No taxi any more.'

'I see.' She got out and passed him ten euros. 'Thank you.'

Taking her bag, she began to walk in the direction he had indicated. Despite the late hour, the sun baked the backs of her legs and arms as she climbed. If this was what it was like in the early evening, it was going to be seriously hot the next day. Maybe this was the wrong time for a fair-skinned Welsh girl to visit Greece. Well, she'd just have to cope with that as best she could.

The town was charming, with streets, lanes and passages that were too narrow for cars. Thick walls bordered each street, houses and courtyards tucked away behind them. Although she could see many bars and tiny restaurants, there wasn't the touristy feeling of the port up here.

It's beautiful, she thought, as she pulled her case past another tiny courtyard lined with wooden chairs and tables, brightened with pink and purple bougainvillea and pale blue clouds of plumbago. She passed through an archway and bumped her case up the cobbled streets until she reached a small shop-lined square where people sat at tables outside a cafe and a small market was selling vegetables, fruit, pottery and all manner of woven things, from baskets to tiny dolls. Going up to a plump woman sitting on a wall by a stall offering bright raffia hats, she said shyly, 'Hotel Joannis?'

The woman nodded towards an alleyway leading upwards in shallow steps from beneath another archway, and pointed with one brown arm.

'Thank you.' *I must be getting closer now*, she thought, climbing the steps and bumping her case up behind her. The alley was lined at intervals with doorways, their thick stone lintels not whitewashed like the rest but left a dark honeyed brown colour. The same brown strip was left above the windows. *This place feels as though it's been designed,* she thought. *Everything is so in tune, so beautifully matched, almost as though we've styled it for a shoot.*

There was such a grace and cohesion in the harmony of white and dark stone, the strips of cobbles, the worn paving stones. Even the chairs and tables in front of the cafes seemed to have been chosen so that their shabby blue wood and woven seats would look delightful against the white walls, the terracotta pots with their spreading plants loaded with bright pink flowers, and the curving lines of the walls and arches. It made her feel peaceful to look at it, as though it was balm for her soul to see something so satisfyingly of a whole, but she wondered if its unchanging perfection might eventually become too much and feel stultifying. For now, though, she was happy to imbibe its well-worn beauty.

At last she saw a painted sign above an arched doorway that read *Hotel Joannis*, so she went through the arch and into a small courtyard where a large wooden door stood open. Inside, a young dark-haired woman in a bright red dress stood behind a desk. 'Hello,' she said with a bright smile in perfect English. 'Can I help you?'

'I have a room booked. Delilah Stirling.'

The woman checked a computer screen on the desk. 'Yes, Mrs Stirling. We have your room ready. Please follow me.'

The room was exactly what she had wanted: quiet and comfortable, with a large bed and a bathroom. A shuttered window looked out over the courtyard below. Before the woman left, Delilah said, 'I'm looking for an address here,' and showed her what she'd carefully written out from the letter.

The woman examined it and frowned. 'Villa Artemis. I don't know it. I don't think it's in the village itself. It may be just outside – some of the larger villas are. You should ask at the post office in the morning – you will find out there.'

'Thank you. I'll do that.'

She was one more step closer to finding Alexandra. She would look in earnest the next day.

Chapter Twenty-Nine

Delilah slept deeply and woke to a cool and almost complete darkness that, for a moment, gave her a shot of panic.

Where am I?

Then she remembered in a rush the whole of her journey the day before. She was in Greece, alone, in a tiny hotel in a small village in the shadow of a great monastery. Last night she had dined alone in the courtyard below and then gone to bed. And today she was going to find a dead woman.

She showered and went downstairs to the dining room where the Greek buffet breakfast was being served. Other guests sat at the tables, poring over guidebooks or concentrating on their food. Delilah helped herself to coffee, fruit and yoghurt and found a table where she could eat undisturbed but another couple soon took the table directly next to her, their plates loaded with the cold meats and cheeses that were put out for German tourists.

She felt stares upon her, and it was not long before the woman leaned over towards Delilah and said in an

American twang, 'Hi, are you all on your own? Do you need some company?'

Delilah looked up and smiled politely. 'You're very kind but I'm fine, thank you.'

The woman was dressed in wide green shorts that fell just past her knees and a black T-shirt, her face open and friendly with large brown eyes. 'Well, I do envy you. I get too lonely if I travel alone! I don't have the spirit for it.' She smiled and said in a firm way, 'I'm Teddie and this is my husband Paul.'

Paul had a lined, tanned face with a thick bristling grey moustache and he wore tinted glasses. He nodded at Delilah and grunted a greeting through a mouthful of sausage.

Teddie spread butter over a piece of crispbread and added a layer of cream cheese as she said, 'We've been to quite a few of the islands now but I like this one a lot so far. It's a little off the beaten track, you know what I mean? It feels like people live here; I don't just mean they run hotels and bars and stuff, but like there are normal lives going on as well. Maybe it helps that it's such a religious place.'

'Is it?' Delilah realised that she knew very little about the island.

Teddie nodded, spreading a dark smear of jam over her cream cheese. She whispered, 'Haven't you noticed all the nuns?' and glanced around conspiratorially, as though there were gangs of nuns in that very room, although Delilah hadn't noticed any.

'I did see a few on the ferry,' she replied, and took a sip of her black coffee.

THE WINTER FOLLY

'Yep. It's easier to spot them than the monks – it's the wimples. They're here because of the Book of Revelation.'

'Oh?'

'Yeah. St John stayed in a cave here and that's where he received the vision of the Apocalypse. That's why it's kind of a special place and why they've got that great monastery looming above us. Plenty of them come on a pilgrimage here to see the cave and get the thrill of being right where that vision happened.'

'I see,' Delilah said, interested. 'Is that why you're here?'

Teddie crunched into her crispbread and ate a mouthful before replying. 'We're not that religious, are we, Paul?'

Her husband grunted again.

'But I like the history of it. We're going to take a tour of the monastery today. I reckon it's going to be the coolest place on the island in a few hours. The sun here is something else. You don't want to be out in the village without sunglasses – I'm telling you, the glare of all these white houses is enough to strike you blind. Are you here to see the sights? You should come with us if you are. You might enjoy it.'

Delilah warmed to Teddie despite her initial desire to be left alone. She remembered that her mission today was to find the Villa Artemis but as the minute approached she felt more like putting it off. 'All right,' she said, almost to her own surprise. 'I'd be happy to come along.'

They walked up the steep road from Chora to the vast fortress above them. Although it wasn't long past nine, the sun was beating down and Delilah was glad of her hat and dark glasses. On Teddie's advice she had changed into a long skirt and made sure her shoulders were covered so that they would not be turned away on the grounds of indecency.

'Will you look at that?' Teddie breathed, gazing upwards. Her husband strode along silently at her side, a small rucksack strapped firmly to his back. 'Isn't it amazing?'

Delilah looked up. The monastery seemed to loom ever larger above them and she wondered just how big it would be by the time they reached it. Would she stand like a midget against its vast doors? Was it really the home of giants rather than men? 'It's huge,' she said breathlessly.

'Cos we're so close to Turkey here, I guess,' Teddie said. 'Gotta protect your church and people when the marauders come, huh?'

'I suppose so,' Delilah said. She thought of the fort at home and how its purpose had once been to shield and defend, a place to shut oneself in and others out. This was much the same but on a larger scale. Here they could have enclosed the entire population of the island behind those walls to keep them safe.

They reached the entrance with its heavily reinforced wooden door, and went through into the courtyard beyond. It was paved irregularly with a mixture of cobbles and stones and in the centre was a round covered structure that looked like a well. All around them were arched colonnades and entrances to rooms and chapels.

Delilah heard a voice from behind her, a soft female voice with a pure English accent. It said, 'There are ten chapels here because the Greek Orthodox Church does not allow more than one sacrament at each altar per day. So in order to carry out all the offices of the religious day, many altars are needed.'

Instantly alert, Delilah looked over her shoulder to see where the voice was coming from but the speaker was obscured from sight by a crowd around her. There was the murmur of another voice raised in question and the same light, mellifluous tone replied, 'No. It looks like a well but in fact it's a jar, a container of holy water. Now, shall we go inside? We'll visit the main chapel first and you'll see the wall paintings of the miracles of St John the Divine.'

The group moved off and Delilah caught a glimpse of a woman in a white dress and a blue headscarf before the throng of people blocked her line of sight.

'Shall we join a guided tour?' Teddie was asking, flicking through her guidebook while Paul stood silently beside them, staring at some distant point.

'One has just gone into the main chapel,' Delilah said. She felt drawn by the voice she had heard. Was it usual for a guide to have an accent like that? Were there many well-bred English women on the island and acting as guides? *Don't get carried away*, she told herself, *you're hardly likely to walk straight into her first thing.*

'We don't want a tour that's already started,' Teddie said. She gestured to a group assembling by the fortified door. 'There's one over there that's about to get going. We'll join them, shall we?'

'All right,' Delilah said, looking back towards the main chapel. Surely the groups would overlap at some point. She felt as though she could still hear that voice ringing in her ears and strained to hear it again, but the interior of the chapel had absorbed it entirely.

She tried to concentrate on the tour and on the marvels that the guide pointed out as they made their way round the monastery. She stared at the lavish Byzantine mosaics, the frescoes, the icons and the altars of the chapels, and heard of the relics kept there and the holy men buried within the walls, but her attention was always on a distant group of people as she tried to catch that voice again. It wasn't until they had made a tour of the entire monastery and emerged back into the main courtyard that she heard it, but this time it was not speaking English.

The musical lilt floated over the still air and Delilah turned to see the woman in the white dress, now free of her tour group, standing with her back to her across the court-yard. She was speaking to a man in a long dark robe with a flowing grey beard and a black hat on his head. An ortho-dox priest, probably.

If I can just get around to see her, Delilah thought, *I'll be able to tell from her face, I'm sure of it.*

'Say.' Teddie's voice broke into her thoughts. 'Do you want to go to the museum here? It costs six euros but it's got old manuscripts and vestments and treasures and stuff. I think it might be worth seeing. Paul's keen. Shall we go and take a look?'

Delilah found it hard to believe that Paul was keen as he'd not yet expressed an opinion on anything and even now was staring into the far distance as usual. He hadn't looked even vaguely interested on their entire tour. 'You go,' she said. 'I might just wander around for a while.'

'It's getting hot,' Teddie remarked. 'You don't really wanna stay out in this, do you? It'll be cool inside. Besides, they're closing soon until this afternoon. It's your last chance.'

'No . . . no.' She was distracted by movement and saw the woman and the bearded man move off together, heading for a different part of the monastery. 'You go, really. I'll see you back at the hotel later.'

'Okay.' Teddie shrugged. 'If that's what you want.' She put her guidebook into her back pocket where it bulged hugely. 'Come on, Paul. We're gonna eat down in the harbour tonight if you want to join us.'

'That sounds good,' Delilah said. 'Shall we talk later? Bye for now.' She turned and craned her neck to see where the guide had gone. A flash of white told her that the woman had disappeared through a doorway towards the older part of the monastery. She walked quickly after her, leaving Teddie and Paul, and keeping her eye fixed on where she had seen her disappear. At the doorway, she made to go inside but a man stepped forward from the gloom within to stop her. He was also in a long dark robe, holding up one hand and speaking in Greek.

'Sorry,' Delilah said, with a smile that she hoped was suitably charming. 'I'm English. May I come inside?'

'You cannot enter,' the man said in strongly accented English. 'This is the library. You must have permission to come in.'

'I'd love to see the books,' she said in a wheedling tone. 'Can I just have a little peek? I've come all the way from England.' She took a quick few steps past him.

'You must be a scholar,' the man said sternly. 'Scholars only.'

She knew that she didn't look in the least like a scholar in her cotton skirt, hat and sunglasses, a guide to the monastery in her hand. She sighed. 'Please?'

He shook his head and pointed to the door. 'You must go out.'

Turning away, she moved slowly to the exit, knowing she could not persuade him. Despite her lingering there was no further sign of the woman and she was forced to return to the brightness of the courtyard, annoyed at her stupidity in not making her move earlier. By being tentative, she had now lost her only chance to get a good look at the guide's face.

But, she told herself, *if that is Alexandra then it's only a matter of time before I see her again.*

She left the monastery, glad to be on her own, and returned to Chora by a different path. This time she could see down the island to the splendid views of the dazzling blue harbour peppered with boats. She caught up with the tail end of a group of sightseers that led her to another small whitewashed monastery that she learned was the one built over the Cave of the Apocalypse. There was no reason to miss the opportunity, so she went inside with the others and found herself in a low underground chamber richly decorated with painted icons that glowed with layers of gilt. On the small wooden chairs, people sat praying and contemplating the holy spot, but she stayed only long enough to absorb the striking decoration and the curious warmth inside before she continued on the path back down to Chora.

She arrived as the sultriest part of the day began, and the village felt as though it was tucking itself away inside the cool stone walls to rest from the heat until the worst was past. In the hotel, it was so quiet she couldn't find anyone to ask about the whereabouts of the post office but she decided that it was probably closed anyway, so she went to the courtyard restaurant for bread, cheese and olives before returning to her room to sleep. It seemed the wisest course with the overpowering heat outside. She lay awake for a while, still amazed that she was so close to Alexandra, perhaps had even heard her voice, and feeling as though she was on the brink of meeting a character from a story who had turned out to be real. The effect of the heat and the morning walk took its course, and she slept. When she woke, it was after three o'clock and the temperature had subsided a little. After shaking off the doziness and refreshing herself with a long drink of cold water, Delilah headed out to find the post office, which was just a few streets away, in one of the pretty cobbled squares lined with shops, many selling art, pottery and icons. It was a small dark shop that also sold postcards and tourist mementoes and she picked up a few cards showing the monastery and the cave. A woman waited to take her money behind the counter. Delilah said, 'Excuse me – can you tell me where to find this address?' and held out the piece of paper.

'Yes, yes,' the woman said, after scrutinising it for a moment. 'I draw you map.' Taking a pen and using the square as the starting point, she drew a simple and very clear diagram of how to the reach the villa.

Delilah sat outside a cafe in the square staring at the map. The villa was not far away. A short walk from the heart of the village and she would be there. Now that she was so close, she almost struggled to remember why she had come. Her life, her world, even John himself, seemed remarkably far away, all of it almost like a dream, while her reality was the warmth of this market square, the iced water in front of her, the shot of bold colour against the white stone where flowers bloomed.

Does that mean, she wondered, *that it's easy to forget?*

She had imagined Alex as a woman struggling to erase her memories but perhaps they had simply faded away as soon as her old life was out of sight. Would she, Delilah, be any different if her life suddenly became this blue and white idyll, a slow and lazy existence on a holy island that seemed closer to the eleventh century than this one?

Perhaps it wouldn't be so easy to storm into someone else's life and demand answers to questions she barely understood. It could be outrageous arrogance to act as though she could force a family's past out and into a new and better future. She remembered Grey's warning about thinking she could make everything right for everyone.

I probably do, she thought. *What if it all goes seriously wrong?*

She had a glimpse of a future where John was disgusted with her actions at tracking down his mother, and their life together came to an end in a morass of accusations, justifications and fury. It would be terrible, heartbreaking.

But then she imagined returning to her morose husband and the monthly rollercoaster of hope and despair – if they even managed to have sex at all – and the certain knowledge that he was pulling ever further away from her, leaving her to cope with life in the house alone. Her plans for the future would never be realised. She could never hope to change or tame the silence inside. She'd be surrounded by all its sadness and mystery again.

That future was just as heartbreaking, in its way. She wouldn't be able to stand it. A sudden glimpse of Ben flashed into her mind. She knew that if she went back to that life, she would surely be unable to stop herself turning to him for comfort.

She stood up, determined on her course. She would get the answers that waited her at the Villa Artemis. It was the only way.

She went back to the hotel and managed to avoid Teddie and Paul. Another night she would have liked to have gone down to the harbour to find one of the restaurants strung with lights, to have sat at a table overlooking the harbour and eaten grilled fish and drunk the local wine. But she would be leaving tomorrow night and had to seize her chance while she could.

It was early evening when she left the hotel with the map held tightly in her hand. She could sense the island coming back to life after the heat of the day. The buzzing of mopeds sounded like a race of giant bees had awakened, and lights were already glowing out over the square and courtyards, the candles on the tables lit in readiness for the sun-reddened tourists looking for their evening meal.

The route led out of the village on one of the narrow roads that widened once it was beyond the confines of the walls. She walked up it, observing the scraggy eucalyptus trees and straggly heather that seemed to cover the rocky ground. Every now and then she passed large villas that faced out over the bay, some with many terraces and surrounded by rich foliage, some with silver reflections from unseen swimming pools glittering on the white walls. Evidently rich people came here to spend their leisure time. She felt obscurely disappointed. She hadn't expected Alexandra to be living in luxury. What kind of penitential exile was that? But then the map showed that she should turn back on herself, following another narrower path up the hill, back towards the monastery, the western side that looked away from the town, and she saw that she was heading towards some smaller houses tucked away at its base, like infant creatures nestling into the warmth of their mother's belly.

Then she saw a sign on the side of a white-painted wall where stone steps led up towards a square building on two storeys with terraces at each level. Above the house, part of the monastery rose up into the cloudless sky, not like the heavy fortress that faced over the bay but a worn wall of sandy stone that turned to the topaz sea to the west. The sign was roughly painted with the words 'Villa Artemis'.

She stopped and stared at it, putting out a finger to trace the letters. The wood was warm under her fingertip. So here she was. Gazing up at the house, she could see no signs of life. All was still. What a very quiet place this was. Perhaps, after all, it was suitable for an exile, this holy island visited by monks and nuns and people wanting to experience its spiritual atmosphere. It was a place of prayer, contemplation, and a quest for salvation.

A cat emerged from nowhere and rubbed its bony body against her bare legs, purring and wanting her attention. She looked down at it, wondering if it had fleas. Then she heard a noise above and a door opened. A woman came out of the house and onto the terrace where she moved about slowly. Delilah froze, hoping she was out of sight beneath the villa's wall. What was the woman doing? There was the sound of pouring water. Plants were being given a drink as the cool of the evening descended.

Her heart was racing. She leaned against the warm stone of the wall, trying to gather her strength and courage. Did she dare? Did she?

If I go up there, she told herself, *what will make her think I've come from home? I could be anybody. Anybody at all.*

Quickly she thought of a story. *I'm lost.* No – that was stupid; she was just below the walls of the most famous landmark on the island. Besides, how lost could anyone be in this place in the daylight? Or else she was looking for a good taverna – could this woman recommend one? No. She had it. *I need a glass of water.* She could fake dizziness, sickness. That's what she would do.

Before she could change her mind, Delilah started up the stone steps, already breathless and outraged at her own nerve, towards the house. The person above heard the slapping of her sandals on the stone and looked over. Delilah saw a flash of blue headscarf and then it disappeared. When she reached the front door, she could see whoever it was had left the terrace and the door that led inside was firmly shut.

She rapped firmly on the door. There was no reply and after a few minutes she knocked again more loudly. Still nothing.

You're not getting away that easily, she thought. Her fear began to harden into determination. She had come all this way. She was not going to leave without seeing Alexandra. She rapped loudly again and called out, 'Hello? Hello!'

She was about to see if there was a back way when the door opened, and the woman from the monastery stood there. Her face was old and lined and the hair tucked under the headscarf was grey, but her blue eyes and the shape of her nose were unmistakeable from the photographs at home. She was looking into the face of Alexandra Stirling.

The older woman stared back at her, examining her face, and then she said calmly, 'So they've sent someone at last. Who are you?'

Chapter Thirty

Delilah opened her mouth to reply and then thought better of it. She had hoped that surprise would be her weapon in making the woman identify herself and already she was about to hand it away.

Alexandra stood watching her, a half-amused look on her face. 'It must be strange,' she said in an almost confiding tone, 'to meet someone you no doubt thought might be some crazy old hermit living in a cave, like poor old St John himself.'

Delilah stared back at her, looking for signs of John in her face. She realised that if she had children, this woman would be their grandmother. Those blue eyes might emerge in a daughter of hers. Did Elaine have blue eyes too?

The woman stood back. 'You're not saying much. Come in. I think you've got some questions for me, haven't you?' She turned and walked inside, and Delilah followed her into a large sitting room with a kitchen at one end. The walls were whitewashed and bare, the only shelf holding painted plates and jugs. Rugs covered the stone floor and a pair of pale sofas faced each other, a rough wooden table between them loaded with books and a vase of pink roses. Between the sitting area and the kitchen was a small dining table with a blue cloth on it. A huge chimney breast sloped down from the ceiling to the floor, as though part of a pyramid had emerged from the wall. An open door led out into a walled courtyard overhung with fig trees and decorated with pots of sweet-smelling flowers.

'Would you like a drink?' the woman asked, turning to Delilah.

She shook her head, thinking of her earlier ruse to pretend to be ill. She was glad now that she hadn't attempted anything so transparent and childish. 'No, thank you.'

'Very well. Let's go out to the terrace.' The woman led the way outside where two comfortably cushioned cane chairs were placed to face out over the wall towards the sea that spread mistily into the distant horizon. Alexandra sat down and waited until Delilah had joined her, lifting one veined hand to shield her eyes from the descending sun. 'It's quite possible to be dazzled by the sunset here,' she remarked. 'It faces west, you see.'

Delilah settled and then waited but when nothing was forthcoming from the other woman she said, 'So – who do you think I am?'

'I don't know. You don't look like a solicitor but as they are the only English people I have contact with, perhaps you are.'

Delilah shook her head. 'No. I'm not a lawyer.'

'All right. Then you must have a connection with . . .

with the place I've left behind. Let me see. Perhaps you are Nicky's child from another marriage.' The old woman went very still as she said this, her hand still shielding her face but showing her mouth tight with fearful apprehension. She said in a strained voice, 'But you are very young for that.'

'I'm not Nicky's daughter,' Delilah said. She leaned forward, suddenly desperate to reach out and tell this woman everything, and make her understand. 'Nicky doesn't have any other children. He never married again after you left.'

'Oh.' She breathed out and seemed to relax. 'I suspected as much. I am not completely cut off. I read newspapers when they come my way and always thought I would discover something like that. But I never wished loneliness on him. Quite the reverse.' The woman fixed a strong blue gaze on Delilah. 'I don't intend to tell you anything more without knowing who you are. You're not Nicky's child. Perhaps another relation? One who has for some reason decided to do a little detective work.'

'In a way. But I wasn't looking for you, not at first.' She sat back in her chair, breathing in the fragrant air of the terrace. The closing day was making the flowers send out a heady perfume and the ripe figs smelled sweet and honeyish. Fixing Alexandra with a direct look, she said, 'I'm John's wife.'

The other woman couldn't help her start of surprise, though she tried to conceal it. She blinked anxiously and looked more closely at Delilah, a frown creasing her forehead with even deeper wrinkles. 'But . . . that can't be right. John is divorced. Isn't he? Unless you are the American girl I read about.'

Delilah laughed. 'Vanna? No. My name is Delilah. John and I have been married almost a year.'

'I see. That news has not reached me.' Alexandra's frown cleared and her expression grew curious once more. 'So you live at Fort Stirling, do you? I suppose you stumbled on things that puzzle you, and you've become a busy bee who has decided to buzz all the way over here to find me out.' She seemed to be attempting an insouciance that she couldn't maintain. Her eyes filled with sadness. 'John. How is he?'

'He's fine – if you can call a man tortured by what happened to him in his childhood fine.' She paused and added, 'He doesn't know I'm here. I discovered your whereabouts by accident and I didn't want to upset him – not until I had more to tell him.'

Alexandra stood up, smoothed out her white skirt, went to the flowerpots and began stripping any withered leaves. 'I thought someone would come one day,' she said in a low voice. 'I thought he might come. John. That's what I've prepared myself for. I've been prepared for anger and accusations. But I also hoped that if Nicky had done his job well, John would never want to see me.'

'Why would he come? They told him you were dead,' Delilah said, stressing the final word and turning to face Alexandra as she bent over the pots.

She stripped a small brown leaf from a stem and crushed it under her fingers. 'Did they? Good. I thought as much. It was for the best.'

Delilah stared at her in astonishment. 'You think that was for the *best*? You think it's a good idea that he's suffered thinking you killed yourself rather than be with him – and all this time you're *alive*?'

'You know nothing about it,' Alexandra said in an unexpectedly stern voice.

'I might know nothing but any reasonable person would think that was an unbelievably cruel thing to do to a child. And the fact you and Nicky collaborated in it . . .' Delilah shook her head, at a loss to explain her astonishment.

'Don't you think we must have had a damn good reason?' Alexandra snapped harshly, her eyes suddenly furious. 'It was the best thing I could do. The only thing that would have been better was if I'd actually died. But I couldn't do it. I meant to . . . but I couldn't.' She turned back to the pots and stared at a flower that held its pink trumpet up towards the last of the sunshine. She reached out one finger and stroked it gently. 'Nicky stopped me. He begged . . . for the children . . . for John's sake . . . that I did not kill myself. So I agreed on one condition – that I would go away and never be a part of his or John's lives ever again.'

'But why?' asked Delilah, unable to hide her confusion. 'I know you suffered a terrible loss. I saw Elaine's grave, and it was heartbreaking. I can't imagine what it must have been like to lose a child. But I don't understand how it could help your husband or your son if you went away. Don't you realise what you left behind? How much you traumatised that little boy? And even if you weren't in your right mind at the time, how could you stay away all this time? Surely after a while you thought about your duty to John.'

Alexandra spun round to face her, her blue eyes blazing.

'How dare you? I live with enough guilt, a kind you cannot begin to understand! My only consolation has been living here, knowing I was keeping my family safe by staying away from them. You have no right to come here and attempt to heap more on me!'

Delilah shrank back in her chair under the force of Alexandra's voice. She felt presumptuous suddenly. 'I'm . . . I'm sorry. I just don't understand . . .'

'How could you?' Alexandra said quietly, the fury passing. She turned back to the flowers. 'No one could. No one. I am the only one.'

'But I understand something!' Delilah protested. Now that she was with the real Alex and realised what strangers they were, it seemed impossible to explain that she had felt such a bond with her. It seemed foolish to think that in some way she had wanted to bring her own problems to Alex and ask what to do. She struggled on. 'I know what it's like to live at Fort Stirling – sometimes I think that house will drive me mad. I've seen that grim old folly. The whole place can begin to invade you, crush you . . .'

Alexandra glanced back at her, her expression startled. 'Yes. Yes . . . that's true. The house . . .' She seemed lost in memory for a moment as though she was once more walking along the corridors and opening the doors of Fort Stirling. Then her face closed off again and she said, 'But there was more to it than simply that. I had Nicky's love. I had the children. I could have survived if it were just the house.' She thought again and a strange look came over her face. She frowned as though half in pain and half in contemplation.

'Was it . . . was it . . .' Delilah hesitated. Planning what to say had been so easy. The reality of approaching the magnitude of the other woman's loss was something else entirely. 'Was it because Elaine died?'

Alexandra returned to the cane seat, sat down and looked over at Delilah. 'Do you know how Elaine died?'

Delilah shook her head.

'I killed her.'

She gasped, her mouth dropping open.

'That's right. I killed her. It was an accident, of course, but one that still tortures me every day of my life.' Her tone was simple and neutral but that somehow made the words more stark and true. 'She was riding her new bike, the one that was still a little too big for her, and she'd been allowed to ride it on the drive. I drove over the hill too fast and I didn't see her in time.' The old woman shut her eyes and then said in a voice drenched with bitter irony, 'I've seen her a million times since, in dreams and visions and flashbacks. That little person on her pink bike, pedalling like mad, her eyes fixed on me. She had utter faith that I would stop or avoid her. She must have been astonished when I didn't. I hope she didn't suffer. I hope she died quickly and didn't have time to wonder why I had done that to her. They tell me she did. They said I got out of the car and held her broken body, crying hysterically because she was already dead, but I can't remember that. I'm glad. At least my memory can't keep torturing me with that vision.'

'I'm sorry,' Delilah whispered, sitting absolutely still. 'I didn't realise . . .'

'Why should you? I'm sure it wasn't spoken of.'

'It wasn't. I didn't even know she existed until I found her grave. No one ever spoke of her.'

Alexandra lifted her head to look at her. 'Didn't they?' she said sadly. 'Did no one remember Elaine?'

Delilah shook her head. 'There are no pictures. No photographs. No memories. Even John's memory is virtually wiped clean. All I found of her was a doll lost at the back of a cupboard in the nursery. She vanished when you did.'

Alexandra seemed to slump down under the weight of this news. 'My little girl,' she said quietly.

Delilah was quiet, sensing she'd delivered a blow of unexpected force.

Alexandra looked down at her hands and said, almost under her breath, 'But Nicky remembers.'

'In a way,' Delilah replied. 'When he saw me in the garden, he thought I was Elaine grown up, so he must be dwelling on her in some way.'

Alexandra looked up slowly, her expression apprehensive. 'What do you mean?'

Delilah felt cruel. What right did she have to deliver news like this? But then . . . if Alexandra could hand out pain, she had to expect to receive it in return. 'He's suffering from Alzheimer's. He barely even knows who John is any more.'

Alexandra's eyes filled suddenly with tears and she bowed her head to hide them. Turning in her chair to face the wall, she sat still for a while until she shook her slender shoulders and looked back to Delilah again. 'I suppose I always knew a day like this would come. His death, perhaps. The final closing of the door. Poor Nicky. He didn't deserve it. He didn't deserve what I brought on him.'

'Then . . . why?' Delilah asked pleadingly.

Alexandra stood up suddenly. 'I think you can go now.'

'Go now?'

'Yes. You've done what you wanted, I suppose. No doubt you wanted to make me suffer in revenge for what John's endured at my hands. You've done that. I didn't think anyone could add to my burden but you have. And now you can leave.'

'I didn't come here to do that!' cried Delilah, feeling that any connection she'd had with the other woman had been suddenly sliced through. 'I had no idea what happened to Elaine, and I feel terrible that I've made it worse for you.'

'Well, you have.' Alexandra began to walk towards the door. 'There are steps that lead back down from this terrace to the road. You can take those. Goodnight.'

Delilah leapt to her feet. 'Wait! Please, I don't want to go yet. There's more to say. Please!'

Alexandra turned slowly at the door. 'What more do you want from me?'

'The truth. I want to know why you went. If you had lost your daughter, why did you decide to lose your son and your husband too? Why inflict that on yourself?'

'My dear girl,' Alexandra said, 'no doubt you want to take something back to John, an answer to all of this that makes sense. Perhaps you want him to forgive me and take me back, and for me to fall into his arms, the sobbing and repentant mother. But life is not so simple. Besides, there is no reason why I should tell you simply because you demand it. I don't owe you any explanation, or indeed anything at all. I simply ask that you believe I have a good reason why I left, why I can never go back and why it's better if people think I'm dead. I made my decision many years ago, and I knew it was irreversible. It is, of course, up to you what you tell John about seeing me but my advice would be to let him go on thinking I left him. It's the kindest way, I promise you. Have children together and pray that they have enough of your blood and Nicky's to dilute mine altogether. I shall be hoping for that.' She turned to leave again and then looked back. 'You ask why I inflicted it on myself. You need to see it another way. I chose not to inflict something on my husband and my son, and that caused me indescribable pain. But it was the only thing I could do.'

She stepped inside the house and closed the door, leaving Delilah alone on the terrace as the sun began to melt behind the brow of the hill, turning the golden evening light to grey.

Chapter Thirty-One

Delilah ordered breakfast in her room. She didn't think that she could face Teddie and Paul, or any of the other guests in the dining room. A tray of fruit, yoghurt and crispbreads was brought to her room, along with a cup of strong black coffee. She poured sugar in and drank it very sweet, wrapping her hands around the cup for comfort as though it was a freezing winter's day back home, and not another blazing day in the Aegean.

She was still stunned by what had happened the previous evening and the interview with Alexandra. Somehow she had imagined that connection she had felt with the young woman in the photographs at home, with her name in the photo albums and in the visitors' book, would carry over into real life, and now she felt a quiet devastation that that had not happened. She realised that she had nurtured secret hopes that she could mend a broken family and help to heal her husband's soul. Instead she had brought more suffering and made a reconciliation even less likely. And the mysteries still remained.

The shutters were open, letting golden sunshine flood into her room along with the sounds from the courtyard below. A light breeze fluttered the strips of veil that served as curtains. She wondered what she would do with this day. The ferry would leave the port tonight and she had a cabin booked for the return to Athens. When she'd imagined that journey, she'd seen herself going back with answers, perhaps even with the woman herself. She'd imagined performing a kind of miracle, bringing Alex back from the dead and taking her home. 'Look, the mother you thought was dead is alive!'

She had made no plans for a future in which she would have found Alexandra but failed to find out the truth and even, perhaps, made things worse.

On top of that, she had to decide what to tell John. Could she put the knowledge of Alexandra's existence out of her mind, go home and pretend that nothing had changed? She couldn't imagine how she could live with such a huge lie between them. The alternative was to confess what she had discovered and tell him what she had done, condemning him to live with the knowledge that his mother hadn't died but had abandoned him out of choice and never shown the slightest interest in him since. How could Delilah convey Alexandra's seemingly absolute conviction that she had acted for the best, in order to protect her son from whatever her 'good reason' was? Delilah felt sure that Alexandra implied it was more than the frightful experience of accidentally causing her daughter's death. Or was that the heart of it? Was it a good enough reason to abandon your other child? That didn't seem to make sense.

'Oh God,' she said, sighing. 'What a terrible mess I've made of this. What a terrible mess.'

No matter how hard she thought about it, she could see no way out.

Delilah packed her things and left them behind the desk of the hotel, and then walked first down the hill to the port, and then along the beaches and bays, following their trails of silver sand and pebbles until she found a place to have some lunch. Afterwards, she retraced her steps, thinking all the while about what she should do. By the time she was climbing the last few steep yards up the path to Chora, she'd come to the conclusion that she really had no alternative. She would have to tell John the truth. Such a large deception had the potential to tear their marriage apart after all. He might be angry with her now for her interference, and he might need all her help and support to get through it, but if he discovered what she had done after the fact, that would be the death knell for them. She felt sick at the idea of telling him but there was no alternative: she would have to take the consequences.

Something that Alexandra had said the night before had been playing through her mind all day. She'd said that she'd had the love of Nicky and the children and so could have survived the house. Her mind kept returning to the words, provoking something wistful and sad that she couldn't identify until, as she stopped on the hill by the village walls and got her breath, taking in lungfuls of warm afternoon air, she suddenly knew what it was.

Without John's love, she herself could never hope to survive the house. Love was all that could make it bearable. Alexandra had known that. That must be the key to what had happened. Was it just the loss of Elaine then? No. It had to be the loss of Nicky's love as well.

Delilah took off her sunhat and brushed her hand through her hair. Her scalp prickled where sweat had cooled at the roots. She shook out her damp hair and turned to gaze out over the island, down the rocky hillside to the magnificent dark blue silver-touched sea, thinking hard. Surely she could work it out. Perhaps one of her early theories about Alex had been correct. Maybe Nicky had been a Lothario, sleeping around and betraying his wife, destroying their marriage that way. But Erryl's words came back to her: that Nicky had been drinking to forget, that Erryl had never seen a man so sad. That was hardly the behaviour of a cold-hearted playboy. Another thought occurred to her: perhaps Nicky had blamed his wife for the death of their daughter and had ceased to love her. Without that, Alexandra had not been able to go on.

'So she abandoned her son forever?' Delilah said out loud. Her voice didn't carry on the still air. She frowned. It wasn't enough. The vital piece of the jigsaw was missing.

Arriving at the hotel hot and thirsty, she decided to take her luggage down to the port and find a place to eat before the ferry left. It would be a long journey back home, with a night on the ferry, a taxi ride back to Athens and then the plane home to Gatwick. She was in the lobby wondering if she could order a taxi when she heard her name.

'Delilah! I was wondering where you'd got to.'

She turned to see Teddie striding in out of the bright sunshine. She smiled. 'Hi. Sorry I missed you since the monastery. Was the museum good?'

'Excellent! You missed a real treat.' Teddie held up a bag of paprika-flavoured crisps. 'I just went out to get Paul a snack. He's really taken to these things. He likes them with some of that Greek beer. Aren't you heading off this evening?'

'I'm afraid so. It was a flying visit for me.'

'Uh-huh.' Teddie nodded, her soft fleshy face beaming at Delilah. 'Well, it was great getting to know you a little. If you're ever in Milwaukee, you know you've got a place to stay. And did you get your letter?'

'My letter?'

'Yup. A lady came in and left a letter for you. I heard her at the desk saying your name – at least, I don't think there'll be many other Delilahs staying here, will there?' Teddie laughed. 'Now, you take care and have a good journey home.'

'Thanks, I will.' Delilah tried not to be distracted but her eyes slid to the desk. 'Give my regards to Paul and enjoy the rest of your stay.'

'Oh, we will. Bye now.' Teddie took her crisps and headed for the stairs. Delilah hurried to the reception desk and rang the small bell. The woman from the previous day came out.

'Hello, madam, can I help you?'

'Yes, I'd like to collect my luggage and order a taxi to the port. And I believe you have a letter for me.'

'A letter? Oh, yes.' The woman started searching behind the desk and a moment later she lifted up an envelope and handed it to Delilah. 'Yes, here it is. I'll have your luggage brought out and order you a taxi right away.'

Delilah was barely listening. She was looking at the delicate script on the front of the envelope that spelt out her name. She tore it open and pulled out the letter inside.

My dear Delilah

I don't suppose you ever expected a mother-in-law like me – one who apparently ceased to be years ago and then turns out to be alive and kicking. Perhaps I'm the best kind. You can at least be sure I shall not be interfering with you and John. It's a very strange story, I know, and you could only understand it thoroughly if you knew secrets that I've decided will die with me. So I'm afraid that I will never be able to satisfy your all-too-understandable curiosity. But what you said about John has tormented me all night. You must believe that I've always loved him dearly and have only done what I thought was right. He will come to know at some point what happened to me. I had hoped by that time I would be dead but if what you say of Nicky is true, it is more likely that I will outlive him. When Nicky dies, John will surely learn the truth, as the estate pays me a living allowance and he will be told of it.

Therefore I would like you to give him the letter I

enclose with this one. It is my final testament to him, not of the things I've vowed to take with me, but of my love for him and my genuine desire to act in his best interests. It is up to you whether you give it to him now or when I'm dead.

There's one more thing you must know. Even if Elaine had lived, I would have left. I had no choice. I'd like you to understand that.

Yours sincerely

Alexandra Stirling

A slim folded envelope addressed to John was inside the one that had held her letter.

There it is, she thought. *John will have to know.*

Delilah drove back from Gatwick as slowly as she could, telling herself it was because she was tired but knowing that really she was afraid of what would happen when she got home. How long could she go before she had to reveal what she'd done? She tried to imagine giving John the letter. 'Oh yes, it's from your mother. Did you think she was dead? Well, here's a funny thing – I've just visited her in Greece actually.'

He was hardly likely to take such news bouncing up and down with joy and wreathed in smiles.

Despite everything, it was wonderful to be home. The sight of the lush English fields and the water-rich green of the hedges and trees refreshed her in a way that the baked rocky scrub of Greece never could. She allowed the mellow warmth to flood into the car and cheer her up, trying to banish her worries, but as she turned the car into the drive-way of Fort Stirling she had a vivid and horrible flash of a girl on a pink bicycle pedalling in the path of an oncoming car, her fragile body not standing a chance against it. She gasped at the vision, overcome not just with the horror of the child's death but the fact that her mother had been behind the wheel. She felt a tiny echo of the guilt and despair that Alexandra must have felt.

But why leave Nicky? And why not take John with her?

As she went over the brow of the hill and began the descent to the house, she noticed a flash of silver as the sun caught the bonnet of a car parked out the front. Was some-one visiting the house? John wasn't due back from his trip for another day. Perhaps it was someone to see Janey, or a visitor for Ben.

She parked her car, got out and examined the strange vehicle. It was extremely flashy, much smarter than most cars around here. John's friends drove battered old Land Rovers and knocked-out Volvos the same way he did. Noth-ing glamorous like this would continue looking so pristine in the country past a week. Once it had been coated in mud, fallen leaves, blossom and bird mess, it would look like all the other cars around here.

Erryl came around the corner of the house with a wheel-barrow full of clippings and stopped short when he saw her. 'Hello, ma'am,' he said a touch awkwardly. 'Mr Stirling didn't say you were coming back today.'

'Well, here I am!' she said gaily. 'How's everything here?'

'Fine, fine.' Erryl's eyes slid to the silver car.

'Whose is this?' she asked.

'Mr Stirling has a . . . er . . . a visitor.'

'But he's away, isn't he?'

'Oh no, ma'am. He got back yesterday. Apparently the trip ended early.'

A chill rippled over her skin. 'That's strange. He didn't ring me.' She picked up her bags, waving away Erryl's approach to do it for her. 'Don't worry, I'm fine. I'd better go in and see who this visitor is.' She hurried up the front steps, anxious to hear that John was back before she'd expected him. Why hadn't he rung her once he was back in range? What had he thought when he'd returned to find she wasn't here? She'd assumed she'd be back before he was. But at least a visitor meant that she was off the hook for a while as to explaining where she had been.

Walking down the hall, she was surprised to hear the tinkle of laughter from the drawing room. John never used that room. She had to force him to use it for drinks when they had guests, otherwise it would stand empty at all times. She went up to the drawing room door and pressed her ear against it. There was the cadence of a female voice and then another burst of laughter. She recognised John's laugh at once.

Well, that's good. He's in a cheerful mood.

She opened the door and walked in, saying, 'Hello! I'm back.'

John was sitting on the old green silk armchair, leaning forward to whoever was on the sofa with its back to the

423

door. The sofa table, with its Chinese vase and pair of alabaster doves, obscured the sofa but Delilah saw the shimmer of golden hair and the white of a spotless linen jacket. John looked up and saw her.

'Darling,' he said, standing up, looking a little flustered. 'You're home.'

Delilah looked at the figure rising from the sofa and turning to her. It was a face she recognised although she didn't quite know how: elegant and slender with chiselled cheekbones and a curtain of perfectly polished blonde hair.

'Hi!' said the woman brightly, and Delilah knew at once who it was before John said anything but she could only stare as John gestured towards their guest and said:

'Delilah, this is Vanna. My ex-wife.'

Chapter Thirty-Two

It was a strange and awkward afternoon. Delilah felt
obscurely betrayed by the fact that Vanna was here, even
though it was all explained very smoothly. She had come to
England on holiday and been invited to stay with friends
who by chance had rented a country house close to Fort
Stirling. She hadn't intended to visit but being in the vicinity
had awakened so many happy memories that she had felt
compelled to drop in. And wasn't it lovely to see John again,
and the house, and also get the chance to meet his charming
wife? Goodness, the place hadn't changed a bit, and neither
had John!

Vanna spoke in a friendly enough way, and smiled and
behaved perfectly pleasantly, but Delilah was ill at ease.

That's not surprising, she told herself. *How many people
would be fine with their husband's first wife dropping in like
this out of the blue? There can't be many.*

But besides that she felt on the back foot. Vanna looked
so polished and glamorous and she wafted through the
rooms of the fort pointing out things she remembered and

exclaiming over how things had either altered in some minute way, or stayed the same. Delilah knew she looked travel-stained and tired. She'd been looking forward to a bath and washing her hair and getting some fresh clothes on, but now she was forced to play the hostess aware she looked a total mess. She could just hear Vanna now, at some charity function, telling all her highly groomed friends about what it had been like to see her husband's new wife.

'My dear, she was a perfect fright. So English in that dowdy way. You'd think she'd never heard of a hairbrush and was a total stranger to the manicurist. Her clothes were things I'd consider only fit for the incinerator!'

Delilah's temper crumbled under the pressure and she could feel a black mood descending, although she tried to smile through it. It was a relief when Vanna said she was leaving as she was expected back at her friends' house for dinner. She kissed John goodbye on the front step, hugging him tightly and murmuring, 'Don't forget what I said,' in a low voice meant just for him before assuming a loud tone for her farewell to Delilah. 'Such a pleasure to meet you! Look after him for me, won't you? He's still precious to me, even after all this time.'

Then she skipped lightly down the steps, climbed into her gleaming car and drove away.

'That was a surprise,' Delilah said, turning to John, forcing out a smile that she was sure looked only half-hearted. 'Did you know she was coming?'

'I didn't. She only called this morning.'

'Quite an odd coincidence,' Delilah remarked, 'that she

should come by at the one time I happened to be away.' She could hear the note of accusation in her voice and wished she could suppress it but her irritation and tiredness were taking control, making her look for some kind of release and resolution to the pangs of suspicious jealousy that had been burning inside her ever since she'd seen Vanna.

'What do you mean?' John said in a cool voice as they went inside.

'I don't know. Just odd. How is she doing? What's she up to? Why didn't she bring her husband?'

'She's just got divorced again, as it happens.'

Delilah pounced on this, letting it feed her fear and jealousy. 'Oh, really? That's another odd coincidence! She's divorced and she just happens to drop by when your wife is away?'

John stopped walking then turned and looked at her. 'Are you saying,' he said in a dangerously quiet voice, 'that I arranged for her to come here while you were away?'

'I don't know!' she said recklessly. 'It just looks pretty strange to me. What does she mean by hugging you and kissing you all cosily like that – and telling you to remember what she said? What *did* she say?'

He said nothing but stared at her, his eyes glittering in the shadow of the hall.

'So?' she persisted. 'What did she say?'

'She said I should take care of myself, that I don't look well. But while we're on the subject of clandestine hugs and kisses and cosy chats, why don't we have a little talk about you and dear cousin Ben?'

She felt the colour drain from her face and she stammered, 'W-w-what do you mean?'

He smiled a horrible knowing smile. 'You think I've been blind to it, don't you? How he's been following you around with his tongue out? I've seen you two, cosying up for glasses of wine together, meeting at every opportunity. I'd be a fool not to notice. I've been waiting for you to tell me about it but you've kept it very quiet, haven't you?'

'John,' she said desperately, thinking as fast she could, trying to work out what he might have seen that would incriminate her, 'you've got it all wrong.'

'Have I?' His expression turned sour. 'You've got a cheek walking in here without so much as a phone call telling me when to expect you, and then treating my guest in the unfriendly way you did. In fact, you were downright rude. For Christ's sake, she's done nothing to you! And then to have the gall to accuse me of arranging her visit behind your back. For one thing, I was only here by chance myself, after our fishing got cut short. For another, I had no idea you'd gone off on your little jaunt.'

Her anger and irritation at Vanna's visit drained away at once and she realised how petty and stupid she'd been to let jealousy get the better of her common sense. Of course he hadn't planned it. How could he have? He was right – he hadn't even known she'd be away.

John had folded his arms and was staring at her furiously. 'Don't you think you'd better enlighten me a little about what's going on between you and Ben?'

Oh God. She wasn't ready for this. She hadn't yet worked

out in her own mind what she felt about Ben. She tried to calm the fear washing around inside her, took a deep breath and said, 'Nothing's happened between us. We're just friends.'

He nodded at her with a bitter, knowing look. 'Okay. So – where have you been for the last few days?'

She was startled at the change in direction of his questioning and then her heart plummeted again. Oh God, what trap had she fallen into? This was the wrong time to tell him about Greece. She wanted to make sure he was in the right mood and this antagonism between them could surely lead to a disastrous outcome.

'Well?' His tone was low and almost menacing. 'I'm waiting.'

She began to stammer. 'Well, I . . . I—'

'Because Janey told me you'd gone to spend a couple of days with your friend Helen in Italy. Sounds nice, I thought. Why don't I go and join you out there? Maybe a break away from this place is what we need to improve things between us.'

Delilah's palms were suddenly damp and a nasty tingle prickled her fingertips, but she could only listen as he went on, all the time staring at her like she was a criminal.

He continued: 'So I called Helen to see if it would be okay. She hadn't a clue where you were. You certainly weren't staying with her, though once she realised that was what I thought, she tried to cover for you. You two really should have got your stories straight.' He looked suddenly very sad. 'I can see by your face that you've been caught out.

I suppose you thought I'd never bother to check up on you, or you'd be back before me. But you reckoned without me coming home early. It was a pretty nasty bloody shock to find out you were not here – or where you told Janey you were going. And then there's the real kicker.' He smiled again but in the twisted way that showed it was anything but good humoured. 'Ben isn't here either. He's not at his cottage. No one at Home Farm knows where he is. Perhaps you'd like to explain that.'

'I have no idea where Ben might be,' she said, her voice coming out in a strangled tone. 'I honestly don't. He didn't even know I was going away. Besides, nothing has happened between us, I promise.' It was true – up to a point.

'Really?' John said in a strange sing-song way. 'After all, he's a good-looking boy. Strong, outdoors type. Your honest farmer sort. I wouldn't be surprised if you were tempted, considering how things are for us at the moment. Did you two decide to slip away together while I wasn't here? A nice little romantic getaway with lots of fiery sex?'

She felt tears of anger and frustration sting her eyes but was determined not to give in to them. 'No! For God's sake, John, stop it! I haven't been with Ben and I don't know where he is! Ask him if you don't believe me. Ring him.' She looked at him miserably and said in a sad voice, 'I want us to be happy, like we were when we got married. Before we came to live here and it all began to go wrong.'

His gaze held the same agonised confusion. 'Then tell me where you were over the last couple of days.'

'I . . . I can't!'

'You *can't*?' He sounded incredulous. 'What do you mean by that?'

She thought of the letter tucked into her luggage. Should she just produce that now? Throw it at him and say, *Here's the proof I wasn't with Ben. I was with your mother.* 'I will tell you. But not now.'

'I want to know right now.'

'No.'

'Come on – tell me where you were.' He suddenly sounded broken. He put his hands to his head. 'For Christ's sake, Delilah, can't you see this is destroying me? Why are you lying to me?'

'I'm not lying to you,' she said wretchedly, wondering how they'd arrived at this sorry situation and all the tangled misunderstandings.

'Then tell me.'

'All right.' Her head drooped and she stared at the ancient carpet, wondering for the hundredth time why it hadn't been replaced years ago. 'All right. I'll tell you. But it's a long story. I'm going to take a shower first. We'll meet at dinner and I'll tell you everything.'

They sat opposite each other in the round dining room where the table had been laid for a formal dinner. Outside the French doors the lawn stretched away, its vibrant green yellowed a little from the long dry spell. There was a hint of coming rain in the fuzziness of the blue sky and the bank of cloud approaching in the distance. Delilah wondered if

Janey noticed the awkward atmosphere as she put the plates of roast lamb in front of them.

'Thank you, Janey,' Delilah said, managing a smile.

'You're welcome. Well, I'm off for the evening now. I hope you enjoy it and see you tomorrow.'

When Janey had gone, the sense of heavy expectation grew. Delilah stared at her plate, and the rich aroma of roasted meat with the strong scent of rosemary and garlic turned her stomach. She didn't think she'd be able to eat anything. The anxiety of how she would tell John the truth had been knotting her insides more and more tightly as the moment grew closer and now she felt sick with it.

John did not seem to be having any problem. He heaped vegetables onto his plate with a kind of determination not to let all this spoil his dinner. When he had had a good load, well anointed with gravy, he sat back in his chair, fixed Delilah with a direct gaze and said, 'I'm ready. Off you go.'

'All right. But I'll need to tell you how it started. Please don't be impatient – it's important.'

She began haltingly, explaining about the clothes she had found in the attic and how she had realised they belonged to his mother, then she described how her curiosity was piqued by the things she stumbled across in the house – photographs and references to the mother who remained wreathed in mystery: where was her grave? How had she died? If she had thrown herself from the folly, why wasn't it known about?

'So you decided to find out more,' John said grimly. He'd been stony-faced and silent until now.

She nodded. 'You seemed to be so unhappy because of it. Ever since I've met you, you've told me that this house is a place that oppresses you, and that the past is all around you here, torturing you. I thought at first you didn't really mean it, that it was a way of dealing with the privilege you were born to. Then I became sure it was the trauma of losing your mother so young that caused your depression and the nightmares. I didn't realise that there was even more than I suspected, until I heard Elaine's name.'

John flinched very slightly, and continued eating as he waited for her to carry on.

'I couldn't think who this Elaine was. It was only because I'd looked for your mother's grave that I found out she was your dead sister. You see . . .' She looked at him pleadingly, pushing away her plate of cooling food. 'I felt that if I knew the truth, I could help you. Then things happened that propelled me along the path. I found the doll—'

'The doll?' he asked, frowning.

'A Sindy, tucked in the back of the cupboard. Who did it belong to? You told me there hadn't been any daughters in your family. And then . . .' She stopped and stared down at the way the light gleamed along the handles of her silver cutlery. 'The letter came.'

John stopped eating and looked at her as if aware that this was the beginning of the real explanation. Everything so far had been groundwork, designed to help understand her state of mind, to show him that she hadn't planned to be deceitful; she wanted him to know that her motives were pure, but events had begun to push her towards concealment.

'A letter came addressed to Lady Northmoor. You'd already left to go fishing so I couldn't show it to you. I was curious – nosy, perhaps – and . . . I opened it.' She glanced at him quickly. What would it mean to him when she mentioned that letter and his dead mother? Wasn't it ghoulish that it should arrive forty years after her death?

He seemed whiter than before and sat stiller in his chair, lifting his eyes to hers with a kind of blank, numbed expression, but otherwise he seemed to take the revelation calmly. He said, 'You opened it.'

'It was on impulse,' she said quickly. 'It occurred to me that maybe it was meant for me – I know that sounds stupid but it seemed a reasonable thought at the time. I opened it before I had time to think. It was from a solicitors' firm, and it was telling this person, Lady Northmoor, that she was getting an increase in her living allowance. The letter had a different address to the envelope. One in Greece.'

John's expression changed to one of complete realisation. He threw back his head for a moment, staring at the ceiling, his arms out wide on the table, then he said loudly, 'And you thought, I know! I've got a wizard idea! I'll just pop over to Greece and see who this Lady Northmoor person is!' He faced her again, his eyes full of accusation. 'That's what you did, didn't you?'

She nodded.

'You went over there and decided to mess with a situation you knew nothing about! Without breathing a word to me!'

'I didn't want to hurt you even more by raking it all up again for no reason. You'd told me your mother was dead and that's obviously what you believed so why would I risk causing you unnecessary pain?' She stared at him pleadingly. Then as she gazed at him, a sudden certainty possessed her, a revelation that as soon as she thought it, she knew was true. She took a deep breath. 'But you already knew, didn't you? You already knew she was alive.'

There was a long, frozen silence and then John got up, throwing his napkin down on his plate, and strode over to the curved French windows that gave out onto the lawn behind the house.

She turned to watch him, twisting in her seat, feeling as though she'd been a fool. All along she'd believed that he was trapped inside a dreadful lie. But that wasn't the case. The only person who hadn't known the truth was her. She tried to adjust everything to this new reality. 'You did, didn't you? You knew she was alive! How long have you known?'

He gave a great sigh, putting his hands in his pockets. At last he said, 'I've known for about as long as I've known you.'

'What?' she said, her lips feeling suddenly dry.

'I've got power of attorney now, you see. I've had it for a while, so my father's business affairs are an open book to me. But he'd left instructions that I wasn't to be told about my mother living in Greece until after his death or her death, or unless there were unavoidable circumstances that meant I had to know. The solicitors managed to cook up one of those unavoidable circumstances between them over the Greek euro crisis and whether or not my mother's allowance would be guaranteed no matter what might happen to the banks there. So they summoned me to London and, in that cold official way of theirs, they broke the news that my mother was living on an island in Greece, and what would I like to do about guaranteeing her allowance?'

She was filled with pity for him. 'You've known since then?'

He nodded. 'I thought I could come to terms with it. But it's been eating away at me ever since.'

No wonder he had been subject to those black moods of despair. No wonder he had wanted his mother's clothes burnt. How could anyone begin to understand something like that? She said softly, 'What did you do when you found out?'

He turned to look at her and smiled his funny lopsided smile. 'I came to find you.'

'I don't understand.' She had the disconcerting feeling that she'd been playing an unwitting role in all of this for far longer than she'd realised, as though she'd been dancing a waltz while asleep.

'I needed something good and true in my life. I'd been thinking about you ever since the day of the shoot. You stood out among all those ditzy fashion people in your normal clothes and in the way you seemed so natural. I liked the pencil in your hair, and the way we laughed together at the madness of everything . . . it struck something in me. That day I found myself walking to your offices and asking to see you. The moment I laid eyes on you . . . it was like the sun coming up after a black night. You were so beautiful and so real, and so untouched by all the darkness. I felt like

I *needed* you. You made me believe I might find love and happiness and all the things I wanted so badly. When we fell in love, I hoped that our relationship would blot out what I'd discovered. I wanted it to make me forget.'

Delilah looked at the table, her heart aching for him. 'And I wanted to make you remember.'

He let out a long breath, his shoulders slumping a little. 'It was wrong of me to ask so much. I should have guessed it was impossible – unfair on you, for one thing. You didn't even know that I wanted you to be the magic fairy who would make all the badness disappear.'

'Oh, John.' She looked back at him, biting her lip. He seemed tired and beaten, his grey eyes full of sadness. She loved him so much. Had she failed him? 'I only wanted what was right for you,' she whispered. 'I was trying to help.'

'I've been a beast to you, I know that. I can't blame you for . . . well, for responding when someone like Ben turns on the charm, not after the way I've been.' *Is he apologising?* she wondered, surprised. But before she could begin to ponder it, he said in a low voice, 'So what happened in Greece? You'd better tell me everything.'

He remained at the window, staring out at the deepening twilight as she told her tale of going to the island, of hearing the English voice at the monastery and then finding the Villa Artemis and finally Alexandra herself.

John stood very still as she recounted everything up to the meeting. 'How was she?' he asked in a curiously flat voice. 'What did she look like?'

'She looked very like her photographs. She wore a

headscarf so I didn't see her hair. Her face was older, of course, and lined . . . darker too from the sun. But her eyes were the same. Very vivid blue, the same shape. She seemed . . .' Delilah thought, trying to find the right word to describe Alexandra. 'She seemed incredibly and deeply alone. The loneliest person I've ever met.'

John turned back to her at last. 'And what did she say?'

'She told me that she'd always loved you. She wouldn't say why she left but she did insist that it was for the best, that it was the only thing she could do. Of course I asked her how she could leave you when you needed her so much, even if she was in desperate pain about Elaine's death. She told me that even if Elaine hadn't died, she would have gone. She even claimed that it would have been better if she'd died but your father begged her to spare herself.' Delilah hoped she was treading as lightly as possible over John's pain while telling him the truth that he clearly needed to hear. 'Do you have any idea why she would think that?'

He walked over to her and sank down in the chair next to her, his shoulders slumped, his hands clasped. He shook his head. She reached out and stroked his dark, silver-threaded hair – more silver threads lately, she thought – and rubbed his shoulder.

'I've got no bloody idea,' he mumbled. 'It's all too much for me to understand.'

'She obviously thinks she's to blame for Elaine's death. I wondered if that was why she felt too wicked to stay here with you but she said that wasn't it. But . . .' Delilah took a deep breath. This was the moment she had most feared. 'She said that you would eventually discover that she hadn't died and she asked me to give you this.' Slowly, she drew the slender folded envelope out of her pocket and held it out to John.

He looked up, frowning, his eyes reddened, and saw what she was holding out. An expression of horror passed over his face and he shook his head, recoiling from it.

'No, no, no!' he said fiercely. 'I don't want it!'

'You don't have to read it now. Perhaps it's best to wait.'

'No, you don't understand. She's not coming back into this house. Not in any way.' John pushed back the chair and stood up, his eyes panicked. 'I can't have that. She can't do that to me, she can't start coming back now. I've spent a lifetime accepting that she's dead and I won't undo it now, do you understand? I won't start all over again like that! I couldn't stand it!' His voice was rising with a mixture of fear and anger.

She rose to her feet, still clutching the letter, holding it out to him. 'But, John—'

'Stop it!' he yelled. She gasped at the ferocity of his voice, staring at him wide-eyed and stunned. 'Haven't you caused enough bloody trouble? Don't you understand what you've done? You can't just go down to the underworld and fetch back the dead and say, There you are, it's all right now, isn't it? It doesn't work like that! Don't you understand that I *want* her dead! She had her chance and she made her choice. She chose death. She chose to be away from me year after year. If she'd killed herself in a moment of madness, I could have understood and forgiven. But to keep rejecting me the way she did ... It's unbearable, can't you understand? I refuse to have her brought back to life to make me suffer in new ways. Don't you see? It's *easier* for me if she's dead.'

He snatched the letter from her and tore it to shreds, scattering the pieces all over the table and the remains of their meal.

'That's it,' he said. 'It's over. It's what I've been trying to make myself believe for the last seven months. She's dead.'

Then he turned and walked out of the room, leaving her staring after him in shock.

Chapter Thirty-Three

In bed that night after the revelation of her trip to Greece, Delilah did what she always did when John was low: she used her whole body to comfort him, wrapping him in her embrace and trying to give some of her life force to him. He lay there, absorbing her comfort for a while, and then he turned to fold her in his arms and take her mouth with his. He seemed possessed by an angry and desperate need as he reached for her, running his hands over her body as if using it only to spur his own desire rather than to cherish it and love it. He squeezed and pinched at her breasts, bit down on her lips and pressed his fingers roughly between her legs, as though his lust needed an element of something hard and fierce. He didn't hurt her, but she felt like a vessel rather than a partner as his hands and mouth moved over her. He tugged at her nipples with his teeth while his hands pushed her legs wider, exploring her with a ferocious need. She did not resist or even attempt to return caresses. She sensed that he didn't require that. His arousal stemmed not from her but from working on her, and all she had to do was be there, his willing object. They had never made love like this before and she found it strange and almost frightening. It had always been the two of them making love to each other, and now for the first time she wondered where he was in his head. He seemed almost absent as he turned her over with needy hands and plunged into her as she knelt on the bed with her back to him. She absorbed the pressure as he thrust forward, his hands on her hips as though to propel her forward and back in time to his own movements. The action began to stimulate her despite her slight sense of disconnection from him. She gasped out loud as he rammed himself home inside her, and that aroused him further to stronger, harder movements. She began to moan without meaning to as each thrust hit her deep and hard, and then she wanted to turn around to him, to kiss him, to have him pressed tight against her so that they could ride this wave of desire together to the end. But she couldn't move. He wanted to keep her there, she realised; he was pressing more of his weight down on her, his hand now on her shoulder and then heavy on the side of her neck. She began to resist the thrusts as they grew harder, but he was caught up in his lust now, producing a guttural noise in his throat with each slam into her. He went faster, pistoning in and out as she gasped for breath and tried to take the shock of the motion without being driven forward into the bed-head. Then he reached his peak and with a grunt of release he poured out his climax into her, letting it subside completely before withdrawing with a sigh. He reached to her night table and pulled some tissues out of the box there, passing two to her and keeping one for himself.

She turned slowly round and lay back, mopping with the tissue while she stared up into the darkness, not really sure what had just happened. He lay beside her in silence for a while, then rolled over, kissed her cheek and said, 'Night, darling,' before rolling back the other way and going to sleep.

The next morning Delilah woke to find John was already gone, and she lay back on the pillows, staring up at the bed hangings with a kind of black despair. The whole of yesterday afternoon had been a disaster, from Vanna's visit to the scene over dinner. She was still astonished that all this time John had known his mother was alive. He had kept that from her. But in a way, she could see why he had. He'd wanted to convince himself that Alexandra was dead. It would no doubt have helped him if Delilah believed the same thing. *But that's it then*, she thought. *There's no way he'll want to see her now. He can't understand why she did it, and until he does he'll never forgive her.*

She wondered what Alexandra had said in the letter that John had ripped up and now would never read. Perhaps she, Delilah, had better write to Alexandra and tell her what had happened. But she shied away from the thought of getting involved again. Things were complicated enough as it was. If she and John were going to have any chance of rebuilding the trust between them, she was going to have to be very careful what she did.

The thought of Ben came into her mind, and she reached over and picked up her phone off the night table. It was very bad luck that he had decided to be away from the fort at the same time as she was. Where had he gone? Should she warn him about John's suspicions or would that make everything worse. She opened a text message to compose something but then, on second thought, put the phone down. Contacting him would only strengthen the impression that there was something going on between them, and she knew now that she didn't want to give him that idea. She put the phone down and went to get dressed. On her way to breakfast, Delilah passed the huge staircase window and saw by the dark dampness of the gravel paths that it must have rained in the night, but the sun was shining again and the gardens were serenely beautiful. Downstairs the estate office door was firmly shut. John must be in there. She wondered if he was on the phone to the solicitors' office, giving them a rocket for that misdirected letter.

In the kitchen, Janey was fretting over a shopping list.

'I don't mind going to the shops,' Delilah offered. 'I need something to do this morning.'

'You're only just back from your trip. I'm sure you've got plenty to do,' Janey said.

'Not really. I might walk there and back. I could do with the exercise.'

'It'll take longer than you think,' Janey cautioned. 'I walk down to the lodge and it's a good three quarters of an hour just to get there. But don't let me stop you if you want to. I'll just finish this list.'

'Okay. Great.' She felt pleased to have a purpose that

would also give her plenty of thinking time. The longer the walk to the village, the better as far as she was concerned.

'By the way,' Janey remarked as she began to complete the list in her neat print, 'there was confetti all over the dinner table this morning. Were you playing some sort of game in there? It was a real fiddle to clear it all away so I could throw it out.'

Delilah took Mungo with her for the walk, and he was excited both to see her back after her absence and to be going on such a long expedition. He trotted along beside her wagging his tail, heading off at odd moments to explore and sniff before returning to her side, as though wanting to check that she was all right and still in the mood for continuing their lovely long jaunt. She checked her phone as she went. There was still nothing from Ben.

As she passed the lodge near the top of the drive, she thought of Elaine again. *This must be close to where it happened.* She shivered, and hoped that it wouldn't always come into her mind at this spot, but it almost felt as if the psychic force of the accident was still shimmering in the air even after all this time.

Walking on more briskly, she called Mungo to heel and put him on the lead as they approached the road. Cars came flying along the country roads, sometimes even on the wrong side of the road, heedless of what might be around a bend or behind an outcrop of hedge, and there were no pavements, only verges to walk on. It was safer to keep the dog close by as they took the hill down into the village. She was just passing the village sign and remembering that she hadn't brought a bag with her – except one for collecting Mungo's mess and did she dare to use that one? – when a car that she expected to pass by stopped beside her, the passenger window sliding down with an electronic whirr.

'Well, hello,' said a smooth American voice. 'What a coincidence.'

She looked round to find Vanna smiling at her from behind the wheel. 'Hello,' she said weakly, not overly happy to see her husband's first wife but mindful that she'd been unjustly cool the day before.

'Very weird. I was just thinking about you,' Vanna said. 'I'm on my way to the airport, but you know what, I'm early. Why don't you jump in and we'll go for a coffee some-where?'

'Well . . .' Delilah didn't find the idea appealing. 'I've got Mungo with me.'

'Don't worry, put him in the back. This is a hire car. I'm handing it back in a few hours.'

There didn't seem to be an excuse not to do as Vanna suggested, so Delilah called Mungo to the car and the next moment they were gliding noiselessly towards the village.

'Where's good for coffee?' Vanna asked. Her air was friendly and good-humoured, and she looked as elegant as she had the previous day in skinny jeans, a white T-shirt and an obviously expensive blue jacket. Her blonde hair was brushed back into a glossy ponytail and gold hoops set with diamonds gleamed in her ears. 'Has this place got any more civilised since I lived here? Ten years ago, you couldn't even get a decent cup in London, let alone out here.'

'There's a tea room just beyond the green,' Delilah said, trying to conquer her awkwardness. 'You can park nearby.'

'Oh, I see it. That's new. Let's try it.'

A few minutes later, they were sitting in the window overlooking the village green with a mug of coffee each. From her seat, Delilah could see where Mungo was tethered outside, watching the pigeons come and go on the green.

'Well, this is a definite improvement,' Vanna said, looking at her cup. 'Real coffee. No decaf, but never mind. We have to be grateful for small mercies, right?' She looked over at Delilah with a smile. Vanna was so impeccable and polished, out of place in the chintzy tea room with its flowery plates and horse brasses on the wall. 'I got the impression you were not that happy to see me yesterday and I wanted to set your mind at rest in case you had any fears about me coming back onto your territory.'

'Oh no,' Delilah said, blushing at the memory of her jealousy the previous day. 'Really. It's fine. I was tired, that's all. I'm sorry if I gave you that impression.'

'That's okay,' Vanna said lightly. 'No problem. But when I left, I had a funny feeling. I could see that something wasn't right with you and John, and I don't want you making the mistakes I made.' She leaned forward conspiratorially and said in a low voice, 'I know what it's like to live in that place. It's not easy. And John isn't easy.'

'No,' agreed Delilah with feeling. 'He's not.'

'But you love him, right? I can see you do – you wouldn't

447

look like you're in such a mess if you didn't. Here's my advice – when things are going badly, get him away from that house. He relaxes when he escapes from it all. I didn't realise it because he resisted me so much whenever I suggested it – and besides, I was always at him to go to the States and he really wasn't keen on that. So we were locked in a constant battle and we never did go anywhere.'

'That's it?' Delilah blinked, surprised. She had half expected Vanna to offer her a complex analysis of John and explain how to solve the problem of his personality.

Vanna nodded. 'Yeah. Honestly . . . the way the British system means you can't sell a house but have to stay there forever no matter how you feel about it . . . It wouldn't happen in the States, that's for sure. I never really appreciated how much John felt the pressure of it. In the end, it got too much for us. We stopped remembering why we'd ever loved each other. I gave up on the whole thing and . . . well, I just wanted to say . . .' She smiled almost shyly. 'Don't give up on him. I think he's worth hanging on for. Just make sure you get out from the shadow of that place from time to time. That's all.'

Delilah smiled back. Could it really be so simple? She felt lighter suddenly, and hopeful. Vanna was right: she did love John, with all the challenges he posed and the burdens he carried. He loved her too, despite what she'd done to the trust between them. She would never forgive herself if she gave up and ran away. 'Thank you,' she said sincerely. 'Really. Thank you.'

'You're welcome.' Vanna looked down at her almost

untouched coffee. 'You know what, I'd better get on my way to the airport. Can I give you a lift back to the house?'

Delilah shook her head. 'No, it's fine. Mungo and I will walk to the shop first. Then go back.'

'Sure.' Vanna stood up.

'There's just one thing,' Delilah said, getting up as well and putting on her cardigan. 'You must have known John's father before he got his Alzheimer's. What was he like?'

'Oh, he was a great guy but kind of sad, you know? A lonely man, I thought. He and John only had each other. They were really connected.'

'Did Nicky tell you that Alexandra had killed herself?'

Vanna thought for a moment and said, 'Well, now, that's the funny thing. John told me she'd killed herself up at that old tower. But once when I talked to Nicky and we mentioned her in passing, he said that his wife had gone away. I guessed he meant died, but it was a funny way to say it. Gone away.'

Delilah nodded. 'Yes. That is strange. I'm glad we had this talk, Vanna. Thank you.'

'You're so welcome. I mean it.'

Walking along the high street towards the village store, Mungo on the lead, Delilah felt a kind of peace descend on her. It was a relief after the high emotion of the day before. She didn't need to fear Vanna at all; in fact, the other woman had suddenly and effectively opened her eyes to the truth.

I've been a fool. I've let myself get confused between John and the house. I loved him first, before I ever lived there.

Our troubles only started when we let that place rule our lives.

She had a sudden image of Ben in her mind, digging in the garden. He wasn't affected by the house – in fact, he'd been an antidote to its darkness – but he was still a part of it in a way. He belonged to the estate and the grounds as firmly as John did. She tried to imagine living a life with Ben away from Fort Stirling. It was impossible. Not only would he never leave, but no matter what scenario she tried to conjure up, there was something missing. She could picture a sizzling attraction and the lure of his physicality, but there was no more than that.

I don't love him. He's sweet and good-hearted, but I don't love him. I couldn't give him what I give John. I would only take from him.

It would be a disaster, she could see that. Now the thought of Ben made her anxious and fearful that she'd got herself mixed up in something that wasn't the answer but had just seemed like a solution at a time when she'd been confused. Even if she and John were far apart from each other in many ways, in others she felt that they were drawing nearer and their bond was growing closer. She was beginning to understand him at last, and perhaps if they got through this, they might be able to heal everything that had hurt them so far.

And yet, there was no real reason to believe that. Nothing had changed, except that Vanna had spoken a few words to her that had given her hope.

*

In the shop, she bought the things on Janey's list while Mungo waited outside, tied to the lamppost, and was just heading out again when the door opened and the vicar came breezing in.

'Hello, Mrs Stirling!' He smiled his crinkly-eyed smile at her. 'How are you?'

'I'm fine, thank you.'

'Any more grave-spotting needed?'

'No, thank you. That's all sorted now.'

'Ah. Did you find out more about the little girl?'

'Well – yes, a little bit more.'

He raised his eyebrows. 'How interesting. I'm just going over to Rawlston now, the old people's home there. I've just popped in to get some biscuits as a present for Father Ronald. Do you remember I mentioned him?'

'Oh, yes,' Delilah said, recalling the name. 'He conducted Elaine's funeral.'

'That's right.' A thought seemed to strike the vicar. 'Why don't you come with me and meet him? If you're not too busy. You could tell me about developments on the way.'

'Oh . . . I . . .' She stared at him, nonplussed. She had not thought of continuing any of her so-far disastrous forays into the Stirling past. 'I've got the dog,' she said, 'and I can't be too long with the shopping.'

'He can come with us,' the vicar offered. 'The old people love to see dogs, you'd be surprised. And we won't be long. I'll drive you back. I'll even take you home.'

'All right then. Yes, that would be very interesting. Thank you. I'll come.'

Chapter Thirty-Four

The drive to the neighbouring village of Rawlston only took about ten minutes but it was long enough to explain the circumstances of Elaine's death to the vicar. He sighed solemnly.

'The loss of a child is always terrible. To feel you're responsible is a burden that not many of us could bear lightly. It's a life sentence. That poor woman. I think we can begin to understand what drove her to do what she did, if that was indeed what happened.'

Delilah said nothing, gazing unhappily out of the window and wondering if lying to vicars was worse than lying to other people. But, feeling that Alexandra's existence was not her secret to share, she kept quiet.

The old people's home was a very genteel place, a Queen Anne mansion of mellow red brick that had once been an important village house but had been sympathetically converted into a care facility. The vicar parked up behind the house and they walked back down to it, Mungo bounding on the lead beside them.

'I come here quite often,' the vicar said. 'Every couple of weeks or so. I don't want any of my parishioners feeling forgotten and some of the people here don't get many visitors. Now – this way.'

He led her inside through a large black-painted front door and Delilah was at once struck by the extreme warmth inside. Despite the summer day, the radiators seemed to be turned up full blast. The vicar didn't seem to notice but perhaps he spent so much time in cold churches that he liked being hot.

He introduced Delilah to the large and glowing lady behind the desk and she told them where they would find Father Ronald.

'May we take the dog with us?' the vicar enquired.

'Oh yes, do, he'll perk them all up no end.' She gestured to a sturdy fireproof door in front of them. 'Through there! Off you go.'

They walked along the heavily carpeted corridor, Delilah already feeling breathless and stifled from the heat. She was relieved when they came out into a lighter, airier room that overlooked the gardens at the back. Someone had opened the windows and a cool breeze wafted into the room. A large-screen television was playing at a quiet volume on a stand, and there were many armchairs around the room, most occupied by very elderly men and women, some with walking frames parked nearby. The vicar began to walk about, greeting people and shaking their hands, talking in a loud, cheerful voice designed to penetrate mild deafness without sending hearing aids squealing in protest. He took

Mungo with him, offering the dog for a pat or a stroke, which was eagerly taken up by most.

'And here we are – Father Ronald, how are you?' He'd stopped by an old man who had shrunk to a small curved shape, and was propped up in an armchair where he could look out over the garden rather than at the television. His skin was withered and liver-spotted, and there were only a few wisps of white hair on his shiny scalp. At the sound of the vicar's voice, he looked up.

'Eh?' It came out croakily. Delilah felt vaguely disappointed. He didn't look as though he had all his faculties after all.

'How are you, Father?' boomed the vicar, smiling broadly.

'Oh! I'm very well. Enjoying this beautiful day, contemplating God's creation. I don't know why they want us to watch that television all day long when there's all this right outside the window.'

'Very true.' The vicar sat down on the low windowsill directly in front of Father Ronald.

He's gone and blocked his view! thought Delilah, wanting to giggle for a moment. Instead she bent and stroked Mungo's silky head.

'Now, Father, I'd like to introduce you to someone,' continued the vicar, beckoning Delilah to come into the old man's eyeline. 'This is Mrs Stirling. She's living up at the fort now. She's married young John Stirling.'

The old man looked up at her, straining his faded blue eyes to get a full picture of her. He nodded. 'Oh yes. How nice. How things do keep moving on, don't they? When I first came here, it was the present lord's parents who were at the big house. Now it's you young things taking it all on.' He smiled up at Delilah and she felt a rush of friendliness towards him. She sat down on the armchair next to him, pulling Mungo close and patting his rear to make him sit down.

'It's lovely to meet you,' she said politely, her voice louder than usual in case of deafness. 'The vicar tells me you remember everything that happened over the years.'

'I don't know about everything,' said Father Ronald, half amused, 'but I know what's what. I've not lost my capacity yet, even if it's not quite as sharp it used to be. It's funny what comes back, isn't it? I woke in the night recalling a poem in ancient Greek quite perfectly. I learnt it up at Oxford in the forties.'

'Mrs Stirling has a particular question for you,' prompted the vicar, giving Delilah an encouraging look. 'Haven't you?'

'Yes.' She coughed lightly, clearing her throat, uncertain where to begin. Less than a week ago, she would have been eager to start questioning but now she felt the danger of dabbling in things she had no right to know about. 'I . . . I wondered what you remember of the death of Elaine Stirling.'

'Ah!' Father Ronald at once looked mournful and he shook his head, his mouth turned down almost to his chin. 'I remember it very well and it was an awful thing, my dear young lady. A truly awful thing. I've never seen a woman more affected by grief than that poor mother at the grave-side of her child. She had lost her daughter, but worse than that she had been at the wheel of the car that killed the girl.'

'Was Lady Northmoor ever charged with dangerous driving?' asked Delilah.

The old man shook his head. 'There was talk of that. But she was in no state to face any charges, poor woman, and by the time they came to think of it, she was gone. And I think words were had, high up, you know. The family could exert pressure when they needed to.' He sighed. 'I've often thought of her. I knew her from a girl, you see. I baptised her children and earlier than that, I conducted her first marriage.' Father Ronald leaned forward, his penetrating eye still on her. 'I feared that would end badly, though I prayed for them both. There was something about that young man that made me think he wasn't made for marriage. God had another purpose for him, but it wasn't that. And Alexandra needed a man who loved her after what she'd been through.'

'Been through?' Delilah asked, frowning.

'Her mother died when she was young. She committed suicide by jumping off the folly.'

A shiver of eerie astonishment flew over her skin despite the heat. 'Alex's mother killed herself like that?'

'Oh yes. It was a great scandal but her father sheltered her from it as best he could. He kept her apart from everyone afterwards and I suspect the girl was told a different story to protect her. I always thought it was his motive in marrying her off so young – getting her away from the village and what happened here.'

Delilah was piecing things together, trying to take in the new information. 'But everyone seemed to think that Alex was the one who jumped off the folly.'

The old man snorted contemptuously. 'Stupid village rumours. Impossible to stop it. They said the family had covered it up in shame and given out that she'd died of grief somewhere.' He gave a hollow laugh. 'People thought it made sense. Her mother had been driven mad too, and so they felt it was simply in the blood. It was history repeating itself.'

'But you didn't think so?'

'I asked Lord Northmoor and he told me that his wife had gone away and would never come back. He asked me not to speak of it, and so I didn't.' He shook his head slowly, looking grave. 'I understood in a way. If you'd seen her at the funeral, so would you. She had no real conception of where she was or what was happening, as though her mind couldn't stand to know. She was the living embodiment of torment. If I hadn't believed in demons then, I would have on that day. She was in hell. If those rumours meant she'd be left in peace, then so be it.'

Delilah felt her nose prickle and drew in a short, sharp breath. Her eyes stung. In hell. That was what hell was, she supposed. Being at the mercy of the unbearable. *All we can do is hope and pray that we're never asked to suffer in that way*, she thought. *And who knows what any of us can stand in the end?*

'But,' Father Ronald said, leaning forward, 'if you want to know more, you should talk to Emily Jessop, who was a maid at the Old Grange. She's in the home here. I believe she's still alert enough to remember. She's often told me how she feels about what happened to poor Lady Northmoor. Tell her I sent you.'

457

Delilah looked over to the vicar, who'd been listening quietly. She felt churned up by all she'd discovered. In a few brief moments, she'd learned so much that was new about Alexandra. But perhaps the puzzle was still not yet complete. 'Can we find Emily Jessop? I'd love to talk to her if I may.'

They found the old woman in a small room, part of a group listening to the radio over cups of tea and a plate of digestives.

'Miss Jessop, might we borrow you for a moment?' the vicar asked jovially, and was quickly shushed by the others. He went on in a quieter voice, 'We want to see if you remember a few things about your old situation.'

'Which one?' asked Miss Jessop, a frown deepening the lines between her brows. She was tiny, a small frail figure almost lost in the depths of her armchair, but her thick white hair was pulled back into a surprisingly sturdy bun and her voice was still strong with a rich Dorset accent.

'The Old Grange,' the vicar said. 'You worked for the old gentleman, didn't you? You knew Alexandra Crewe before she married?'

'Ah!' The old woman sighed. 'Yes, yes.' She glanced about at the other people. 'But I'd rather not say here.'

By the time they had Miss Jessop up on her walking frame and had found a place down the hall where they could sit in privacy, Delilah was growing increasingly eager to ask her questions but she had to wait until they were all settled.

'Now, Miss Jessop, this lady is married to Alexandra's boy, John,' the vicar said.

Miss Jessop turned her bright eyes on Delilah. 'Is she? That's nice.'

'She wondered what you remembered of the old days.'

'It's lovely to meet you, Miss Jessop. Thank you for seeing us. Father Ronald said to say he sent me,' Delilah said, hoping this would be enough to win the old lady's confidence.

'I'm glad someone wants to talk about Miss Alexandra!' said Miss Jessop unexpectedly. 'They only ever spread nasty gossip and lies. It's about time the truth was heard.' The old lady's voice was strong despite the cracked notes in it. 'She was treated so badly by that wicked father of hers. It's lain hard with my own conscience all these years that I didn't speak up. I've always feared that I could have stopped it and that's a hard thing to live with.'

'Stopped what?' Delilah asked quickly.

Miss Jessop fixed her with a defiant gaze. 'Why, all of it.' She shook her head. 'She was tormented beyond endurance, just like her poor mother before her. It was no wonder she couldn't live with it.' The old woman leaned towards Delilah and said in a low voice, 'But it was a wicked lie! And I knew it. Cook and me, we both knew it.'

Delilah tried to follow Miss Jessop's train of thought. 'You mean, the lie that she jumped off the folly?'

Miss Jessop tutted impatiently. 'No – not that. I'm talking about the lie that caused the trouble. You see, I tended the old devil in his last illness. God knows, many a time I've wished I had taken up a pillow and put him out of the world before he caused any more mischief, but I didn't. We'd already seen him destroy poor Mrs Crewe, his wife. I know some would think she did wrong to be with Lord North-moor and no doubt she did. They both did. They were promised to others and they broke their vows to be together. I don't know about the old lord, but you could hardly blame *her* for looking for some kindness from somewhere. But when Mr Crewe found out, there was merry hell to pay – excuse me, Vicar – and he drove that poor woman to her death.'

'Alexandra's mother had an affair with Nicky's father,' said Delilah in a wondering tone, trying to absorb this new information and what it might mean. 'And then she killed herself.'

The old woman nodded, her white bun bobbing on the back of her head. 'That's right.'

'So . . . what was the wicked lie?'

Miss Jessop looked down to where her hands were twisted together in her lap. The knuckles were prominent and her fingers bent with arthritis. She seemed to be battling with herself, as if now the moment was here, she wasn't sure she could tell what she knew after all.

'Please, Miss Jessop,' urged Delilah quietly. 'It might help very much if you tell me what you know.'

'It can't cause more pain than has already been caused,' the old woman returned crisply. 'It's something I promised myself I would do before I go. I want to tell you – but it's not easy to remember. You see, the old man treated that girl terribly. Poor motherless thing! He visited the sins of the mother on her. After what had happened with Mrs Crewe, and the way she'd left this world, he could hardly bear the sight of their daughter. We all saw it and our hearts bled for her. And when she left that man he made her marry and ended up living at the big house with a title and everything the Stirlings could offer her, it made him sick to his stomach. It was like his wife had come back and triumphed after all. Like she'd won through the girl, you see. And he wasn't having that. So then he did it.'

'Did what?' Delilah leaned forward, not wanting to miss a word. Here at last was the heart of things. 'What did he do?'

Miss Jessop paused, then said slowly, 'He told a terrible lie. Miss Alexandra came down to the house to see him when she heard he was dying. She wanted to make peace with the old monster, which was more than he deserved. And he took the opportunity to curse her with his dying breath.'

'What did he say?'

The old woman's voice sank to a whisper but it was almost clearer than her speaking voice. She took on an expression of deep gravity as though this was a message she had been waiting many years to pass on. 'When she sent me out, I left the door ajar so I could listen. I knew it was wrong to eavesdrop but everything in me told me that old wretch had something up his sleeve to make sure she suffered. I heard every word. He told her that she was not his child. He told her that she was the result of her mother's affair with Lord Northmoor and that she was cursed like her mother.'

Delilah gasped. 'Wait – he said that she was the child of Lord Northmoor? Nicky's father?' She closed her eyes at the implication, her insides clenching in shock. 'You mean, he told her that she and Nicky were half-siblings – that she'd married her own half-brother!'

A sense of revelation washed over her. She was sure beyond doubt that this was the secret Alexandra wanted to die with her. What could it be but this?

Emily Jessop nodded. 'That's right. He sent her mad in his own way. He knew how to do it. He was cock-a-hoop when she left, delighted with himself for spoiling her life. That was the very day the little girl was killed.'

'But that's terrible!' Delilah said, appalled. It made an awful sense that Alexandra, in a state of horror and shock, would be driving recklessly enough to cause the accident.

The vicar was shaking his head, his expression solemn. 'It's unbelievable.'

Delilah said urgently to Miss Jessop, 'But you don't think he was telling the truth?'

Emily sat up straighter, invigorated by her indignation. 'Cook and me knew it wasn't true! Cook had been there years and was privy to everything. She told me that Mrs Crewe started her love affair after Miss Alexandra was born. And it gave the poor woman a few years of happiness at least, and I don't begrudge her that, Vicar, even if you do!' The old woman fixed him with a beady stare.

The vicar said softly, 'I understand human frailty, Miss Jessop, and so does God.'

'How did that horrible man feel when he realised he'd

caused the death of his granddaughter?' asked Delilah, outraged at the events of the past. She felt real anger bubbling up inside.

'He never knew. His illness took its course quickly and he died the next day before the news was out. And no one cared a jot that he'd gone, not in the face of the loss of the precious child.'

Delilah reached out and took the knobbly old hand with its papery skin. 'Thank you,' she said quietly. 'Thank you so much for telling us what you have. It's made everything clear now. And I truly think it will help.'

'It can't bring her back, though, can it?' said Miss Jessop and her eyes were suddenly red-rimmed and full of tears. 'I've wished so hard I could have told her before the little girl was taken and before she felt the only way was to end it. They all said that was what she'd done and I cried for weeks when I found out. You can't think how hard I wished I could have changed things!'

Delilah bent down to hug the frail body, suddenly moved. Her anger disappeared and she felt happiness and hope take its place. 'I think you must have wished hard enough. I think you might be able to bring her back.'

Chapter Thirty-Five

'Madam, madam!'

The little piping voice came up from the narrow street below, floating into the kitchen like birdsong.

Alexandra left the worktop, where she was making a salad of ripe red tomatoes, long slices of wet cucumber and torn shreds of lettuce. A piece of damp salty feta cheese sat on a wooden board, waiting to be chopped into rough cubes and added to the bowl. She went out onto the terrace and looked over the white wall. Down below a small brown face surrounded by thick dark hair gazed back up at her.

'Tina, hello,' she answered in Greek. 'How are you?'

'I've brought bread,' the girl said. She lifted a basket that she was carrying over one skinny arm. 'Mama told me to come.'

'Come on then.' Alexandra beckoned her up. 'Bring it here. You're just in time.'

The girl scampered through the gate and up the stone steps to the terrace.

'Thank you, Tina,' Alexandra smiled at the girl. The local

children always seemed enchanting. She'd watched a couple of generations now, growing from urchin-like children with sun-darkened skin, spidery arms and legs and tough sandy feet, to a kind of graceful adolescence that she was sure did not exist in England. The inhabitants of the island seemed to have a secret that made them scrambling adventurers one day, and ripened young women or strong young men the next. And in almost no time there would be another wedding and she would be astonished to learn that tonight they would be dancing for young Yannis who last week had been climbing her fig tree to get the fruit for her, and this week was the handsomest man in the village and marrying the beautiful Alida, only just transformed herself from a skinny thing playing hopping games in the road. So many of the young ones left now, heading to Athens for work or trying to move abroad where life would be better away from the terrible economic conditions. At least the island would always have a steady stream of tourists and pilgrims come to see the holy sites, and the beauty of the place meant that people with money would always want to live here. Sometimes she worried about her job as a tourist guide at the monastery, fearing that she was taking work from someone who needed it more, but as she refused a salary she hoped it was not so. She asked the monks to donate what they would have paid her to charity or any family in particular need that month.

Tina came into the kitchen, looking about curiously as everyone always did when they came to madam's house. Alexandra wondered what they all said about her. No doubt there were rumours. They always called her madam, as though they had found out that she had once had a rank back home. Not that it mattered now, of course – or, indeed, had ever mattered.

Tina took out two loaves of bread and put them on the counter. 'Here you are, madam.'

'Thank you, Tina. Do you have something else for me?'

She giggled and said, 'Of course.' She produced a small cardboard box that held four pastries filled with a sticky concoction of honey and nuts.

'Delicious! Your mama is a wonderful pastry cook.' Alexandra bent down towards the girl. They both knew the routine but enjoyed it just the same. 'But you know, I don't think I'll be able to eat all this on my own. I can hardly manage one of these rich pastries, let alone four. I think you should help me. Why don't you take one?'

'Thank you, madam,' Tina said, eagerly plucking one out of the box. 'May I have it now?'

'Eat it before you go back. Then you can wash your hands here. Come onto the terrace and you can enjoy it outside.'

They both went back to the warm scented outdoors. Summer was at its height and Alexandra could already sense the year on the turn. The freshness was leaving the air, the season of dust was beginning and then she would feel the plants starting to age around her, tiring of the great burst of energy they had expended since the spring. Tina munched happily on her sticky treat, licking her fingers as she went along. Alexandra watched her, enjoying the girl's simple pleasure in the sweetness of the honey and the crisp layers of golden brown pastry. The sound of a horn blasting out below them somewhere made them both look towards the sea.

'The ferry must be arriving,' she said. It was invisible from where they were, approaching from the south and sliding into the harbour below the hills. But she always heard the horns as they announced the approach and departure of the great vessel.

She had grown so used to the sound over the years that she barely noticed it now. That was, until the woman, Delilah, had come here. Now she realised that the horn was a harbinger of change and always had been. Growing deaf to it had been a mistake. Any day might bring a stranger here, one who intended to change her life in some way. She'd existed so long in this place untroubled by the outside world except on her terms – when she chose to read a newspaper or watch a television programme – that she'd begun to forget that it might still have an interest in her. In fact, that it certainly would one day or another. And so it had proved to be. The question was whether it was done with her now or not.

She turned to the girl who was licking the last traces of honey off her fingers and from the corners of her mouth, like a cat might clean itself after eating. 'Now, Tina, rinse your fingers, then you'd better be getting home. Thank your mother. Tell her to give me the month's bill.'

'Yes, madam.' Tina was already on the steps to the kitchen. 'Goodbye, and thank you.'

'See you soon!' Alexandra waved to her, knowing that it wouldn't be Tina next time who came with the bread. It would be one of her brothers or sisters, taking turns to walk up to the English lady's house and be given a cake.

She went back to her salad and finished assembling it. She cut a slice of the fresh bread, covered the pastries with a towel against the marauding flies, and took her meal outside to the terrace as she usually did. She liked to eat her supper slowly, without reading or listening to the radio, absorbing the sounds and smells around her and savouring each mouthful. The years were moving so quickly now that it made sense to open her eyes as much as she could to every season, catching it and living it before it sailed past and was gone.

The memory of that woman came back to her as it so often did. She had imagined that she would find it easy to shut Delilah out of her mind. After all, she'd had many years of practice closing herself off from what was happening beyond her immediate existence. Eventually, she'd even been able to stop herself returning home in dreams – except for those regular nightmares that still came to punish her – although occasionally she was unexpectedly ambushed. She would be in a perfectly normal dream and would turn to find John as a boy standing there, staring up at her with his huge grey eyes, demanding to know where she had gone, or she would realise she was standing at the door of Fort Stirling, with everyone expecting her to go inside and take over her old life. Sometimes she would see Nicky and he would be furious with her, or else blankly detached, happy with a new life that didn't include her. Those dreams were almost unbearable, but at least they were easier than the nightmares.

Still, she had assumed that her little tricks for forgetting would work as well as they had for years. And that was wrong. The vision of Delilah on the terrace, her face strained between anger, pity and confusion, was so strong she couldn't shake it from her mind.

Was I right to write that letter? she wondered, putting a sliver of creamy feta on her tongue and letting it melt there saltily. A picture came into her mind of John opening it, reading and then . . . what? It was hard to say as the image in her mind was of the boy John. He was so young in her imagination that she saw him stumbling over the big words, as he had when she'd heard him read from his storybooks, and bursting into tears with frustration at the end.

'But, Mummy,' he shouted, stamping his foot as he had when he was seven years old. 'I want you to come back, don't you understand?'

Her heart twisted in pain at the image.

'Stop it!' she ordered herself out loud. 'None of that, do you hear? What good will it do?'

Since Delilah had come – *my daughter-in-law*, she reminded herself – some of the things she had always clung to as certainties had not seemed so immoveable as they once had. Her absolute conviction that she had done the only thing she could for her family began to shimmer and look hazy, like a mirage when one begins to get close and realise that it is something unsubstantial. She could not afford for that to happen. She had built her entire life and everything in it around her certain knowledge of what was right. While Delilah had been here, she had been as convinced of it as ever. It was only after she left that the doubts began to come.

Perhaps it had been writing that letter. She hadn't intended to leave anything for John, nothing to explain why things had turned out the way they had. Her promise to herself had been to take everything with her, good and bad. No complaining, no explaining. And yet she had found herself sitting down and writing that letter, then phoning around the hotels until she found the one where Delilah was staying so that she could deliver it there.

It's no good regretting it! she said to herself. *You've done it now. It's gone, she's taken it back. He'll have read it by now.*

Why did remembering the letter give her such a cold feeling? Perhaps it was because of how cold she had felt when she wrote it. She had thought herself back into the state of mind that had enabled her to leave home all those years ago. *For the best*, she had told herself. *No other way.* And that was how she had framed it: a letter with no apology and little explanation. *I loved you*, it said, *but that was not enough. You won't believe me but I did it for you. I suffered too. It was the only way. Your mother, Alexandra.*

How could she ever begin to write of the pain? It would take more paper than there was on the island and more hours than she probably had left to live. How could she convey the deadening despair of feeling herself at the mercy of a malevolent fate that had sent her into a cursed marriage

470

that would taint all of them? If it were ever known, what would happen then? She shuddered to think of it. John would have lost his inheritance in one fell swoop, and been tainted by his parents' disgrace.

And Nicky . . . her heart twisted with the thought of him. The pain was still so acute that she had been even more successful at shutting him out of her mind than her children. What had she done to him? She'd had to save John's right to the house, knowing how much it had mattered to Nicky to pass his legacy on to his son. Their marriage was over – it had to be over – but he didn't have to suffer seeing John lose the family inheritance that mattered so much to him. And at least he didn't have to live with the knowledge that he'd spent eight years in an incestuous union with his own sister. She could spare him that.

It was hard to remember those dreadful hours when Nicky had gradually come to accept that she was going – forever. He'd pleaded with her, shouted and wept. He'd begged to know her reasons for leaving and she wouldn't give them. He'd told her over and over that he forgave her for Elaine's death and that leaving him and John would only make things a hundred times worse.

'Is it me?' he'd asked, his voice cracking and his eyes full of anguish. 'Is it me you hate?'

'No,' she'd said, knowing that if her heart were not already broken, this is when it would have shattered. 'It's not that. I can't explain. You have to believe it's for the best.'

The truth had to remain concealed. It had already destroyed so much. She couldn't let it continue its rampage, taking Nicky's life and work, and John's inheritance, with it. She could give him a future at least.

'I want you to be happy,' she said, 'and that can't be with me.'

'Don't you understand, Alex?' Tears spilled out of his eyes. 'I'll be nothing without you. We'll be lost if you go. Don't leave me and John, I beg you. We need you. We love you.'

It was almost more than she could stand to witness his grief but she could not be moved. She longed for things to be different but she knew their secret now, and she had to sacrifice herself to keep it. At last, in bewildered pain, he'd had to give in and accept her terms. The agony of leaving John had felt like tearing her heart out. It had only been bearable because she believed wholeheartedly that she was doing what was right for him. Losing Nicky had been like cutting off half of herself and trying to live without it. But for them, there truly was no other way. She could not embrace him as a wife again. She couldn't kiss him and think of making love to him. That was over forever, no matter how much her wicked self might yearn for him. She'd woken up from dreams of indescribable pleasure, where they had met again and he'd kissed her, stripped her naked and made intense and extraordinary love to her. She'd woken shaking and crying out as she'd shuddered around him, pulling him deeper into her, desperate to possess him again. She'd lie back on her pillows, panting at the vividness of her physical experience, still in the grip of the aftermath of her climax, but as the pleasure of being with him waned, she became sickened by her own desires. She knew who he was and yet she still wanted him, and that made her worse than she had been before. She'd spent most of her life now fighting against her deep need to have him again. It was her life's challenge to subdue that desire and accept it as base and evil. It was not the pure love that made John and Elaine but a perverted thing that tainted her children after all.

She got up and took her dishes back into the house. Tonight would be a night like most others. She might go up to the church for the late mass, where she often went to get comfort and strength. Or she might sit here as night fell, listening to the night sounds and reading by candlelight until it was time to sleep. Since Delilah had come she hadn't been able to read so well. Images of Nicky kept floating into her mind. He was sick now; he had begun to lose his memories. The images of her life as it had once been were disappearing. While they lived in Nicky's mind, they had a kind of three-dimensional quality, a roundness that came from existing in two memories simultaneously. Now they were melting away from him, they were turning flat and unreal in her own head. Could she trust that she recalled everything as it was? And then . . . she remembered what Delilah had said. 'When you vanished, Elaine vanished too' – or words to that effect. Their daughter had lived on after death in their hearts and minds. But now that Nicky was forgetting, there was no one left to bring Elaine to life with their memories. She couldn't be resurrected. And when Alexandra died, Elaine would finally be snuffed out completely. She'd join the hordes of the past who now had no one to remember them as they were. They had faded to names and then beyond that to something even less defined. Elaine was too young and fresh to become one of them, wasn't she? Didn't she deserve to live on a little longer?

I don't know why you insist on thinking this way! she rebuked herself. *What can you do about it now? It's far too late! What's done is done.*

And yet she couldn't help wondering about Delilah going back to Fort Stirling and taking the news of their meeting back to John. How had he taken it? She could only imagine him feeling hatred, anger and bitterness. And who could blame him?

On impulse she went to her bedroom, climbing the wooden staircase to the second floor of the house. By her bed was a small cabinet and she opened the door and took out an old book of poetry. Inside the cover was a folded piece of torn newspaper. She unfolded and smoothed it out. It showed a wedding party, a groom and his elegant bride, the gawky young best man, the father of the groom standing beside the mother of the bride in all their finery. It was the only picture she had of John as an adult, taken at his first wedding and printed in the paper on some society page. She put out a finger and touched his face, trying to imagine it mobile, speaking, frowning, crying. What had he said when his wife had broken the news that his mother was still alive and continuing, with every day that passed, to abandon him?

'Oh, John,' she said, sitting down on the worn rug that covered the stone floor. 'You will never understand. I can never tell you why.'

Chapter Thirty-Six

Delilah could barely speak on the way back to Fort Stirling from the old people's home. The vicar, sensing her turmoil, did not try to talk to her as he drove her through the village and up the hill towards the house. She knew, at last. The secret that Alexandra had decided to take with her to the grave was now in Delilah's possession. It was a terrible, life-destroying secret, except for one thing. It wasn't true. All she could think was that she had to get this lie out into the open and rob it of its potency.

As the house appeared in front of her, she was struck anew by what had happened here all those years ago.

I was right, she thought, feeling as though a mist inside her mind had finally cleared. *Alex said she could have survived the house if she'd had Nicky's love. Her father destroyed that for her. He made it impossible for her to have that love.* Delilah felt as though she could see it all now: Alexandra thinking that she could no longer live with Nicky as his wife, and the grief of losing him as well as Elaine would have been too much to stand.

And yet, she wondered, her mind playing over the pieces of the puzzle and re-examining them, *why did she leave John behind? Couldn't she have taken him with her? Perhaps she couldn't do that to Nicky. Maybe she gave John to Nicky, and renounced him for herself. After all, she felt such terrible guilt about Elaine's death – she told me that on Patmos. She might have felt that after taking his daughter, she couldn't take his son as well.*

It made a kind of sad sense. What a terrible trap Alex must have been in. No wonder she felt the only answer was something as extreme as trying to wipe herself out. But . . . Delilah remembered the portrait of Alexandra in the hall. Once a Stirling, always a Stirling. There was no way to be entirely erased.

I want to make it right, she said to herself determinedly. She thought about how disastrous her attempts had been so far. She had increased Alex's sense of guilt, estranged her husband and made herself miserable enough to wonder about leaving her marriage. Wasn't it madness to go on? She should have listened to Grey, and left everything alone. *Perhaps I should just get out of John's life and stop meddling.*

The knowledge rushed in on her, like a blinding revelation. No. She knew she mustn't do that. Alex had thought the same. She'd thought life would be easier for everyone if she hid the truth, if she vanished. She decided to leave it all alone – and look what pain it caused. Perhaps if she'd stayed, Emily would have told her years ago that the old man had lied to her, and she could have been restored to her husband and her child. When she left, she only made all their misery certain.

As Fort Stirling loomed huge above her, Delilah thought, *I won't do that. I can't let it all go on. I don't care what happens afterwards, it's better than letting this lie carry on poisoning everyone's life.*

'Are you all right?' the vicar asked kindly, as he brought the car to a halt in front of the house. 'You're awfully quiet.'

'What? Oh – yes, fine, thanks. Thanks for the lift.' She barely registered him beyond the thoughts pouring through her mind. She opened the back door and let Mungo out onto the gravel. 'Goodbye, Vicar.'

'Goodbye, Mrs Stirling. I hope you sort everything out.'

'Thanks. I'll try.' She managed a smile as he set off back up the drive, then she ran up the steps and into the house, Mungo at her heels. 'John! John!' she called. 'Where are you?'

She ran to the estate office, knocked on the door and flung it open, but it was empty, the desk scattered with papers and ledger books. In the kitchen, she found Janey at work. Mungo trotted to his bed by the range and curled himself into it. 'Have you seen John?' she asked breathlessly.

Janey looked up. 'He went out a little while ago. I think he was going over to the coach house to visit his father. He's been spending quite a bit of time there lately.'

'Thanks, Janey.' Delilah dashed out of the back door. She walked briskly along the gravel path, the red-brick wall of the kitchen garden ahead of her. It was early afternoon and the air was distinctly humid as if there was a storm not far off. Insects buzzed furiously around her as if working hard before the rain arrived. She wondered what she would say to John and how she would break down the barriers between them and make him listen to her.

The old wooden door into the kitchen garden opened and, to her surprise, Ben appeared in the doorway, fresh and vital in jeans and a red T-shirt, his light brown hair spiked. He saw her at once and a broad smile illuminated his face. 'Delilah!'

Her heart sank. She didn't want this to happen now. She was desperate to get to John. 'Hi, Ben, you're back. How are you? Where did you go?'

'I took an impulse trip to Cornwall to see some fantastic gardens there. It was great. Really inspiring. I can't wait to tell you all about it.' He had been walking towards her and now he was close, his body radiating an animal energy that made the air around him buzz. 'Sorry I didn't let you know where I was,' he said in a low, intimate tone. 'I wondered if you'd miss me. I thought it might be fun to surprise you in person.'

Delilah felt strangely impervious to his presence in a way she hadn't just a few days before. He was smiling down at her, his eyes tender and knowing, as though they shared a special bond. *Do we?* she wondered. She couldn't feel it. Whatever it was she'd once felt towards him had completely vanished. *Oh my God, I've been an idiot.*

He frowned, sensing her distance. 'Is everything okay?'

'Of course,' she said, wishing she could find a way to stop this from happening now and be free of him so that she could get to John. Everything in her yearned to find her husband and tell him what she knew.

'Come and sit down then,' he said, gesturing to the bench up against the brick wall. 'I've missed you. I want to talk to you.'

She tried to hide her eagerness to be gone. She owed Ben something, she felt, after what had happened at their last meeting. She'd implied that all he had to do was be patient and she'd eventually fall into his arms. She'd felt it then but she didn't feel it now. There wasn't a trace of it.

Why is the human heart so strange? We're capable of such constancy and such mutability at the same time. But something's changed for me – I know I want to be with John. Did I decide that in Greece? Or was it just today when I talked to Vanna?

All she could be sure of was that it had happened.

Ben sat down on the worn wooden bench and watched expectantly as she joined him, sitting far enough away that there was a stretch of the seat between them. There was a pause and as it grew, his expression became troubled. 'Delilah, is something wrong?'

'No . . . no, of course not.'

'I get the feeling you don't particularly want to be here.'

She looked away, flustered for a moment.

'Ever since I left, I've been thinking about what happened between us at the pool,' he said in a low voice. 'I tried to tell you what I'm feeling for you and I got the impression you felt the same. Did I get the wrong message? Have I made a dick of myself?'

She felt awkward and guilty, as though she was breaking a promise. *But I never did promise anything*, she reminded herself. It had all been unspoken. She turned to him, her expression beseeching. 'Ben, all I can say is that was a very bad moment for me. John and I have had our troubles lately and I was feeling sorry for myself and very vulnerable. I shouldn't have given you the idea that anything might happen between us. You're a lovely guy but we can't be more than friends and I'm sorry if I made you think any different.' She looked straight at him and said firmly, 'I love John.'

'Do you?' Ben frowned. He leaned forward so that his elbows rested on his thighs, and clasped his hands. He looked so young suddenly. 'Do you? I wish I could understand it. You're so warm and full of life and so beautiful. He's so morose, so cold, so unfeeling. Look, he has all this and he has you and he's still not bloody happy!' He turned to face her, and took a deep breath as if about to deliver a speech he had rehearsed. 'Listen, if this is what matters to you, you should know that if John doesn't have kids, I'm the next in line to inherit Fort Stirling, after my dad. I would be the owner of all this. If you felt something for me, you could still have it! The house, the gardens, the title. You don't have to give that up. We could share it all together. Can't you see it? We'd be great together, once John was out of the way.'

She stared at him, horrified. 'Ben – how can you say that?' she whispered.

He looked sheepish. 'I'm sorry if it came out brutally, but I had to say that if losing this is what's stopping you from being with me – well, it's not the case. I can offer it to you, as long as John doesn't have kids. Please, I'm asking you to think about it.'

She straightened her back, furious with him now. 'There's nothing to think about! It's none of your business but I didn't marry him for the house or the gardens, and I wouldn't be with you for them either!' She stood up. 'I'm sorry you think I'm the kind of woman who would do that.'

He couldn't look at her but stared at the ground intently.

'I think you've got me wrong, Ben,' she said. 'There's really nothing between us, just a friendship that we fleetingly mistook for something else. I love my husband and I'll do everything I can before I give up on my marriage.'

'Is that your final word?' he said, looking up, his eyes now cold.

'Yes, it is.'

'Fine.' He got up and strode away over the gravel. She watched him go and sighed. That was over now, and she was relieved. Now she had to find John.

The doors to the old coach house stood open, letting the afternoon sun in. Delilah could hear the mutter of low voices as she came near and paused at the open doors for a moment to see Nicky, white haired and stooped, sitting opposite John, who leaned towards his father, listening intently to what he was saying and occasionally answering. She felt moved suddenly by the strength of their relationship and how close they evidently were, and was sure again that

Alexandra had renounced John for herself so that Nicky might have this precious bond with his only child.

John looked up and saw her, and his eyes turned cold and stony. It seemed that he was still in no mood for listening to her. Her heart sank but she said as cheerfully as she could, 'Hello, you two. How are you?'

Nicky looked at her, startled by her arrival. 'Hello, dear. You're . . .'

'Delilah,' she supplied, smiling at him.

His brow furrowed and he looked thoughtful. Then his faded grey eyes lit up and he said, 'John's wife!'

'Yes, that's right.' She was touched by his sudden recollection of her. 'I wonder if you'd mind if I steal John away for a while? I need to talk to him.'

'Of course not,' Nicky said. He seemed very lucid. 'You two ought to spend some time together. I've wondered why I never see you. Will you come by next time and have some tea and a chat?'

'Of course,' Delilah said, touched. She thought of his loneliness, remembering what Erryl had said about Nicky's sadness. He had lost half his family, for nothing. Tears pricked her eyes and she blinked them away. 'I'd love to.'

'Off you go, boy,' Nicky said to John, flapping a hand at him. 'Go and be with your lovely wife. Don't waste a minute.'

'See you later, Dad,' John mumbled, disconcerted by his father's command. He stood up and glanced at Delilah, then walked past her out into the garden. She went after him, trotting to catch up with his stride. He stared straight ahead, not looking at her. 'What's all this about?' he asked curtly.

'John, please – stop. I need to talk to you. It's important. It's *really* important.' She put a hand on his arm. He stopped and turned to look at her.

'What is it?'

'I need you to listen properly.' She saw his expression change to exasperation. She needed to be quick, she could see that. Any moment now, he would stride away and it would all be lost. She might never get another chance like this. She took a deep breath and said, 'I know why your mother left you.'

He frowned at her, puzzled, as he took in what she said. 'What are you talking about?'

She clutched at him again, desperate to convey the importance of what she had to say. 'I've found out! The vicar took me to the old people's home in Rawlston and your mother's old maid was there and she told me – she told me *why*! My God, John, you won't believe it, it's too incredible.'

He stared at her suspiciously, thrusting his hands in his pockets. 'The old people's home?' He gave a cold, contemptuous laugh. 'Have you dug someone up to tell me that my mother was an angel after all? Because I warn you, it isn't going to work. I told you. She's dead. As far as I'm concerned that's the way it's going to stay.'

'If that's how you want it, then fine,' she said gently. 'But before you make your final decision on that, why not make sure you know everything?'

He shrugged as though uninterested in the idea that there might be anything he didn't know. 'All right. Tell me.'

'Let's sit down.' She led him to the nearest bench, a stone

one that faced a small fountain spouting four twinkling arcs of water into the pond below. 'I need you to listen carefully. You know that your sister died in a hit-and-run, and your mother supposedly killed herself – at least, so you thought until you found out a few months ago that she was still alive?'

'Yes.' His voice was studiedly blank.

'Who told you she'd killed herself?' Delilah asked, suddenly diverted. 'Was it your father?'

John seemed to be remembering despite himself and after a moment he murmured, 'No, no . . . he never said that to me. He told me she'd gone away. It was Nanny who told me that she'd jumped off the folly. Well . . .' He frowned as if with the effort of pulling up old memories. 'She didn't know I was listening, to be fair. They were talking about it – her and the nursery maid – and I was awake and I heard them say, "Well, she jumped off, didn't she? She jumped off the folly." And I knew that they meant my mother.'

'You didn't ask your father?'

He laughed mirthlessly. 'I would have sooner stabbed my eyes out than talk about the thing that so evidently destroyed my father. I never mentioned any of it, and I knew he would lie to protect me too. I assumed he'd told me she'd gone away in the same way that our dogs "went away" – they'd died but he tried to pretend it was something else. And I had no reason to think my mother was alive. I never heard from her, there was no prospect of her returning.'

She took his hand and held it gently, glad that he was letting her do so. 'John, it wasn't your mother who jumped off the folly. It was your grandmother. The rumours in the village managed to turn your mother's sudden absence into a mysterious death. That must have been what your nanny was talking about. But it wasn't true.'

He looked pale and strained as he took this in. 'Right.' He shook his head. 'Good God, no wonder I hate the damn place. I always knew something vile happened there.'

'I'm just sorry you heard all that gossip and believed it. That must have made it much worse for you.' She stroked the back of his hand. 'But I'm glad your father never lied to you.'

There was a pause and then John said roughly, 'So why? You said you know why. Why did my mother leave?'

'I think . . . she did it for your father.'

'What?' he snapped. 'Don't talk rubbish.' He went as if to get up, but Delilah stopped him, speaking quickly.

'It wasn't just any hit-and-run driver that killed Elaine. Your mother was behind the wheel of the car and she killed Elaine in a terrible accident.'

John pulled in a sharp breath and recoiled as if struck.

'You didn't know . . .'

'No! No, of course not. Christ, how dreadful. Oh my God.' He groaned and put his hand to his head. 'I can't believe that.'

'It's appalling,' she agreed wholeheartedly. 'Ever since I found that out, I can't stop seeing it. That poor child – and your poor mother. But it's more understandable when you know what happened to her earlier that afternoon. She was in shock. Emily Jessop – the woman who'd been a maid at

485

the Old Grange – she told me what happened. Your grandfather specialised in making your mother's life a misery and he was particularly furious when she married your father. So furious that eventually he decided to do his best to wreck her life once and for all. And the hell of it is, he succeeded.'

John had gone very still now, listening intently. When Delilah paused, wondering how to tell the next part, he said abruptly, 'What did he do? I knew my father always hated him.'

'I don't think your father knew about this final act of wickedness,' Delilah said quietly. 'The old man told a lie that exploded your mother's marriage and took away the only good things in her life – you and Nicky. He told her that she was the child of an affair between her mother and Nicky's father.'

The implication took only a moment to sink in and then John drew in a breath with a hiss of shock. 'Fuck!' he swore. 'Fuck.' He looked dazed under this new and terrible idea. 'You mean . . .'

'An incestuous marriage. Illegal. Invalid.' Delilah said the words slowly and with emphasis. She felt that they carried with them all the force that had impelled Alexandra out of John's life.

'Oh God,' John said. He closed his eyes and when he opened them again, he said in a low voice, 'So that's why she went.'

Delilah nodded. 'She wasn't in her right mind, I think that must be true. The old priest who conducted Elaine's funeral told me she seemed to be in hell. But it wasn't just Elaine's death, it was this ghastly knowledge. I think she did what she thought was the only sane thing – she released Nicky from his marriage to her. But she decided to leave you behind, to be his comfort and probably to protect you too. I don't know for sure – when I saw your mother, she said nothing about all of this. I think she wanted to take this secret to her grave. I only know because of Emily Jessop.'

John turned to her, his expression suddenly agonised, obviously deeply shaken. 'But it was true?' he whispered through dry lips. 'Were my parents . . . related?'

Delilah shook her head, her heart bleeding for him. 'It wasn't true. Emily will swear to it.'

'Oh God,' he said again, his voice shaking with emotion.

'I'm so sorry.' She wrapped her arms around him, and hugged him to her. This time he crumpled into her arms and let her comfort him.

Once John had absorbed what she'd told him and recovered from his initial shock, it was all they could talk about. They discussed it through the evening and into the night, barely sleeping before waking again to talk more. She could never have imagined that he would have so much to say on a subject that had once appeared to be absolutely closed. He seemed to feel dazed by the extent of the grief his grandfather's wicked lie had caused. It had reverberated down over decades and, like a huge wave, had washed away lives with it.

'You must see he can't be allowed to get away with it,' Delilah said to him as they lay in bed, side by side.

'He was a vile old man,' John said in a heartfelt tone.

'Well, he must have been very miserable,' Delilah said, trying to be noble.

'Let's hope so.'

'But either way, you mustn't let him win.' She ran her hand over his arm, feeling his warm skin under her fingertips.

'What do you mean?'

'If you go on hating your mother and not forgiving her, if you go on wishing she were dead – then he's won.' This had been the conclusion she had felt sure they must eventually reach but even so, she held her breath after she'd said it, half fearful of his reaction.

'I know,' he replied after a moment, his voice more normal than she'd heard it for a very long time. 'I suppose I'm beginning to accept that. She had an awful time, I can see that. I've never really thought before about her pain. I can do that now.'

'So . . . would you be prepared to see her again?' She held her breath, her stomach fluttering with excitement.

He turned to look at her. 'Do you think she'd be prepared to see me?'

'Oh.' She thought for a moment, realising it would not be that straightforward. 'Of course, she still believes that Nicky is her brother. That's what she's punishing herself for and why she doesn't think she can see you or Nicky again.'

'We'll just have to convince her she's wrong.'

'How? Shall we wheel Miss Jessop all the way to Patmos?' They both laughed at the ridiculous image. Then Delilah said softly, 'Why don't we go back and tell her ourselves?'

He turned to her suddenly and wrapped his arms around her, hugging her tightly to him, pressing his face against her cheek. She felt a tremendous lift of happiness, drinking in his nearness as a wash of relief flooded over her. He was back, she knew it for sure. It was going to be all right between them.

He put his mouth to her ear and whispered, 'Thank you. Thank you, Delilah.'

Chapter Thirty-Seven

'Welcome back.' The woman behind the desk of the Hotel Joannis did not try to hide her surprise. 'I'm very pleased to see that you must have enjoyed your stay here to come back so soon.' She smiled at Delilah and then looked across to John. 'And you've brought your husband this time.'

'Yes, that's right.' Delilah beamed at her.

'I'm pleased we have some availability for you. The cancellation meant I could find you a double room.'

'Thank you so much.'

'Please, follow me.'

This room was a larger double and almost twice the price, but Delilah thought it was worth it. From the wide windows they had a view of the beautiful sea stretching away, and the hummocks of the island and a glimpse of the yachts moored at the edge of the bay. She went to the window and gazed out, breathing in the hot salty tang of the air, then turned to John. 'Isn't this wonderful?'

'Yes,' he said. He had a slightly bewildered air about him as if he did not quite believe where he was. 'It is, actually.

It's gorgeous. I can see why you fell in love with this place.'

'Why your mother fell in love with it,' she reminded him.

'Hmm.' He came over to her and wrapped his arms around her, tucking his chin in beside her neck. 'I'm nervous about this.'

'Don't be,' she said stoutly. 'We've got our plan. I'll see her first and explain and we'll see how it goes from there. One step at a time.'

John looked out again, shaking his head. 'She's here – on this island. I can't believe it.' Then he nuzzled into her neck and kissed the soft skin there. 'But . . . I'd rather think about you right now. Do you know, you taste of honey?'

Delilah sighed luxuriously. 'I feel strange. Relaxed but keyed up. Excited and yet completely languorous.'

'I know what you mean. I feel the same way.' He pulled her around so that she was facing him, wisps of her hair being lifted by the light breeze coming in through the window. 'Just in the right mood for . . .'

'Really?' She laughed a little. 'Are you?'

'I'd like to very much,' he said. 'I feel very close to you right now. I want to be as close as I can.'

She softened in his arms. 'Yes,' she said simply. 'Yes, please.'

He unbuttoned her light cotton shirt and pushed it open to reveal her white bra beneath. He slipped one hand over her left breast, cupping it and then pushing back the lace to reveal her dark pink nipple, shrunk down to a tight bud. 'Oh, you're so beautiful,' he breathed, and bent his head to kiss it. She breathed in as he ran his tongue over it and tugged on it gently. He moved to her mouth, kissing her lightly on the lips as his hand moved to her other breast, testing the hardness of her right nipple with the ball of his thumb. He kissed her harder as her arms snaked around him, pulling him closer. He smelt of warm linen and the muskiness of skin reacting to summer heat. She kissed him back harder, pressing herself against him, wanting to feel the whole of his body, lean and strong, against hers. She recalled the way they had made love the night she confessed about her trip here, the strange impersonality of it. The distance between them had been a shock. The experience of having sex without making love had frightened her deeply.

We're so lucky to have it back, she thought, running her hands under his shirt and across the broad expanse of his back. *We so nearly didn't.*

They made slow and delicious love in the afternoon heat, the veil curtains blowing in and creating wafts of air to cool them as their skin pressed together, hot and sticky at times, smooth and soft at others.

When it was over, she sighed happily. 'I'm so glad we're here. It's a different kind of homecoming isn't it?'

He nodded. 'Yes. But it's what happens tomorrow that counts.'

'I'm sure it will be fine,' she said, stroking his hair. 'You're here. I know it's going to be all right.'

'I hope so,' he said. 'It all depends on whether she'll listen or not.'

*

The next afternoon they walked together up the steep road from Chora towards the west, taking their time, each of them filled with a fluttering excitement that was a mixture of apprehension, fear and hope. Perhaps Alexandra wouldn't be at home – she had the job at the monastery taking tourists around but that might not be every day. Her life was only vaguely known to them. But at least Delilah knew where she lived.

'We're close now,' she said, a sudden tension in her stomach. There was so much potential for this to go wrong. Alexandra didn't know what they knew.

They walked on in silence, panting a little at the heat that made their efforts to climb the hill all the more strenuous. They stopped at last near the top, passing a water bottle between them to quench their thirsts, but it was also to put off the moment to come just a little longer.

Delilah pointed up the hill to where the square villa rose among the pine trees at the foot of the monastery. 'There it is. That's hers.'

John followed the direction of her finger and stared at the house. It looked like so many of the others but this one was different. It was where his mother had lived unknown to him for years on end, perhaps all the years that she'd been absent.

'Come on,' she said encouragingly. 'We're nearly there. Let's do it.'

She strode on up the hill to the narrow street where the gate to the Villa Artemis stood slightly ajar. *Now*, she thought, *we really are at the end of our journey.*

John said, 'You go up. I'll wait for you to call me.'

'All right.' It was what they'd agreed. She turned and mounted the white stone steps until she'd reached the door. Pausing for a moment, she took a breath, then knocked. She waited, the tension squealing in her nerves, and then the door opened. Alexandra stood there, clear-eyed and calm, and gazing straight at her. When she spoke her voice was low and musical, vibrating with emotion.

'I knew you'd come back,' she said. 'I'm ready. Come in.'

They sat together in Alexandra's sitting room. The heat on the terrace was too blazing at this time of day. 'There's another on the other side of the house,' Alexandra said, 'but we'll be more comfortable here.'

A dish of marinated olives and glasses of cool citrusy iced water stood ignored on the table between them.

'You were expecting me,' Delilah said, feeling jumpy with adrenaline and excitement. The knowledge of John's proximity made her edgy and she knew she must calm down.

Alexandra nodded. She was quite different, Delilah thought, flushed and glowing with an excitement that made her look almost girlish. 'Ever since your last visit, I've not been able to see things in quite the same light. You changed things for me, I'm not quite sure how. If you hadn't come, I think I would have done my best to reach you somehow.' She smiled over at Delilah. 'I was convinced nothing could change my mind and yet . . .' She looked a little shamefaced suddenly. 'That's why I wish I hadn't written that letter. I would have done anything to take it back afterwards.'

'It's in a bin in Fort Stirling somewhere,' Delilah said cheerfully. 'In fact, it's probably in the compost by now. John didn't read it.'

'Good.' Alexandra looked relieved. Then she said worriedly, 'Was he very angry?'

'Furious.'

A troubled expression crossed the other woman's face. 'I thought as much,' she murmured. 'I can understand that. Why should he forgive me? I shouldn't ask it of him. All I can do is explain a little. I thought perhaps if I tried to make it clearer to you – to him – it might ease his pain. What you said stayed with me – it haunted me. I can't bear to think he's still suffering after all these years. Somehow I convinced myself that he didn't feel the pain of losing me anymore.'

'You're so wrong,' Delilah said gently. 'I think he's felt it every day since he was a boy.'

Alex flinched. 'Of course. I ought to know that. Why should I be spared?'

'But he's ready to forgive you, I think, and meet you again.'

'You mean, I should return to Fort Stirling?'

'Yes – perhaps. If you can.'

Alexandra sat back in her chair, her expression strange. 'That house. I gave up so much for it in the end. I thought I'd never go back. But . . .' She hesitated and then said, 'But if you think John wants it, then I'll go back. Besides, there's something I want to do. But I can't return at once. In my own time. In a week or two. I need time to adjust. My life has moved at a very different pace to yours for many years.

I can't simply up and leave, you know.' She stared at the floor for a moment, then she looked up at Delilah and fixed her with a steady gaze. 'There is one thing I cannot do. Please do not ask me to see Nicky again. It is too much, for me and for him. It's too late now for him ever to understand why what happened had to happen. And it would break my heart to see him. May I ask that simple favour? From what you said, I understand he may not know I'm there in any case.'

Delilah felt a wave of sympathy wash over her. She said simply, 'You don't need to stay away from Nicky. I know why you thought you had to leave him.'

Alex looked almost fearful. 'What do you mean?'

'The secret you wanted to die with you. I know what it is.'

The other woman paled, and she gave a sudden, shallow gasp. 'How?' she said in a whisper. 'What do you know of it?'

'Please, Alexandra, I don't want you to suffer any longer,' Delilah said. She leaned towards her, her eyes earnest, she hoped, and full of the sincerity she felt. 'I want to set you free, if I can. For all of our sakes.'

'Tell me what you know. Quick,' Alexandra said, closing her eyes, her hands clasping the arms of the chair.

Delilah got up and went to sit next to Alexandra's. The older woman sat very still, keeping her eyes closed as if preparing herself for an onslaught. Delilah kept her voice low, even and comforting. 'I've got something to tell you. It's not easy but it's easier than the burden you've struggled under all these years. You see, years ago, someone told a lie. A very wicked lie. It was a murderous piece of deception and it ruined your life. It ruined Nicky's life. It almost ruined John's – but now we know the truth, and we can defeat it.'

Alexandra opened her eyes and stared back at her, frozen. She looked terrified.

Delilah went on, 'I think you know the lie I mean. It was the reason you had to leave and never come back. It is the reason you don't think you should see Nicky again. It's why you gave John up for good.'

The old woman had begun to shake. Delilah leaned forward, full of pity for her as well as hope that this release would bring her a joy that would overwhelm the despair and save her from collapse. She put an arm around her to steady her. 'You know what I am talking about, don't you?'

'Yes,' Alex whispered, her voice cracking. 'I thought no one else knew. No one! How do you know? Who told you?' Then she wailed, 'How do you know it's a *lie*?'

'Because it is,' Delilah said firmly. 'I've heard the whole story and I'm going to tell it to you now. Do you think you're strong enough?'

Alexandra pulled in a shaky breath, clasped her hand tightly around Delilah's and looked her in the eye. 'Yes,' she said. 'I'm strong enough. I'm ready. Tell me now.'

Delilah emerged from the house, calm in the way that comes after a storm of tears, even though she hadn't been crying. She'd been shaken, though, by witnessing Alexandra's reaction to the news: a deep and seismic realisation and a strange dignified acceptance of it. 'John!' she called and ran down several steps towards the bottom.

He came up through the gate, anxiety flickering in the depths of his eyes. 'Is everything all right?'

She nodded, smiling. 'Yes. I think so. Come up.'

'Are you sure?'

Delilah nodded and put out her hand to him. 'Absolutely.'

John walked slowly to her, and then stopped. He took her hand. 'I'd like you to be with me.'

'I'll be right behind you, I promise. But you should go first.'

He took a deep breath, fiddled with the cap of the water bottle he was holding and then passed the bottle to her. 'Okay. Here goes.' He went up past her towards the terrace. Turning back, he looked at her and she smiled encouragingly so he took another step and then another. A moment later he had reached the top. Delilah stood still, watching, clutching the bottle hard in her hands. She nodded at him and mouthed, 'Go!'

He lifted his hand, paused for a moment, then walked up onto the terrace.

Delilah watched as Alexandra appeared, held out her arms and said, 'Hello, John. You've come.'

She watched her husband move slowly into his mother's embrace, the old woman's arms not meeting around her son's back, her grey head only just visible above his blue linen shirt. Delilah closed her eyes and released a long breath that she had not even realised she'd been holding.

It was done, at last.

Chapter Thirty-Eight

Fort Stirling was filled with a sense of madness and incipient celebration, and for once the house seemed alive. It was already buzzing with people and later today it would be full to bursting.

Delilah was racing around trying to organise everything and everybody at once. There was a marquee going up on the back lawn that was almost complete and the caterers were itching to get in with their tables and chairs, while the florists were standing about moaning that the flowers were wilting in the sunshine and could they please get into the marquee to set up?

Meanwhile, the DJ had just arrived with his decks and the chemical lavatory people wanted to know where their loos were going to be put. Delilah had forgotten how much of this kind of thing she had done as a day job and she was simultaneously loving it and hating it. In a way, she could now see John's point about Fort Stirling being invaded by other people. She remembered how she had felt about the place the day she'd first come with Grey and Rachel all that time ago to do the photo shoot. She'd thought it was virtually a public space to be treated as she liked and had rather resented the idea that the owner might have an opinion. But now she was in the opposite position and she knew exactly why it was so irritating.

She threw open a window and shouted at an electrician who was sitting on a stone wall and idly kicking the heads off the flowers: 'Hey! Stop that, please! Thank you!' then slammed the window shut and went up to find John.

Upstairs the house was stuffy with late afternoon heat that had risen up into the bedrooms. John was lying on the bed with the windows shut and a pillow over his eyes. He pulled it off as he heard Delilah come in.

'What a bloody racket!' he said loudly. 'I thought this was supposed to be my birthday. Where's my lovely long lie-in and my peaceful day pleasing myself?' He reached out an arm and grabbed her as she came close to the bed, ignoring her screech and pulling her down beside him. 'And you, my love.' He snuggled into her, covering her with kisses. 'Where have you been?'

'Organising your bloody party,' she said, giggling as he tickled her.

'I didn't want a party. You're the one who wanted the party.'

'For you! To celebrate. To mark this rather special occasion.'

'The rebirth,' he said, hugging her tightly. 'Of us.'

'Mmm. Yes. Of us. And of your relationship with your

mother. But that's not all.' She turned to face him, trying to make him be serious. 'Now. Listen. I've got something important to tell you. A kind of birthday present.'

'Oh? I hope there's going to be something I can unwrap as well.'

'Yes, yes, later . . .' She pressed him away as he tried to nuzzle into her neck again. 'Let me get this out – I want to say it. I've been thinking about it ever since we came back from Patmos.'

'What is it?'

'Darling, whenever we've been away from here, we've been at our happiest. The house is wonderful but it's also the place I've been most miserable, and I think that goes for you too. And so I thought that we ought to make some plans to go away ourselves. For your birthday, I want to give you your freedom.'

He frowned. 'What do you mean?'

'You've always said how much this place oppresses you. Well, let's go away. Give it to Ben, for the time being at least, and let him do all the things he wants to do.'

'Ben?' John turned his eyes up to heaven. 'He's in a funny mood at the moment.' He gave her a sharp look. 'Do you know anything about that?'

She cast him a glance. 'It's nothing to worry about, you know that. He'll sort himself out and what better way than to do some of the things he'd really love to do here?'

'Hmm,' grunted John. 'I'm not sure.'

She said, 'But don't you understand? We can go away from here if you want. Live anywhere we like. Do something different. Get away from the weight of your inheritance before it crushes you.'

He turned to look her straight in the eye. 'You're serious about this, aren't you?'

'Yes. I'm deadly serious. Because I want you to be happy and if this place makes you unhappy, then we should leave. It might make Ben happy, you never know. Or he might be as miserable as you. And you can come back when you need to. Or maybe we could live somewhere else. In the village perhaps.'

John lay back on the bed, pressing his pillow down behind his head. 'I'm stunned.'

'Really?'

He stared up at the carved top of the four-poster with its drooping orange hangings. 'You'd do that for me?'

'Of course.'

He started to laugh suddenly, a jerking sound that gradually grew louder and richer until he was laughing as hard as he could.

'What? What?' she said, laughing along with him, infected by the hilarity. 'What's so funny?'

'You really have decided to wave your magic wand, haven't you? A missing mother? Oh dear, that's no good. Bing! Here she is. Now, what else? Your house weighing you down? Kapow! I'll make it vanish just like that. I'll overturn all the traditions and all the lineage and make it go away.' His laughing tailed off a little, and then he sighed. 'Oh, darling. I really love you. I always knew I did but I've just realised it all over again.'

She smiled at him happily. 'Whatever you want, I'll help you every step of the way. Just let me know whatever you want to do.'

'Thanks, darling.' He grinned at her. 'That's a lovely birthday present. I do hope you got me some aftershave, though. To go with it.'

She threw the pillow at him, laughing. 'Get up, you rascal. You should phone your mother at the house and see how she's settling in.'

'I can't believe she's not coming to the party.' John made a face but he wasn't serious.

'You can see why she wouldn't want to be there,' Delilah said. 'A bit much really, after all this time, to suddenly appear in front of all your friends and family. Much nicer the way she's planned it, don't you think? Now, have a bath and get ready! People will be arriving soon.'

By the evening the house had been transformed into a magnificent party venue, the marquee shining on the lawn and the garden illuminated by hundreds of lanterns. It was a beautiful summer evening and the guests milled around the gardens drinking champagne and fruit cocktails as they chatted.

Delilah was dressed in a shimmering sequined silver sheath and a pair of vintage heels, a feather headdress curling over her head.

'You look stunning,' Grey said as he came wandering up. He was wearing a plum velvet smoking jacket, evening trousers and matching plum monogrammed slippers.

'So do you,' Delilah said. 'Love all the velvet.'

'I'm a little hot is the only thing,' Grey remarked. 'It's such a warm evening. I hope it's going to get cooler later.'

'It won't on the dance floor. I'm hoping to see you move your tail feathers on there later. I've got the DJ to line up some of your favourite tunes specially.'

'Oh, it'll be fine by then. I've got a string vest on under this. I think I'll cut rather a dash on the dance floor.'

'As long as you've waxed.'

'Oh, you're perky, aren't you?' He looked at her more closely. 'You know, you really do look happy. Last time I saw you, I was worried about you. But now that you've turned into a veritable Miss Marple and have solved all the mysteries, you're very pleased with yourself. So . . .' He stretched his eyes and gazed about in an ostentatiously secretive way. 'Where is she, the mysterious mother who's come back from the dead?'

Delilah laughed. 'She's not here.'

'What a disappointment. I wanted to see her.'

'She only arrived today and she's staying in a house down in the village. She didn't want to come and face a barrage of attention after having seen no one for forty years or so. I think you can understand that.'

'I suppose so. Look – champagne!' Grey snatched two glasses off the tray of a passing waiter. 'I'm desperate for a drink. Here you are.' He handed one over to her and raised a glass. 'Here's to you, and John, and the fruit of your loins, you lovely people.'

Delilah flushed. 'There's no news on that front yet.'

'No, but I think there will be before too long. You two look like you can't keep your hands off each other. Just one thing – can I be a godparent? I've always wanted a lord as a godson.'

Delilah laughed and smacked his arm playfully. 'You wicked man. We'll see!'

The guests were called into dinner in the marquee and when it was over and the coffee was served, John stood up, took a microphone and called for order.

'Delilah tells me that I oughtn't to make a speech as it's my birthday, but I want to say a few words. They're not really about me so I think it's allowable. About a year and a bit ago, there was a wedding. I'm afraid not many of you came to it because it was a very small affair and held in London, and that's why I want to take this opportunity to say something about it.' He gazed down at Delilah who smiled back at him. 'I just want to say that I made the right decision that day, and with every day that goes by I'm more aware of what a lucky man I am. In the coming weeks there are going to be a few surprises. I hope you'll bear with us as we work out some of the changes that are coming. Don't be afraid – it's nothing drastic. There will still be Stirlings here, trying to keep this magnificent place going. And the changes are good, positive ones. We're looking to the future now and not the past. But . . . well . . . I won't say more at the moment. I've had a wonderful birthday and I'd like you to toast the woman who made that possible. Delilah. My lovely wife.'

Everyone raised their champagne glasses and murmured, 'Delilah.'

As John sat down, she said in mock indignation, 'But it's your birthday! They should be toasting you!'

'It's what I want,' he said simply and put his hand over hers. 'I don't need anything else.' He leaned over and kissed her as the room burst into applause.

Chapter Thirty-Nine

Alexandra felt as though the entire village was still asleep, as though the whole place was under a spell of slumber. Last night she had seen a riot of fireworks in the distance exploding on the night sky, and had thought about the night on a beach in Goa years before when she'd given birth to John, and how happy she and Nicky had been. She'd imagined the celebrations up at the house and wondered if Nicky knew what they were for.

She woke in her old room, though it looked quite different now. The flowered wallpaper was long gone, replaced by a tasteful shade of vintage-pink paint. This was where she had spent her girlhood and she never expected to see it again. She still couldn't quite believe that John had inherited this house – it had gone to Aunt Felicity after her father's death, and Aunt Felicity had left it to John. He had asked if she would like it to be her home in England for as long as she wanted it.

'I should think you're used to your own company after all

this time,' he'd said. 'I don't think it will suit you to be in the big house.'

He was right. But at first, she'd been afraid to come here. The memory of what had happened the last time she'd been in this house felt almost like a poison inside her mind. But, she told herself sternly, she had to learn to stop thinking in that way. Places didn't cause sadness, people did. There was nothing more evil about this place than there was about the folly on the hill and she wanted to reclaim her old home from those nightmarish recollections. She'd insisted on coming here alone, even though John and Delilah wanted to accompany her.

She had stood on the front step for some minutes, her hand shaking as it held the key. Then she'd gathered her strength, turned the key in the lock and pushed the door open so that she could step inside. It helped that everything looked different, with all the old possessions gone and the decor changed and modernised. It was a lovely family home now and rather wasted on her, all alone. She hadn't yet made any firm plans about how long she would stay in England or, if she went back to Patmos as she intended, how frequently she would return. *But*, she reminded herself, *there will be grandchildren. Perhaps, if I'm here, they can come and stay, the way my children never did.* She tried to imagine being a grandmother. It was an odd yet comforting feeling that she might yet get a chance to resume something of her interrupted motherhood.

That was a pleasing thought. She held on to that. Upstairs, she stood on the landing outside her father's bedroom, remembering what had happened the last time she'd been here. She could almost hear the sound of her father's laboured breathing from inside and the sound of Emily moving about as she tended to him. Then she turned the handle and threw the door open to a pleasant bedroom with a brass bed and pretty flowered curtains at the window. He was gone. He'd been gone forty years. And he couldn't hurt her any more. Ever.

She decided to take her old room for herself. Yes, that's where she wanted to wake up on her first morning. Somewhere she felt truly connected to her old self.

It was only just after dawn. Alexandra got up, dressed and let herself out of the front door. As she walked down the path to the main road that went through the village, she stopped, took out some scissors she had brought specially and cut some roses from the bush that flowered by the front gate. Then she turned right and made her way towards the church. This was what she had promised herself she would do first of all.

It was far too early for anyone to be up and about and she walked undisturbed along the main road, noticing that everything looked the same but subtly different. She wondered who lived in these houses now and if anyone was left who might remember her from all those years ago. The old biddies who loved to gossip about her would be long gone.

You see, she told herself, *only people can hurt you. And they can only hurt you if you let them.*

She wished she'd learnt that lesson years ago. No doubt there would be plenty of chat about her and speculation about her return, but she wasn't going to care about all that.

'I'm going to look forward,' she said out loud and was startled by the way her voice carried along the road. *I might have to get out of the habit of talking to myself so much when I'm in England*, she thought.

There was the church gate just the same as it was the last time she was here on that terrible day. She unfastened it and went up the path to the churchyard, then made her way between the sloping gravestones to the yew tree at the back. Her heart began to thump hard as she got closer. It was not fear but a strange kind of excitement. The grass was long under the tree as though the caretaker's mower had not been able to negotiate the awkward place, but she saw that it had been pushed aside not that long ago. A small square of grey lichened stone was clear to see among the pale green fronds. She breathed in sharply and then knelt down by it, pushing the grass completely clear. There was the inscription. She'd never seen it before. When she'd left this place the ground had been open, the white box still visible six feet down. Nicky must have arranged for this stone. She had a sudden memory. Nicky had said Elaine must be buried in the family vault and she had sobbed that she couldn't bear her little girl to be shut away in that dusty cold room with all those bones. So he had chosen this place instead, close to the churchyard wall with the open fields beyond.

She read the words aloud slowly.

'Elaine Stirling, 1969–1974. "In one of the stars I shall be living."'

Reaching out, she stroked the stone and moved her fingers

around the carved inscription. She closed her eyes and tried to create the most vivid picture of Elaine she ever had, from her soft brown hair to the curve of her nose, her wide blue eyes, the body that was just losing its baby plumpness and growing strong. She heard her high voice again and her peal of laughter. She put all her strength into creating the image, breathing life into her memory with everything her imagination could summon. She wanted to feel Elaine's presence again and for a moment, she almost did.

Opening her eyes, she smiled at the gravestone and began to put the roses she had brought into the marble flower urn. 'I've come home to you, darling,' she said as she slipped the stems into the holes of the urn's cover. 'And I'm going to bring you back to life in the only way I can. We will talk about you and remember you. I will tell John everything he's forgotten. I'll pass my memories on to him, and he will tell his children. I shan't let you disappear.'

She sat for a long time at the graveside and when she left, the stone was clear of grass and the little vase of pink roses made a bright spot in the shade of the yew tree.

Alexandra had wondered if she would be strong enough for the walk up to the fort, remembering the hill out of the village, but it turned out that her climbs up to the monastery on Patmos had kept her fit and the way to Fort Stirling felt almost gentle. It took a while, though, and by the time she was on the brow of the hill and looking down towards the house where it sat on its green cushion, as beautiful as ever, the sun had risen high in the sky. So there it was, that house.

It was for that house that she'd made her sacrifice, so that Nicky could stay there and pass it on to John. She'd let Nicky keep his son and heir, partly to compensate him for the daughter he'd lost and partly so that the great house would not be lost for John. Nicky believed in it all so whole-heartedly, she hadn't been able to destroy it.

But perhaps Nicky would have been happier if she had told him the truth and let him choose between her and the house. But, she reminded herself, it hadn't been possible. She'd believed that they were related. Their relationship had to stop no matter what. But if she took the secret away with her, the house could go on, move from Nicky to John, and no one would ask any questions.

Thank goodness for Delilah, she thought. Delilah had told her that all of them were more important than the house, and Alex had the feeling she meant it and would stick by her guns. *This place will never destroy her the way I let it. And she has John's love. That will help her.*

It was almost mid-morning but no one had yet surfaced. A large white marquee sat brightly in the garden, and in nearby fields were rows of cars and a collection of tents. There were not many signs of life but it would be busy here later. Perhaps she'd ask John to take her back to the Old Grange and return when it was quieter.

She continued on, down the long curving driveway, the house growing larger and more imposing as she approached. A place like this was so immutable, designed to outlive centuries of owners, sheltering them one after another but always waiting for the next custodian. Her time here was over and she did not feel like this house had once been hers but rather as though she'd stayed in it a long time ago as a guest. As she crunched across the gravel at the front, she went to the side of the house and began to walk around it to the back, where she could rest a while in the gardens. There was party detritus everywhere: burnt-out lanterns, abandoned glasses, cigarette ends. The marquee came into sight, looking empty and abandoned, its opening flapping a little in the morning breeze. She didn't want to sit among the remnants of the celebration so she kept moving along the paths, through the formal garden and past the red-brick walls of the kitchen garden. She was approaching the old coach house and she stopped to examine it, frowning. It looked different somehow, smarter and more modern. There were proper windows and a front door.

Of course. The realisation broke on her. John had told her that Nicky lived here now. The old place had been converted for him.

Just as she thought that, she saw him. Her heart lurched. He was in the garden at the side of the coach house, sitting on a bench that was bathed in morning sunlight. His face was turned up to the sunshine, his eyes closed, and he appeared to be asleep.

She stared, her heart beating rapidly. So there he was. The last time she had seen him, he'd been the Nicky of her past: tall, dark-haired, good-looking, alive with easy charm. Now he was stooped, thin and his hair was reduced to a short brush of white over a shiny scalp. His wild energy had gone but it was still him. He was still handsome, and he sat with the same grace he'd always had.

She wondered what to do. Should she approach him? Was it right – or fair?

As she stood there, he opened his eyes, turned his head and looked straight at her.

She smiled, although it was a struggle to make her mouth do what she wanted as her lips were trembling. 'Hello, Nicky,' she said, her voice shaking.

He said nothing but only stared. She began to walk towards him, stepping carefully as she felt so weak.

'Do you remember me?' she asked gently. 'It's been a long time. A very long time.'

He was frowning now and his grey eyes, lighter than she remembered, were puzzled.

'I went away after Elaine died. I thought there was a reason why you'd be better off without me but I was wrong. I've come to say that I'm sorry for everything you suffered.'

She was near to him now, and could see every detail of his face. It was an old man's face and yet, to her, it looked strangely young. Nicky was there – her vibrant lover, her incredible husband.

Nicky pushed himself up onto his feet. Now she saw that he was still tall, despite the stoop. He spoke at last. 'Alex. Is that you?'

She nodded, smiling. 'Yes. It's me.'

He scrunched up his face, closed his eyes and opened them again. 'Is it really you?' he said. 'Or am I dreaming you?'

'You're not dreaming.' Her eyes filled with tears. She could see that it was her Nicky but he was not the same. That old Nicky was gone now and she would never see him again. But this Nicky was still here and she loved him too. She held out her arms to him. 'I'm here. I've come home.'

Acknowledgements

I'm so grateful to everybody who helped me with this book, in particular Wayne Brookes, my wonderful editor, Louise Buckley, Katie James, Jeremy Trevathan and all at Pan Macmillan. Thank you to Lorraine Green for a brilliant copyedit and to Myra Jones for splendid proofreading.

Huge thanks, as always, to my magnificent agent, Lizzy Kremer at David Higham, who worked so hard with me on this book, and to Harriet Moore, who helped enormously with many excellent suggestions.

Thanks to Gill Paul for her encouragement, sage advice and gracious willingness to help whenever I asked.

Thank you to everyone at Albany House for looking after me so well. I loved being able to write this book in such a wonderful place.

Thank you to my family and friends for their endless support, in particular to James Crawford who puts up with far too many glassy stares and half-finished sentences as I disappear into other worlds!

And thank you to everyone who reads and enjoys these books. I love to hear from you.

Lulu Taylor
www.lulutaylor.co.uk
@misslulutaylor

extracts reading groups
competitions books new
books discounts extracts events
competitions extracts reading groups
books new discounts
events extracts reading groups
books new books
new titles reading groups
interviews extracts events
books events extracts reading groups
discounts new books books
new books events interviews
events new books extracts
discounts extracts discounts books
www.panmacmillan.com
extracts events reading groups books
competitions books extracts new